Hordes

an FFSG novel

Bill Dughaille

Contents

Tuesday Morning, Early October
Yes, nurse; Yes, darling; Yes, mum

'Now what are you doing in here again, Inspector Summers?'

Detective Inspector Frank Summers cringed at the voice of Nurse Brien behind him. Nurse Brien came from Dublin. She was unlike any nurse Frank had ever met. She had a soft voice with a hint of Irish in it that managed to castigate with such an air of hurt sadness a saint would feel guilty. She moved with a silence which defeated Frank, a man who could instinctively sense the slightest threat of authority from five miles. She was also impervious to his schoolboy smile.

'I was just chatting to Aggie,' he replied, turning around and wasting a schoolboy smile on her.

Nurse Brien shook her head, went to the head of the bed and plumped up Aggie's pillows.

'You're supposed to be relaxing and taking things easy,' she said. 'And Aggie here also needs her rest.'

That was Nurse Brien all over. Outflank the other from both sides. While he could counter her protest about his need for relaxation, his other flank regarding Aggie was left wide open.

'Aggie –' he began, scrambling for resources he didn't have to shore up that flank.

'It's not visiting hours and she'll be needing her strength for then. And you're in the ladies' ward outside of visiting hours, when everyone needs a little privacy. And if Matron finds out I'll be in trouble. Again.'

Outflanked on four sides, then.

'Oh, er, sorry about that.' He looked around at the other beds in the ward. When he had entered the ward the other women had either not seemed to mind him, being asleep, or had

1

welcomed his cheerful greetings. Now they pretended not to notice him. The ceiling had become a point of focus. Nurse Brien had that effect on people. 'I'll pop off, then. I'll see you later, Aggie.'

Aggie slowly waved a thin, wrinkled hand as he was escorted away by Nurse Brien. Nurse Brien was making sure that he returned to his ward. She didn't trust him not to lose his way. He was the type of man who could get lost in five yards. He had done just that a few days before when she had shooed him out of Aggie's ward then. Matron had been fuming when she discovered him later sitting in the kitchen chatting to the chefs while he devoured a cheese and piccalilli sandwich they had made for him.

With freshly made bread and real butter. He had really being enjoying that sandwich up until he had been interrupted.

And Matron fuming was not a sight you'd like to wake up to too often. If ever.

Okay, perhaps they had a little, teensy-weensy point. After all, he was in hospital after a massive anaphylactic shock, and they had yet to identify the cause. It could just as easily have been something found in piccalilli, cheese, or the bread. Which was one reason his nose had led him to the kitchen. The food he was permitted to eat had been as boring and bland as any food he had ever had, anywhere, including his couple of years at boarding school. For a man whose love affair with take-away pizzas and curries had only recently ended along with the termination of his bachelor status this was a heavy blow. While he wasn't an excessive eater, he did need some herbs and spices in his daily intake. With a dash of garlic salt. Pepper. Chives were nice ...

And liking one's grub did not make one an excessive eater.

Apart from which lying around in a hospital was so extremely boring. There was a world of difference between lying around at home reading and relaxing when you had a chance to do so and having to do so in hospital when you had no choice.

And then Frieda, his wife, had found out when she had come during visiting hours, and she had not been best pleased either. Between Frieda, the Matron and Nurse Brien he was feeling more than outnumbered. In fact, it felt as if just one of them on their own would outnumber him.

And there was still his mother to have her go.

The only consolation was that Frieda's mother was recovering from surgery on a broken ankle and had been unable to join in the general mothering. She had however promised to come down as soon as she was able, mentioning "quiet nights in with a bridge foursome". That had done absolutely nothing for Frieda's equanimity: her mother set her teeth on edge as it was, now she felt obliged to find a bridge fourth who would be prepared to put up with her mother's forceful but erratic bridge playing.

'Will you find the people who did it?' asked Nurse Brien as they walked. 'The people who attacked Aggie? And the others?'

Frank turned to look at her, surprised.

'Oh, we'll find out,' he assured her. 'The question is, will we be able to prosecute? And if that's successful, will we get a guilty verdict? And if we do, will the judge send them away for twenty years without the option of parole?'

Nurse Brien nodded.

'What do you know of her?' she asked. 'Aggie, I mean.'

'Probably as much as you do. She's somewhere in her sixties, maybe even seventies or eighties. She thinks she's twelve. It's not that she's retarded in any way, she just thinks and acts like a twelve year old. She was probably attacked at some stage, years ago, which is where she got that horrendous scar on her face. She's had some form of religious background. She believes that God is going to call her to join her little brothers and sisters in heaven in October. Fortunately it looks like that won't happen this October.'

He looked out the windows as they continued walking down the polished corridor. It was an unusually warm October's day. The sun shone.

'I understand she lives in the cemetery,' Nurse Brien said.

'Yes. It's a long story. I'm surprised she hasn't already gone back there. She doesn't like being indoors.'

'I suspect she's only staying here while you're here. She seems to trust you.'

Frank grimaced.

'I don't know why. I wasn't exactly friendly towards her when we first met. I almost arrested her for theft in the cemetery. I'm afraid I lost my temper.'

'Tell me about it.'

Frank paused and looked at her. She too paused and looked at him. It made him glad that he was married, otherwise he might have thoughts about Nurse Brien.

'One day shortly before Christmas a couple of years ago,' he said, resuming a slow walk, 'a Mrs Fuller found Aggie living in her garden shed. Mrs Fuller had been playing records of Christmas carols, and Aggie had crept up to her window to listen. Mrs Fuller spotted her and Aggie fled to Mrs Fuller's garden shed. Mrs Fuller is quite a woman. Anyone else would have called us in, the police. We'd have arrested Aggie and put her in the cells so that she could enjoy a warm Christmas inside a police cell, complete with automatic central heating, but lacking such things as windows which you could open to smell the fresh evening air. Mrs Fuller thought it was some young neighbourhood girl fooling around. She went off to the shed to investigate. Inside she found Aggie trying to hide under an old tarpaulin. God knows what she thought when she ripped the tarpaulin back and found a skinny little woman of about seventy with a scarred face.'

He pulled his earlobe at one of his own memories.

'Anyway, Mrs Fuller, it appears, has a mind of her own. When she had questioned Aggie, and she realised that Aggie thought she was a twelve-year-old waif, she insisted that Aggie have a hot bath and a hot meal. She tried to convince her to sleep in a spare bedroom, but, as I said, Aggie hates being indoors. She preferred the shed. And then, the next morning, Aggie insists that she should do something to pay for the meal and the bath. Not money, she doesn't have any, and anyway, she believes that a personal favour should be repaid with a personal favour. God's work in loving labour, you could say. In the end Mrs Fuller says that she's going to the cemetery to look after her husband's grave, and that Aggie can give her a hand if she wants. Mrs Fuller suffers from twinges of rheumatism, so she's quite glad of the help.'

He stopped to look out of a window.

'The day following the visit to the cemetery Aggie's gone. Mrs Fuller's a bit upset, but she shrugs and carries on with the festive season. Not much of a festive season for her, she's more or less on her own, old folks' get-togethers, but that's about it. All the same, she can't get Aggie out of her mind. Mrs Fuller hasn't much, but she has a roof over her head, Aggie doesn't even have that. Anyway, on New Year's day she again goes off to visit her husband's grave as usual. And there, on the grave, are some fresh flowers. And behind her Aggie says, 'I hope they're okay. The shop didn't want them,' or something like that.'

He swallowed.

'Aggie, you see, had decided that it had become her job to look after Mrs Fuller's husband's grave. And she had seen all the graves that weren't looked after, especially the children's graves. Those, she decided, were her little brothers and sisters. The good Lord had given her a job. To look after their graves until her time came to be called to heavenly paradise. She's even found a little shed to live in.'

He noticed that his hands were clenched.

'Well, that was it, really,' he said, turning around and trying to smile. 'From then on she had her own little world. Her own meaning in life. She was happier than most people. The people who visited the cemetery were mostly old and grieving. Of course her face frightened them initially, the scar, but Mrs Fuller explained things to them. They accepted her as a strange little twelve-year-old. They'd give her spare change. She spends it on food for stray animals, cats mainly. She's had a number of visits from social workers, but they're stumped. She doesn't want anything from them.'

Nurse Brien nodded.

'Until one night someone – or a group of people, kids, most probably – threw stones and bottles at her. Gave her a few new scars.'

Frank frowned.

'We'll find the bastards,' he said softly. 'I'll find them. It's not just Aggie. Other elderly women have also been attacked. But Aggie – that has put whoever it is beyond the pale. She's defenceless.'

'Inspector Summers, you need to relax. Forget your job. We'll look after Aggie. Your colleagues will – do what is necessary.

For the moment your good health is just as much my concern as Aggie's.'

'Sure, Nurse Brien, and isn't all of this a little silly?' Frank asked, trying to adopt an Irish accent. 'After all, I just had a little headache is all.'

That was a mistake. On all counts.

'Inspector Summers, your little headache landed you in hospital. I'm sure the doctors have told you that the next one could be fatal. It's not just a little headache, it's a combination of things, and it is serious.'

She took his arm and gently but firmly, as only Nurse Brien could do, directed him on towards his ward.

'I've never had a patient die on me yet,' she said. 'And you wouldn't want that on your conscience,' she added. 'What with your wife being pregnant with your first baby and all.'

He stopped and turned. He looked at her, beaming.

'Bloody marvellous,' he said. 'I can't believe how much I'm looking forward to being a dad.'

'That's probably because you're such a child yourself. You're looking forward to the company.'

'Nurse Brien, nothing you can say can faze me. Oh, by the way, don't mention it to anyone, it's not confirmed yet.' He paused. 'How did you know, though?'

Nurse Brien gave the world one of her rare smiles. It had the Mona Lisa quality.

'Inspector, I'm a nurse and a woman. You detect crime, I can detect a pregnancy. Now, here we are, Inspector Frank Summers, your bed. Get in and relax.'

'It's okay, I get released at lunchtime,' Frank said, sitting on the bed.

'Yes, and until then I need you alive. And the word is "discharged". I wish you wouldn't make it sound as if you were getting out of jail.'

'We'll have dinner sometime. With my wife and me.'

Nurse Brien paused. She looked at the sheets as if wishing to tuck them in. As Frank had no intention of getting in to bed it was a wishful look.

'She was a nurse at some stage,' she said softly. 'You can tell. She showed the cleaners how to clean properly one day. An old-fashioned nurse. One who saw cleaning and washing as part of their job. They don't, these days. More's the pity.'

'Aggie?'

Nurse Brien nodded.

'I'm not saying we should go back to those days. Nurses often specialise, and their time is valuable. What I am saying is that Aggie was a nurse of the old school. And, wherever it was, it was probably a small hospital a one-doctor, one-nurse outfit.'

'Why do you think that?'

She gave him the full force of her powerful eyes.

'My mother was a nurse, as was my grandmother, and my great-grandmother, and, for all I know, seventeen generations before that. We can recognise other nurses and their types. My great-grandmother nursed the wounded from both sides in the Easter Uprising. The only side we ever take is that of the ill and the innocent.'

Frank ran a finger along his chin. Despite Nurse Brien's soft voice he was sure that she would never allow doubt to enter her world. Doubt was his constant companion. Not showing it was part of the job description.

'If you should find whoever was responsible,' she said, 'for what happened to Aggie. If they should end up here – we would give them the professional treatment they could expect.'

She gave Frank a last look and left. The look left no doubt that Nurse Brien was capable of tough love as far as Aggie's attackers were concerned. Without the love ingredient.

'So, the beautiful Nurse O'Brien caught you,' said the man in the bed next to him, one Anthony Sampson, a man wearing his pyjamas buttoned to the neck, thick pebble glasses revealing a squint.

'You could say that,' Frank replied. 'Time I was getting dressed.'

'Ah, that's right, you're getting out. I shouldn't be here more than a few days more.'

Frank nodded and took his bag to the bathroom to get changed. He rarely found a problem chatting to anyone, but Anthony Sampson had been that one over the past days. He was a salesman, and not a very good one, Frank guessed. Everything he said was designed to be in agreement with whoever he was speaking to at any particular time. He had invited Frank to call him 'Sampson, just Sampson, everyone calls me Sampson', which was awkward enough when he called Frank 'Frank', but as soon as he discovered Frank's job and rank it had become 'Inspector', and Frank had no choice but to address him as 'Mr Sampson'.

Anthony Sampson was just the unfortunate type who tried to be agreeable to all and ended up in being irritating to all. He called Nurse Brien "Nurse O'Brien" without realising his mistake. He repeated words unnecessarily. He nodded enthusiastically at whoever was speaking to him if the subject was cheerful, or shook his head sadly if it wasn't. Altogether you might have expected him to be in hospital for treatment of neck strain. Instead he was there after an unexpected need to remove his appendix. Why it hadn't left him years before was a mystery.

And then there was that silly article in the Wellbury Herald. Frank rather liked Phil Walthers, editor and almost the entire staff of the Herald. But Phil Walthers had a bad habit of printing encomiums about a certain Frank Summers, a Detective Sergeant as was, and now a Detective Inspector. The latest had been about how both Inspectors Summers, Frank and Frieda, had been such a magnificent boon to the local French police where the Summers had been on honeymoon, helping them to solve an almost impossible case. The truth was that neither they nor the French police had had a clue, and the case had solved itself. But Phil Walthers was a good journalist: much as Frank hated the article, he had to admit that there hadn't been a single mistruth in it. Just far too much bias in the favour of Wellbury's finest. Which in itself was, in Frank's experience, a rare thing. And not, when it had his name throughout, a very welcome thing. Frieda had thought it excellent, but she always did when something promised to boost her prospects of promotion or her team's efforts. She was ambitious, Frank achieved success through good luck and pure curiosity – and keeping out of the way of superior officers, when he wasn't marrying them. Frieda would have won the battle of Waterloo through perfect planning, he would have won it because of something like an oak tree accidentally dropping on Napoleon while being carried overhead by a flying fish.

The oak tree being carried, not Napoleon.

But with Frank the latter would have been entirely possible.

When Anthony Sampson had read the article his attitude had gone from servile to almost grovelling. Even worse, it turned out that he had once applied to join the police, but had been rejected on health grounds. Frank's better nature had allowed him to bear the heavy load of listening to Mr Sampson alternating between self-pity on his own part, and hero-worship on Frank's. Trying to stay polite when he dearly wished to throttle the poor little man had not been easy.

Still, Mr Sampson had been even more lucky than he knew: the reaction on Frieda's face to his ingratiating style did nor auger well for his near future. Had she found herself having to endure much more of him not even the thickest shell of positivity could have survived her withering putdowns.

But at least now Frank was to be free. He whistled to himself as he dressed. He returned to his bed and packed everything he was going to take. He had hoped to end his brief relationship with the other man with a wave, but it was not to be.

'I shall follow your career with great interest, Inspector,' Anthony Sampson said. 'I've already arranged with the editor of the Wellbury Herald to have the newspaper sent to me. Of course I travel a lot, but it will give me an added reason for looking forward to getting home, to find out how well you're doing with the sad case of the poor little old ladies.'

Frank did his best to come up with a reassuring smile. Anthony Sampson lived with his elderly mother in a town some miles north of Wellbury. Apparently she was an angel on the dear Lord's earth. Just the thought of some maniac attacking little old ladies made Anthony Sampson weak.

Frank could not help but wonder if Mother Sampson wasn't in truth a demanding, dominating old ogre. It would explain a number of things.

'I can't promise anything, Mr Sampson, but we'll do our best as we always do,' he said.

'I have every confidence in you and your men, Inspector. Hard work, as The Lord says, brings its own reward,' Anthony Sampson said, holding out a limp hand. Frank shook it, and looked into the other man's eyes, trying to work out what was really there behind the meek smile and pebble glasses. The man held his gaze for a split second before turning away. Frank was stunned by what he had seen in that second: laughter.

Anthony Sampson was laughing at him?

It must be the glasses, he decided.

'Best of luck,' he murmured, and left as rapidly as he could. He had sufficient problems without trying to analyse the character behind a travelling salesman who would be leaving Wellbury for good in a day or so. Minus his appendix.

He opened the swing door of the ward, took a careful peek both ways, and slipped out, heading along the polished floor towards reception. There was an hour until Frieda was due to collect him, and he was absolutely sure that Nurse Brien would turn up five minutes before then, pushing a wheelchair for him to sit in, telling him to be a good boy and do as he was told, not to get himself tired or excited, and remember that he could have another attack at any time. He had enough worries on that score himself, he didn't need everybody else reminding him of what could happen. They were worries he intended to keep to himself. He had no intention of sharing them with his wife. She would have enough to concern herself with her first pregnancy.

He gained the corridor leading towards reception without being discovered. Being at the main entrance to the hospital, and outside visiting hours, it was quiet, as he had banked on. He recognised the one nurse sitting behind the reception counter, a pleasant, middle-aged woman he had had a conversation with two days before, who had warned him at the time that Nurse Brien was on her way, giving him time to escape. Now he strode up to the counter, confident that she would do the same if necessary.

'A pity the bookies wouldn't take the bet,' said a voice behind him as he emerged into the reception area. A voice with a lilt of Irish in it.

'You can't blame them, really,' said another voice behind him, a voice with the lilt of wife in it. He turned around to find Nurse Brien and his wife sitting on a couch, looking at him in a manner reminiscent of his primary school teachers after they had found his missing frog in the staff room, inside the milk jug.

'Free!' he exclaimed. 'Give your old man a kiss. He's been dying for the lack of you.'

'Frank Summers,' she replied, standing up, 'you are a thorough-going ... thorough-going ... Oh! Nuisance!' She put her arms around him and gave him a passionate kiss. Nurse Brien stood up and smoothed down her uniform.

'I must be off,' she said. 'Duty calls. Look after the nuisance, won't you?' She stroked Frank's cheek and left.

'Mum not here?' asked Frank, deliberately avoiding the look Frieda was giving him, a look which included the question 'You and Nurse Brien?'

'She's at home, chewing her fingernails. Along with dad. He really should have returned to the university. He tries to pretend that he's not worried, but it's obvious that he is. For some reason they dote on their only child. I can't imagine why.'

'Dad' was Frank's father. Frieda's father had died when she was a teenager. She had hero-worshipped her father. Frank's father was a professor, and she couldn't help but respect such beings as demi-gods. Her father, a dominant and assertive man, and Frank's father, an apparently absent-minded visitor from Olympus, had almost nothing in common. At times she wondered what she and Frank had in common to fall in love and get married. Now they were, she was pregnant with Frank's child – she was pretty certain she was pregnant – and calling Frank's father 'dad' was a step into a world she was totally uncertain of, a world which looked attractive but was full of lurking dangers. And Frank was suffering from something that could kill without warning.

'Free, there is nothing wrong with me,' Frank said. 'I just had an unexpected reaction to something. Anaphylactic shock, as they call it. Once we work out what it was, all I have to do is avoid it. It's just a different sort of peanut allergy. Except I'm not allergic to peanuts. Or nuts, because I know peanuts are actually lentils, not nuts. Or something. String beans, possibly. Who knows? But they aren't nuts. And anyway I eat nuts on a regular basis. As well as most other things, and I've never had an allergic reaction before.'

Frieda looked at him. She was beginning to suspect that Frank, her new husband, was in a form of denial. He could see the weeds in the garden, but insisted on looking at the flowers. His impetuous decision to fall in love with, and become too quickly married to, a fellow police officer was typical of him. Not that she could overly criticise him for that, since she had been the one he had proposed to, and she had accepted without a second thought.

However there were two problems. Firstly Frieda had very formed views about Eden, and weeds had no place. Frank might not be able to tell the difference, but she could. He would just have to learn.

Secondly, it was October. The blossoms had long gone. It was time to face up to reality.

The reality being that Frank's career as a police detective could well be over.

As Frank's, technically, boss, she could not allow him to continue working when he might, at any moment, succumb to an attack such as the one which put him into hospital. It would endanger him and those he worked with.

As Frank's wife, she wanted to put him in cotton wool and only allow him out at night. For a limited time. The trouble was that she knew he would never accept that.

She was extremely efficient. He was extremely lucky. Of such things are the battles between gods made.

'So what's the latest on these attacks?' asked Frank as Frieda drove.

'Percy's looking after that. You are booked off for three weeks. Doctor's orders. Forget about work, Frank. You are going to spend three weeks taking things easy. At least until the test results come back.'

'Percy? With all due respect, Free, Percy's not bad at what he does, but I'm sure – well, I could at least give a hand.'

'No, Frank.'

They continued in silence.

'Your mum and dad are leaving this afternoon,' Frieda said finally.

'This afternoon?'

'Your mum said she just wanted to see you home and safe, and then they'd leave us alone. She said she knew that you'd feel uncomfortable if she was hanging around fussing over you.'

There wasn't much Frank could say to that, as it was perfectly true.

'Maybe I'll take up fishing again,' he said. 'Not much else to do.'

Frieda glanced at him. On the one hand it sounded like a good idea. On the other hand both Inspector Percy Hanson and the Chief Inspector could often be found along the river bank with a fishing rod, and it would hardly be a coincidence should Frank bump into them and just happen to start discussing work with them. However she could have a word with them. It would be easy enough to convince Percy not to get involved with such a discussion. He was terrified of her and they both knew it. The Chief Inspector was a different question. Still, he was a sensible man.

And she was quite confident she could make him as terrified of her as Percy if he didn't behave himself.

'Yup,' said Frank, stretching his legs as far as he could in the Landrover, 'leisurely mornings spent fishing, a pint or two at lunchtime with a newspaper, stroll back for an afternoon siesta, then I'll cook dinner for us in the evening. I could get used to that.'

Frieda allowed a reasonable pause before saying, 'Just remember to go easy on the spices, Frank, we have our little one to think of.'

That was so obviously an attempt to limit Frank his access to lively foods in case they should prove themselves to be to cause of his anaphylactic reaction it would have required a character of Herculean patience not to respond in a perfectly understandable sarcastic tone.

Or a newly married husband.

'Free,' he replied, his voice going the extra mile in being reasonable, 'I've got the epi pen, I've eaten spicy foods all my life, I love peanut-butter-and-jam sandwiches which I've also had all my life. We don't know what caused the reaction, but I'm not going to let it control our lives. In fact, I've been given something others would kill for, if they thought about it. Three weeks sick leave, full pay, I can indulge myself. Percy would be confused without the job, Pete would have mental spasms and withdrawal symptoms. Me, I intend to enjoy myself.'

Frieda gave him another glance as they pulled up at their house, another bone of contention for her since it had previously been just her house. She wanted them to buy a new house together. He insisted that he was more than happy in what had been her house. He made it sound convincing, just as he now sounded convincing as he claimed to be looking forward to three weeks off. He might even believe it himself. But she knew that there was just no way Frank could settle into such a life. He would get bored very quickly. His curiosity would get the better of him. That was the rub. Even if she managed to keep him away from police work, he would only end up doing something silly. Fitting an engine to a canoe and crashing it into someone's waterfront cottage. Uncovering a major smuggling ring on the canal purely by accident. Discovering Lord Lucan's decomposing corpse by chance, perhaps because he happened to trip over a tree root which no other person had ever tripped over.

That gave her an idea.

'Frank,' she said as they got out of the Landrover, 'why don't you get yourself a metal detector? If Wellbury is the central point of ley lines the Romans must have travelled through here quite often. Apart from the Old Roman Ruins. You might discover a hoard of coins from the time of Octavius.'

17

That came from another article in the Wellbury Herald. Phil Walthers had overheard a teasing comment by Constable Sam Nightingale, the Wellbury police station's resident witch, about ley lines in the area. It gave him a filler for the newspaper: 'Wellbury: Ley Line Centre?' It included little titbits such as the fact that the theory of ley lines had been first suggested by amateur archaeologist Alfred Watkins in his book 'The Old Straight Track', published in 1921. Examples from around the world were supplied, from the Nazca lines and Mexican pyramids to Stonehenge. It allowed him to use words such as geodesy, and point out that some people believed that UFOs used the lines as cartographical markers.

It was the sort of article a modern journalist might cobble together off the Internet, but Phil Walthers did not use the Internet for that sort of thing. He had his own private library and indexing system. He had an original of Watkins' book. And his own personal memory. And his own personal vanities. He believed in quality, and he believed that quality believed in him. However he wasn't a luddite: the Herald had its own website, initially built by one of his regular brand new journalism graduates and maintained by himself thereafter. The ley lines article had been snatched up by several national dailies in exchange for a small encomium; Phil Walthers remembered the days when to have a story bought by a national newspaper was a prize beyond pearls. These days, however, for the national dailies it was cheaper than employing real journalists – and Phil Walthers could actually spell and string two sentences together, which was an added bonus.

That also irritated Frank: Phil Walthers could write articles in such a way that sceptics would think he was critical of the ideas, while believers would read his words as if they were the gospel truth. And there were more than enough Wellburians and others from outside gullible enough to fall for that. But he grinned at Frieda as they walked up to the door. She had been even more vociferous about idiot editors who wrote nonsensical rubbish likely to attract the more weird and anarchic elements to her domain. The phrase "I'm going to have a word with him" had been uttered, and with Frieda that didn't involve either the singular nor the possibility of the other person being invited to join in the discussion. And when Frieda discussed something with someone, they stayed discussed.

'You don't believe in ley lines any more than I do,' he said, putting his arm around her waist. 'And the archaeologists have given Wellbury a good look and decided that the Old Roman Ruins are the only sign of Roman occupation, and even then they aren't convinced that they weren't brought here after the Romans left. Quite possibly by some Victorian land-owner. A form of Piltdown Man. You're just trying to find something to keep me occupied. Which shows that you love me just as much as I love you.'

Frieda's blushes were saved by Frank's mother's opening the front door, purely coincidentally, not at all as if she had been waiting and watching out of the front window for a few hours.

'Frank! Frieda! Come inside and sit down. I've just made a pot of tea. We have time for a cup or two before your father and I leave.'

'Now, mum, no fussing. You can see I'm perfectly fit. The doctor says that the chances of my having an attack like that again are incredibly slim.'

'I'm not fussing, Frank, you have a wife to do that now. And very lucky you are too, if I may say so. Now, come into the lounge, your father's discovered a television show that actually interests him.'

'The history channel?'

'Don't be silly, Frank, you know what he thinks of that. It's some talent contest or something. I'll get the tea things.'

'I'll give you a hand,' Frieda said. Frank left his overnight bag in the hall and wandered into the lounge. His father was sitting on the edge of the couch, his eyes fixed on the television.

'Frank, my boy! Sit down. Have you seen this? It's fascinating. Perfectly normal people – or I think they're supposed to be perfectly normal – without any talent go up in front of three judges who then insult them. Singers, apparently. I'm trying to work out whether they're actors or not. They're very good at being bad.'

'I don't think they are actors, dad,' Frank said, sitting down. As he did so his growing kitten, Squishy, came haring into the lounge, eager to see him back and ready to forgive him for deserting her for almost a week. As a small sign of her hurt feelings she dug her claws into his legs as she scrambled up onto his lap and miaowed at him.

'Ah! Careful, Squish, don't use your claws now, there's a good girl.'

'But why? Why would any sane person go on a television programme to be insulted? There was a young girl a few minutes ago who ran out crying. Most strange. Do they only show this in Wellbury?'

'No, dad, you can get it anywhere,' Frank said, trying to control Squishy who had ascended his chest and was intent on licking his face clean.' You just don't watch much television.'

'Well, that's true, my boy. I don't normally have time for it. Do you watch this sort of thing?'

'Not if I can avoid it, dad. I'm normally too busy myself. I often wonder whether it's worth having a television.'

'A good question, Frank. Your mother couldn't live without the opera shows, but I can certainly imagine myself without a television.'

'Opera shows?'

'He means soap operas,' Frank's mother said, coming in with a tray of tea items, Frieda behind her. 'Now switch that thing off, Frank, it's very unsociable.'

Frank's father switched the set off reluctantly and turned his attention to his son.

'So, my boy, fully recovered then? You certainly look it.'

'A hundred percent, dad. It was just one of those things that happen in the best of families.'

'Exactly. Just what I said to your mother. Just an unfortunate combination of circumstances. A mixture of pollen and the wrong sunlight and some other things, as the doctor said. Probably won't happen again for another thousand years.'

'Any news on when the tests will come through?' Frances Summers asked Frieda.

'By next week at the latest. So they say. I think they're being optimistic for our sakes.'

'And then,' said Frank, 'all will be revealed, I'll know what to avoid, and I can get back to work again. Protecting the honest citizens of Wellbury as I'm paid to do.'

'Or endangering them and yourself as you normally do,' commented Frieda. Frank made a face at her.

'It's a pity you're leaving, dad,' he said. 'I'm going to get myself a metal detector and spend the next week looking for hoards of buried Roman coins.'

'Are you? My goodness, that does sound interesting. I wonder if I could get the university to agree to extend my leave.'

'Frank!' warned his wife.

'Yes, dear?'

'Yes, mum?'

Frances Summers shook her head and sighed.

'You know, Frieda, each of them on their own can often appear to be grown up, but when they get together they're like a pair of incorrigible schoolboys.'

'Actually, if I am going to be off for a few days, I might just start something I've often thought of.'

'And what is that, Frank?'

'The definitive book of Epicurean philosophy. I think I might call it "I party, therefore I am".'

'So you mean your idea of the definitive book of Epicurean philosophy,' said Frieda.

'Of course. It wouldn't make any sense just to repeat what someone else has written.'

'Well, my boy, I'll send you the books I have on Epicurus,' said his father. 'Though I think you'll have a tough time finding anything new to say. There is really very little left on his philosophy, you know. And you'll have an uphill battle. Very few people today understand Epicurus's original philosophy. I'm afraid the early Christian church did what I can only describe as a hatchet job on him. Not that his fellow philosophers were that enamoured either.'

'You're probably right, dad. But it will give me something to do while I'm not digging up those hoards of ancient Roman coins. At least Frieda won't worry so much.'

'You're very lucky to have Frieda to look after you,' his mother said. She turned to Frieda. 'But don't let him have too much spicy food my dear, he's always been one for spicy food. I don't think it's ever been good for him. His father never has spicy food.'

Frank's mouth twitched. His father took a sip of tea with a look of utmost innocence.

Wednesday Morning
The Cult; General Frieda; Along the riverbank

It was a novel experience for Frank to kiss his wife goodbye as she went to work and he stayed at home. Admittedly it was still a novel experience being married, but somehow he had always presumed that, when he did get married, if anyone was going to see anyone off to work he would be the one going to work. While being an admirer of the strangeness and ironies of life he was also one to take advantage of them when they happened. Five minutes after Frieda had left he was ready to be on his way himself, to begin his enforced absence of duty by purchasing a metal detector. He had absolutely no intention of using it. But, if Frieda and his mother would feel happier with the sight of him waving one around every so often, he was quite happy to do so. He had always been a very thoughtful boy that way.

In the hallway he put on a heavy jacket and looked back at Squishy sitting on the stairs.

'Coming, Squish?' he asked. Squishy tucked her front legs in underneath her and half closed her eyes to indicate that inside here was nice and warm and no way she was going out into the October cold out there no matter how sunny it might be. Besides which Frieda's house had a cat-flap at the back, so she was no longer reliant on Frank for getting in and out. And if she got bored she could go find Colonel Midnight, a thug of a black cat which Frieda often fed, a cat afraid of nothing except being indoors and little kittens who wanted to be friendly. Plus there was the neighbours' six-year-old girl named Tammy who was much better at playing games than Frank.

But she'd wait for him to get back very patiently, anyhow.

'Okay, Squish, be good, see you later.'

The door-bell rang as he was about to leave. He opened the front door to find two smartly dressed men carrying briefcases. One held a stack of leaflets in his hand. He recognised the type at once. He had no doubt that he was about to be given a leaflet eulogising the joys of Jesus and being invited to join with them in finding the one and only true way to The Light. Involving, no doubt, a small financial contribution to aid them on the Path. The man with the leaflets held out one for him to take. He was about to smile, apologise politely and close the door firmly when the title caught his eye.

'The Cult of the Clueless' it read. He blinked and took it.

'I'm sorry, we don't know,' said the man. Frank blinked again. 'Sorry?' he asked.

'Yes, we are too.'

'We don't know,' added the other man. 'Sorry.'

Frank looked from one to the other. The man with the leaflets was trying to look miserable, but had a twinkle in his eye. The other was doing a good impression of a man trying hard to do a good impression of a man overwhelmed with doubt and angst, and feeling quite pleased with himself at the effect. Frank looked back at the leaflet in his hand. Apart from the title there was nothing. He turned it over. The other side was blank apart from the words: 'Men only'.

'I'm sorry,' he said, 'I'm afraid I don't understand.'

The two men looked at each and sighed dramatically. They enjoyed it so much they repeated the sigh. Then they turned back to Frank.

'A true brother,' declared the second man.

'Well, now, it's quite simple really, to be sure,' said leaflet man with an Irish accent, an accent Frank found it difficult to tell whether real or put on. 'You see, we get so many people coming to our doors claiming to know the truth. We, on the other hand, only know that we don't know. And there we were, one day, sitting in the pub, discussing these important issues, when we said to ourselves, to be sure, why shouldn't we form our own group, you know, of people who don't know. And go out and not spread the word.'

'Are you a believer?' asked the second man.

'A believer?'

'Do you have faith?'

'Sorry?'

'Sure now and he's only teasing,' said leaflet man. 'What he's asking is whether you firmly believe in a deity of some form or fashion. You know, a god or some-such. Chap in the sky, beard, white robes, that sort of thing, you know. Normally has angels floating around, harps on clouds. Sometimes lightning, or the odd trident being thrown.'

'Well, I don't really know –'

'Ah, praise the wotsits, we have a convert!' exclaimed the second man.

'Hush now, Jaimie,' the first man told him. He turned back to Frank. 'He gets a bit carried away. I'm Seumas O'Brien-O'Murphy-O'Connor-O, by the way. I would say that it isn't my real name, but who's to know, to be sure? I might well have been in a previous life.'

Frank looked from one to the other. He was beginning to wonder whether it was time to call for the men in white coats carrying a couple of padded jackets that buttoned up securely behind the back.

'Sure now, and I recognise that look,' said Seumas O'Brien-O'Murphy-O'Connor-O. 'You think we're loopy.'

Frank nodded.

'The thought had crossed my mind,' he said.

'Well, think about it. Most people don't know. But there's this small minority who go around trying to convince people that they do know, and that minority gets all the attention. On the television. That radio programme, Thought For The Day. They'll have a priest of this, a pastor of that, a rabbi of the other, an imam of the fourth, but do they ever have one of us who doesn't know? No, never. So we thought we'd set up a group to give ourselves a voice. The Cult of the Clueless.'

'We spent some time on getting the title right,' put in Jaimie. 'I wanted us to be called The Latter Day Church of the Truthfully Clueless And Bewildered – Men Only. But it was Seumas's round, so I didn't want to argue the point too much.'

'Ri-i-ight,' Frank said slowly, drawing the word out while scratching his jaw. 'Could you explain something to me? Why men only?'

'Women know everything,' said Jaimie. 'Ask my wife. And, in the almost inconceivable situation of her not being a hundred percent sure, you can bet your last fiver her bloody mother will know.'

'O-k-a-y,' said Frank.

'We don't want to take up too much of your time, so we'll leave you,' said Seumas O'Brien-O'Murphy-O'Connor-O. He pressed a clutch of leaflets into Frank's hand. 'If you are interested and want to know less, you'll find us in the Fisherman's down the river most evenings, and definitely Saturdays and Sundays before lunch. Afternoons if Liverpool are playing and they've got it on the telly.' He smiled and adopted a deeper tone of voice. 'The day of the great showdown between the Clueless and the Know-alls is coming. There will be gnashing of teeth and rending of clothes. And water bombs. And flour bombs.'

'Water bombs?'

'Well, we wouldn't want to hurt the poor wee little lambs, now would we, Inspector?'

The men raised each raised a hand in a departing salute, turned and began walking away. Seumas O'Brien-O'Murphy-O'Connor-O turned back for a second and called,

'Oh, and bring a six-pack and a folding chair if it's before opening time. We might even be charging tickets, sure we might. When the wotsits hits the fans like.'

Frank watched until they were out of sight before closing the door. He read the title on the leaflets again, turned it over, and studied the phrase 'Men only' on the back. Then he put the leaflets on the sideboard and grinned. Suddenly he was very glad that he had been booked off. People like Jaimie and Seumas O'Brien-O'Murphy-O'Connor-O were undoubtedly law-abiding citizens. The worst crime they would ever commit in the eyes of the law would be that of singing badly in the early hours of the morning after having been kicked out of the pub. But if they got together enough like-minded souls they could cause havoc by poking fun at people who had no sense of humour whatsoever. It would be those people who took to the streets demanding that their beliefs be respected. They would be ready to kill others to defend their right to tolerance.

The fur would fly. And once the fur started flying the Friends of the Furry Creatures would get involved. And there were some even more dangerous people amongst that lot.

As for the 'Men only' bit: it would be easier to get life assurance for someone whose hobby was to light matches in dynamite factories. That would have the feminists going, and there didn't have to be many of them to start a fight.

And if there was one place on earth where people were likely to get thoroughly incensed and start demonstrating loudly and stridently, that place was Wellbury. Once they had finished weeding the flower patch, done the shopping, finished the washing and ironed the net curtains, they would find enough time on their hands to become Highly Indignant. They would even say "Sorry about this" before throwing the first punch.

Well, the men would, anyway. The ladies tended to have fewer scruples.

What made the two Clueless particularly dangerous was the fact that the first one had addressed him by his rank. They knew who he was. They weren't just randomly handing leaflets out, they had some sort of plan.

No, he was definitely glad to be off for the next couple of weeks. If Jaimie and Seumas O'Brien-O'Murphy-O'Connor-O got enough support and publicity Wellbury was not going to be a peaceful place to live in.

But by all gods or none it would be fun watching. From a distance.

First he had to sort out this nonsense about someone attacking little old ladies. If the Cult of the Clueless were still spreading mayhem after that he might buy a ticket. Until then they had better keep out of his way, or be someone else's problem.

A serving police officer who wasn't booked off duty, for example. Percy would be ideal. Percy, nice chap as he was, shared that in common with the two strangers; an element of cluelessness.

Frieda's first action on getting to work was to carry out what any general would recognise as a priority: assemble your senior officers and come up with a plan. She would have no shortage of troops. She had a whole police station of them. Most of the women police officers would act in sisterly solidarity. Most of the male police offices would act in fear of the ice-queen who could kill with eyes of fire. From the first moment she had arrived in Wellbury she had acted as what she considered to be a strict but fair disciplinarian. The rest of the station had initially considered her to be a raving bonkers nutter with a hair-trigger temper. They had since learned that hair-trigger was a slight exaggeration. Along with that she had earned the nickname "Frigid" for her rigid self-control, which had made a kind of sense to them.

Her senior officers consisted for that moment of her secretary Tricia, Detective Constable Giggling Gertie and pathologist Susan 'Doctor Death' Pleadle, the latter two of whom had been at one time in competition with Frieda for Frank's romantic attentions. Some might say they still were, in a way. Either that or they were being nice until the day came to settle his hash for him properly.

'Plan of action,' Frieda said. 'First, Frank is not to hear of any ongoing investigations. Definitely not interesting ones.'

'Such as the highly suspicious death of Count Alfiera of Thuringia,' said Susan. 'More commonly known as Bernie Brown who ran a confidence trick operation selling Romanian titles, and was found hanging from a stairway bannister by the silk cord of his pyjamas, even though it was mid-afternoon.'

'Exactly. That's precisely the sort of –'

'And whose partner in crime, the so-called Countess Alexandria, a young bottle blonde with an Essex accent, disappeared the day before and hasn't been seen since.'

'Exactly –'

'What about this gang targeting small shops and post-offices?' asked Gertie.

'Definitely not. Now –'

'Or Gerald Bolton, the notoriously stingy ageing multi-millionaire found poisoned in his bed a couple of weeks ago?' continued Susan. 'For which we have six suspects who had the time, motive and opportunity to drug his midnight cocoa with the fatal dose?'

'Especially not him. There's nothing more guaranteed to get Frank going than the chance of grilling suspects. But what I –'

'He won't be interested in the march of the English Independence League,' noted Gertie.

'If I have my way there won't be a march of the English Independence League. Most of them are German and Swedish in the first place. They can have their march in London, they're more cosmopolitan. Now –'

'Then there's the mystery of how Steven Jenkins won the Wellbury half-marathon even though he was last at the half-way point, and disappeared off all the cameras for the following half hour,' Tricia pointed out helpfully.

'That would grab Frank's attention without a doubt.'

'And BKOTT,' Tricia added. 'He'd love that.'

BKOTT stood for 'Bible, Koran, Old Testament and Torah'. Someone was going around selling hefty tomes which were "Guaranteed Genuine Leather Bound Original Copies Of

The Original Work". The "Leather" was fake, and, after a first page which gave the title along with apparent encomiums from The Times, The Literary Review and other worthy publications, was followed by printed characters which could have been Old Aramaic, Hebrew, Arabic, Sanskrit or even Greek to anyone who couldn't read those languages, but had been pronounced total gibberish by most scholars. The real killer was that every page was an exact copy. For every book. The problem from a police point of view was that the people who bought such things didn't buy them to read, they bought them to point out to guests and friends that they now owned a Guaranteed Genuine Leather Bound Original Copy Of The Original Bible/Koran/Old Testament/Torah as an investment. By the time they realised that it was worthless, even in recycling terms, the offenders would be long gone.

'Still,' Frieda had mused when the issue had first come to light, 'anyone who hands over money for something described by the seller as genuine deserves to be taken for a ride.'

'November the Fifth is coming up,' Gertie said. 'That means the Friends of the Fifth are going to start their annual nonsense.'

The Friends of the Fifth could more accurately have been described as the Enemies of the Pope, as their annual message was a call to celebrate the hanging, drawing and quartering of the 'Catholic traitors', with no effort being made to distinguish between Guy Fawkes and the Gunpowder plotters and Catholics in general.

'November is weeks away,' Frieda said, 'we'll worry about that when it comes.'

'Not forgetting Jane Doe,' said Susan. "Jane Doe" was the name given to the body of a young woman discovered in a room in the Railway Station Hotel. She had nothing to identify her and there were no clothes in the room, apart from an American flag she had been wearing as a wrap. That had been enough for the American embassy in London to promise to send down a representative. That meant being polite to the Americans, something difficult for a town where hospitality was as much prized as despising foreigners. And Americans were worse than foreigners, they were colonials.

'What about Godfrey de Boulloin,' said Gertie. 'International jewel thief, just out of jail, believed to be hiding out somewhere around here. They think he hid his last heist in or around Wellbury.'

'Please do not mention that to Frank. He's said he's going to buy a metal detector and look for Roman hoards. No, no mention of buried treasure of any sort.'

'Then there's the Wellbury Independent Prostitutes Society' Tricia added. 'Or WIPS for short. They've been campaigning for more protection.'

'I don't think Frank will be too interested in that, there isn't much of a mystery involved.'

'No, but it all takes up resources. Like the tour of Wellbury's famous boy band returning to their roots. Apparently the tickets have all been sold out to teenagers, pre-teeners, and their mums. The last time that happened they broke their way through to the stage and ripped the clothes off the boys. Five adult women arrested and jailed overnight. And the band members were charged with indecency in a public place, but it didn't stand up.'

'I prefer Tom Jones, myself,' mused Tricia.

'And there are various nutters and tourists following Wellbury's famous ley lines,' said Gertie. 'Vic Brown's got a nice little business going selling photographs of the spirits of the areas the ley lines pass through.'

Frieda sighed.

'Not to mention the rumble of discontent from various feminist, gay, lesbian, bi-sexual and other groups who all seem to have interpreted these recent attacks on elderly ladies as the start of some personal campaign against them. I spend so much time listening to their complaints I don't have time left to do anything about the actual attacks. I swear there's a group for each feminist in town.'

They contemplated this in silence for a few moments. They were individually strong women. The only reason none of them had started their own movement was because they hadn't been able to find any other feminist who would bloody well do as they were told.

'But, anyway,' said Frieda, brightening up and rubbing her hands, 'back to the task in hand. To protect Frank from harm.'

'We've been here before,' Susan pointed out. 'The last time we decided Frank needed protection we nearly killed him ourselves.'

'Yes, but that was trying to protect him from someone else,' Frieda pointed out. 'This time we have to protect him from himself.'

'Now that sounds like a lost cause,' Gertie noted.

'There has to be a way,' Frieda said. 'Just occasionally bump into him every so often to make sure he's not doing something silly.'

'Not that he'll suspect anything, or notice anything,' Gertie chipped in, 'not when a patrol car just happens to pass him or call in on him every half an hour or so.'

'I was thinking more of every five minutes,' said Frieda.

They looked at her.

'Okay, we could make it hourly,' she offered. The silence this was met with told her all she needed to know about what they thought of that idea. 'We only need to do it until his results come through,' she added.

'I've often thought he would have done really well in the army. He has a natural talent for camouflage.'

'Why don't we try reverse psychology?' suggested Tricia.

'Make him believe that we're trying to avoid him?' asked Gertie.

'It could work,' Frieda said with little optimism. 'I'll make sure that everyone knows they must avoid Frank at all costs. And if they do bump into him, not to ask him how he's doing, or what he's doing.'

There was a silence of deadpan faces.

'When did you say the results are due?' asked Susan.

Five minutes after the two strange anti-evangelists had left Frank was on his way to the large shopping centre which Wellburians had graciously agreed should adorn a neighbouring town, preferably on the far side. Before eleven o'clock he was the owner of a new, lightweight and, in the right hands, inconspicuous metal detector which the salesman had assured him would detect the slightest hint of metal up to three metres below ground. Much as he had been tempted to get the salesman to prove this highly dubious claim – in the shop, through the concrete floor – he had decided against it on the principle that he wasn't really interested in finding anything. It was merely a device to give him an excuse to be in places he shouldn't be. Or, rather, places that Frieda would think he shouldn't be in.

He began with the river bank, strolling along as if looking for a place to begin detecting. Purely by chance he stumbled upon the Chief Inspector hidden in a clump of willow trees next to the river bank, sitting on a folding chair with a fishing rod in his hands, his eyes closed, a man at peace with the world, meditating on the greatness of nothing.

Was.

'Morning, sir,' Frank said. 'Any luck?'

The Chief Inspector started, looked at Frank, looked around him to see where his cover had been breached, and sighed.

'Up until you turned up, yes. I'm under orders from Frieda to keep you away from anything resembling work. How are you feeling?'

'Top of the world. Fully fit and raring to go.'

'So I see. What's that gadget?'

'The most modern line in metal detectors. It's my new hobby. It's supposed to keep me out of trouble. It was Frieda's idea.'

The Chief Inspector laughed as Frank switched the machine on, put an earpiece in his ear, and waved the metal detector along the ground, pretending to have a serious desire to locate buried treasure.

'I think she might regret that. It looks just the thing for doing the exact opposite.'

'What worries me is that I might actually find something while Frieda's around. I'd end up having to dig a hole to find whatever it is. And it would probably turn out to be a water pipe or something.'

'Or an unexploded bomb from the war. It's amazing how many they still find after all these years.'

'Well, from what I understand Wellbury was reasonably unscathed during the war. Yanks dropped a few by mistake, but that was it. However, as interesting as the subject is, I was wondering about something more up to date. These attacks on old ladies, for instance.'

The Chief Inspector smiled. There was a hint of nervousness in the smile. He was used to playing the all-knowing elder statesman. He was confident when Percy Hanson approached him. He was comfortable with Frieda. He enjoyed Frank's company. But a mixture of Frank and Frieda with himself in-between was a new and rather disconcerting experience. A tug of war isn't any fun when you are the rope.

'Now, Frank, you know that we can't discuss that,' he said. 'You're supposed to be off work on grounds of ill-health. Apart from the fact that Frieda would not be happy, I am also your senior officer. It is my responsibility to make sure that you take things easy.'

'Do I look like I need to take things easy, sir?'

'No, but I'm not a doctor. Frank, forget it. You aren't going to get anything out of me.'

'That's okay, sir, I understand.' He switched the machine off. 'I suppose I'll just get along and do some metal-detectoring. There's a patch of land behind the cemetery which looks promising. Oh, by the way, this thingy picked up a signal just next to you. Who knows, maybe there is something buried there.'

The Chief Inspector smiled as Frank left. He returned to his contemplation of the river. He was far too old and wise a bird to fall for that one. If Frank thought that he was going to rush off for a spade and start digging up the riverbank, well, it just wasn't going to happen.

Frank also smiled as he walked away. He had been honest about the detector giving off a signal. However, mentioning it had merely been a little red herring to divert the Chief Inspector's attention. Otherwise the Chief Inspector might have stopped to think for long enough to realise that, if Frank was going looking for information, his next port of call was a bit of an obvious one. There was one man outside of the police station who would know the most about what was going on: Phil Walthers.

So long as Frieda hadn't got to him first.

And removed his ley lines for him.

Thursday

The Press; TOBs; The allotments; Cordon Bleu

Frank looked through the large front window of the Wellbury Herald as he approached. Phil Walthers had had a history of employing young girls straight out of university journalism courses to look after reception and take on all the odd tasks required by a local newspaper. Unfortunately, for some inexplicable reason quite possibly to with the water supply, the young girls had a bad habit of falling in love with the gaudy-waistcoat-wearing editor. It would no doubt have been an ego-boost to many a man easily old enough to be their father, but Phil Walthers' interests had lain almost purely in his newspaper. Now he also co-ran the night-club The Blue Bliss, on the outskirts of Wellbury, with Mrs Blower, a woman whose stream of consciousness speech was like a tornado passing through a small bathroom with an open window and door. Frank wondered whether their relationship had changed the style of receptionist cum odd job person Phil Walthers now employed. Through the window he could see a young girl behind reception wielding a pair of scissors with a certain air of viciousness. He opened the door and entered.

'Good morning, is Mr Walthers available?'

'He's in his office. Who shall I say wants him?'

'Frank Summers.'

'Hokay.' The girl picked up a telephone and dialled a number. After a few words she put down the telephone. 'He says you know the way,' she said, and resumed her cutting.

Frank raised his eyebrows and went through the internal connecting door behind the girl. He passed along a corridor, came to the editor's office, knocked and entered.

'Inspector Summers!' declared Phil Walthers, rising from his chair. 'You're looking good. Over the attack, or whatever it was? You had us all extremely worried, I must say.'

'Perfectly, Mr Walthers, just a bit of a scare. The doctor reckons it was just an incredible combination of circumstances that probably won't happen again until Haley's Comet flies past wearing a tuxedo. Or they prove that Wellbury is the centre of ancient ley lines.'

'Ah, yes, take a seat,' the other man replied, slightly embarrassed. 'That was just one of those fillers, you know. A bit like the astrology section. People don't really believe that sort of thing.'

'Some do. Trouble is they're the sort of nutters who end up wasting police time and interfering with Frieda's efficiency drives.'

'Ah, yes, well, certainly, if the Inspector, Inspector Gar ... Inspector Summ ... you are enjoying yourself, aren't you, Frank, winding me up.'

'Of course,' Frank replied, smiling. 'However that's not why I dropped in. Little old ladies getting attacked. I was wondering whether anyone had perhaps let slip any information to you that we might be interested in.'

Phil Walthers raised his own eyebrows.

'Really, Frank, you know that if I knew anything I could tell you I would have, and anything I can't tell you, I can't, can I?'

'Of course not. To tell the truth – and this isn't for publication – I'm at a bit of a standstill. It's a problem when you're discussing a case with other police officers, you all end up seeing the same thing. I thought I'd find someone who had a different viewpoint and just toss things around. But, same rule applies. It's not an official visit. No stories about the police seeking the help of the press, okay? Not yet, anyway.'

'Of course,' replied a puzzled Phil Walthers. What Frank said made sense. And they had often discussed cases. But Frank had never before deliberately sought him out for the purpose. It was normally – invariably – the other way around. But one of his other vanities was a delight in discussing media issues, which is to say he loved explaining how a modern newspaper should and did work to lesser-informed mortals.

'Right, so the first question is, is there really someone going around attacking little old ladies? Or are the facts such that can be vaguely linked to make a plausible news item?'

Phil Walthers rubbed his jaw

'I don't know, to be honest. There is a certain similarity, as I'm sure you've noticed. Take Martha Shaw, for example –'

'Just a second,' said Frank, taking out a pen and notebook, 'I want to try a technique I read about a few months ago. I haven't had the chance up until now. What you're supposed to do is write everything down as if you're hearing it for the first time. Draw diagrams and links, that sort of thing. And then go back and compare them with your original notes.'

Phil Walthers nodded in interest and made a note on his own pad in front of him. 'Wellbury's finest continue to use exciting new methodologies' he wrote, following it by circling the word 'methodologies' and adding a question mark. It sounded a bit foreign for Wellburian ears.

'Right, Martha Shaw,' he said. 'She lives in a house in Lords Acres. She's lived there all her life, the house was owned by her parents and by their parents before and so on – it's supposed to be the oldest house there, dating back to the 1500s, but heavily modernised over the years. It's an exclusive area, as you know, all manicured lawns and freshly painted walls, extensive gardens backing on to fields with ponies and horses, type of place they polish the roses once a week. Or at least their servants have to. But her house is run down. The garden is a mess. Whether she's a wealthy miser, or the family fortune has run out and she's living on the last few pennies is open to rumour. We do know that her front window was broken by someone throwing a hefty stone, almost a small rock, through it. Now –'

'Kingston Avenue,' Frank interrupted.

'No, she lives in Dukes Avenue.'

'Yes, I know, I was just trying to remember something that happened a while ago in Kingston Avenue. Anyway, carry on.'

'Kingston Avenue? Can't remember anything recent. Now where was I? Ah, yes. Anne Summers in the Grovelands, similar sort of thing. And then poor little Aggie in her shack in the cemetery. Only she heard a noise, came out to see what was happening and caught a rock in the side of her face, knocking her out and putting her in hospital. The attacks all happened in the space of three weeks. Just a coincidence? Possibly. Possibly not.'

'And what does your journalist's instinct tell you?'

'My journalist's instinct tells me that there's a story there. My other, logical, self tells me that there isn't sufficient information to go on. It's quite possible that it was a neighbour throwing things through Martha Shaw's window. Everyone in the neighbourhood thinks that her house is a disgrace. You've seen the way the garden has been left to grow wild. People in Lords Acres just don't do that sort of thing.'

Frank nodded as if the image of Martha Shaw's garden was fresh in his mind.

'That entrance ...' he said as if sharing a common memory.

'Precisely. Two wrought-iron gates rusted into position, half-open. Looks as if it was abandoned twenty years ago. Longer.'

'But how do you explain the others, then? The one with a name that sounds like some kind of foodstuff, for example.'

There was a pretty good chance someone would have a name which could perhaps sound like a foodstuff.

'Pearl Ginger in Old Merrick, an ex-prostitute now self-styled wise woman,' Phil Walthers replied. 'Holds séances for the gullible. Sells secret potions on the Internet. Another woman the neighbours would like to see the back of, but in her case it's because they suspect she's a witch. A real witch with real powers. Anne Summers – well, she keeps getting calls from people who think she's the Anne Summers of the sex-catalogue fame. It wouldn't take much for some idiot to reach the same conclusion and try to make an anonymous point. As for Aggie – well, I don't know. I just don't know. I really cannot understand it. Who would do that sort of thing to Aggie? All I can think of is some kids who use the old road at the back of the cemetery as a short cut, and thought it was a bit of a joke to frighten her. If it is I hope you find them and beat seven bells out of them. If I find out who they are their names will be on the front page, and they or their parents can sue me if they like. I've had enough of this nonsense of school children being allowed to run wild. Frank, Aggie was the final straw. Under-age can go hang.' The usually easy-going editor's face was grimly set above his canary-yellow waistcoat.

'I agree,' said Frank, standing up. 'But it's the usual situation. We have to find the proof. Otherwise we're just as bad as they are. Time I was getting on with things. Oh, by the way, do me a favour and don't mention to anyone that I was here. I think it best for the moment that nobody knows. That's everyone, regardless.'

Phil Walthers shrugged a surprised acknowledgement.

'If that's what you want. I need to be getting on myself. I have a luncheon appointment at the Fisherman's down by the river. Top secret. You'll be able to read it in the paper on Thursday.'

'Cult of the Clueless?' asked Frank as they walked out.

'How on earth did you know?'

Frank grinned.

'I'm a copper. I'm paid to know everything. Take my advice and avoid them. They're trouble. Better to concentrate of things like little old ladies being assaulted.'

'I'm a journalist. They sound like good copy. I might as well advise you to avoid criminals.'

'I do try to avoid criminals myself, they're messy characters and normally not very interesting. The difference is that I can lock the criminals up. You can't put the genie back in the bottle. Imagine if the Cult of the Clueless became the lead story while elderly ladies being assaulted was relegated to the middle pages. We wouldn't want that, would we?'

'You worry too much, Frank,' Phil Walthers said as they came out into reception. 'Well, Marie, how's that story coming?' he asked the girl now working at her computer.

'It isn't,' replied young Marie. 'It would do if you let me use the goalkeeper's affair with the coach's daughter. It would serve the bastard right.'

'And I repeat: you can't. I've told you the old saying, it might interest the public but it isn't in the public interest. Try another angle.' He turned to Frank as they stepped out into the street. 'Wellbury football club,' he explained. 'The goalkeeper is forty-two, married, and apparently having an affair with the coach's twenty-one year-old daughter. We always have an article about the club in the paper. Unfortunately they didn't play last weekend – or perhaps fortunately, otherwise we'd be printing the usual excuses for why they lost, yet again. Young Marie's an aggressive type. Stalked them for a week of nights until she got the footage. Perfect stuff for a tabloid. But the Herald isn't a tabloid. It's a local newspaper.' He paused. 'Though I must say there's something about her ... I'm not sure if it's misandry, but she does seem to have a bit of a chip on the shoulder about men.'

'You've finally found one that doesn't fall in love with you, then?'

'Oh, ever since I met Mrs Blower I seem to have been employing a more discerning type of young girl. I like to blame it on Mrs Blower. Otherwise I might have to admit that whatever strange sexual or other allure affected the others has somehow gone.' He turned to Frank and smiled. 'I seem to recall that those young girls also went weak at the knees whenever you turned up. Marie doesn't appear to be affected in the same way.'

'She recognises a happily married man.'

'All of a few weeks happily married. Well, must be on my way.' He put a hand out and Frank shook it. 'Pass my regards on to your wife.'

'Will do.'

'She is not, of course, on the list of those who should not know of your visit here?' asked Phil Walthers, holding on to Frank's hand. Frank looked him in the eyes.

'Funny you should mention that, Mr Walthers. She happens to be at the top of the list.'

'For some strange reason I thought that might be the case, Inspector.' He released Frank's hand and pulled his coat around him. 'It's a dangerous game we're playing, Frank.'

'Dangerous?'

'If Frieda finds that you're hiding something from her, you're in for the high jump. If C finds out I'm hiding something from her there's no height I could jump to gain her forgiveness.'

'C?'

'Mrs Blower, Frank, Mrs Blower. Her first name is Cornelia. The only way she'll forgive me is if it helps in catching the bastards who put Aggie in hospital.'

He paused.

'I distrust the word love, Frank,' he said. 'But I'm happier with Mrs Blower than I've ever been. Much as – much as – well, much as I respect you, some things have to come first, you know.'

'I know that, Mr Walthers. I married the person who came first in my life.'

'Well let's try not to cock up both our lives then, shall we?'

Shortly after they had left the phone in the Herald's reception rang. Marie answered it. After an initial greeting she listened to a question.

'Sorry, Inspector Summers, you've just missed Mr Walthers. He's just left with a – well, that's a coincidence, the man's name was also Summers.'

'Rubbermats,' said Frieda. She paused. 'Pass a message on to Mr Walthers, will you?'

'Certainly, Inspector. What is it?'

'Tell him I'll be coming to have a word with him about ley lines at some stage. Soon.'

Somewhere in a large house in the suburb of Old Merrick a newspaper flapped. It made a cracking sound, the sort that might be used in a film when the five-million-year old dinosaur egg begins hatching.

'Attacking old women! Disgusting!' boomed the voice of Mrs Georgette Scythe. Sitting in the easy-chair opposite her, her companion of the past twenty-five years was placidly knitting. Whereas Mrs Scythe was built along the lines of an aged and slow-moving juggernaut – she had been very fast in her youth – Miss Mildred Smith had been designed from her teenage years to be a timid, little old lady. It had taken her all her life to get there, and now that she had finally achieved this state her only wish was to be left in peace to enjoy it. Over the years she had become accustomed to Georgette's outbursts and now rather enjoyed them. She knew exactly what was coming next: Georgette would announce that they must do something.

'We must do something!' announced Ms Georgette Scythe.

Miss Smith smiled and continued knitting. It was such a well-worn ritual that she no longer need to ask what. There had been a time when Georgette would have been serious about doing something, but these days she merely identified the people responsible – normally the government – excoriated them soundly for five minutes, complained about her taxes being wasted, and then moved on to some other story, normally repeating the process. The last time Georgette Scythe had actually done anything about something had involved making jam. It had not been a pretty sight.

'We shall form a self-defence group,' decided Georgette Scythe. Mildred Smith looked up in alarm.

'A self-defence group, Georgette?'

'An association. A self-defence association. Of women. Of more mature women.'

'But, Georgette, don't you think we should leave that sort of thing to the appropriate authorities.'

Georgette Scythe's eyes sparkled.

'We are the appropriate authorities,' she said. 'We are little old ladies, after all.'

Georgette Scythe was indisputably a lady. A lady, indeed, of the old school, perhaps even of Empire. The sort of lady who could quell tribal rioting with no more than a severe look. She had also unarguably passed retirement age several years before. And perhaps she was no longer the same strapping hockey-player she had been. But if there was one thing Georgette Scythe would never, ever be, it was a little old lady.

'But, Georgette –'

'No buts, Mildred. The time has come for action. Those youngsters have had it too easy for too long. It is time to reclaim the streets. The judges will only give them a slap on their wrist. We will do far more.'

The fecklessness of youth, their criminal ways, and the laxity of judicial sentencing was one of her favourite topics. Georgette Scythe considered the Daily Mail to be a limp-wristed, liberal rag. She was in favour of bringing back hard labour. And the birch. She was prepared to accept that the death penalty had the drawback of not allowing restitution in the case of a mistake, and made a second birching a waste of resources, but would admit nothing else. Not that she would ever make a mistake, but it was obvious the judges – invariably men – were only too fallible. Mildred Smith had agreed with her, just as she always agreed with everything Georgette said.

'But who will you get to join your association?' she asked.

'Our association, Mildred, our association. There's the two of us for a start. And we'll advertise. We'll use this new social media thing I keep reading about.'

'But Georgette, you know my joints. I could never join a self-defence association with my joints.'

'Nonsense! Do you the world of good. Told you so many times. Exercise, that's the key. You should take some of those purple pills for your joints, I keep telling you.'

Mildred Smith sighed internally. She wondered if Georgette had somehow contracted whatever the older version of a mid-life crisis was called. She would be buying a motorbike next.

And Georgette knew full well the purple pills made her break wind uncontrollably.

'And I tell you something, Mildred. It won't be so much defence as offence. Take your battle to the enemy, that's always been my motto!'

Mildred had never heard of a self-offence association before. But she knew from experience that Georgette's idea of taking things to the enemy included creating an enemy if one couldn't be found.

Indeed, Georgette Scythe's philosophy of life could be summed up in her approach to driving: she aimed the car and pressed the accelerator flat. On the odd occasion she remembered to take the handbrake off first. If she didn't it got taken off through natural force anyway.

'Says here one of the victims was a Ms Shaw. This Ms stuff – absolute nonsense.' She frowned. 'Knew a Marti Shaw at school once. Went off to Australia to run a camel farm, I heard. She was a right ball-breaker.'

Mildred Smith dropped a stitch. That was never a good sign.

'And while we're about it, we can tackle the cyclists.'

'The cyclists, Georgette?'

'The ones who ride on pavements.'

Mildred Smith paused. She loathed pavement cyclists. Pavement cyclists were dangerous to little old ladies minding their own business while out shopping.

She smiled.

She dropped another stitch.

That was because she was looking at her knitting needles in a new light.

She hated cyclists.

There was a sunken old road just beyond the wall at the back of the cemetery where Aggie lived. Next to the road was a set of allotments. Alongside them were the tennis courts which Frieda's tennis club used. Since Frank had been contemplating joining the club it was only to be expected that he might pause in passing and decide to have a look. He walked past them admiringly, noting how well they resembled tennis courts in their tennis-court essence, went around the back, and noticed a small wall at the back of the allotments. He hopped over the low wall and strolled towards the allotments, idly waving the metal detector to and fro.

'And just what do you think you're doing, my lad?' asked a voice from one of the lean-tos. Frank turned. A short, burly man of about seventy was standing in the entrance regarding Frank with the suspicion of a Victorian hanging jury toward a homosexual witness.

'Looking for buried treasure.'

'Not around here, you aren't, my lad. This is – council property, this is, and we're in charge of it.'

'We?' asked Frank, looking around for any others.

'Us what works here. This is allotments, this is. But I expect you know that. That's what you're really here for. To see if you can nick some of our hard work. Well you can take that metal detector of yours and walk away right now, otherwise we'll shove it where it's most uncomfortable. You aren't allowed on here.'

'Want to put some money on that?'

The man stepped up to Frank and looked up at him with one eye closed, the other ranging over his face.

'Now when someone says that to me he's either bluffing or I'm about to lose some money.' The closed eye opened. 'And by the look of you it'll be the money being lost. Where do I know you from? I know I know you from somewhere.'

Frank took out his warrant card. The man nodded.

'Ah, so you're that Summers bloke. Saw your picture in the Herald once. You looked younger. Didn't have that –' He pointed at his head to indicate the quiff of white hair left by a bullet.

'I've managed to avoid the press photographers since that picture was taken. But, do me a favour. If anyone asks, you haven't seen me.'

'Undercover?'

'You could call it that. I want to have a look around here without anyone knowing.'

'Your lot have already tramped all over here. Because of that old woman being attacked in the cemetery. Poor cow.'

'I know. I want to have a quiet look without trampling all over the place, and without an audience. Quite often you see things differently when you aren't being interrupted by seventeen other people giving you their opinions.'

The man nodded.

'True enough. I'll walk around with you. Otherwise everyone else will be popping out to ask who you are and what the hell you think you're doing. We tend to be a suspicious lot, especially at this time of the year. Harvest time. You'd be surprised at how many people who wouldn't think of shoplifting vegetables from the supermarket seem to think that nicking what we grow is acceptable. We don't tend to win medals, but compared to the supermarket rubbish our stuff is leagues ahead, taste-wise, know what I mean? And there's kids just destroying things for a laugh.'

'You don't grow herbs and spices, do you?'

'Herbs, yeah, course. Spices? You're having a laugh, arntcha?'

'Private joke. I thought the harvest would in in by now.'

'Mostly. But we've had to have someone on guard for the last month and a half. Takes a while to relax.'

'Someone on guard? Was there someone on guard the night Aggie was attacked?'

'Aye. Jack Green, it was. I'm John Higgins, by the way.'

'Did Mr Green see anything?'

'Didn't you interview him?'

'No, not personally. That's one of the problems. Everything I've got is second hand. A lot tends to get lost that way. People think they're writing down what they think they heard from what they think the other person meant when he said what they think he said. If you see what I mean.'

John Higgins nodded.

'I do. My mother in law used to be like that. Told her hundreds of times I couldn't stand Brussel Sprouts, and what did we have every time we went around for lunch? Brussel Sprouts is what.'

'So? Did Mr Green see anything?'

'Aye. Well, Jack reckoned he saw something. A man dressed in black skulking in the road over there. Trouble is, it was about midnight, no moon, Jack's eyesight isn't what it used to be, and he'd brought a few friends with him to keep him company. Bishops, in fact.'

'Bishop's brew?'

'That's the one. Keeps a man warm enough, but let's the imagination run a bit wild, as you could say.'

'You don't think he saw anyone?'

'He didn't phone for help. That's part of the plan. See anything, you phone for help. Don't try to tackle anyone on your own, most of us aren't trained for it. But then, he said the man stayed in the lane, he didn't seem interested in the allotments. Jack reckons he turned away for a moment, and the man was gone. Then he heard the old woman – Aggie – cry out, waited for a while, and went to investigate.'

'Why did he wait?'

'Probably not sure if he was hearing right or the Bishops was getting to him.'

Frank gave a wry grin.

'Sounds like a definition of sobriety. If you think you're pissed you're still sober. It's when you're three sheets to the wind that you're confident you haven't had too much.'

'True enough.'

'So, Mr Green finally goes to investigate. What happens then?'

'He grabbed his torch and hopped over the wall. He found the old woman on the ground, blood coming from her face. Then he ran back here for the phone and called an ambulance. Then he grabbed the first aid kit and went back to help her.'

'The phone?'

'An old mobile thing we share. Can't remember whose it was originally. I think someone's nephew gave it to them and it became sort of everyone's. This time of the year we even remember to keep it charged. Most of the time. It's a right bugger dialling a number, though, those keys is tiny.'

Frank nodded. John Higgins was from that section of a generation that had never had mobile phones and didn't see the point of them even now. Apart from securing their allotments from thieves and random vandals. And his description of Jack Green 'hopping' over the wall and 'running back' was probably far more energetic than the reality.

'So what happened next?' he asked. 'The ambulance turn up? The police?'

'Ambulance. Police weren't told until the next day. See, we didn't know she'd been attacked until then, Jack thought she could have done it to herself, falling over or something.'

'Let me guess, a couple of uniforms who wandered around for a few minutes and then left?'

John Higgins gave him a look.

'Why do I get this feeling that you're fishing, Inspector? You'd get a better answer by asking them.'

Frank nodded, smiling.

'Got it in one, Mr Higgins. I'm booked off work for the moment, sick leave. If I go anywhere near the station my wife will give me hell. Which is a particular problem as she's also my boss.'

John Higgins paused and then burst into laughter.

'Well, I've been married more than forty years, five grown up kids, dozens of grand-kids, and my wife has always been the boss at home, but she wasn't at work with me. Not sure I could have handled it at work as well.'

'It certainly makes for an interesting life. Now, Mr Higgins, this man your Mr Green thought he saw. And these thieves and burglars you're guarding against. How many, how often?'

'You mean how often do we catch people trying it on?' He paused to think. 'Difficult to say. After the old woman was attacked – after we found out that's what it was – we doubled the guard. Standing patrols every two hours. Torch inspection.'

'Over the wall, into the cemetery?'

'Aye, a quick look just in case someone was hiding there.'

Frank nodded in understanding.

'You wanted them to know you were here and awake, you weren't actually trying to catch anyone.'

'Aye, lad, got it in one. We prefer to frighten them away rather than get into a fight. Not that some of us would object to a fight, mind, but when it's night and dark you can never be sure what it is you're getting into a fight with. It could be a young drunk with a knife or even that old Aggie. She likes wandering around at night.'

'Do you know if you frightened anyone away at any time?'

'Dozens.'

'Dozens?'

'Dozens of shadows. Some of the chaps don't know how to use a torch properly, especially the youngsters. And they have lively imaginations.'

'Youngsters?'

'Well, some of the people here are hardly over fifty.'

'I see. What about you personally? What's your take on this dark stranger?'

John Higgins looked at him for a few moments before replying.

'I wouldn't say this on oath, mind, but I'm pretty sure there's been someone out there in the cemetery when I've been on. See, I had to do National Service back in the day, infantry. One of the last call ups. We were trained how to use our eyes properly. It's little things you either see or don't see. Outlines which don't look natural. Things that should be there, but aren't because something else is getting in the way. That sort of thing.'

'But not enough to make an identification.'

'Nowhere near.'

'And whereabouts was – or were – these outlines?'

'Well, when I saw them they were in the cemetery around Aggie's shack. Or the graves nearby. Trouble is, if they had been further away I wouldn't have seen them if you know what I mean. There could have been an entire company doing the goose-step just beyond the first line of trees and I wouldn't have seen them. Heard them, yes, but I don't think our nocturnal visitor – or visitors – are interested in making a noise.'

'Skulking?'

'That's the way I read it.' He grinned with little humour. 'Course we were trained to move silently. Wouldn't have called it skulking.'

'Well, thanks for that, Mr Higgins. I think it could be quite useful.'

'My pleasure, Inspector. And if you ever need a hand with your undercover work, let me know. So long as it doesn't involve too much exercise.'

'I'll remember that, Mr Higgins.'

'So, what's your next step, if you don't mind me asking?'

Frank checked his watch.

'Time I put the dinner on,' he said. 'While I'm booked off I'm on cooking duty.'

'Well, in that case – what would you say to some fresh baby cauliflower?'

'Fresh baby cauliflower? I'd say hello and welcome. But I thought you –'

'Sign of appreciation for our hard-working police force.'

'I don't suppose you have any recommendations for cooking?'

'Lightly boiled, little salt, cheese sauce at the side. Don't drown it. Don't cut it up before, either.'

'Pepper?'

'Loads. That's the way I like it. Mother in law wasn't too fond of it. Bloody Brussel Sprouts.'

Frank whistled as he checked the dials on the stove, peering in to make sure the oven was still cooking. A noise from the front door indicated that someone had opened it and entered. Squishy, who had been happily napping on the windowsill woke up and miaowed. She sensed the presence of the one human who appeared to understand the correct portions to feed a growing little kitten under the table during dinner.

'Aren't you supposed to call, "Honey, I'm home"?' Frank called out.

'How are you, Frank?' asked Frieda, standing in the kitchen doorway, coat on, her briefcase in her left hand.

He turned, a surprised look on his face.

'Never felt better. I've got dinner on the go. Don't you want to take off your coat, put your briefcase down, kick your shoes off, put your feet up, relax?'

She put the briefcase down, came into the kitchen, and gave him a hug. Squishy miaowed. She turned and stroked the kitten's head.

'Fancy a glass of wine, Frank?' she asked, opening the fridge. It was bare of any suggestion of wine.

'No, I'm fine, thanks.'

She looked at him.

'What happened to the half-full bottle that was in here? The Riesling?'

'That? Oh, I put it in the cupboard. Seemed a waste, keeping it cool. Using up electricity needlessly, you know.'

She shook her head.

'You can be daft sometimes, Frank. Just because I'm not supposed to be drinking doesn't mean you can't. Anyway, I'm going to have half a glass of red. Doctor Meredith said that there's nothing wrong with a drink now and then when you're pregnant. Everything in moderation. That is,' she added, almost superstitiously, 'presuming I am pregnant, of course. It might be a false alarm.'

'She did?'

'Yes, she did.' She took a bottle from the wine rack and inspected it before opening a drawer to look for the cork screw. 'As she pointed out, there's more danger to the baby in fretting about every single thing you eat or drink than there is in actually eating or drinking whatever it is. The poor little thing will grow up neurotic. Fancy a glass?'

'Well, now you come to mention it ...'

Frieda poured the wine, smiling.

'Maybe I should go see Doctor Meredith,' said Frank. 'She sounds eminently sensible.'

Frieda stopped pouring and smiling.

'Stop it, Frank,' she said. 'Anyway, Doctor Meredith is a gynaecologist. Now I'm going upstairs to change.'

'Hokay. Dinner ready will be ready when you are. No rush.'

When she came back downstairs, wearing civilian clothes – hair down, a skirt with a suggestion of something floral, and a blouse which didn't look like it had been trained from infancy to stand to attention – Frieda looked at the kitchen table. The places were ready. Knives and forks out. Napkins in place. Side plates. Bread rolls in a basket. The only contribution she could make was to put their wine on the table. Somehow it didn't seem right.

Sideplates? Frank?

His mother's influence must have been stronger than she thought possible.

She sighed and sat down as Frank brought a steaming pot to the table.

'Goulash,' he said. 'Everything in one pot, or slow-cooker. But, as one of your five a day, and for a little variety, lightly parched baby cauliflower with a soupçon of cheese sauce alongside if you wish to vary the flavour.'

'Mmm, that does smell nice. This cauliflower smells really fresh, where did you get it?'

'I travelled many highways and byways in search of the perfect cauliflower just for you, my precious one,' he said, sitting down. 'Tuck in while it's still hot.'

'I can think of someone else around here who's precious. Where did you get the recipe for the cheese sauce? It's really good.'

'A girl I went out with years ago was a chef. She had a complex about her sauces, she could never believe they were any good. Had to practice at least three a day. I got roped in so often I could make them blindfolded.'

'Well, I suppose there is something to say for ex-girlfriends.'

They ate in silence for a few moments.

'So how was your day at the office, darling?'

'Boring. Absolutely boring.'

He smiled at her.

'Well,' he said, 'if you aren't going to tell me anything about work, we'll have to discuss world politics instead.'

She glared at him.

'I think Squish needs a new flea collar,' she said.

He nodded.

'What colour?'

'Transparent.'

He smiled innocently.

The smile reminded her of someone. She just couldn't place whoever it was.

Friday

Martha Shaw; Riverbank II; A Kite; £10; COTC meet

The following morning Frank repeated the acts of a dutiful husband kissing his wife goodbye as she left to earn the daily bread. He had left the metal detector in the hallway as a reminder that he was happily indulging in his brand new and fascinating hobby. On the way out she had given it a look which said she didn't buy that story in the slightest, and it was likely to get a severe talking to if it didn't behave itself.

Once she had gone he tidied up and put his heavy jacket on again. He raised an eyebrow at Squishy on the stairs.

'Walkies?' he asked. Squishy gave him the special cat look which translates as 'No thank-you, and I am not a dog. Dogs do walkies. Cats perambulate at their leisure. Like queens, but more so.'

'Okay, Squish, see you later.'

He put the detector on the back seat of the car and set off to Lords Acres. It was easy enough to work out which was Martha Shaw's house. The tall front gates were indeed rusted into a half-open position by years of lack of use or maintenance. He parked opposite them and surveyed the entrance for a while. It was not an entrance which radiated menace. It radiated a total lack of interest. It was almost as if the entire property had turned its back on the world. And was giving the world a huge "Whatever".

As he walked up the driveway he could see why the neighbours might complain. The driveway was pot-holed and riddled with weeds. What once must have been smartly kept gardens were overgrown with tall brambles. The high walls surrounding the house might hide some of it, but those too showed decades of neglect. Compared to the other wealthy and smartly-kept houses in Lords Acres, Martha Shaw's stood out like some form of Gothic apparition. He half-expected to see bats coming home to roost in the attic.

Old, tattered, dusty bats.

He tried the door bell, but that made no sound. He knocked and listened for the echo in an empty house. There wasn't one. But a woman's voice came from behind him, demanding to know what he wanted. He turned, but couldn't see anyone.

'Mrs Shaw?' he called. 'I'm Detective Inspector Frank Summers. I've come about the attempted break in.'

There was a slight clinking sound as if something metallic had been put down. Then a thin, grey-haired woman of an indeterminate but elderly age appeared out of the undergrowth.

'Well, have you caught the bastard who did it?' she asked in a peculiarly emotionless and disinterested tone.

'I'm afraid not, Mrs Shaw. I've just come to have another look at the crime scene. Get things fixed in my head as it were.'

She looked at him.

'You were in the papers. A few years ago. An old photograph.'

'I'm afraid so, Mrs Shaw.'

She scrutinised him, from his shoes to the quiff of white hair.

'You look a bit casual for a police office. Thought you lot all wore suits.' She shrugged almost imperceptibly. 'Well, I suppose I'll have to trust you. For the moment. Come around the back.'

She disappeared back into the undergrowth. Frank followed, trying to avoid the brambles while walking along what appeared to be the only way through. Eventually he came out at the back of the house into a wide open area. It resembled a huge vegetable patch, squares and rectangles dedicated to different produce.

Martha Shaw was waiting for him, an old rifle in her hands.

'Don't worry,' she said, 'it isn't loaded. Even if it was it wouldn't work. The barrel's rusted through in the inside. It would burst if you tried to use it. I use it to frighten off nosy visitors.'

'I suppose asking if you have a licence for it would be a waste of time.'

'It would. This is a museum piece. One of my uncles brought it back with him after Dunkirk. Unfortunately he left his head back there.'

'His head?'

'Went doolally. Couldn't stand being inside. Took to living in the fields. Died of pneumonia eventually.'

'Ah, I see.'

'The neighbours think it runs in my family. They think I'm mad as well.'

Frank nodded. He looked around.

'You grow your own vegetables?'

'Yes. Seemed a waste, keeping the lawn all neat and pretty. Especially when people stopped coming to visit.'

'People stopped coming to visit?'

'Come in, I'll make some tea.' He followed her into a large kitchen. Apart from the huge size it had the feel of a busy farmyard kitchen, kept practically clean, but without any polishing or shining. A garden spade and fork rested against one wall. Seedlings were growing in containers on a work surface on top of a newspaper.

'About fifteen years ago,' Martha Shaw said, filling an old kettle, 'my son was sent to prison. I'd like to say that he got in with the wrong crowd, but he was a feckless little layabout just like his father and the rest of that family. His father only married me because he thought I'd bring a nice little fortune. Of course there wasn't a fortune. Just this big old house where I grew up. So off he went, disappeared to Australia or somewhere. Leaving me with a son to bring up. Well, I thought I'd managed that quite well, until the son and a few friends decided that robbing people was easier than working for a living. One day they tried robbing a jeweller's, an assistant was killed and my son and his friends went to jail. It had been bad enough before, with a missing husband, but with a son a common criminal nobody around here would speak to me. If it have been fraud, white collar crime as they call it, that would have been acceptable.'

'What happened to him?' asked Frank as she poured strong tea into two mugs.

'Hanged himself. Couldn't take prison life. Soft as well as stupid.' She put a mug of tea in front of him, sat down, pushed a sugar bowl across, and looked Frank in the eyes. 'In a way I was glad. Didn't have to pretend to be a loving mother any more. I tried to be, at one time, but it was obvious that he was just a thieving little low-life. So, that's the story. I decided that, if society didn't want me, I didn't want it. No need to waste money keeping up appearances. Let the front gardens do what they want. Brambles grow nicely here. Keeps people out. Use the back for growing vegetables. I can also sunbathe in the nude without worrying, too. It's very relaxing. You should try it.'

Frank managed not to choke on his tea.

'I'm afraid our garden wouldn't allow that,' he said. 'The neighbours would complain. My wife might not be too impressed either.'

'You're married? That ring isn't just for show, then? Not divorced? I thought you policemen weren't the types for a family life. In fact you've reminded me now, one of the policeman who arrested my son was also named Summers, a Detective Sergeant, I think. Not you, of course. I seem to recall he was divorced.'

'I've managed a few weeks of married life. I'm planning on a lot longer. But back to this attempted break-in. Where did the rock come through?'

'The front lounge. Come through. I've boarded it up. If it was the kitchen I'd have it replaced, but there's no sense in wasting money on the front.'

She picked up a heavy walking stick. As he followed Frank noticed that she had a limp.

'Arthritis,' she said without looking back, guessing Frank's thoughts. 'It gets worse when I'm in the front of the house. The damp.' There was definitely a musty air as they got further away from the kitchen. 'I try not to let it show outside. Those things they call neighbours would love a reason to get me moved out. Poor old biddy can't cope on her own, they'd say. Get the social services in to take me to a home. A mental home, no doubt. History's full of it. Women locked up. Called insane just because they prefer to live their life as they want. There you go, that's where it came in.'

Frank looked up to where she was pointing. There was a section of old board across the topmost of the windows.

'I showed the others where it was thrown from. They wouldn't take my word for it. Probably thought a mad old woman wasn't worth listening to.'

'Out in front as close as they could get through the bushes?' guessed Frank. 'Which is not that close, looking at the undergrowth.'

'That's it. I could tell where the brambles stopped them. It was a thinnish man, about five foot ten.'

'You saw him?'

'No, I could tell from the way the brambles had been pushed back. Quite a bit of force used, but you can't push past brambles no matter how much force you use. Only way is to cut them down entirely, or burn them.'

'Do you have any suspicions about who it might have been? One of your neighbours? A kid fooling around?'

She shook her head.

'I can't see them doing that sort of thing, the neighbours. Firstly they'd get their hands dirty. Secondly it isn't the way they'd go about it. Get lawyers in to prove that I'm doolally, yes, throwing rocks around, no. And if it was a kid he'd be a tall one. Also, kids work in packs. This was someone on his own.'

'What makes you so sure of that?'

'Each time it's only one rock or piece of brick, at most two. A quick throw and whoever it is runs like hell. That's the way I see it, anyway.'

'Each time? There was more than one?'

She looked at him speculatively in the near gloom.

'I always thought the police made reports when they were called out. Either they don't or you haven't read those reports.'

'Ah, yes, I've, er, just got back from leave. I haven't had a chance to thoroughly read through everything. I thought it better I have a look in situ.'

The look on her face showed a distinct lack of belief.

'Out in the vegetable garden,' she said. 'I'll show you.'

He followed her back to the kitchen and out to the back garden.

'There you go,' she said, motioning to a pile of about five or six rocks and half-bricks. 'The first one landed in the frame over there, broke the pane of glass. I found the others all over the vegetable patch.'

Frank looked at the frame, a low kind of greenhouse, and then at the high back wall some distance away.

'All in the same night?' Frank asked.

'No. The first one was the night after whoever it was threw the rock through my front window. I found it in the frame the morning after that. The following morning there were two, then another two the morning after, then one yesterday morning. I've reported them all, but I think your constables have decided I'm imagining things. Finding rocks in my vegetable patch and inventing stories about them. If they knew anything about vegetable growing they'd know that you don't suddenly find rocks on the surface when it's harvest time. Not normally.'

'Hell of a distance to throw if they were aiming at your back windows,' Frank noted. 'It's about half the length of a cricket field. I could probably throw a cricket ball that distance, but not with that high wall in the way. And not something like one of those pieces of brick.' He paused, pulled his arm back and went through the motion of someone throwing a cricket ball. 'I could probably hit the wall from here,' he decided. 'I don't suppose you have a cricket ball handy, do you?'

'No. You know what I think?' asked Martha Shaw.

'I'd love to know what you think,' Mrs Shaw, Frank replied with a grin. 'I always enjoy it when other people do my work for me.'

She gave him a puzzled look.

'Unusual in a man. And a policeman. The rest of your lot don't.'

'You probably know far more about where you live and what might have happened than I ever could. Go on, what do you think happened?'

'Whoever it is throws a rock through my front window to scare me away. Leave town, as they say in the movies. The police turn up and everyone gets to hear about it. So then the front is out of bounds, too much chance of being noticed, people are watching out now. The neighbours all have security cameras and the like. But the back fence backs on to open fields, mainly used for horses, plenty of trees and cover. So the following night our friend, I don't know, maybe he has a look first somehow. Pulls himself up the back fence enough to get a look. Finds himself a nice little rock and throws it with everything he's got. He hears the sound of glass breaking, thinks he's done it, and runs.'

'I see what you mean. Not the sound of a window breaking, but rather the sound of the little pane of glass in the greenhouse. That's much closer to the back wall.'

'Precisely. Then he returns the following few nights because I haven't got the message. Only he misses the frame those times, so no breaking glass. Means he gets a second throw, but still no joy. He can't see what's happened, but he knows he can't stick around for too long, so again runs.'

Frank nodded.

'Seems a likely scenario,' he agreed, silently filing away the possibility that it could be an accurate analysis, or Martha Shaw could be indeed just plain batty. 'Well, I'd better be going. I think I've seen enough for the moment.'

'Aren't you going to give me advice about how to protect myself? Or move out until it's over?' she asked as they made their way back towards the hazardous front garden.

'Will you take it?'

'No.'

'Well, there you go, then. I would ask one thing. I'll give you my number. If anything else happens, report it to the police station, but do me a favour and let me know as well.'

She looked at him as he used his knee as a desk while he wrote out his number.

'I would ask why your constables couldn't just tell you, but I can see there's something funny going on so I won't.'

'Very kind, Mrs Shaw,' He said, handing the note over.

'So why are you here? I thought you lot would have filed it away and forgotten about it.'

'Something similar happened to an old woman in the cemetery. I'm trying to work out whether the two incidents are related.'

'The one called Aggie? The simple one?'

'I don't know if you'd call her simple. She thinks she's twelve years old.'

'Don't know if I'd want to be twelve years old again. Still, I suppose it's one way of coping.'

She looked at him.

'I don't buy this rubbish about all women together,' she said. 'My experience is that most women are more than prepared to put down their so-called sisters if there's a man involved. But, Aggie – I've never met her, but from what I've read she needs looking after.'

'She needs a certain amount of protection. She has a very simple life, which she's happy with. But it doesn't involve being attacked.'

Mrs Shaw nodded.

'In which case I need to get to know her. I might even clean the old rifle. Who knows, it might work.'

'Don't do that, Mrs Shaw.'

She looked at his quiff of white hair.

'Inspector Summers, I know who you are. I know how you got that. I still get the Herald delivered. But you had better get whoever it is before I do. I will not sit on my arse and be a helpless little old woman. I wasn't born that way. I've never lived that way. I have no intention of starting now.'

'I'll do my best, Mrs Shaw. But my hands are a little tied, I'm afraid.'

Martha Shaw looked back at him with no-nonsense eyes.

'You're not telling me the whole truth, Inspector,' she said. 'I just hope that whatever it is you're trying to conceal doesn't end up in tragedy for someone.'

Frank looked at her. Then he smiled.

'Want the truth?' he asked.

'I prefer it.'

'I'm supposed to be off sick. I'm not supposed to be on this case. If my wife found out I'd be – in deep trouble. The trouble is that she's also Inspector Summers, and my boss.'

'Your wife is also Inspector Summers? Was that, what was her name, Inspector Garold?'

'That's the one. Tell me, you don't have a recipe for cabbage in white sauce, do you? They used to make it at an Irish pub close to where I worked once. Had ham or bacon in.'

'Don't tell me that's part of your case.'

'No, while I'm off work I'm on dinner duty. Thought I'd multi-task and try to pick some recipes up while I'm at it.'

Martha Shaw shook her head slowly.

'A man doing the dinner. And they think I'm the mad one,' she noted. 'Come on inside, I'll copy the recipe out for you. Just remember it can be very filling. I'll give you a couple of baby cabbages, you don't want to buy that rubbish they sell in the supermarkets, it's all Frankenstein food, genetically modified.'

'Keep that thing switched off while you're around me, Frank,' the Chief Inspector said as they walked along the river bank, the Chief Inspector weighed down with his fishing impedimenta.

'This?' asked Frank, looking at the metal detector in surprise. 'Why's that, sir?'

'Because you had me digging a big bloody hole yesterday. And you know what I found? A rusty old nail, that's what.'

'You dug a hole?'

'Just where you said that thing had given off a signal. I wasn't going to fall for it, but they do say that there's no such fool as an old fool.'

Frank considered this.

'Well, with all due respect, sir, the machine was right, and you did find the cause of the signal. So it proves it does work.'

'That's not the point. You had me thinking I might find some lost hoard of Roman coins or something.'

'Did I? I don't recalling saying anything like that. I just said I'd found a signal.'

The Chief Inspector glowered.

'Yes, exactly. That's what makes it worse. Bad enough being fooled by someone else, fooling yourself is – really irritating!'

'I suppose there's a certain art to it. Or skill, or experience, perhaps. You'd get used to the amount of signal coming through. I've been getting loads of readings, some strong, others weak.'

'Just don't tell me where you got them, okay? Enough, already.'

'Of course not, sir. Actually, I thought I'd just bring you up to speed on the investigation. See what you think.'

The Chief Inspector groaned.

'And hope I'd accidentally mention something, no doubt. Forget it, Frank, I'm not playing. You're on sick leave. Go enjoy yourself. Go watch a film, or – go dig bloody holes yourself. Big ones. The bigger the better. I've found myself in one, and, as the saying goes, stop digging. You carry on if you want to. In your own bloody hole.'

'That was a Bairnsfather cartoon in the First World War – If you knows of a better hole then you go to it.'

'Ole. Now go away, Frank.'

'Sorry, sir?'

'It's "If you knows of a better 'ole". The character saying it was known as Old Bill. Now go away, Frank.'

'Okay, sir, if that's what you want. Pity, it's an interesting one.' He made a face and switched the metal detector on. 'Anything biting, sir?'

'No. Nor am I. Switch that bloody thing off.'

'Oh, sorry sir, I wasn't thinking. Though there is a strong signal coming through. You haven't got some heavy metal in your fishing bag, have you?'

The Chief Inspector sighed.

'I can see why you got posted to Wellbury. I'm not going to get any peace, am I? Go on, tell me what you've found out.'

Frank switched the machine off and gave the Chief Inspector a quick summary.

'I'd like to have a look at the rocks that were used. See if there's any similarities. Maybe try to work out where they came from.'

'There aren't,' the Chief Inspector said. 'They were probably picked up from near to each incident. One was a small half-brick which was taken from a wall. It was coming loose.'

'What about size?'

The Chief Inspector nodded.

'All much the same. Which suggests that the culprits are similar, or the same person. Almost definitely a man. Too heavy for your average woman. Unless we're looking for a powerful woman. That's presuming that the incidents are related.'

Frank nodded.

'That's the feeling I'm getting. Some of them will be coincidences, some accidents, some tomfoolery, but some are linked. Now if I could get access to all the files ...'

'Forget it, Frank. I'm not going in to smuggle out a caseful of old files like that chap in the le Carré book. I've already told you enough to get on the wrong side of Frieda.'

'But you're her boss.'

'Indeed, Frank. And she's your boss. Which makes me your boss as well. And she's your wife. And you've been booked off sick because you have an extreme allergy to thing or things unknown. And being your superior I'm responsible for your wellbeing. And answerable to Frieda for the same.' He sighed. 'When I was young I wasn't sure whether sure whether to go into the police or the army. Sometimes I wish I had chosen the army. It would have been easier to explain the casualties. Or at least to hide them.'

'I tell you what, sir, how about a little bet.'

The Chief Inspector looked at him through suspicious eyes.

'I somewhat doubt that Frieda would approve of gambling,' he noted, carefully avoiding rejecting the offer.

'Oh, I would imagine the same sir. So we won't tell her.'

'Okay,' said the Chief Inspector slowly, 'what's the bet?'

'I bet you ten quid I'll be inside the station within a week.'

The Chief Inspector laughed.

'No chance, Frank. I won't take your bet because I know some things you don't, so it wouldn't be fair. Trust me, you have absolutely no chance of getting past reception. They'll be renaming the place Fortress Frieda as far as you're concerned.'

Frank grinned.

'That's okay, sir, I wouldn't worry about those things you know. I don't know what they are, but I still reckon I can get back in there within a week. Seven days from now. So, are we agreed on ten quid or do you want to take it higher?'

He held out a hand to shake on it. The Chief Inspector reluctantly took it and did so.

'Why do I have this feeling I shouldn't be doing this?' he asked himself. Frank turned to leave and then turned back again.

'Oh, by the way, sir, why did you get posted to Wellbury?'

'I beat a Chief Constable at poker. Took him to the cleaners by pure bluff.'

Frank chuckled. He turned to go and then turned back again.

'Frank, you're being irritating now. Go, just go.'

'Yes, sir. Oh, by the way, Frieda was thinking that we should have a bridge night now and then.'

'I haven't played bridge for years.'

'Her mother will be coming down next week or the week after. Apparently she's a bridge fanatic.'

'Frieda's mother?' He paused. 'You know, I used to be not bad at bridge. I'm sure I'll be able to pick it up again quite quickly. What night were you thinking of?'

Frank returned home for lunch. He would have, as Frieda suspected, taken lunch in a burger bar or pizza place, but Squishy was at home and needed some TLC as well as food, despite having Colonel Midnight and the neighbour's daughter for company. True to form she met him at the door, pleading starvation of food, drink and love. He filled her bowls in the kitchen for her, checked to see that Midnight's bowls out the back weren't empty, and made himself a piccalilli and ham sandwich.

'So what do you think Frieda expects me to do now, eh, Squish?' he asked as he ate. The kitten turned and gave him a look that said 'I'm eating/You shouldn't be speaking with your mouth full/I should have thought that was obvious/Silly man/Keep your mouth full.'

'Indeed, Squish. Pumping people. And I know just the one.' He finished the sandwich, put the plate in the sink and went to the phone in the hallway. He dialled a number from memory.

'Hello, Susan, it's Frank here.'

'Frank. How are you feeling?'

'Absolutely marvellous. Don't know why people keep on asking me. In fact, I feel so good I thought I'd see if you fancied lunch some time.'

'You must think me simple, Frank. Frieda warned me that you might call. You want to know if I found any useful forensics in these cases where old women are being attacked.'

'Well, now that you mention it ...'

'No, Frank, I'm not going to tell you anything. You are supposed to be off duty. Was there anything else?'

Frank sighed.

'No, I suppose not. How's the love life going?'

'Tom is coming down for the weekend, so it's going very well, thank you.'

'And Gertie and Wilf?'

Tom, an ex-rugby player and Gertie's brother was going out with Susan. Wilf, a would-be Romantic poet and Susan's younger brother was going out with Gertie. They had been stand-in partners at a wedding soon after Frank had proposed to Frieda.

'Well, since that isn't police work, I suppose I can tell you. Wilf will be down on the weekend too.'

'Excellent. Er, going out shopping, by any chance?'

'Shopping?'

'If I know Gertie, she'll be wondering what to wear, followed by an urge to go shopping for a new outfit.'

'We have arranged to do a little shopping, as it happens.'

Frank gave an exaggerated sigh.

'You know I don't like to stereotype,' he said, 'but some people have this image of women who will always shop. Even when they hit eighty or a hundred, they will always shop. Which isn't, of course true about you. After all, you're a professional, and –'

'Frank?'

'Yes?'

'Stop fishing. I'm not going to tell you anything about the case. You are supposed to be taking things easy. Some of us do actually care about you, though God alone knows why.'

'Okay, okay. Say, fancy coming around to dinner one night?'

'Dinner?'

'You and Tom. Maybe Gertie and Wilf too, if they're available. I'm getting quite good at cooking.'

There was a pause as Susan considered the idea.

'No use trying to pump Tom,' she said. 'I don't discuss my work with him.'

'You should. Couples should share their lives. It's important.'

'Frank?'

'Yes?'

'You're a total shit. But I like Frieda. Shall we say a week Saturday?'

'Saturday a week it is. Must fly, speak to you later.'

Having sent up a kite he was about to leave when the phone rang.

'Frank? It's Frieda.'

'Hello, Free, what's up?'

'Frank, were you expecting something to be delivered to the station? A large-ish parcel?'

'No. Why would I have anything delivered to the station? If I was expecting something I would have mentioned it.'

'That's what I thought. But one has been delivered, along with an envelope with "Personal and Confidential" on it.'

'What's inside? What does it say?'

'Frank, I can't open something addressed to you marked as personal and confidential.'

'Course you can, Free, we're married. Go on, open it and tell me what it says. I'm intrigued. It isn't my birthday or anything like that.'

'Are you sure, Frank?'

'Course I'm sure, Free. Anyway, if it was interesting it wouldn't be labelled private and confidential. The only people who do that are the tax people. Really interesting envelopes don't even have a name on.'

Frank listened to the sound of Frieda opening the letter. There was silence as she read it.

'It sounds rather threatening, Frank. It says, 'I hop the enclosed will light your life up, Inspector Summers. I will give you a few days to set him up. Then I will email you the rule of combat. Let the best man come out victoria's. I tossed, you are black.' And then it ends with a scrawl, a signature of sorts. A Mason. Or Amazing. Actually, it might even be A Salad.'

'Did you say "Victoria's"? As in belongs to the queen?'

'Yes, Frank, exactly.'

'I hop the enclosed? Rule of combat? What sort of a language is that?'

'Either someone unfamiliar with the English language or someone who wants us to think they are. Doesn't sound like any masons I've known. Do you know any masons, Frank?'

'I knew a plumber once who was a mason. As far as I could tell it was an excuse to have large dinners while dressed up in strange regalia – a bit like cross-dressing, really.'

'You never met any in the force?'

'Oh, yes, of course. Loads. I used to take the Mick out of them.'

'Why did I ever doubt that, darling? You were never tempted to join?'

'My grandmother on my father's side was Catholic. I've yet to discover a lodge that welcomes anyone who has a Catholic relation later than Henry VIII.'

'Maybe it's a case of revenge. For you ... taking the Mick.'

'Well, I'm not sure what it is they're threatening. But it is most intriguing. Any idea what's in the parcel?'

'No. I've had it put in one of the interview rooms just in case it goes bang. Eric Johns said it didn't seem heavy enough to be a bomb, but you can never be too sure.'

'Eric Johns suddenly knows something about the weight of bombs?'

'Eric Johns always suddenly knows something about everything, darling, you know that.'

'True. I never cease to be amazed by the way he explains the computer systems in reception to new constables despite never using them himself.'

'What worries me is that he's almost always entirely wrong. Which means the parcel is probably a small nuclear device that could take out a minor city.'

'Point. I'll be straight over.'

'Now, Frank, you're off duty.'

'It's my parcel.'

Frieda sighed.

'Okay, Frank, you can come in and open your parcel. But that's all, you're still not on duty. I'll have someone meet you in reception.'

'Free, I'm sure I can remember my way around still. It hasn't been that long.'

He could hear Frieda smile.

'I've disabled your security access, Frank, you don't think I'd leave it still active so you could accidentally wander back into work, did you? See you shortly, sweetie.'

Frank put the phone down. He hadn't considered the possibility of Frieda de-activating his security access, but that was only because he hadn't intended to use it. The strongest and weakest links in any building weren't the locks, they were the occupants. That's why computer hackers found it so easy to break into companies who had forgotten that fact.

'Afternoon, Eric,' he greeted as he breezed into the reception area of Wellbury police station, holding the metal detector just the way an enthusiast wouldn't. 'I believe I have a minder waiting.'

'Indeed you do, Frank,' Eric replied with a good deal of worry in his voice as he picked up a phone and dialled an internal number. 'The Inspector was very precise about that. Hello, constable? Inspector Summers has arrived. Frank, that is, not – Well, you know what I mean.'

He put the phone down. Frank grinned.

'Frieda threaten to amputate your lunch hour if you let me wander around on my own?' he asked.

'Not funny, Frank. There is a definite tension in the station at the moment. The women.'

He nodded as if that made everything clear.

'The women what?' asked Frank once it was clear Eric wasn't going to expand without prompting.

'They aren't happy. They've been going around saying that these attacks on old women are a sign of the pate ... pate ... pate-ree-arky –'

'Patriarchy?'

'Of men oppressing women.'

He leaned towards Frank confidentially.

'And then Pete was in his office upstairs. And a police van turns up and parks out in front, "Dog Section" written on the side. Only it's driven by two WPCs. And Pete says, without thinking, "I don't think they look that bad". Only Alison Wheately had just walked in when he said it. So she looks outside to see what it is, and she didn't see the funny side, I can tell you that. Has a word with her union rep. Who turns out to be Mary East.'

'Oh, dear,' said Frank, 'Mary, Mary quite contrary?'

'That's the one. Built like a br – Well, better not go there, walls have ears. So she demands a meeting with Frigid regarding casual sexism in the workplace.'

'Who does not quite have the patience of a saint when it comes to such matters.'

'A very good way of putting it, Frank, a very good way of putting it. Anyway, she hauls Percy and Pete in, Percy because he's Pete's superior officer, of course, and asks Pete what he's got to say for himself. Pete apologises, says he wasn't thinking. And you know what happens next?'

'Frieda hangs him out of the window by his more tender areas?'

'No. that's what's so strange. She says, 'Good, that's cleared up. Was there anything else? No? Well, close the door on the way out, will you? And try not to do it again, there's a good lad.' And that's it. Well, apart from the women wanting more revenge. They think Frigid, I mean the Inspector, was too easy on Pete.'

'Well, well,' Frank chuckled. 'Sounds like she's playing the long game.'

'The long game?'

'She's conserving her bollocking resources for things that really matter.'

'Such as?'

'Oh, I don't know, someone who lets me out of sight while I'm in here, perhaps. Someone who accidentally lets me see reports in this log book of yours that I've just been reading for the last five minutes.'

'Now, Frank, stop that, give that back here –' Eric began. Just then the internal security door opened and Sam Nightingale walked into reception.

'Sam!' cried Frank, 'you're looking ravishing as always. Eric's just told me I can go in. Interview room four I believe it is.'

'You're looking pretty good yourself, Inspector,' Sam replied, letting Frank in before following him closely. 'The Inspector has given me orders to make sure you don't get lost.'

Frank grinned. He had vaguely wondered who Frieda would choose to baby-sit him. His money would have been on Gertie or Pete Phillips. Gertie because she was more experienced in Frank Summers' ducking and diving, Pete because he would be too terrified of getting in Frieda's bad books to let Frank out of sight. But he was impressed. Sam Nightingale was an excellent choice. She was a lesbian, so while Frank's flattery wasn't unwelcome it would never have the same effect as on Gertie. She had also been given the job of baby-sitting Frank before, with the order not to let him out of sight for a second. She had done just that, and Frank had disappeared for the night on that occasion. She would never make that mistake again. She might like Frank Summers, she just wouldn't trust him an inch, unlike Pete who would fall for any gag going.

'So, how's your mother keeping, then?' Frank asked as they walked down the corridor towards the interview rooms.

'I wasn't aware you'd met my mother, sir.'

'Didn't you mention her at the wedding? Or am I getting my mothers mixed up?'

'I think you might be getting your little old women mixed up, sir. And your innocent young constables, if I may say so.'

'Damn, you're good, Sam,' Frank enthused.

'And getting better with experience, sir. Here we are, interview room four,' she said stopping short of a door. 'The Inspector will be here shortly.'

'Why don't we go in?'

'The Inspector thinks we should err on the side of caution in case it does turn out to be explosive.'

'Ah, well, good point. If it is, we can discount our stone-thrower.'

'Why do you ... Good try, sir, you almost had me there.'

'Oh, come on, Sam, you know I'm going to wheedle it out of you sooner or later.'

'In your dreams you will, Frank, darling,' said a voice coming along the corridor.

'Hello, Free,' Frank said, turning to meet his wife. 'Ten more seconds and I would have got there.'

Frieda smiled as she inserted a key into the lock. A number of his past reviews had contained coded language which translated as 'lacks confidence'. That certainly wasn't the Frank Summers she was coming to know.

'I'm sure you would have, Frank, I'm sure you would have.' She opened the door to let him in. As he passed she winked at Sam.

'So, where's this parcel, then?' he asked as she closed the door. 'That thing over there?' He pointed to a package at the end of the interview table, something about three feet square, badly wrapped in cardboard with far too much adhesive tape and string.

'That's the one,' agreed Frieda.

'So what are you doing in here?' he asked. 'I don't want you in here if it's likely to go bang.'

'I wouldn't want you to accidentally climb out of the window and find you wandering the corridors chatting to people about work. Someone has to be in here with you, it might as well be me. As you said, ten more seconds with Sam and she'd have been singing like the traditional canary.'

He gave her his Clint Eastwood look. Just then the door opened and a man rarely seen around the station walked in, the Chief Inspector, wearing his fishing gear.

'What's this about an unexploded device, Frieda?' he asked. 'Frank!' he exclaimed, 'how the devil did you get in?'

'That will be ten quid you owe me, sir,' Frank reminded him. The Chief Inspector scowled, took out his wallet and extracted a ten pound note.

'And just what is all that about?' asked Frieda, in the double note of a wife who does not take kindly to her husband indulging in dangerous practices such as gambling, and a Detective Inspector who does not take kindly to a Chief Inspector who associates with her officers while they were on sick leave and should be avoiding anything to do with work. Especially since said sick police officer was her husband and said Chief Inspector was her boss, both of whom should be doing as they were told.

But also with that slight hesitant note that, if it were a gamble between her husband and her boss, she'd back her husband the whole way. And he'd better bloody win or he'd be in deep trouble.

'He bet me he'd be back in here within a week,' said the Chief Inspector with a touch of acerbity. 'I put my money on your keeping him out.'

'Well, really,' said Frieda, 'he's not here to work, he's here to collect a parcel. So he's not really here, is here?'

The Chief Inspector glowered at a grinning Frank.

'So where is this blasted thing? Is it that bunch of string and brown paper?'

'Indeed, sir,' replied Frank. 'Reminds me of a great-aunt I had. Her eyesight was going, and she had a bit of a phobia about parcels falling to pieces. She'd use half a ton of cellotape and enough string to outfit the Cutty Sark. The WI set aside a day a month to cutting open her parcels.'

He ran the metal detector over the parcel.

'It's giving a reading in the corner over there,' he said. 'Not much, about what you'd expect from a couple of nails.'

'How do you know what a couple of nails sound like?' asked Frieda.

'Someone I know dug up a place where I found a similar reading. They found a rusty old nail.'

The Chief Inspector gave him a look daring him to reveal the name of the 'someone'.

'They actually dug a nail up?' asked Frieda. 'Honestly, some people.'

'Don't have the sense they were born with?' suggested Frank.

'Frank, here's my fishing knife,' the Chief Inspector said, handing over a rather vicious-looking sheathed knife. 'Open the bloody thing before I think of other things to use the knife on.'

Frank grinned and began the process of cutting away enough packaging to wrap a mechanised brigade. Slowly the contents became visible. It appeared to be something made out of wood, a squarish piece of wood and some legs. Frank eased the main bit out.

'It's a chess board,' said Frieda.

'It's a very strange chess board,' said the Chief Inspector. 'Too many squares. It looks like a square coffee-table. The top of one, anyway.'

Frank looked into the box and took out four legs. One pack of screws. And four boxes. He opened the boxes. There were four sets of chess pieces, two white, two black.

'Double chess,' he said.

There was a pause.

'Double chess?' asked Frieda.

'Count the squares. I'll bet there are sixteen by sixteen. Normal set is eight by eight'

They counted. It was sixteen by sixteen.

'How did you guess that, Frank?'

'Chap I knew at university came up with this idea one night at the students' uni. There were four of us who played the odd game of chess. I used to win most times, purely by bluff, really. The others all knew every single move ever invented, and their names. Their problem was that they couldn't handle anything unorthodox, so all I had to do was make a few strange moves – the one time I told them that a move was known as the Heimlich switch. They never did cotton on. Strange, because they were extremely bright people.'

'Not women. then,' said Frieda. 'A woman would have sussed you out straight away.'

'No, they were all blokes, as it happens.'

'I don't understand,' said the Chief Inspector. 'I don't see the point.'

'Well, one evening one of them – Adam Manson, that was his name – came up with this idea of double chess. Just like this. Except for one small point.'

He paused, chin in hand, looking at the set in reverie.

'Frank, darling, would you mind putting your wife and the rest of us out of our misery and explaining?'

Frank pointed to the pieces.

'Our double chess had four different colours. It was designed for four people to play at the same time. A bit like that game, Risk, where you try to take over the world. Trouble is you're facing other people who might attack you while you're busy attacking another player's pieces. This one only has two colours. Which suggests that it's been designed for two players. Two kings each. Have to checkmate twice.'

'Interesting,' said the Chief Inspector. 'It certainly means using a totally different strategy. Very interesting indeed. I wouldn't mind a game.'

'So this is probably from one of them? The people you knew at university?'

'God, no, I haven't seen them for years. Unless somehow one of them has landed up in Wellbury. But then they'd give me a call, they wouldn't send this along without warning. At least, I wouldn't have thought so. No, I reckon if it was one of them there'd be four different chess sets.'

'These friends of yours,' said Frieda, 'they were quite sane, weren't they?'

'Perfectly normal students,' said Frank.

'In that case, not quite sane. What were they studying?'

'Computer science, mainly.'

'Oh, dear,' said the Chief Inspector. 'I've yet to meet one of those who isn't a bit ... eccentric,'

'Battier than the battiest bats ever,' agreed Frank. 'I really enjoyed their company. We had some great times.'

'And the university computer systems never quite worked properly afterwards?' suggested the Chief Inspector.

'No, but that was okay, they never really worked properly before.'

'Frank,' noted Frieda, 'if whoever it is is going to email you the moves you'll need to redirect your office email to your private one.'

Frank grinned at the chessboard. She caught his look.

'But that would mean you'd be getting all your other emails, and you're not supposed to be working. I'm sure there's a way to redirect only those from a certain sender. Tricia will know.'

'And the sender's name will be ... Mason? Salad? Amazing?' asked Frank.

She sighed.

'Yes, we won't know until he sends an email, will we.'

'There's a very simple answer, Free.'

'Which is?'

'I'll give you my password. You can keep an eye on my email account and let me know if anything comes through.'

'Frank, it's a sackable offence to share passwords, you know that.'

'We're married, Free. We're supposed to share everything. Anyway, there's nothing confidential in my in-box, just the usual guff, your memos about time-sheets and other rubbish.'

'Very funny, Frank. Not.'

'Think of it as an operational exigency, Free.'

'Yes, I know your operational exigencies, Frank. Anything you disagree with.'

'Okay, I tell you what, I promise to change it again when I'm back on duty and not tell you the new one. Happy?'

Frieda frowned at him. He was being much too reasonable. And helpful. Of course breaking rules was his forte. But sharing passwords? That wasn't the sort of rule he'd break. But then he was right, they were husband and wife, if you can't trust your spouse who can you trust?

Well, her first marriage had taught her that your spouse was quite likely to be the last thing you should trust.

She sighed again. It reminded her that his mother seemed to do a lot of sighing when talking about him and his father.

'Frank, you can be really infuriating, you know, especially when you're being helpful. Okay, what's your password?'

He leaned over and whispered in her ear, ending with a snatched kiss on the cheek. She coloured at whatever he had whispered.

'I might have known, Frank, I might have known,' she said, smiling.

Frank rubbed his hands.

'Now, all we have to do is wait for our Mason's first move.'

'Or the Salad's,' pointed out the Chief Inspector.

The Fishermans was a pub with both a history and a reputation. The history was mainly one of being burnt down at times of crisis or just when the beer ran out, which could arguably be defined as a crisis. The reputation was that of being a place reputable people did not go near. It wasn't that it was a hive of insurrection, criminality, dark deeds or other nefarious practices, they just liked having a reputation which kept the boring people out. It was the sort of pub where the regulars would choose their side in a civil war based on which army looked like it would have more fun. And dressed better.

In fact a better name for it in previous centuries would have been the Smugglers Inn, but that would have been a dead giveaway.

And woe betide anyone who started a discussion on whether "Fishermans" should have an apostrophe in it. People had ended up in hospital after discussions about that.

The Cult of the Clueless was having its regular Saturday morning meeting which that week was taking place on the Friday evening due to the fact that its two founder members had decided to go for a pint. That sort of thing had been happening ever since they had their first regular Saturday meeting, but they felt that tradition was worth upholding. Besides which, it marked out anyone pointing out that it was Friday rather than Saturday as a stranger and someone to be treated with contempt, if not to have a pint of slops poured over his head. Should the stranger happen to be an attractive young woman they had agreed to be rather magnanimous and use a pint of relatively clean water instead.

They had been joined by one of the locals known as "Major Tom" on account of his looking like a major and being named Tom. At the time Major Tom had first appeared they already had a Tom, known as Uncle Tom. There had been much debate about whether Major Tom should be called Tom-Tom, or even Two-Tom, on the grounds that anyone asking where he was could be told, "Two-Tom Coming". "Tom-Two" offered promise of the start of a badly made and sung song, but in the end it turned out that he had once indulged in LSD, which made him a spaceman, which confirmed him as "Major Tom".

Post-graduate sociology theses have been created out of much thinner material.

Also at the table was "Oh And Litmus", so called because he lived in his own world and was only remembered after everyone else. His parents, when queried as to the number of their progeny would reply, "Two. Oh and Litmus." Anyone asked who had been in the night before would be given a list of names, a pause, and "Oh, and Litmus". This had become "Oh, and Oh And Litmus, and some had bets on when that would first become, "Oh, and Oh And Oh And Litmus", or whether it would simply resolve to "Oh And".

The four of them (and partially Oh And Litmus) were involved in a war council, or what could be described as three-parts drinking to one-part thinking.

'Well, this door-stopping and leafletting business isn't working as well as can be expected,' the man calling himself Seumas O'Brien-O'Murphy-O'Connor-O sighed, once he had time to enjoy the first slaking of his thirst. 'It's a lot tougher than we thought.'

'How many drops have you made?' asked Major Tom.

'Bricks,' said Oh And Litmus.

'Three,' replied Jaimie. 'The vestry at the Catholic church while Father Brown was doing his holy stuff with sick people at the hospital, Inspector Summers, and that pokey little flat that presumptuous little Bible Thumper lives in. We left a bunch of them at each place. Hopefully they'll share them out with their friends and neighbours. Apart from the little Bible Thumper who won't have any friends and whose neighbours avoid him like the scabies.'

'It's a start,' Uncle Tom said.

'Don't want to hurdle your jumps before you pass them,' agreed Major Tom.

'I have a feeling we might have to try a different tack,' said Seumas. 'Ignorance is a hard sell.'

'Maybe we should award degrees,' suggested Jaimie. 'Anyone who wants to join has to do an exam. If they show they know nothing they get a nice piece of parchment saying so. For a price.'

'Ice-cream,' added Oh And Litmus. "Mint and chocolate."

'Expensive stuff, parchment,' noted Major Tom.

'Can't remember the last time I saw parchment,' offered Uncle Tom. 'Doesn't the queen read her speeches from it? Or is that vellum? From goats.'

'What we need is a mass audience,' said Seumas.

'Hate mass,' decided Oh And Litmus. 'Ruins a good wake.'

'We need to get on radio to spread the word,' said Seumas.

'What about television,' suggested Jaimie.

'What about the Internet?' asked Uncle Tom.

'Twitter,' suggested Major Tom. 'Everybody's on Twitter these days. Except me.'

'And the rest of us here,' said Seumas. 'No, the people we're trying to reach aren't the kind to waste their time on Facebook or Twitter or whatever that other one is called. I think we have to go for the old-fashioned option.'

'Telegrams?' asked Major Tom.

'Someone died?' enquired Oh And Litmus.

'No one died, And,' said Seumas. 'Finish your pint.'

'One of those cars with a loudspeaker on top. I remember old Harry Flanders doing that. Stood as an independent in the general election, 65 it was,' recalled Uncle Tom.

'What happened?'

'He came last. Tory chap won.'

'Wait a minute, there wasn't an election in 65. You must be thinking of 64 or 66.'

'Soapbox. Like John Major.'

'No. Radio. Like I said, radio. Doesn't anyone here listen?'

'No.'

'Radio?'

'You mean that Zack Pratt? Or do I mean that prat Zack?'

They considered the idea of the locally despised radio DJ in gloomy silence.

'He is an idiot,' noted Seumas.

'If they did degrees for ignorance he'd get a first.'

'Summer come lord,' said Oh And Litmus.

'But a lot of people do listen to his show,' pointed out Uncle Tom.

'A lot of people used to watch the test pattern on the telly,' Seumas replied.

'My goodness,' said Major Tom, 'that takes me back. Haven't seen the test pattern for ages.'

'Fish paste,' said Oh And Litmus. 'And cheese. Sandwich.'

'Ages since I had a fish paste sandwich,' said Jamie.

'Well, look on the bright side, he might break a leg before. The Pratt.'

'I think we should take some teddy bears with.'

'To give to him?'

'To beat him to death with.'

'Isn't that a bit harsh? On the teddy bears?'

Seumas sighed and took a deep sip of beer.

'I think our next meeting should be in the brewery.' he decided.

'Why's that?'

'To prove that we do have certain organisational skills.'

The others brightened up at this thought.

'Would you fecking gentlemen mind if I joined you?' asked a soft voice behind them. They turned to find a mild-mannered, elderly looking man dressed in brown slacks, white shirt, brown tie and dark brown jacket.

'Well, now,' said Seumas, 'that depends. Do you believe?'

'Christ, yes, of course I fecking believe. I am fecking god after fecking all.'.

'You are fecking god?' asked Uncle Tom. 'I always did wonder what a fecking god looked like. Never quite saw you as wearing a brown tie, though.'

'We are all, fecking god, my fecking son,' said Brown Man politely.

'Ranter,' said Oh And Litmus.

Seumas clicked his fingers in delight.

'You're a Ranter!' he exclaimed. The man smiled brightly.

'You recognised it!' he exclaimed back. 'Oh, you don't know how happy that makes me. You know, every day I force myself to go around swearing – sorry, fecking swearing – and trying to commit sin, and all they say is, there's that weird old man swearing again. And me trying to save their fecking immortal souls.'

'Take a seat,' said Seumas. 'We don't normally accept the religious, but a Ranter – well, they were once declared atheists, weren't they? What's your name?'

'Tom. Just fecking Tom.'

'Oh fecking great,' muttered Major Tom, 'another one.'

'What's a Ranter, Fecking Tom?' asked Jamie.

'Is committing sin a requirement of your religion?' asked Uncle Tom. 'And if so, where do I join?'

'The Ranters,' said Seumas, 'if I've got my dates right, appeared around Cromwell's time. They claimed that god was in everyone and everyone was part of god. And because god created everything he also created sin. But god could never create sin so there was no such thing as sin. So the Ranters went around sinning and swearing and cussing to demonstrate that there was no such thing as sin. Correct, Fecking Tom?'

'Oh, yes, but don't forget the fornication. They were quite into fornication.'

'And you been keeping up the traditions?'

Fecking Tom sighed.

'I try, I try. I can handle the swearing, though I need to remind myself from time to time. But I could never get the fornication right. It's ironic since I'm probably a descendant of Laurence Claxton, the most famous of the Ranters.'

'Probably a descendant?'

'He had affairs with barmaids and such. They didn't tend to leave many official records.'

'And there were the Diggers and Quakers and Shakers,' said Seumas, misty eyed. 'Must have been great days.'

'Oh, my goodness, no,' said Fecking Tom, 'we wouldn't have anything to do with the Diggers, Quakers or Shakers. They were more or less respectable.'

'Splitters,' suggested Oh And Litmus.

'Well, the Diggers could have been, I suppose,' admitted Fecking Tom. 'Or am I thinking of rail-splitters like Abraham Lincoln.'

'Pickled onions,' added Oh And Litmus.

'Didn't they go around in the nude?' asked Uncle Tom.

'The Splitters?'

'The Ranters.'

'Well,' said Fecking Tom, 'it depends on who you believe. My father always said that they were very well dressed. But then he liked being well dressed. If you read what was written at the time, fecking however, there are plenty of reports of them going around without doublet or breeches. But that doesn't mean they weren't wearing hose, and, fecking anyway, you can't trust them, the reports, I mean. The only people who could write in those days were the educated and the scribes, and they had it in for the Ranters. The Ranters didn't bother writing anything down because they thought their truths were too self-evident to need recording. Bit of a fecking own goal, really.'

'You know, that's a very good point, Seumas,' said Uncle Tom. 'You're going to have to do something similar or history will portray the Clueless as ... well, clueless.'

Seumas contemplated his pint bitterly for a few moments. Then a not very nice smile began to creep across his face.

'What we need is a riot,' he decided. 'A battle between the Clueless and the Bible Thumpers. Something that will get us noticed. Recorded for posterity. On that U-Tube thing.'

'Now wait a minute,' said Jaimie, 'you said that all that talk about a showdown was just that, talk. I'm not averse to a bout of pugilism, but that Father Brown is built like a brick shithouse on stilts. And he's too forgiving afterward.'

'Ah, no, Jaimie, my son, we don't want to take on the Church, not the Catholic Church, Father Brown would have us back in the confessional before you could say Forgive Me Father. No, no, we have to play it clever. We have to find Believers who don't believe but do so devoutly. People who are so certain they won't be forgiving.'

'You mean like the Bible Thumper who got you so wound up in the first place?'

'Precisely, Jaimie. Thumper. Little Thumper.'

'You could always burn a Koran,' suggested Major Tom.

The others looked at him in alarm.

'Well, I didn't mean a real Koran,' he said hastily, 'I meant one of those genuine fakes that's going around.'

'Don't be daft, Major Tom,' said Seumas. 'Doesn't matter how fake it is, they'll see it as an insult on their religion anyway. And we don't have a dog in that fight. Let the Muslims have their own fights between them, the Sunnies and the Shi'its, we've got enough of a problem with Christian believers.'

'Fecking right,' said Fecking Tom.

'You think we should burn a Christian Bible?' asked Major Tom.

'Certainly not,' replied Seumas. 'Burning books is for barbarians. What we will do is quite simple.'

'Which is?' asked Jaimie.

'We will simply quote from it.'

There was a silence as this was absorbed.

'You mean like that bit about stoning your wife if she eats cuttlefish?'

'That and the rest. Especially the anti-homosexual paragraphs.'

'And women being obedient. That'll get them going'

They clinked glasses, grinning, some broadly, some maliciously.

'Fecking brilliant,' said Fecking Tom. 'Would you like to go on the radio to do it? I've got some contacts at radio Wellbury. Sorry, radio fecking Wellbury.'

'You mean fecking radio Wellbury.'

'No, I think he means fecking contacts.'

'Who gives a feck?' asked Seumas.

They looked at him.

'We've had that discussion before,' said Jamie. 'And bloody depressing it was too.'

'Pancakes?' asked Oh And Litmus.

Saturday
Frieda's overtime; More voices stir

'I'll be back by lunchtime,' Frieda promised as she buttoned up her coat. 'Unless something unexpected happens.'

'You mean like the Chief Constable not turning up?' asked Frank.

'He said it would in the morning if he did pop in.'

'You'd think he could at least say for definite whether he was going to turn up. You're probably wasting a perfectly good Saturday morning for nothing.'

'Has to be done, Frank. We'll go house-hunting next weekend. Percy's on duty.'

'Okay, I'll get the domestics sorted this morning.'

She gave him a suspicious look.

'You didn't make any sarcastic remarks about looking forward to next Saturday, Frank.'

'Well, Free, I've decided that, if it has to be done, it has to be done. Get it over and get on with more important things.'

'Mmmm,' she said. She gave him a kiss. 'Don't cause any disasters while I'm gone, Frank.'

Frank looked at Squishy once Frieda had closed the door.

'Ten quid says the Chief Constable doesn't turn up,' he told her. Squishy miaowed agreement.

'And another ten quid says absolutely nothing happens the whole day. Apart from the usual minor crime.'

Squishy stayed silent.

'Cult of the Clueless,' said a voice slowly as it read the words on the pamphlet in a dank little basement flat. 'Heresy! Cults are an abomination in the eyes of The Lord.'

There was a pause as the man waited for the next thought to arrive in his head.

'We must fight this as true Believers,' it announced.

Pause.

'They are the anti-Christ.'

Pause.

'Who can I get to join me in this Holy Quest?'

Pause.

'I know. Mohamed Mohamed. He'll be at the mosque now.'

Pause.

'We are People of the Book. They are Unbelievers.'

Pause.

There was a sound of a (probably) human hand softly patting a Guaranteed Genuine Leather Bound Original Copy Of The Original.

Pause.

'Unfortunate he's so thick, though.'

There was the sound of an old-fashioned phone being picked up and a number dialled.

'Hello, is that Wellbury Herald? It is? My name is Danish, Deacon Danish, and I would like to announce a forthcoming demonstration. How many? Thousands, young lady, thousands, if not more. All those who have seen the light and will be taken up in the Rapture.'

Pause.

'No, Rapture, not rupture.'

Monday

Queen Frieda; the Mason's first move; TOBS is GO;

Tom Gregson and Wilf Pleadle sat on the bench in the reception of Wellbury police station. Wilf was waiting for

Gertie to come off duty. Susan had told Tom that she would meet him there as she had something to drop off. Wilf had the air of someone looking forward to all the delights a police reception could presumably offer for the innocent, the curious and the mickey-takers. Tom sat with his elbows on his knees and the attitude of someone who had once, in his younger days, been arrested during a fracas after a rugby match, following an unfortunate but wholly innocent misunderstanding, and had ever since had a distinct dislike for police reception areas, and police officers' knees. He also found the occasional glances from the constable behind the reception desk off-putting. There was an element of a snigger in the young man's face. It brought back memories of a time he had been going out with a school teacher, and had unwisely agreed to meet her at the school gates.

Little children and young coppers can be very cruel.

'Should have been here by now,' he muttered, checking his watch for the third time in a minute.

'I wonder if Gertie is tied up with some fascinating crime,' Wilf said in a rather loud voice as Sergeant Eric Johns came in to relieve the young constable. 'I can't say I've been very impressed with what we've had so far.'

Eric Johns glanced at him. The two of them presented him with an unusual problem. As they were civilians he could adopt his patronising "well, young man" attitude. But Tom definitely looked the type who should be addressed as "Sir". And he was going out with Doctor Pleadle, a woman best left alone. Wilf was going out with Gertie, who was a mere constable, so that could work.

Then again, she was a woman, and those things were dangerous at the best of times. They could go bang at any moment. For absolutely no reason whatsoever.

'I was planning on becoming a police officer once,' said Wilf, checking his cravat as if he hadn't noticed Eric Johns' look. 'But they said I had to start in the ranks. I mean, with all my abilities, I expected to begin as a commissionaire at least.'

Eric Johns paused mentally. He had a horrible suspicion someone was Taking The Piss.

'It's the quiet time,' he decided to say. 'Not much happens this time of day.'

As so often with Eric Johns's announcements this was immediately proved false as the doors burst open and constables Sidney Feeler and Steve Wright staggered in carrying a man who appeared to have adopted the lotus position, with long hair and a beard, sandals on his feet and a guitar in his hands. Behind them came four young women, flowers in their hair, who seemed to be beating the two constables with lilies.

The sight would have been discombobulating on its own, but what made it more so was the disparity between the two constables. They were almost always paired together because firstly they were best friends, secondly because Steve was the tallest and thinnest beat bobby in the station and Sidney the shortest and stockiest. Neither was of an aggressive nature, but they never seemed to have a problem with people not co-operating: most people's confidence would be undermined by having to face questions coming alternatively from above and below, however polite.

They managed to get him to the bench and put him down on it, next to the two bemused young men.

'Causing a public nuisance outside the police station, Sarge,' Sidney Feeler explained in a breathless voice to an open-mouthed Eric Johns. The desk sergeant scratched his cheek.

'And these four have been assaulting police officers,' said Steve Right. 'Oi! Now stop that! I've got a pollen allergy I'll have you know.' The four women drew back. Eric Johns looked from them to the two constables, and then to the bearded man.

'In what way?' he asked. 'The bearded bloke, I mean, what's he been doing?'

'Refused to move on, Sarge. He was sitting on the pavement playing his guitar. We told him to get out of it but he wouldn't'

'Ah, begging in public, then.'

The two constables looked up and down at each other.

'Well, not quite, Sarge. Leastways he didn't have a sign asking for money or anything.'

'Or a cap next to him, that sort of thing.'

Eric Johns scratched his cheek again.

'Was he playing badly?' he asked.

'Sorry, Sarge?'

'Was he playing badly? What I want to know, son, is, how was he causing a public nuisance?'

The two constables exchanged another look.

'Well, Sarge, we'd just got back from patrol, and we were just about to go to the canteen for a cuppa, when we met the Inspector in the corridor. And she told us to sort out whoever was, and I quote, making that damn awful noise below her office.'

'Ah, yes,' said Eric Johns, nodding. 'Hindering the police in the lawful pursuit of their duty. Not to mention upsetting a superior officer who is also of a womanly persuasion. Now, son, let's start with your name.'

The bearded man looked directly ahead and chanted 'Ooohhhhmmmmmm'.

'Right,' said Eric Johns, licking the tip of his pencil. 'Ohm. Is that your first name or surname?'

'Ooohhhhmmmmm'

'Yes, son, I've got that bit. I want to know whether it's your first name or surname.'

'Ooohhhhmmmmm'

'I think he's chanting, Sarge.'

'Chanting? Ohm Chanting? Funny sort of name.'

'No, Sarge, chanting. As in, well, chanting. You know, like religious people do. Priests and that sort. Singing sort of thing.'

'He's a priest? I don't see no dog collar.'

'It's his pranayama,' said one of the women.

'His prawn what?'

'His pranayama. His holy breath control.'

'Don't know what's holy about it, it sounds bloody awful.'

'He is our master. He is a man of peace.'

'Well, love, at the moment he's facing a charge of breaking the peace.'

'Don't you use that word to me, you patriarchal sexist dinosaur!' the woman shouted. Eric Johns blinked and stepped back. The other women muttered 'Sexist! Sexist! Sexist! Ssssexissssst!!!'

'Look, this is a police station, you can't come in here and start siss-siss-ing at me, you know.'

'Pigs! Pigs! Piiigggsss!!!'

'Right! That's it! Lock 'em up in the cells, you two.'

Sidney Feeler and Steve Right looked at the women. They had closed ranks and were shaking their lilies in a most aggressive manner.

'Just what exactly is going on here?' asked Frieda, entering reception. 'Sid, I asked you and Steve to sort out that rumpus outside, not to create a cacophony in here.'

'Er, well, you see, Inspector, the, er, rumpus was this bloke here on his guitar. Only he wouldn't move on, so we arrested him.'

Frieda raised an eyebrow.

'You arrested him for playing a guitar in public,' she said slowly. 'I see. And these women? What were they doing?'

'They were listening to him.'

'I see. And you arrested them as well? For aggressive listening, perhaps?'

Steve and Sidney looked at each other. Then back at Frieda.

'No, ma'am, they sort of followed us in. They were attacking us with them plants.'

'And Steve has a pollen allergy.'

Steve sneezed to prove it.

Frieda noticed that the bearded man was staring at her.

'Your guitar needs tuning,' she said. 'The E string is way out.' She turned back to the two constables. 'Put him back where you found him. Or a few yards further down. And take that lot out with him too. We have much more important things to do than arrest out of date hippies for playing a guitar badly.'

She skipped back as the man suddenly went down on his knees and bowed to her. The women immediately followed suit.

'My queen!' the man moaned.

'Our queen!' the women echoed.

Frieda stared at them, speechless.

'Your throne is holy,' the man cried.

'Your head is flippin barking mad,' muttered Eric Johns.

'Now stop that!' Frieda ordered. 'What's this nonsense about a throne?'

'Your office is on the conjunction,' one of the women said, looking up.

'Conjunction?'

'Conjunction of the holiest of ley lines. That's why the master was playing where he was. It's the closest he could get.'

'Oh, for crying in a bucket,' muttered Frieda. 'Ley lines! I'm going to kill Phil Walthers.'

'Your words are our command,' moaned the man.

'Don't tempt me,' said Frieda.

'Our command,' agreed his cohort.

'They are?' asked Frieda. 'Right, this is what my command is: get out of here and go play in the park or somewhere. Somewhere green and far away from other people. Go find some ley lines there. Got it? Find an old oak tree to play under. A very, very old oak tree. And while you're about it, tie some yellow ribbons around it. And dance around it a few times.'

'We understand and obey,' cried the man, following this up by retreating out of the door backwards on his hands and knees, the guitar bumping along the ground. His followers did the same.

Frieda turned to Eric Johns.

'Sergeant Johns, in future you will not clutter reception up with – with – members of the public such as that. Understand?'

'Yes, ma'am!'

Frieda's angry glance looked around reception for someone else to bark at. Her eyes alighted on Tom and Wilf who both immediately quailed.

'Has my husband being talking to you?'

'No, Miss.'

'No, Miss.'

'Good. keep it that way.'

With a last glare directed at Eric Johns she turned and left.

'Whew!' said Wilf. 'Suddenly I don't fancy being a copper after all.'

'And we're having dinner at theirs the week after next. I think that will be what is known in the business world as "challenging".'

'Frank's okay.'

'It isn't Frank I'm worried about.'

White: The Mason's Move: 1. m2-m3

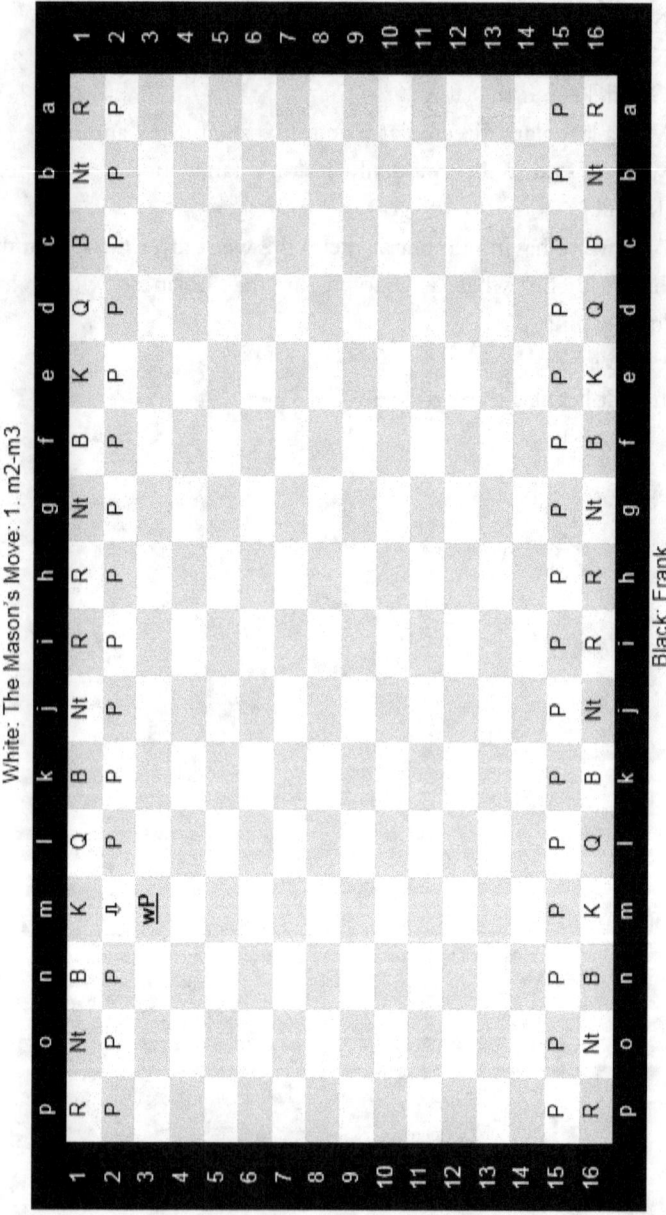

Black: Frank

104

'Wellbury ley-line centre,' Frank announced as he answered the phone. 'If you're calling about the Ioana directed ley-lines, please press one. If it's the Canterbury lines you want, that's the South Coast you need to contact. For Glastonbury, press sixty-nine. If you –'

'Frank, it's Frieda.'

'Free! You just caught me. I was just about to go to my place – the old flat – to start sorting things out.'

There was a pause on the line as Frieda's attention was temporarily diverted to the question of whether Frank was being honest or blatantly lying. And if the latter what he was really planning on doing.

'Frank, this mason friend of yours, he's sent the first move.'

'Right. What's he got to say for himself?'

'He or she, Frank, it could be a woman.'

'Mmm. Can't be a woman mason, they don't allow women in. But it would be a neat trick to pretend you're a mason if you're a woman.'

'There's more to it, Frank. First, this time he – or she – signs off as 'Manston'. Ring any bells?'

'Manston? Manston, Biggin Hill, Crawley. Manston was a fighter aerodrome during the war. Silly buggers built it too close to the coast, so the Luftwaffe shot it up as a matter of course as they were flying past. Some ground-crew went into the shelters and refused to come out. Can't say I blame them. Might as well have painted a sign, "Please bomb here" on it.'

'Yes, I know that, Frank, but what does it mean? Why first "A mason", and then just "Manston". Do you think it could be a clue?'

Frank made a face.

'Stop making faces, Frank.'

Frank didn't ask her how she knew.

'Who knows, Free? We've got too little to work on. Could be a clue, could be a spelling mistake. After all, maybe it was Amazing, or A Salad, like you said. Was it hand-written like the first?'

'Well, that's the second thing, Frank. It was sent as an email. Only it was sent to me.'

Frank paused.

'Sent to you? Now why was that?'

'Precisely. Whoever it is must know that you've been booked off. They must have found out since sending that chess set in the first place, because that was addressed to you. Which means it's someone who has inside knowledge of what's going on in the station.'

'It's not so much that, Free. They don't seem to realise that I really will kill anyone who tries to bring you into harm's way. Remember that mugger in France?'

'Yes, Frank, vividly. The difference is that there we were free to act as citizens, here we're police offices. And the mugger was drunk as a lord.'

'I'll still kill the summer beach.'

'Frank,' Frieda said in a warning tone.

Frank made another face, this time at Squishy, who had set up throne on the stairs and was watching him in case he produced more tuna from somewhere, or perhaps a saucer of milk.

'If they were able to find out your email address – well, that is a give-away. Should be, anyway. How did they find out your email address?'

'I've been trying to work that out. They aren't published, they aren't public, it isn't on the police website. The only think I can think of is that it was included in the cc list on an email that got sent outside. Can't think what or when. I've asked Tricia to go through my emails and see if she can spot anything.'

'Good luck with that. It should only take about ten weeks. Including all the meeting invitations for meetings which were sent to Uncle Tom Cobley and all.'

Frieda sighed.

'I know. Trying to discipline people in the correct usage of digital communication is difficult. So much easier to scatter it like shotgun shot than pausing to take a little care.'

'Well, there's another thought. Was it only addressed to you, or was anyone else included?'

'Just me, Frank. And there's the third thing. The message. It's in code.'

'Code? Excellent. A mason from Manston writing in code. Just what I need to make my day that bit more interesting. What's it say?'

'It says, 1, that's numeric 1, full stop, m for Mother, numeric 2 , hyphen, m for Mother, numeric 3.'

Frank chuckled.

'1. m2-m3? That's not code, Free, it's his first move. He's moving a pawn one space forward. Column m, let's see, that will be on his far right. Interesting.'

'Frank, I never played chess. You might as well be speaking Greek to me. Actually, I'd have a better chance with Greek.'

'You never played chess? Free, you're joking me.'

'Well, not exactly never, but hardly ever. What does it mean?'

'Have you got the set he sent in front of you?'

'No, it's still in the interview room.'

'Have a look at it when you get a chance. In chess notation normal chessboard columns are annotated a to h at the players' ends, left to right. The rows are numbered one to eight from the white to the black end. It's a bit like nominating squares in a game of battleships. My guess is that, with a double set, he'll be thinking of it as columns a to, um, let me see, p, I think it must be. And the rows will be numbered one to sixteen. So, when you start, space a1 has the white left-hand rook on it. Rook meaning castle, of course. So m2 is the pawn in front of white's King. He's moving it to space m3, which is one space forward. The number 1 at the start stands for the first move. My response will be number 2, his next number 3 and so on. He might have had the lines and columns annotated on the chess board, though I can't recall noticing that.'

'And you're black,' said Frieda, drawing a double-chessboard on a pad, 'so your pieces are currently on lines ... sixteen and fifteen, pawns on line fifteen, major pieces on line sixteen, at the back.'

'Exactly. What he's doing is advancing a pawn a single space, opening up his, let me see – ' he made a few notes. 'Queen and the Queen's Bishop on his right flank. It's a defensive move. Normally you'd advance two spaces. Especially as white. Get your infantry out ready to engage as soon as possible. That's known as the King's pawn opening. What he's doing is the Van't Kruijs Opening. Not very popular, that one.'

'That's what you'd do, is it? The King's Pawn one? Not the one that sounds ... well, sounds, you know.'

'Hmmm. Difficult to say, Free. Trouble is, you're working in a different dimension in double chess. More distance to cover. Hmmm. Let me think.'

Frieda allowed Frank two seconds' cogitation time.

'So how do you want to run this one, Frank?'

'I've just had a thought. What's his email address?'

'Just a second – the username is AS1234567 at jeejawjaw dot net.'

'Great. About anonymous as you can be. Different version of the post restante drop. Okay, let me see ...' He made some more notes on an advert in the Herald, quickly sketching a rough outline of a double chess board.

'Okay, Free, do a reply ...'

'Okay.'

'And send this. 2. h15-h13. That's numeric 2, full stop, lower-case h for Hotel, numeric 15, one-five, hyphen, lower-case h for Hotel, numeric 13, one-three. Got that?'

'2. h15-h13. Got it. Why lower case?'

'Sometimes, especially once the pieces are out, the notation indicating the space on the board is prefixed with the initial of the piece being moved, just to clarify exactly what is moving where. So a capital B would be shorthand for Bishop. B followed by lower-case e and number 4, Be4, would mean the Bishop on space e4. If there's actually a knight on e4 then it's obvious someone's got mixed up. It's pretty much a necessity when you're playing someone by post, say, or email these days. If you're writing the places down rather than using a board you also have to prefix the pieces with a lower-case b for black or w for white.'

'Post? Now that would be a novelty. I presume this is an international standard used by everybody?'

'It's the international standard as far as I understand it. I've come across variations, but I've never bothered to get involved with the detail. Life's too short. Oh, and the letter for the knight is N, because K has already been taken by the king. Some people justify that by saying the piece is actually the nightrider. Other people use a capital K followed by a small t.'

'How very untidy. Though nightrider sounds interesting – all flowing black in the moonlight.'

'As in eighteenth century horseman rather than that American television series?'

'Horsewoman. Shall I send this?'

'Absolutely. Let's see what he's got to say to that.'

'Frank, darling?'

'Yes, my sweet?'

'Would you be kind enough to let your little wife know what your move is supposed to mean? I guess that you're advancing one of your central pawns two spaces. Why?'

'It should be my right-hand Queen's knight's pawn, that would open up the bishop. But if I moved that two spaces he could take it with his bishop for free, that's the problem with double chess, he couldn't do that normally. And if I moved it one space that would give him the idea that I was as cautious as him. Instead I'll begin by advancing as many pieces down the centre as possible.'

'You're going to advance with your centre?'

'No, I'm going to feint with my centre. I'm going to hit him wherever he leaves himself open, as soon as possible, and as hard as possible. I might even invent a couple of moves that are impossible. That'll keep him guessing.'

'Frank, you've lost me. What are you talking about?'

'Free, like I said, if he's playing by email he can't see my board. So if I move my left queen to a space it can't reach on his board, he won't know if we're looking at the same board. Keep it going for ten moves and he won't have a clue what we're looking at. My guess is that he will reply to an email saying, 'You can't do that', and I'll say, 'Well, according to what I'm looking at I can'. Means we have to sort out the mess. He has to get in touch more often. Giving us more chances to nail the bastard.'

There was a pause as Frieda considered this.

'I suppose you'll have to come in to the office to play the moves on the board.'

'Nah, Free, you make the moves on the board. I normally do it in my head.'

There was a very long pause.

'You play the game in your head.' It was a resigned statement. 'Doesn't everyone?'

There was that special silence that a wife makes when she really, really loves her husband, but is trying to work out, for the umpteenth time, why.

'Frank, has anyone ever told you that you can be insufferable?'

He chuckled.

'Nope. Not that I remember. Not in the past week. But I've thought of something.'

'What's that.'

'The next time we're on an operation where we have to use code words for each other, I know what I'll call you.'

'And what will that be, husband, dearest?'

'M-Mother.'

There was a pause.

'I've sent the email, Frank. I'll make the move on the board downstairs. And you are still off duty. See you later, darling.'

Frank looked at the phone and then at Squishy.

'Typical woman, always wants the last word.' Squishy miawoed. She was a she and all she was interested in was the last tuna. And then seconds.

'Let's find ourselves a large piece of paper, Squish,' Frank said, 'There's no way on God's earth I'm going to remember these moves. Just don't tell anyone, Squish, especially Frieda. I've got a reputation to live down to.'

White: The Mason

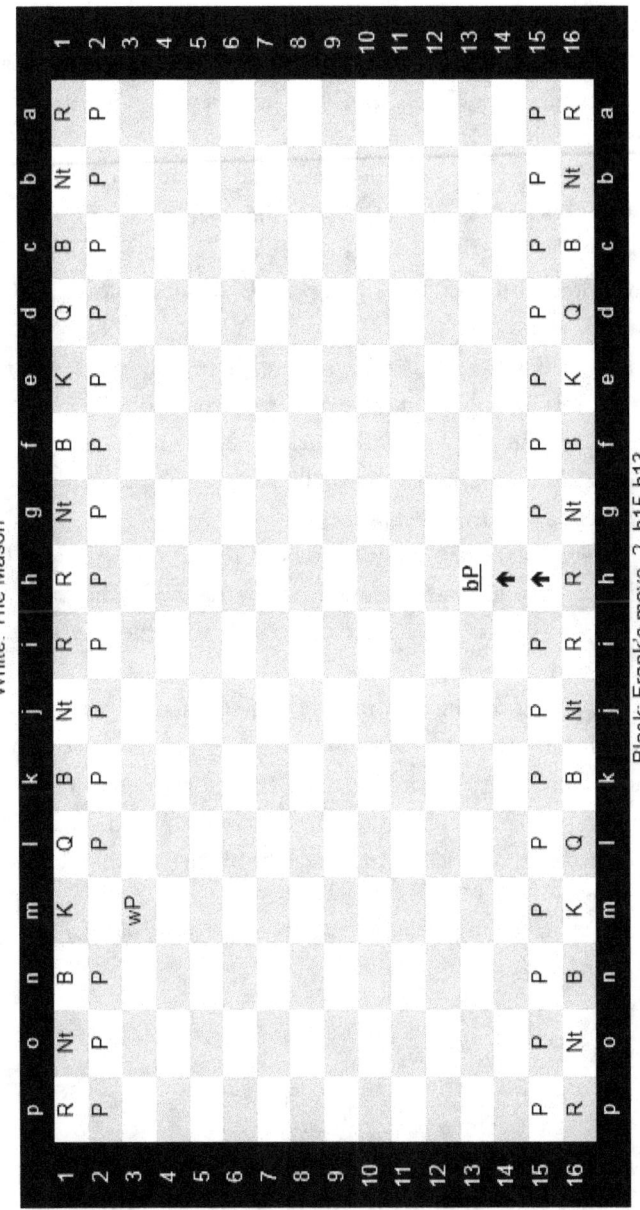

Black: Frank's move. 2. h15-h13

Frank whistled as he prepared dinner. The radio was on. Wellbury's local DJ, Zack the Man as he called himself, Zack the Prat as others knew him, was interviewing what he off-air described as his latest victims.

'Now, Mrs Smythe, I understand that you and Mrs Smith are forming a ladies' defence league?' he was asking in what he claimed was a friendly, breezy tone, a claim that had prompted some of his support staff to label him The Old Fart.

'I'm Mrs Scythe. This is Miss Smith here. I'd advise you not to get that wrong again, young man. I won't tolerate rudeness from the likes of you. This hockey stick isn't for show, you know. And Mildred's umbrella has a point that's been sharpened to bayonet sharpness.'

'Ah, terribly sorry, I must have been giving the wrong notes. I'll fire my assistant immediately afterwards, ha, ha, ha. Anyway, Mrs Scythe, I understand it's called the TOBs. That isn't another error, is it?'

'No, we are forming a women's counter-offence unit. We plan to call ourselves The Old Birds' army. A group of women of more mature years united in countering these quite despicable attacks on senior citizens of the female sex. The police won't do anything. We will. And we'll be taking the fight to the enemy, you'll see.'

'I see. I mean, I will see. I mean – just who are the enemy, Mrs Smy – er, Mrs Scythe?'

'Men.'

'All men?'

'All those who are not with us are against us, Mr Zack.'

'So you'll allow men to join?'

'Certainly not. We are an all-female organisation, we have no intention of permitting the joining of male members.'

'Er, yes, interesting phraseology. But surely if men can't join, they can't be with you, which makes them the enemy automatically, doesn't it?'

'That's their choice, Mr Zack.'

'Well, folks, you heard it here first. The women of Wellbury are rising like Boadicea did, taking to the streets, led by Mrs Smythe here. Now I see the lines are lighting up, there's plenty of callers out there waiting to give us their opinion, so after a short commercial break we'll be back – Mrs Smythe, what are you doing with that hockey-stick? Now wait a minute, Mrs Smythe, you can't -Scythe! Scythe! I meant –'

A commercial for the new cleaning wonder-liquid EasiBriteLite extolled the power and reach of the product, covering whatever interaction was taking place between Mrs Scythe (Commander, TOBs) and the enemy (Zack, a Man).

Frank heard the front door open, followed by the sound of a briefcase hitting the carpet. He switched the radio to Radio Classical.

'You have not had a good day, I take it,' he said as Frieda entered the kitchen.

'Oh, I had a marvellous day,' she replied, sitting down at the table to take her shoes off, then picking a miaowing Squishy up and stroking her. 'In fact I was promoted – to queen.'

'Queen?'

'By a hairy old hippie who believes that my office lies directly on the conjunction of ley-lines.'

Frank chuckled.

'Oh, dear, they are coming out of the woodwork aren't they. I've just been listening to Zack the Prat on the radio, interviewing The Old Birds' Army. That Georgina Scythe sounds like someone you don't want to meet down a dark alley.'

'I was listening on the way home. I think I might have to have a word with her about taking the law into her own hands. Before she really gets going and does something silly. And I really don't have the time. We have ... a lot of more important things to do.'

'Interesting dilemma,' Frank said, laying out knives and forks. 'I'm not sure she'd listen to another woman, though she sounds as if she thought men even less worth listening to. Maybe you should send Percy around.'

'Percy? He wouldn't last five seconds with a woman like that.'

'No, but it would be fascinating to hear his account of what happened. If he ever makes it back.'

'Our problem is that we have plenty of officers who can deal with reasonable honest people and unreasonable crooks, but hardly anyone who can cope with unreasonable honest citizens.'

'Why don't I pop around and have a word with her? It would give me something to do.'

They looked at each other.

'Free, we need to knock this nonsense on the head and concentrate on the important stuff. Aggie and the old ladies.'

'I told you, you're off duty, Frank.'

'Oh, come on, Free. I'm hardly likely to injure myself going round for a quiet natter with Mrs Scythe.'

'That, Frank, is exactly what you're likely to do.'

'Ten quid says I don't.'

'I don't know why people think you aren't ambitious, Frank. I've never met anyone so determined to win. When your curiosity is aroused, that is.'

'Now, Free, you know I'm a team player. It's just that I've had my team taken away from me.'

She frowned at him.

'Just don't let me hear of your going around to Mrs Scythe.'

'I won't,' he promised ambiguously.

'Did you know,' Frieda said, changing the subject, 'there's a new shop open in Little Glastonbury? It's called the Porridge Place.'

'Little Glastonbury. The arcade of little shops in the Old Town that caters for all your spiritual needs? Where everything comes from Glastonbury, even the stuff labelled "Made in China"?'

'That's the one. This new Porridge Place sell bowls of cereal or porridge for about five pounds a bowl.'

Frank's eyes shot up.

'Five quid for a bowl of cereal? What's it made of, rare South American bat droppings?'

'No. Apparently it's just normal sugary cereal you can buy in any supermarket for about two-pound-fifty – for a family-sized box. You can get No-name All Bran for twenty pence a pound, and that's a lot of bran –a bowl of that at the Porridge Place will set you back four pounds, and that's a small bowl. They sell the international stuff for about five pounds a bowl. Milk is extra.'

'Muesli?'

'Oh, now you're talking expensive. There's Swedish muesli, Andorran muesli, Brazilian muesli, pretty much name your country. I think the Japanese muesli is the most expensive.'

'Do they sell bacon butties?'

'Don't be a heathen, Frank.'

'And this shop, it's doing extremely well, I take it?'

'Indeed, apparently the hipsters love it.'

'Hipsters? Men with beards and pony tails?'

'Those are the ones.'

'Well, thank goodness we live in a democracy where people can freely choose to look like idiots and pay over the odds for bowls of milk-soaked cardboard.'

'Have you ever thought of growing a beard, Frank?'

'Not a chance. Goes against my philosophy of not standing out in a crowd.'

'You mean trying to remain anonymous.'

'That's the one.' He grinned. 'When I first became a detective we had one chap who desperately wanted to do undercover work for some reason. Anyway, he grew a beard to disguise the fact that he was a copper. Trouble is, it made him stand out at the station because everyone else was clean-shaven. People began calling him Serpico – well, polite people, that is. There were some more descriptive terms some of the senior officers used. He used to get the worst jobs going. And the kids on the estates began shouting 'Here comes that copper with the beard' every time he turned up. Eventually he shaved it off, but then all the senior officers recognised him as that hippy without the beard. So he still got the lousy jobs.'

'The moral of the story being that it is better to be outstanding than to stand out.'

'Well, kind of. I prefer to think of it being a case that, if they don't know you they don't know what you're doing wrong.'

She looked at him for a few seconds. She had a feeling that she knew him well, which is why she knew he was doing something he shouldn't be doing. But she didn't know what it was.

'And what is it you're doing that I should know about, Frank?'

'Nothing. Absolutely nothing. Apart from cooking dinner. Now, tell me something, this cereal shop – it isn't one of Vic

Brown's schemes, is it? Our good old faux-Cockney schemer and the most honest criminal in the neighbourhood?'

'No, I'm pretty sure it isn't. It isn't his style. What's for dinner?'

'Chilli con-carne with fresh banana slices, topped off with grated cheese.'

'Yum, that sounds good.'

'Fresh baby cabbage in a white ham-and-pepper sauce on the side.'

'Oh, god, I could live on that, I love cabbage in a white sauce. How fresh?'

'Picked this very day. Oh, and not forgetting, strawberry ice-cream with hot custard for dessert. And wafers.'

She sighed.

'Frank, I'm tempted to sign you off duty permanently. Only I'd have to go on a new diet every other week.'

'It's quite interesting, actually. There's a certain logistical challenge to cooking meals which might have to be kept warm for some time. And also minimising the amount of effort required, and the number of pots and pans.'

'Welcome to a woman's world, Frank.' She sniffed. 'That does smell good.'

'Try some,' he said, picking up a teaspoon, dipping it into the pot and handing it to her.

'Mmmm, that is nice. A little bit mild, though.'

'Mild?' asked Frank. Frieda looked up.

'Perfect,' she decided. 'Quite possibly a little hot.'

'Liar,' said Frank.

Tuesday

Cult go radio; Feminist nick; Mason (3); TOBS fall in

The following morning Frank switched on the radio to see if
Zack had found any new movements or groups likely to
enliven Wellburians' lives.

'This is another reason I absolutely have to get back to work
as soon as possible, Squish,' he told Squishy, 'if I carry on
listening to Zack every day I'm going to morph into a Zombie
and start devouring the neighbours.'

Instead of Zack's voice there came the sweeter sounds of his
assistant.

'And that was an advert for Pootle, the company promising a
solution to your pets' scent problems, or smelly poos as some
might call them. And this is Julia, taking over Zack's morning
slot while he has remedial treatment for an aversion to
hockey-sticks applied to the head. And do we have a
programme lined up for you. Later I'll be interviewing the
latest boy band to hit the airwaves, Wellbury's own The
WellBoys. Before then there's a discussion on whether the
congestion on Wellbury Old Road is due to traffic or to repair
work. But first, let's have a drum roll ...' she played a recorded
drum roll '... allow me to introduce the TCoTC, short for The
Cult of The Clueless. They did try to get me to call them Cult
of Cluelessness, but we aren't that clueless at radio Wellbury.
Now, gentlemen, why don't you introduce yourselves and
explain a little about the cult.

'And the top of the morning to yourself, Julia, surely the Jewel
in the crown of Wellbury's local radio. And the top of the
morning to all the listeners out there, sure if you could see
Julia as I can see Julia you'd be wishing that this was
television.'

'I can see the surgery hasn't worked,' Julia noted.

'Surgery, my turtle dove? What surgery?'

'To remove the Blarney stone from wherever it ended after you've swallowed it. Perhaps, if you've finished with the soft-soap you could introduce yourself?'

'Ah, well I'm Seumas O'Brien-O'Murphy-O'Connor-O, and this is Jaimie.'

'I'm Jamie,' another voice confirmed. 'I'm the tird in command.'

'And who is second?'

'Sure and we don't have a second in command,' said Seumas. 'We're a very democratic cult. But we felt we needed a tird in command.'

'Very amusing, Mr O'Connor. Perhaps you could elaborate on what your cult does, preferably in the next twenty seconds before we go to another commercial break and you'll be replaced by a reminder of illegitimate toothpaste diseases.'

'Illegitimate – Ah, sure, and you're just having us on, tis a wicked woman you are, Julia, and one so young and beautiful.'

'Ten seconds.'

'Sure, and it won't take ten seconds to explain. We, you see, know nutting.'

'You know nutting? You're squirrels?'

'No, no, no, the knowledge type of nutting. And we know nutting. Nutting at all, at all. You see, every day we meet others who are confirmed believers. The Christians, the Jews, the Muslims, Buddhists, bankers, that sort of ting.'

'Bankers?'

'We just don't like bankers, after all even the word rhymes with –'

'And hold out there audience while we have a short interruption for our commercial supporters to get their special messages across.'

Frank looked at Squishy sitting next to the radio with the half-closed eyes of a cat which is quietly enjoying the comforting sound of something it can't understand and prefers it that way.

'Squish, I would dearly love to know what she's saying to them right now. I suspect she's as powerful as Frieda with a bollocking, but with a different style. I think our friend Seumas has met his match.'

As the commercials ended a slight giggle escaped from Julia which suggested that this might not be the case. Squishy opened one eye as if to say 'Got that wrong, didn't you?'

'And welcome back, listeners. I've had a severe word with Mr O'Brien-O'Murphy-O'Connor-O and Jaimie here and they have promised to behave for the rest of the interview. Otherwise I'll replace them with a turnip, and we all know how boring it can be listening to a turnip answering a question on radio. Now, Mr O-O, could you repeat what you've just being saying about the Cult of the Clueless.'

'Well, Julia, most fairest of the fair sex, as I was saying, there are some people who are very certain about the meaning of life, why we're here, if we're here, when's the next bus to paradise, that sort of malarkey. We, on the other hand, believe that we don't have a clue. We don't know if there is a god, we don't know if flying saucers are real, and after the fourt pint we aren't even too sure if we're real. Now we believe that we aren't in the minority, in fact we're sure – well, not that sure, of course, to be sure, but pretty confident in a not-all-knowing way – that we're in the majority. Only thing is, how do you get people together who don't know? Easy to cry

"Follow the Holy Weevil" and people will start to believe in the Holy Weevil, especially if you threaten to kill them if they don't. Sure, tell a people they will burn in the infernal regions after they die if they don't believe, and they'll be burnt to deat in this one too if they refuse, and, hey presto, a religion.'

'And you wouldn't believe some of the things they come out with,' said Jamie. 'For instance, chapter 22, verses 28 to 29 in Due To Ron O'Mee. It says that anyone raping a virgin must pay the father fifty shekels of silver because she's damaged goods.'

'You're joking. Fifty shekels? I mean —'

'Don't take our word for it, Julia,' said Seumas, 'you've got researchers sitting around idly, doing nothing, get them to work.'

'I'll do that. In the meantime —'

'And did you know that you could be stoned to deat for eating prawns? That's in that Levvy Tick Us, chapter eleven. You wouldn't believe what you can and can't eat.'

'Locusts,' said Jamie, 'they're okay.'

'You like locusts?'

'No, I wouldn't touch them, but Levvy Tick Us reckons they're kosher.'

'Seagulls is also out, along wit ravens, the horned owl, the screech owl, storks, herons vultures, them sorts o tings.'

'And pigs, of course. And if you so much as touch any of those you're unclean.'

'Unclean?'

'Women are unclean a lot of the time, of course.'

'I beg your pardon?'

'I mean that's what they say, them religious types. We in the Cult of the Clueless think women are marvellous people. Most of the time.'

'And we don't believe most people believe in things like not wearing two types of clothing together.'

'Two types of clothing?'

'Oh, no, that's definitely against their rules. And then there's that Timothy. He didn't think much of women who dressed up.'

'I want women to adorn themselves with proper clothing, modestly and discreetly, not with braided hair and gold or pearls or costly garments,' quoted Jamie.

'I do not permit a woman to teach or have authority over a man,' added Seumas, 'she must be silent. And that's in the New Testament.'

'But to be fair to the man he did say that people should give up on the water and start drinking wine.'

'So we want to unite all those who don't believe so that we can conquer the minority believers. Before they can impose their menus on us innocent civilians.'

'R-i-g-h-t,' said Julia slowly, 'so you want to conquer the believers before they conquer you?'

'Well, in a manner of speaking. We wouldn't be unnecessarily cruel to the poor little lambs. Maybe put them into institutions according to their faiths. Let them each have their little glass bubbles where they can be happy.'

'Won't work,' Jamie said with a burp. 'Buggers need something to call heretics. There'll be schisms before you can fart.'

'And time for our commercial sponsors to remind us not to use naughty words like fart,' said Julia. The radio immediately switched to the product for pet flatulence.

'You know, Squish, if they don't promote that Julia to lead interviewer ahead of Zack the Prat they don't know what's good for their radio station.'

Squishy opened her eyes wide enough to suggest that Frank was talking cobblers and he should know it.

Frank sighed.

'Yes, I suppose you're right, Squish. People will phone up and email to tell the radio station how much they hate Zack the Prat. They aren't going to do so because they like Julia the Jewel. Which means the figures will show more people listen to the Prat than the Jewel. Apart from that it don't make no sense, as our American cousins would say.'

He put on his jacket.

'Right, Squish, I'm off out. You coming, or you happier staying in?'

Squishy closed her eyes and purred with the sound of Julia coming back from wherever she had gone.

'Something I should mention to our listeners as you can't see it on radio: Seumas and Jaimie have brought me two lovely, huge teddy bears, quite heavy ones. Now you were explaining why you brought me these even though you couldn't have known I'd be doing the interview rather than Zack, who, listeners might not know, is allergic to artificial fur.'

'Sure and we didn't know that, more's the pity. But the ting is, oh fairest Julia, we of the Clueless, well, because we know nutting, and we honestly admit we know nutting, we develop a kind of sixth-sense.'

'A kind of feminine intuition?'

'Ah, that's it, precisely. We're in touch with our feminine sides, as it were.'

'Wouldn't mind being in touch with –' Jamie said before he made a sound of someone with an elbow in his stomach.

'Time to bring in our listeners, and we have a caller on line one,' Julia said, 'I believe it's Father Brown, from Wellbury Catholic church.'

'Oh, Jaysus,' came the voice of Seumas O-O, 'not him. Especially not him.'

'I think Seumas and Jamie have a very good point to make,' Father Brown said with a quiet Irish brogue. 'Indeed, I could see as they were growing up they were going to be good thinkers. Until the alcohol got them. And from the sound of it they're well into their communion whine now.'

'See you later, Squish,' Frank called as he opened the door to leave. 'Let me know what the final score is.'

Detective Sergeant Pete Phillips sat at a table in the police canteen trying to enjoy his lunch. He couldn't help but feel that every female eye in the room was fixed on him, just waiting for him to say or do something sexist, or possibly just say or do anything, which, because he was doing it, would by definition be sexist. The male constables were also nervous, and showed their sympathy and appreciation of their colleague's situation by keeping well clear of him. To be fair, he had started his time at Wellbury by throwing his weight around just as a sergeant shouldn't, and while that period was over and largely forgiven, if someone was going to be a sacrificial victim, then Pete Phillips was an ideal choice in that they weren't him.

'Mind if I join you, Pete?' asked Desk Sergeant Eric Johns in a very low voice.

'Glad of the company,' Pete whispered back, forgetting that there was a good reason he normally avoided the other sergeant. 'I'm beginning to feel like a pariah. Can't these women take a joke?'

'No, is the honest answer to that,' Eric Johns whispered, sitting down. 'I've never met a woman with a sense of humour. Unless it's at a man's expense.'

'It's a bit much,' Pete Phillips whispered. 'I get it in the neck from the missus night and day. You'd think I could get away from it at work.'

'Steve Right and Sidney Feeler got screamed out of a shout this morning,' Eric Johns whispered back. 'Some old biddy – I mean, a woman of approximately sixty-five of the opposite agenda – reported a break-in. Steve and Sidney went around to investigate and she claimed that they were going to oppress her. Said she'd only speak to female officers.'

'Oppress her? Steve and Sid?'

'Exactly. Steve and Sid couldn't oppress a paper bag, let alone some poor dear old duck.'

Pete considered this. He was pretty sure calling a woman a dear old duck would fall well within the range of descriptions police sergeants should never, ever use. If he were to agree with Eric Johns and it got out ... He came up with the only thing he could think of before Eric Johns could say anything else.

'I'll bet Frank would get away with it. He doesn't seem to think of himself as a man. He's just your just being normal, average bloke'

'That's it. You've got it there, Pete. It's all about being just your average bloke. But it's an English thing, too. Take your Scots, now.'

Pete Phillips looked at Eric Johns, his stomach contracting. If Eric said anything derogatory about the Scots, and Eric Johns was not known for his compliments, then Pete Phillips would be found guilty by association. Someone would turn out to have Scots ancestry. And be highly offended.

Thinking of it, Agnetha who effectively ran the canteen was Scots. You wouldn't want to offend her. She made the best food this side of the grave. If she decided to serve you the worst food the other side of the grave you'd probably be happy to jump into it to get life over with. Pete had a feeling between his shoulder blades that she was actually watching him at that moment. And listening. Or lip reading. While sharpening a butcher's knife.

'See,' continued Eric Johns, oblivious of the desperation in Pete Phillips's face, 'to a Scot being a Scot is important. Crucial, in fact. An Englishman doesn't think of himself as English, but a Scot – well, he lets you know he's a Scot in the first thirty seconds. Same with women.'

Pete Phillips pushed his half-full plate away

'Women always think of themselves as women first,' Eric Johns continued. 'Modern women, that is. A bloke, well, he's just a bloke. He doesn't wake up and think, I'm a bloke. Women do.'

'Women wake up and think their husband is a bloke?'

'Nah, Pete, you don't understand. Whatever a woman does, she does it because she's a woman. Like voting.'

Pete Phillips prayed that he could sink into the canteen floor. He would have got up and left, but Eric Johns's theories were always mesmerising.

'Now a bloke, when it comes to voting, looks at the essentials. Better health care. You know, brighter schools. More police on the beat, that sort of thing. A woman, well, her first thought is, what does it mean for women? See what I mean?'

'I have to go. There's a report I have to get out this afternoon. And there's the time-sheet to do.'

'I reckon you're coming down with something, Pete,' called Eric Johns as Pete left, 'you've left half your lunch. But you're right about the Scots.'

White: The Mason's move. 3. e2-e3

Black: Frank

'Frank? It's Frieda. Our friend the mason has emailed his next move.'

'What's he calling himself this time? Maxwell? Madman? Masonite? Margarine?'

'It's back to 'A Mason'. Maybe he's a plasterer or builder or something.'

'Could be. What's his move? Anything interesting?'

'It's 3. e2-e3. That's numeric 3, full stop, e-Echo, numeric 2, hyphen, e-Echo numeric 3. And he's added a comment. 'I see you're adopting a very aggressive approach, Inspector. Not one I would want to try. Softly-softly, Inspector, that's my tomato.'

'My what?'

'Tomato. As in round red fruit.'

Frank frowned for a few moments.

'If there's any fruit involved I think it's our friend on the other end of that e-mail. E2 to e3, you say? Let me think about that.'

He took out the piece of paper and unfolded it silently. He marked the move.

'Cautious little bugger, isn't he,' he said thoughtfully.

From the other end of the line there was the sound of a strong character holding her silence despite a deep wish to throttle her husband. Eventually Frieda's strength gave in.

'What, Frank, are you talking about now?'

'Well, you've made the move on the board there, I take it.'

'Of course I have, Frank. I'm in the interview room looking at it now. I just don't have your experience to make sense of it.'

'He's inching his pawns forward, opening up a line of attack for his queens and bishops, but he's not advancing his pawn line as far as he could. It's a very defensive approach. Unusual for white.'

'And what's the name for that move?'

'There isn't one. He's playing a pawn on column that doesn't exist in normal chess.' He looked at the paper in front of him. 'Well, to be pedantic it shouldn't exist from where I'm looking at it. From his side it was his first move that can't happen in normal chess.'

'I'm beginning to think I was lucky not to play chess at school. This double-chess must give normal players a headache.'

'Didn't you have a chess club at school?'

'It was that or violin lessons. I decided I preferred the violin.'

'I would have decided to take chess based on the theory that I could learn the violin later.'

'Hmmm,' was Frieda's comment. Frank had tried playing Frieda's violin once. It had taken half an hour of pleadings and an extra-large bowl of tuna to get a spitting Squishy down from the top of the curtains.

'Okay, Free, let's try this: 4. i15-i13. That's numeric 4, full stop, lower-case i-India, numeric 15, one-five, hyphen, i-India, numeric 13, one-three.'

'4. i15-i13,' Frieda said. She made a note of it and moved the piece on the board. 'Aren't you leaving those two pawns rather exposed, Frank?'

'That's what I want him to think.'

'You mean you're lulling him into a true sense of security?'

'I've got two rooks behind the pawns, the heavy cavalry just waiting to pound into action. I think of it as emulating Grant's attack on Vicksburg.'

'Probing through the lagoons, around the mountains, until you find the weak spot followed by a full-on attack? By which time Grant's opponent, General Pemberton, or in this case our friend A Mason, will be nervous as can be, not knowing where the next attack is coming from?'

'That's the one. I'll give him flolloping bananas or tomatoes or whatever fruit he wants. From all directions.'

'Okay, Frank, I'll have to go now. You are looking after yourself, aren't you?'

'No, Free, I'm taking the afternoon off to go skydiving.'

'Sarcasm is the lowest form of wit, darling. See you later, bye.'

Frank looked at the phone.

'Now why on earth shouldn't I go skydiving?' he asked it. He thought about skydiving for a few seconds.

'Maybe tomorrow,' he decided. 'After I've sorted out our stone-throwing friend.'

In the interview room Frieda tapped her mobile softly against her chin as she looked at the chessboard. Gertie, Sam and Susan were with her.

'If I were putting money on this game,' Susan said, my money would be on our Mason friend.'

'Frank is adopting his usual plan,' Frieda said.

'Smile, be friendly, wait until the Mason drops his guard and then clobber him?' asked Susan

'He's planning on out-confidencing the Mason. He's very good at it. Unfortunately it requires the other person being able to see how confident you are. I'm not sure it works as well over the Internet.'

'Frank's the sort of man who would look the Devil in the face and flatter him while dealing the cards in a winner-takes-all poker game,' noted Susan.

'True,' said Gertie, 'but he'd have a dodgy pack of cards and he'd be dealing off the bottom.'

'And,' said Sam, 'he'd take the first chance he had to kick the Devil in the goonies. I know I would.'

'Maybe you should include a couple of emojis the next time you send an email,' suggested Gertie.

'Good idea, Gertie. I'll ask Tricia if there's one of the Hangman.'

White: The Mason

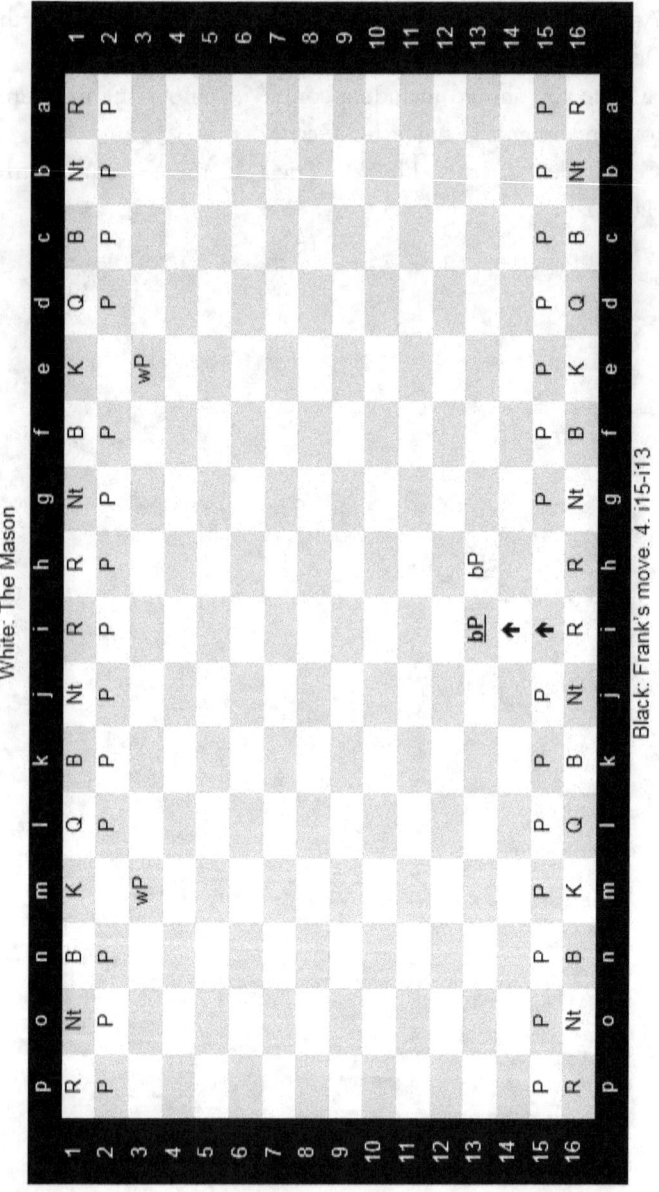

Black: Frank's move. 4. i15-i13

134

'My goodness,' said Mildred Smith, peering out from behind the stage curtains at the church hall, 'it looks as if we might have a full house.'

'Let me have a look,' Georgette Scythe said, moving Miss Smith out of the way by sheer force of personality. 'Ah, just as I expected, Wellbury's women rallying to the clarion call of justice. What the –' She spluttered for a second in as far as she could splutter. 'There's a man out there. A man! Get these curtains open, I'm not going to skulk behind curtains.' She turned around, searching for someone to order about. 'You! Vicar-what's-your-name! Do you know how to open these curtains?'

'Well, I, er, yes, I, er ...'

'Well, don't just stand there stuttering, open the damn things!' The vicar was a wise man who knew when to surrender. He pressed a button and the curtains rolled back.

'Right, you can go, now vicar, won't be needing you anymore.'

'Right,' said the vicar and promptly disappeared. Mrs Scythe turned to the congregation below her.

'Marjorie Willcox!' she called. 'I thought it was you. What's that man doing behind you? No men allowed in the Old Birds' army. I thought I had made that quite clear.'

'It's my husband,' came back Marjorie Willcox's high-pitched voice. 'Someone's got to push my wheelchair.'

'Well, someone else will have to do it while we're in meeting. You'll have to leave him outside.'

Marjorie and her husband had a short interchange which ending with him patting her on the arm and leaving the hall. A few other men who had been performing similar wheelchair duties took the opportunity to disappear.

'Probably go down the pub and not come back,' muttered Marjorie, a concept supported by the speed and alacrity with which the men had left.

'Have to get some of the motorised things,' Mrs Scythe called. 'See if we can get blades fitted to the wheels. Right, settle down you lot. Settle down. Those nearest the doors close them and make sure there's no one skulking behind them, especially no men. Right, you all know why we're here. Someone's going around beating up little old ladies, and we're going to put a stop to it. That means self-defence, pre-emptive self-defence. Any man who looks like he might be about to assault a little old lady gets walloped before he gets the chance. Understand? That means we have to be prepared. Remember, any object is a weapon if you've been trained in how to use it properly. A pair of scissors, A knitting needle. A bag of pepper in the eyes will slow a man down. An iron in his knee will stop him for a good few seconds if you can't hit him somewhere softer. We can all think ways to hit them where it's painful, but that's no good if you don't do it automatically. We've got to train ourselves to respond to the merest touch with as much effective force as possible. If someone looks at you sideways you split his skull without a second thought. So the first thing we're going to do is to divide ourselves into sections for training. Ten women to a section, give or take. We'll start by streets. Everybody who lives in the same street or close by move together until there's about ten of you. Come on, come on, move, move!'

The women looked around to locate others from their street, getting up hesitantly, not knowing if they should join their neighbours of vice versa. Mrs Scythe did not wait.

'Come on, come on, move it,' she bawled. 'This sort of tardiness is exactly what's keeping us women back.

Indecision. I won't tolerate it. Get moving or I'll get my hockey stick out.'

Whether or not the resulting sections were actually from the same streets was open to question, but their new-found speed was admirable. Within less than a minute there were five groups of ten standing awaiting orders.

'Right, ladies,' said Georgette Scythe, 'you see those dummies I've set up there at the back, the ones stuffed with straw?'

They turned to look. There was a row of stuffed dummies dressed up as men, all wearing hats. Most wore glasses. One had a dog collar. A couple were carrying books. Three had walking sticks.

'They're the enemy! They're thinking of attacking little old ladies! Get them! Now!'

There was only a slight hesitation. Then a burst of enthusiasm as they took up their training, having just realised there was no one around to restrain them, such as their mothers or their own good manners. The stuffed straw dummies lasted about twenty five seconds.

'And now,' said Georgette Scythe to Mildred Smith as the last piece of straw floated down, 'the question is whether we can get the buggers to do that in real life to real men.'

Mildred Smith didn't say anything. She was wondering who would have to clean up the mess they had made. She didn't want to think of the real life mess they were planning.

Then she thought of the cyclists and smiled.

Wednesday

The Righteous Once; TOBs v TCoTC

Squishy miawoed as Frank finished emptying the sachet of kitten food into her bowl, indicating that he hadn't emptied absolutely everything, and she was sure she could still get a mouthful out of that packet if only he'd let her try.

'You finish that first, Squish, I'll feed you some more if you're still hungry.'

He looked up at the radio as Squishy decided, okay, she'd finish this lot first and complain later. A lot. At least Frieda knew how to treat a poor starving kitten. Especially one who needed all the food she could get as she grew into a full, real-life cat.

Zack the Pratt had heroically overcome his injuries and returned to service before he lost his job to Julia. He was introducing his new guests.

'And that was our special sponsor's message from Petit-Poo. Now, we have a special group of people to introduce, the very latest in religious groups. I have in front of me Deacon David Danish of the Ultra Reformed Faith, and Mohammed Mitzi Mohamet Bruce Mohumed Muhamed Jack Black Mohomed Smith Muhamet Sundance Kid of the East Wellbury mosque. That's a lot of Mo-type names, isn't it?'

'I named me myself,' said a voice which sounded rather like Bluebottle sitting on a stool.

'Well, do you mind if I call you Mo-Mo, then?'

'No-no.'

'Excellent. Now, tell me, Deacon and Mo-Mo what is this new outfit you've invented?'

'We have formed a group of believers called the Righteous Ones,' said Deacon Danish.

'No Mo-Mo, Righteous Ones,' cane the echo from below.

'Righteous Once? Yes, I can see once might be enough. It would be for me.'

'Eh?'

'Eh?'

'Now, am I right in that this is in response to the Cult of the Clueless who my former assistant allowed to speak on radio Wellbury this morning?'

'Exactly. Cults are forbidden by God's law.'

'Coleslaw.'

'Right, I see, Mo-Mo, I think. Okay. Deacon Danish, I understand that you are the leader of this group.'

'Well, I wouldn't quite say leader. You see, we are a broad church of believers who cover pretty much the spectrum of all religions. All real religions. As such I think words such as 'leader' would be inappropriate. Our real leader is Jesus, or, in the case of Mohamed, his prophet.'

'Innit proper it,' echoed the voice.

'You don't see yourself as creating a new religion?'

'Sorry?' asked Deacon Danish.

'Sorry?'

'Er, well, all religions started somewhere. You might not intend to, but since you come from two different faiths, don't you think it might be the start of a new religion? A brotherhood, as it were. The Righteous Brothers.'

'I see what you mean. However we have not come together to start a new religion. We merely wish that our deeply held beliefs, and those of like-minded believers, should be respected. We plan on demonstrating for religious tolerance.'

'Lotto-tolerance.'

'Well, I can't see anyone disagreeing with that.'

'And after that we will destroy the Cult of the Clueless.'

'Destroy.'

'Destroy the Cult of the Clueless?'

'They are unbelievers. They are a danger to us all, of whatever belief. We must destroy them. Cults are the work of the devil.'

'Unlebievers.'

'Are you sure that's legal?'

'Legality is for those who do not believe. Believers have their own laws. Higher laws. Much, much higher.'

'We believers. Me dad not so much.'

'Well that's an interesting belief which I think I've only heard from accountants and lawyers before. Now, something the ladies out there will be eager to know, I'm sure: what do your wives think of your movement?'

'We do not allow women members. True religion has always been run by men. Women are a weaker sex. As the Bible says, "On her forehead is written, mystery, Babylon the Great, the Mother of Prostitutes and of the Abominations of the Earth".'

'My wife on order still.'

'Okaaay. Now you are deacon in the Church of England, I understand?'

'I was an assistant deacon in the Church of England. I re-aligned myself to the Presbyterian church when the Church of England decided to ordain women priests. Then I discovered the true faith and became a Muggletonian.'

There was the quick intake of breath of someone trying desperately not to laugh.

'A Muggletonian? You're joking!'

'I am deadly serious. Our group started in 1651. We are the only ones who know who is damned and who will be saved. It is quite obvious that the true word of the true God was truly given to us to pass on. The true religions recognise this.'

'I'm a Muslim, I am. I was born one. True.'

'Er, yes, right, got that, Mo-Mo. So, if you're no longer a deacon, what is it you do as a job?'

'What do I do? Well, I'm a sheet metal worker, but I don't see —'

'A shit metal worker? Don't worry, I'm sure you'll improve with practice. Go on, Mo-Mo, I can see you're dying to tell me what you do for a living.'

'Eh?'

'I work as a waiter. Inner bar.'

'A bar? What, with like, alcohol?'

'Yes. But I don't drink myself, that is forbidden for us Islams. But it's okay to sell alcohol to infidels because they're going to hell anyway, may as well let them enjoy the journey.'

'I would point out,' said Deacon Danish, 'that most true Christian churches forbid the use of alcohol.'

'They do? Well, let me ask you then, Deacon Danish, which religions do you admit? Catholics, of course.'

'Certainly not. Catholics are the messengers of Satan, led by the anti-Christ in Rome. We can see through their lies. No, we are seeking strong Puritans, Calvinists, Methodists, Muslims, Orthodox Jews, all the old religions.'

'No unorthodox Jews,' said the other voice. 'They not very nice.'

'Unortho – right, yes, I see, Mo-Mo. And what is your plan?'

'Our way is that of peace and tolerance. And respect, especially respect. After all, that is what we are demanding, respect. And our democratic right to free religion. And if we do not get it –'

'Er, yes, Deacon Danish? If you don't get it?'

'Are you Magog, Mr Zack?'

'A god? No, I know some of my girlfriends over time have –'

'Are you a believer, Mr Zack?'

'Well, not in the religious sense, though I –'

'We shall smite the unbelievers!' Danish announced, his voice fading slightly as he stood up and his voice left the microphone's comfort zone.

'Smite! Smite! Unlebievers!'

'Now, deacon, that's a large bible, you want to be careful – Arrggh! No, not the Muslim book as well! Aaarggh!'

'It's a Koran, that's what it is,' said the other from a distance. 'A genuine copy. And me not Mo-Mo, you so-so.'

There were several sounds repeated at intervals of Zack's head being hit by large books, and his cries and groans diminishing until someone who sounded like a security guard announced, 'Here, you can't do that here, mate, you're making a right mess, you are. Jimmy, come give us a hand getting rid of these nutters.' Deacon Danish's voice disappeared into the background crying, 'We will smite the unbelievers! Vengeance is mine sayeth the Lord!'

'Vengeance!' came the disappearing voice of his colleague. 'The Lord! No, wait a minute ...'

'Well, Squish,' said Frank, 'old Zack isn't having a good week of it, is he? Or whack of it, you could say.'

Squish looked up, decided her food was more interesting than Frank's puns and carried on eating. Anyway, once you had heard Zack being beaten up once ...

'Right, Squish, so we now have hordes of people stirring it up all over the place. We have the Old Birds army preparing for pre-emptive strikes on anyone, or any man, who looks sideways. We have the Cult of the Clueless trying to wind everyone up. And now the horde of believers calling themselves the Righteous Once are threatening pretty much everyone else. Down the station the women police officers have become raging feminists, and I hear the local lawn tennis club might be revolting. While what we really need to be concentrating on is who has been attacking little old ladies. You know what that reminds me of, Squishy?'

Squish looked up at him with a face that said 'More tuna?'

'General Foch, Squish. In World War I he was in charge of French forces during the first battle of the Marne. Things were going pretty badly, so he sent a message to Marshal Joffre, "my centre is giving way, my right is retreating, situation excellent, am going into the attack". And, that, Squish, is what I intend to do. Straight after my doctor's appointment. You coming with, or staying here?'

Squish gave him a brief look which translated as 'Do I look like trench fodder? And don't come complaining to me when you get hurt again.'

'Come in and take a seat, Inspector,' said the doctor after Frank's name had been called. 'We're running a bit late, but we always do after about eight-thirty.'

'Not much you can do in ten-minute slots, doctor. If we had to limit our interviews to ten minutes a suspect we'd never lock up anyone.'

'True. I presume you've never tried it.'

Frank grinned.

'You've just given me an idea for next April First. I'll send a memo out instructing officers to limit their interrogations to ten minutes. Sign it as the Chief Constable.'

'Well, I can see you've fully recovered. From a number of things. Last time I saw you you were recovering from a bang to the head not too long after getting shot. Now it's anaphylactic shock.'

'Yes. Any results come through?'

'Nothing yet. You're scheduled for further tests, aren't you?'

'Next week. I was hoping something would have come through. I'm booked off work until they find the cause. I'd quite like to get back to work sooner rather than later.'

The doctor looked at him over his glasses. He sighed.

'If I was booked off work I'd take the time off and have a holiday in somewhere like Barbados. But then I'm somewhat older than you, and more jaded. Anyway, you're looking fit enough.'

'I feel almost as fit as I've ever been.'

'Almost?'

'There was a stage when I used to run five miles before breakfast religiously. And I've always played sports. But that seems to have taken a bit of a back seat since I came to Wellbury.'

'I'd get back into it as soon as you could, if I were you. Without breaking confidences I can assure you that at your station you will find people who postponed exercising for one reason or another, and never quite restarted.'

'Point taken.'

The doctor stroked his jaw.

'Be interesting if your attack was due to not keeping fit. The body stores some really nasty toxins in fatty cells. Can come as a really bad shock when they break down.'

'But you don't know? What causes it.'

The doctor shook his head regretfully.

'We can identify what causes individuals to have reactions in most cases, but we don't know why. Still, it's a step forward from ascribing it to devils in the body.'

'That gives me an idea.'

'Another idea?'

'Devilled ribs. For supper. I'm on kitchen duties while I'm off. Maybe tomorrow.'

'I hate it when people do that sort of thing. Now I'm hungry.'

Frank whistled as he prepared dinner. The radio was on. Julia had once again taken over Zack's post due to his being held for investigation in the local Accident and Emergency. They were treating it as more Accident than Emergency.

'Good evening Wellburians!' Julia's voice sang. 'And have we a special programme for you, yes we do. I have in front of me the leaders of The Old Birds' army and The Cult of the Clueless, and they aren't fighting – yet. Now, Mrs Scythe, you are opposed to the Cult of the Clueless on the grounds that it does not allow women to join?'

'Exactly. It's absolutely ridiculous. A men-only group in the twenty-first century. Ludicrous.'

'And what do you say to that, Mr O'Brien-O'Murphy-O'Connor-O-O-O?'

'Ah, well I'd like to ask the lovely Mrs Scythe, a lady of formidable persuasion and one who can only be given the greatest respect and admiration as befits a lady of her station, a little question if the dear lady wouldn't mind, and may I say what a handsome lady she is, to be sure.'

'Impertinence!'

'Now,' Seumas O'Brien-O'Murphy-O'Connor-O continued, 'Mrs Scythe, you're quite certain that we should admit women?'

'Of course. There's no question about it.'

'Ah, to be sure, there's the pity now. You see, we couldn't admit such a fine, upstanding and outstanding representative of the female race on the grounds that you're too sure. You see, we admit only the clueless.'

Julia turned her attention to the leader of The Old Birds army. 'Mrs Scythe, your group, The Old Birds: you only let women join, don't you?'

'Well, naturally. We could hardly call ourselves The Old Birds if we permitted men to join.'

'Surely then the two movements would make ideal allies? The Old Birds army admit only women, and the Cult of the Clueless admit only men. Then if you have meetings where a member of the opposite sex is there, they're attending as a member of the allied movement.'

'Sure, and that's a good idea,' said Seumas O'Brien-O'Murphy-O'Connor-O. 'I must confess to having had doubts about our women-only policy. Not many, but some. In our club you have to.'

'And,' Julia pointed out to Georgette Scythe, 'I presume you wouldn't want to be affiliated to the Righteous Once.'

'Good grief, what a ridiculous suggestion!' erupted Mrs Scythe. 'That nitwit little headed small-brained reptile calling himself Bacon Danish and his little side-kick? I heard him on the radio earlier. Pompous little idiot. Thinks women are inferior to men? Wait till I get my hands on him, he'll soon find out what women are capable of.'

'Sure, good lady, you will let me know when that's going to happen,' requested Seumas O'Brien-O'Murphy-O'Connor-O. 'I'll bring me camera along.'

Thursday

Mason (5)

Frank was about to pick up the metal detector before driving to his flat to start moving his property out when the hallway phone rang.

'Frank, your mason has emailed me his next move. Only his signature isn't A Mason this time, it's A Monster.'

Frank almost sighed. Then he brightened up.

'Okay. Listen, I'm just down the road from the station. What say I pop in?'

There was a suspicious pause.

'You haven't got another bet with the Chief Inspector, have you, Frank?'

'No, I just thought it might be quicker. I'm in the pet shop, getting a collar for Squishy.'

'Okay, Frank. I'll ask Gertie to meet you in reception.'

'See you soon.'

Frank put the phone down and looked at Squishy.

'Let's get going very quickly before Frieda realises something, Squish. Coming along? You'll be able to see Tricia.'

Squish miawioued a definite yes. She wasn't going to be in to answer the phone when something clicked with Frieda.

Frieda put down her phone and looked at Tricia who sat in front of her desk, notebook at the ready.

'Frank is in the pet shop down the road, buying a new flea collar for Squishy,' she said. 'He'll be in shortly.'

'Is he bringing little Squishy in? I haven't seen her for ages.'

'He didn't say. But I've just realised.'

'What?'

'How could he answer from the pet shop when I telephoned my home landline?'

Tricia considered this for a moment.

'Good point,' she said.

'And when his mobile phone is almost permanently switched off.'

'Even better point.'

Frieda sighed.

'You get so used to being able to contact people wherever and whenever they are you miss the obvious. Frank even sounded like he was talking on a mobile phone, that's the way I pictured him as I was speaking.'

'Me too.'

'I think we need to change that question, snog, marry, avoid? It should be snog, marry or murder.'

'Hmm. But you've already married him.'

'Maybe it should be "and" instead of "or". Get hold of Gertie. Tell her she's on guard duty, and to stick to him like glue.'

'Will do.'

'And go down yourself. If Frank's bought Squishy along I want someone to babysit her also. He's probably attached a radio and video camera to her collar.'

White: The Mason's move. 5. n1-m2

Black: Frank

	a	b	c	d	e	f	g	h	i	j	k	l	m	n	o	p
1	R	Nt	B	Q	K	B	Nt	R	R	Nt	B	Q	K	↻	Nt	R
2	P	P	P	P		P	P	P	P	P	P	P	**wB**	P	P	P
3					wP								wP			
4																
5																
6																
7																
8																
9																
10																
11								bP	bP							
12																
13									bP							
14																
15	P	P	P	P	P	P	P	R	R	P	P	P	P	P	P	R
16	R	Nt	B	Q	K	B	Nt	R	R	Nt	B	Q	K	B	Nt	R

'Gertie! Tricia!' exclaimed Frank as the door behind reception opened.

'Squishy!' exclaimed Gertie and Tricia, petting the kitten who greeted them with the desperate miaows of a starving little feline. Tricia took Squishy off Frank and Gertie took his arm and held it firmly to her chest as they marched to the interview room.

'Gertie, do you mind? I am supposed to be a happily married man.'

'Supposed to be?' asked Frieda from the doorway of the interview room. Gertie pouted.

'I was just trying to look after him,' she said, releasing his arm. 'You said he needed looking after.'

'I didn't mean in the same way you'd want to look after Wilf.' Gertie brightened.

'Actually the last time I held Wilf that way I was demonstrating an arm lock. He didn't believe I could throw him.'

'Does he believe now?' asked Frank as they entered the interview room.

'Oh, yes,' said Gertie, 'he's thoroughly converted now. He's even promised to get someone in to fix the dents in the plasterwork.'

'I printed out the email,' Frieda said, passing Frank a piece of paper. 'We'll start the paperless office project next week.'

'I try not to crucify the English but study as she goes,' read Frank. 'What the hell is that supposed to mean?'

'Sounds like the sort of English some Indian computer helpdesk people use,' Tricia said, stroking Squishy. 'It makes sense when you know what they mean.'

'Thanks for that, Trish,' said Frank. 'I shall bear that in mind. Any idea of what he might be saying before I know what he means?'

'Nope. What about you, Squish-Kitty? Aren't you gorgeous?' Squishy licked her chin in agreement.

'Right,' said Frank, 'if we can't decipher his comments, let's see if we can make sense of his moves. Bn1 to m2. That's Bishop n1 to m2.' He moved the white bishop. 'Well, well, he really is a cautious little soul, isn't he.'

'He's going for an early castle,' said Gertie.

'My thoughts exactly, Gerts.'

'Castle – that's where the king and castle are changed over,' said Frieda.

'Indeed. He's just got a knight to get out of the way and he's free to castle.'

'That's the way I play. Wilf prefers to charge in.'

'Wilf plays chess?'

'Yes, of course. Why are you looking at me like that?'

'Wilf has a very ... strangely developed sense of humour,' Frieda pointed out.

'He wouldn't ... I suppose he might,' concluded Gertie.

'I don't think it is Wilf,' said Frank.

'Why not?'

He waved a hand at the board.

'This was specially made. You can't buy them in a shop. So he would either have had to make it himself or pay someone to do so, quite an experienced carpenter, from the look of it.'

'No, that's not Wilf,' conceded Gerty. 'He's very good at painting so long as it's a few brushstrokes, but he'd never have the patience for something time-consuming like that. And as for paying for it, well, no, I can't see him doing that either. A cravat or scarf or waistcoat or something like that for himself, yes, a chess board, not a chance.'

'But it is personal,' said Frank. 'Whoever is out there playing this game knows me. I don't know who it is, but they've met me. I'm sure of it.'

'Wellburians can be daft,' noted Gertie, 'but not daft enough to spend their own money like that.'

'Free, they're using your e-mail address. How did they get hold of it, and how did they know that mine wasn't being used?'

'Tricia hasn't found anything obvious. No personal email addresses go outside, and there's nowhere anyone can access them. The only email address given to the public is a generic one.'

Frank leaned his hands on the desk and studied the chess board. He reached a hand out to touch one of the pieces and pulled it back quickly.

'J'adoube,' he said.

'Quoi?' asked Frieda.

'I touch,' Frank translated. 'In tournaments, if you touch your own piece you have to use it for your next move. Unless you say "J'adoube", which means you're intentionally adjusting it without intending to use it.'

Gertie looked at him as if worried he might be having some form of mental breakdown.

'I'll make sure he's aware of that when we nick him,' she noted.

'That's part of the problem,' said Frieda. 'A bit like my hippies. They haven't actually broken any laws. Nor has our Mason friend. He's just made implied threats. With added fruit and nuts. Or tomatoes.'

Frank rubbed his jaw.

'I think I'll advance my left-most Knight's pawn one space,' he said.

'Only one space?' asked Frieda. 'What happened to General Grant charging on Vicksburg?'

'Well, to be fair he kept trying to outflank Lee on his way to Richmond instead of full-on frontal attacks. You have to use a mixture of strategies to keep your opponent off balance. I need to get my bishop out to do a bit of damage on Mason's pieces. And castle my king on the left side. Then I can let rip with all these central pieces.'

They looked at the closed ranks of the white pieces.

'I think it's time to open up my left flank,' Frank said. He leaned forward and advanced his left-hand knight's pawn one space. 'There: o15 to o14, Free.'

'One space?' asked Frieda. 'Are you sure? You wouldn't want to get a speed wobble, would you?'

Bill Dughaille

White: The Mason

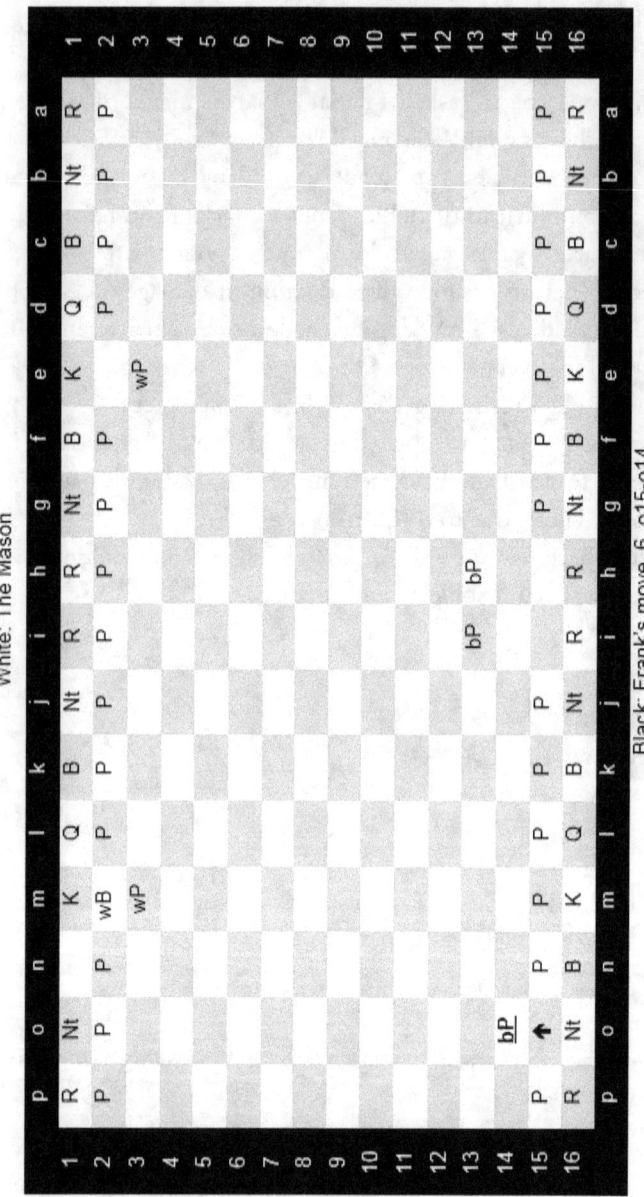

Black: Frank's move. 6. o15-o14

154

Friday

Radio Ranting; TOBs talk; Aggie; Mason (7); Dinner

'Yes, folks, that was indeed an advert for enemas for poodles, and this is Julia welcoming you back to Wellbury's favourite local radio station with all the news and grooves that behooves. And today I have another scoop for you as we beat the Herald to interview the leader of a modern movement which has allied itself to the Cult of the Clueless, the one and only Tom Ranting. Now, Tom I've been reading up on the Ranters and they sound quite a bizarre fad from Cromwell's day.'

'Well, I'm not sure about bizarre, Julia. They succeeded the Levellers, and were followed by the Quakers. You could say that the Quakers are actually Ranter apostates.'

'I don't think I will say that, Tom, we get enough complaints in our email in tray as it is. But the Ranters, didn't they go around, well, ranting?'

'Yes, ranting and swearing and such, going around in the nude, pretty much anything that was considered sinful. It was an attempt to prove that there was no such thing as sin. Because God created everything, which meant that he would have created sin, and God couldn't create sin, of course.'

'Couldn't she?'

'Sorry?'

'I was asking whether god – as a female – couldn't have created sin. After all, wasn't it Eve who caused Adam to eat the apple which resulted in a mortal sin?'

Tom laughed.

'Oh, my goodness, no, that's Sunday school stuff for children. And it goes to show how organised religions have perverted peoples' understanding of God. After all, what sort of god would deliberately put temptation in front of someone knowing that they would succumb to that temptation? God is, after all, omniscient.'

'Good question, Tom, I've often wondered about that. But here's another question: aren't you supposed to be effing and blinding like a sailor who has been too long at sea?'

'Well, technically speaking, yes. I do do my bit when I'm amongst friends, but to do so on radio would be very impolite.'

'You're worried about being impolite?'

'Of course. It's one thing to go around committing what others claim is a sin, quite another matter to be impolite. This is Britain, after all.'

'Well, it's Wellbury, so I suppose you've got a point. But, seriously, Tom, please don't tell me that we've gone to all the bother of having you on air and you're not going to rant a bit? I mean, think of our listeners. They need something to be offended about.'

'Well, Julia ...'

'Yes, Tom?'

'As it's for you and the listeners, well, what I could do – well you know I mentioned some Ranters going around nude? I could take my clothes off for you.'

'Er, well, Tom, now that's a –'

'So, here we go, start off with the jacket, and then the shirt, and here, just a moment, need to undo my shoe laces ...'

'Ladies and gentlemen, our good listeners, I don't think you should be hearing this ...'

'Trousers, and finally –'

'So we'll go to an advert break. Be back shortly, and be grateful you can't see what I'm seeing.'

The airwaves were filled with an advert for a brand of new and improved fruitcake made "just as mother nature intended".

Julia looked at Tom.

'You didn't even so much as loosen your tie,' she pointed out.

'Well, you didn't think I was going to take all my clothes off in front of you, did you? I'm old enough to be your father.'

'You're as big a bullshitter as my father, I'll say that.'

Tom's eyes twinkled.

'Would you say that people out there who have mentally imagined me taken off my clothes have sinned?' he asked.

Julia steepled her fingers and looked at him.

'The trouble with people like you is that you cause havoc and leave the mess for people like us to clear up. Before lunchtime we'll have hundreds of emails, half of them complaints and the other half from elderly women asking for pictures.'

'There's an advert for some aftershave that shows a man in his underpants. You could send them that.'

Julia shook her head.

'You know, between you and that lot from the Cult of the Clueless, you could start an awful lot of trouble.'

Tom stood up.

'We aren't going to start trouble, Julia. The trouble is in peoples' minds, waiting to start.'

'You're not leaving us, are you?'

'I'm leaving before the phone calls come in. It's a struggle between being polite and being honest. Would you like to hear a joke?'

'Oh, go on, then, make it quick, the commercials are about to end.

'This young chap is being interviewed for a job. The interviewer asks, 'What are some of your bad points?' the chap replies, 'Being honest.' 'Oh,' says the interviewer, 'I don't call being honest a bad point.' The chap replies, 'I don't give a feck what you think.'

And with that, Tom was gone.

Frank rang the doorbell to the house where Mrs Scythe and Miss Smith lived. Despite the lateness of the season there were still window-boxes with flowering plants in them. The small front garden was full of carefully tended rose bushes. Everything spoke of a tidy little house inhabited by two tidy, elderly women. The door opened and one of them looked out.

'Miss Smith? Inspector Frank Summers. I wonder if I could come in for a moment?'

Mildred Smith looked back at him with the frightened face of someone who had never had a police officer turn up on the front doorstep and really didn't want to start now.

'Who is it, Mildred?' boomed a voice within.

'It's a policeman,' Mildred squeaked back.

'Well, don't just stand there. Bring him in. I want a word with him.'

Mildred Smith opened the door wider to let Frank enter. He made sure that he wiped his feet extra carefully. It was that kind of hallway.

Inside the lounge Georgette Scythe was attacking a jigsaw on a board lying on her lap. The box showed it to be a copy of Poussin's "The Rape of the Sabine Women". She was making sure the correct pieces were going in the correct place by pounding them in. She glared up at Frank.

'Would you like a cup of tea, Inspector?' asked Mildred Smith.

'Do we have to feed the thing tea?' asked the other woman. 'Thought we paid enough in council taxes without having to feed and water them.'

'I'd love a cup, Miss Smith,' Frank said, sitting down in the chair obviously reserved for occasional visitors. He smiled at Georgette Scythe as her friend scurried off to the kitchen.

'What brings you here? Shouldn't you be out catching criminals?' Georgette Scythe demanded, forcing the head of a Roman soldier onto the body of a horse.

'Only when I'm on duty, Mrs Scythe. I'm not at the moment. I heard you on the radio. I was most impressed.'

'So you decided to come around here and warn me off. That's it, isn't it? I know what you lot are like.'

'You could say that. I promised my wife I'd pop around for a chat. More or less.'

'Your wife?'

'Inspector Frieda Summers. We're both in the force, you see. She's actually my boss.'

Georgette Scythe paused to look at him in the way a lion may pause when their dinner donkey has unexpectedly said hello.

'And she's an inspector? Well, I'm glad to hear that there's some equality these days. I've always said that women make better policemen than men. None of this namby-pamby nonsense. A quick clout across the head, that sorts most things out. Men are too afraid to do it these days.'

'Ah, thank you,' Frank said, accepting a shaking cup of tea from Miss Smith. 'I dare say there are those that would agree with you, Mrs Scythe. However I'm afraid we have to obey the law, being police officers.'

'That's it! We don't have to worry about such nonsense. Do we, Mildred?'

'If you say so, my dear.'

'I do say so. Leave it to us, Inspector, leave it to us. You just turn a blind eye and we'll sort these hooligans out. Mark my words. The girls are in fine fettle, just raring for the fight.'

'Now you know we can't do that, Mrs Scythe. And I'm sure you'd rather have us concentrating on the villains than having to spend time on a group of normally law-abiding citizens.'

'Don't worry, Inspector, we shan't do anything illegal. Simple self-defence, that's all. If that's still legal these days.'

'Self-defence.'

'Precisely, Inspector. We shall defend ourselves to the death. '

'Let's hope it doesn't come to that, Mrs Scythe.'

'Oh, I didn't mean my death, Inspector. I was speaking of anyone who tries to attack us little old ladies.'

Frank paused.

'Okay, Mrs Scythe, I'll be honest with you. I'm not here officially. Actually I'm booked off sick. I did tell my wife I'd pop in and see you, and she told me I wasn't allowed to.'

Mildred Scythe's eyes opened as widely as they ever might.

'You're disobeying your wife's orders? And she's your boss?'

Frank grinned.

'I'm interpreting an order from a superior officer on my own initiative in light of unexpected events, Mrs Scythe, I would never disobey my wife's orders. Though she would never give me an order as my wife, just as I would never give her an order as her husband. It's what keeps our marriage going.'

Georgette Scythe shook her head in disbelief.

'It's times like these that I realise that my husband did the sensible thing early on in my marriage,' she said.

'Which was?'

'Killed himself trying to jump a fence. On a horse, of course, he would never be silly enough to go running around the countryside on his legs.'

'I'm sure he was a wonderful man, Mrs Scythe.'

'He wasn't. He was stupid, arrogant, ignorant, sexist – everything bad you can think of. Got a house-maid pregnant when he was sixteen. I never did find out whether that was a case of his stupidity or hers. She got paid off not to tell her story to the newspapers, so maybe she knew what she was doing all along.'

'And yet you still married him?'

She glared at him.

'You don't suppose they made any of that public, do you? All I knew was that he was a dashing young subaltern in a very prestigious regiment. It's only after you're married they tell you all the things they should have mentioned when the vicar asks whether anyone has any objections. We bring up our girls to dream of being princesses when we should be showing them films of birthing rooms.'

Frank's mouth opened and closed temporarily.

'I can't say I've thought of it that way, to be honest.'

'Well, you should. These defenceless little old ladies being attacked, once upon a time they were little girls who dreamed of meeting their prince. Now look at them, all of them, too afraid to go outside.'

'A bit of an exaggeration, Mrs Scythe. There are some women who would like to fight back.'

'Name me one. One other than ourselves. Just one.'

'Well, there's a Mrs Shaw I was speaking to just a few days ago, lives in Lords Acres. She'd like to hit back if she could.'

'Not Marti Shaw? She used to live out in Lords Acres. Went to school together, only girl tougher than I was. Last I heard she'd gone out to Australia.'

'That's her. I think it was her husband who went to Australia. But she is pretty resilient.'

'Well, there you are. Lost touch with her after school. Must look her up again. See if she wants to join TOBs. She'd make a good battalion commander.'

'Okay, Mrs Scythe, can we reach an agreement? I'm just as concerned about the little old ladies as you. Give me two weeks. If I haven't worked out what's going on and who is responsible, well, you can do what you want.'

'One week.'

'Ten days.'

Georgette Scythe glared at him again.

'Inspector Summers, you're the first person I've met who can talk me out of something I'm determined on doing. Very well, you have ten days. And then, to quote Shakespeare, or probably his wife, we shall let slip the dogs of war. No man will feel safe walking the streets alone.'

Frank sighed and stood up.

'You know that will be illegal, of course. Well, then, I'd better get moving. Good day, Mrs Scythe, Miss Smith. Thank you for the tea.'

Once he had left Georgette Scythe smiled at Miss Smith. It wasn't a pretty sight.

'Silly man. We won't be ready for a good ten days, if not a fortnight. TOBs are just not ready. They have to react immediately, instinctively. The moment a man touches you on the shoulder you smash your heel into his instep. Carry a boiling hot coffee in case a man gets too near. Carry a butcher's knife, because a woman's place is in the kitchen.'

'But you said –'

'Yes, I know what I said, it's the sort of thing leaders have to say.'

She sighed.

'Why is it that men find it so easy to lead? Nelson, Wellington, Napoleon. Men followed them through rain, hail, sleet, starvation, you name it. Try and get a bunch of old women to follow you, all they can do is come up with excuses.'

She smiled grimly.

'Still, mustn't grumble, eh? Inspector Summers has given us ten days. In ten days we have to blood the troops.'

'Blood the troops?'

'Yes, give them a taste for blood, and a confidence in attack.'

'Georgette, what on earth are you thinking about?'

'Religion. Religion, the bastion of patriarchy. These men demanding their rights to march and be heard, well, we demand to be heard too. And felt, might I say.'

'I'm sorry, Georgette, I don't understand.'

'I promised Inspector Summers that we would delay our main campaign for ten days. That gives us ten days to get the girls battle ready. Hitting the religious demonstration will test our resolve, clarify our tactics, and get the girls used to the sight of blood.'

'But, Georgette, it's a religious demonstration.'

'Well, where do you suppose priests come from? Vicars, bishops, cardinals, they're all men aren't they?'

'Well, strictly speaking, Georgette, no, it's not unusual to see a female priest these days.'

'More fool them, then. If there are any on the demonstration they'll just have to take their chances.'

'But, Georgette, what I mean is, well, they'll be the mild sort, not, well, not like these ruffians we read about.'

'Good,' said Georgette Scythe. 'Once they've got used to beating up the mild ones they won't be so worried about the real brutes.'

'So, Aggie, all quiet on the western front?' asked Frank, sitting on a clump of bricks outside Aggie's shed in the cemetery.

'There's a police car which passes every few hours,' Aggie replied, stroking the head of a skinny black cat which was looking at Frank with distrust. 'They often stop to say hello and look around.'

Frank nodded. The one thing the station did agree on was that Aggie was to be protected.

'You've got all you need? It's not too cold at night?'

'I don't get cold. I've got blankets. And the police officers bring me hot food in the evenings.'

Frank nodded again. Uniformed coppers could be criticised for many things, but not knowing the best places for cheap and tasty food wasn't one. Similar to an army marching on its stomach, uniformed police officers would forgive many things, going hungry wasn't one of them. You had to become a plain-clothes detective to join the elite who thought bad diets and ulcers part of the job. Normal coppers valued their food above their careers and married lives.

'Get any feelings?' he asked. 'About whether there's someone still out there?'

Aggie nodded.

'He's still there, waiting. He's scared of the police, and the men in the allotment come over at different times, he's scared of them too. But I can feel him out there. Not every day. Most days. Every second day, perhaps.'

'Definitely a 'he'? Not she?'

'No, it's a he.'

Frank nodded again. He knew that Aggie believed what she was saying. But she also believed that she was twelve years old and going to meet her little brothers and sisters in heaven soon. She was well over sixty, and she wasn't about to pass on if he and her other friends had anything to do about it. For all he knew she was imagining this anonymous "he".

On the other hand, if she wasn't, there was someone out there who needed to be stopped.

'Can you choose where you get buried?' she asked suddenly.

'I don't know. It isn't something I've ever thought about. I think people sometimes do.'

'I want to be buried next to him,' she said.

Frank looked towards where she was pointing. In the twilight it was an anonymous grave.

'Any specific reason?'

'He's unhappy. He's a ghost, he walks the cemetery at night. I can bring him to the Lord. He will walk in the ways of the Lord.'

'To walk in the path of the righteous, and the path of the just,' suggested Frank.

'He's just a boy, a silly boy who did something wrong once. When the final judgement day comes there will be those who will lead many followers who have seen the light. I just want to be able to lead that poor boy to the Lord and ask, Please Lord, forgive this boy and admit him to your paradise.'

Frank nodded.

It was the sort of nod a person gives when they haven't a clue what the other person is on about.

Bill Dughaille

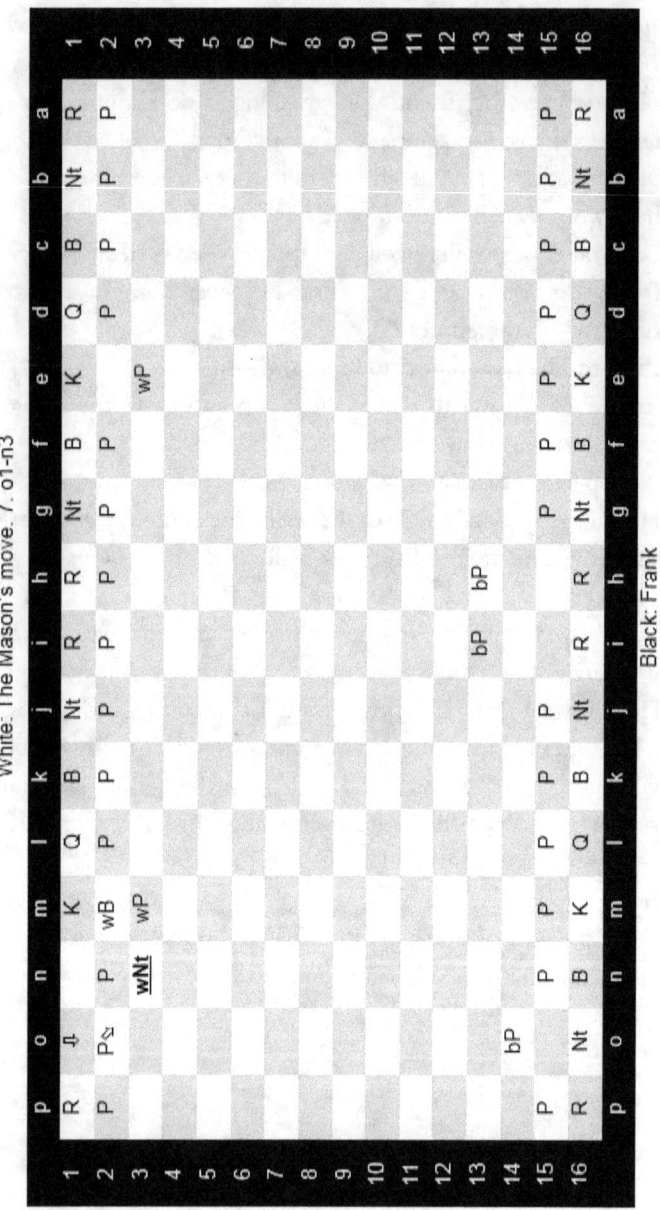

White: The Mason's move. 7. o1-n3

Black: Frank

166

'Frank? Where are you?'

'On my way home to cook dinner, Free. What's up?'

'Pull, over, Frank. Let me know when you're safely parked.'

'Hokay, Free, just a second. There, now, safely parked in a no-parking zone, just waiting for a traffic warden to turn up. You can do that with a police warrant. What's up, my one true love?'

'It's our mason friend again. Calling himself Mason once more. Do you want his move or his latest attack on the English language?'

'Go on, tell me his latest pearl of agricultural produce.'

Frank took out his large paper and unfolded it.

'The vintage is mine, sayeth the lard.'

'The what is what?'

'The vintage is mine, sayeth the lard. And don't ask me what that means, Frank, I haven't a clue.'

'Ah, but it is a clue. It must be. Doesn't make sense otherwise.'

'Well, the real saying, if I recall correctly, is vengeance is mine sayeth the Lord. Or something like that.'

'Yes. So instead of vengeance we have vintage. And instead of the Lord, we have the lard. Which obviously means ... ?'

'Sour grapes?'

'Fatty grapes? Maybe that's his real name, Fatty Grapes.'

There was a pause on Frieda's side.

'Frank, have you ever, ever heard of anyone called Fatty Grapes? Even a rock band?'

'Sylvester and the Fatty Grapes. No, can't say that rings any bells. I'll mull it over. In the meanwhile, what's his move? Does it make any more sense than Fatty Grapes?'

'He's moved his right-most knight; o1-n3. That's o-Oscar, numeric one, n-November, numeric three.'

'Well, well, well, Mr Mason, so you're using a knight, eh. Well, that's a bit obvious.'

'He's planning to castle, like you predicted?'

'Exactly, Free. Allows him to move his king towards a corner, reduce the number of pieces needed to protect it, cover its flank. Right, let's see. A riposte is called for, I think. Let's trundle out the left hand bishop: n16-p14, Free. November 16, numeric one six hyphen p-Peter 14, numeric one four.'

'You're setting up to castle yourself?'

'I'm letting him think that that's what I'm doing. But what the master does and what he intends are as different as white knight to black bishop.'

'Dear god, now he thinks he's Wellington,' muttered Frieda.

Hordes

White: The Mason

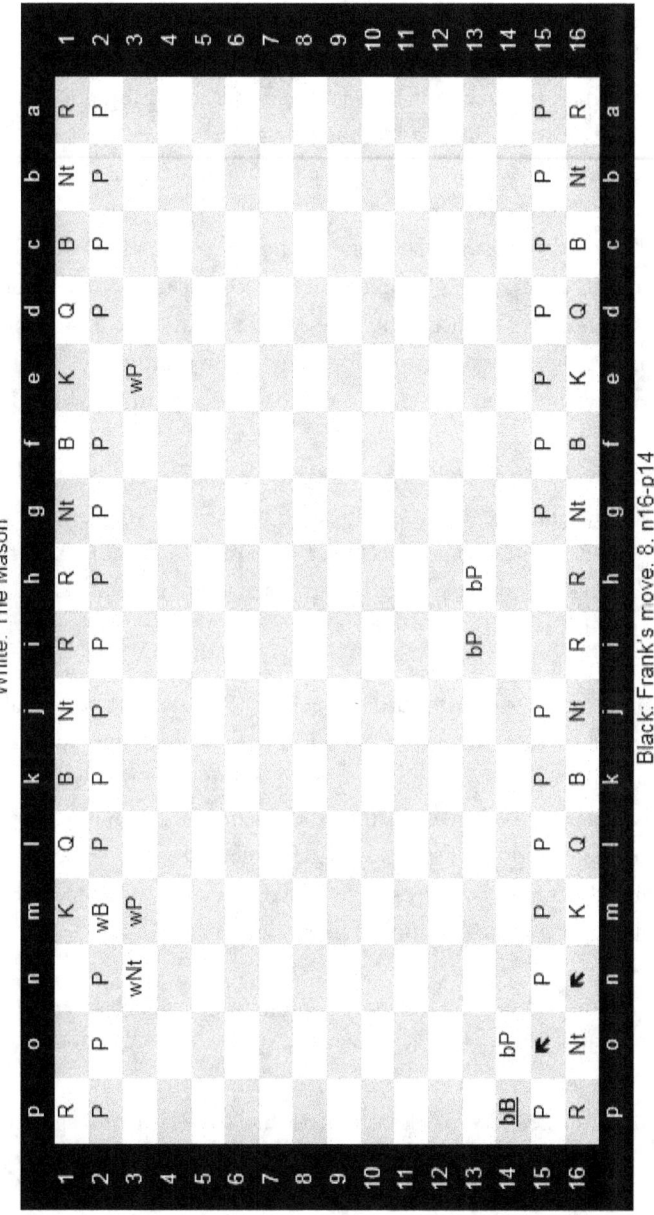

Black: Frank's move. 8. n16-p14

169

Frank heard the front door open and close. The sound of a briefcase being gratefully dropped came through to the kitchen. A few seconds later Frieda appeared in the doorway.

'Good day at the office, darling?' he asked.

'Remember, second golden rule of our marriage, Frank. No shop talk out of hours.'

'Hokay. Only, since I'm off at the moment, that wouldn't seem to apply. It's a bit like those 1950's manuals on a happy marriage. The spouse should always be ready to listen to their partner's work woes after a long day at the grindstone.'

Frieda scowled at him, sat down, took a shoe off and kneaded her foot.

'Julia was on the radio again today,' he continued. 'Seems like Zack the Prat is still off after being mugged by that inter-faith group called the Righteous Once who plan to demonstrate for religious tolerance. They want the Cult of the Clueless banned.'

'I know. I had them in my office today, insisting they were going to demonstrate Friday-week. They claim that they have a right to demonstrate. Each time I explained that we have the right to ban a demonstration if we think it might cause a disturbance they insisted that they were peace loving people and that it wouldn't cause a disturbance unless the unbelievers caused offence by disrespecting them. It's quite obvious they fully intend to cause trouble whatever happens.'

She sighed.

'And then those two from the Cult of the Clueless came in immediately afterwards. I'm sure they were following the others. Seumas O'Connor and all the rest, and Jaimie No-surname. They wanted assurance that they had the right not to demonstrate. It was all I could do not to have them thrown out into the street.'

'They seem to be picking up quite a following. They've even got themselves a Ranter.'

'A following of people who would normally keep their protests confined to their local pub. Really, Frank, this whole business is becoming very irritating.'

'Oh, I don't know. I was thinking of joining the Cult of the Clueless.'

Frieda glared at him.

'Well, even if I am a police officer, surely I have the right to join a club that doesn't believe in anything? In my off-duty hours?'

'Frank, I've just realised that I've been discussing work with you. I shall have a word with the doctor tomorrow. The sooner you get back to work the better. You're likely to cause more trouble outside of work than in it.'

Frank winked at her.

'I love you too, darling.'

Frieda wasn't smiling.

'Your problem is that you don't realise that other people care about you, Frank. I just know you're going to do something silly and land up in hospital again. Or maybe just not come home again. You really are a right uncaring bastard.'

With that she left the room and swept upstairs before he could see her tears.

Frank looked at a wide-eyed Squishy.

'Bollocks,' he finally said, softly. He stood silently for a few seconds. 'Squish, you do realise that, if your mother doesn't come down in ten minutes I'm going to have to go up and get her?'

Squishy cocked her head in the friendly sort of commiseration that said she was glad it had nothing to do with her.

'Make it fifteen minutes, Squish. No need to rush these things.'

Fifteen minutes passed.

Sixteen.

Seventeen.

Squishy miaowed.

Frank sighed.

'Okay, Squish, once more unto the breach,' he muttered. As he walked out of the kitchen Frieda was coming down the stairs.

'I was about to ask,' he said, 'are you coming down for dinner, or shall I bring it up?'

Frieda paused.

'I hope that was an accidental pun, Frank.'

'Oh, entirely accidental, oh mighty one.'

'Good,' she said, continuing down, 'I'm still angry with you. Just not angry enough to miss dinner.'

'The way to a woman's heart, and all that,' he noted as they re-entered the kitchen.

'Plus flowers, Frank. And jewellery. And perfume.'

'I suppose chocolate falls under the and-all-that banner.'

'No, it's another extra. So what is for dinner?'

He put his arms around her.

'Well, you know what they call Beef Wellington? Puff pastry around a slice of fillet steak?'

'I know what Beef Wellington is, Frank.'

'Well, I thought I'd do that, gratin dauphinoise with leeks, and carrots and peas - but the Beef Wellington without the puff pastry.'

She looked up at him.

'Now why didn't I think of that? Beef Wellington without the puff pastry. I've never understood why people insist on ruining a perfectly good fillet steak that way.'

'I agree. Steak should be out in the open. Maybe a wee bit of mushroom sauce, but even that should be alongside, not on top.'

'Yes, in my experience the only reason for hiding meat under anything is because it's gone off. But why gratin dauphinoise? I would have thought barrel potatoes would be better with fillet. Not an idea of another of your ex-girlfriends by any chance?'

'Nope, my very own. Every time I have any kind of steak it always comes with some form of roast or fried potato. So I thought I'd try something different. And I like gratin dauphinoise.'

'So do I. Unfortunately I like almost all food.'

'Apart from take-aways.'

'No, Frank, I like take-aways too. I just disapprove of the concept.'

'So, am I forgiven?'

She sighed and buried her head in his chest.

'Only this once, Frank, only this once.'

And the next three hundred thousand times, she could have added.

Saturday

Father Brown; Vic Brown; FFSG + Tom + Wilf

'You sure you'll be okay?' Frieda asked that morning as she pulled a leather glove on.

'As okay as I was the last time you asked, Free. First I wait until the spaceship arrives, then –'

'I did listen the last time, Frank,' she said, slapping his arm with the remaining glove.

'Well, there you go, then, it's classic Come Dine With Me time. Spend the morning shopping at some esoteric little shops, start the dinner in the afternoon, pause to go to the hairdresser's to have my nails done, then return just in time to finish off the perfect meal for our enchanting guests. Either that or down a couple of bottles of red, burn everything and keep asking them if they're enjoying themselves while they try to hide most of it behind the aspidistra.'

'Good thing we don't have an aspidistra.'

'I think we should get one. And call it George.'

'Okay, Frank, we'll get an aspidistra and call it George. Now, I'll be back as soon as I can, okay? Probably around three this afternoon.'

'Okay, Free, see you then.'

Frank waited until the door was definitely closed and Frieda had definitely left before turning to Squishy.

'Right, Squish, time to go sort out some of this nonsense. Coming?'

Squishy put her head on one side as if to ask where he was going, because if it was somewhere interesting she might come along.

'I think we can start with the Catholic church and that priest,' Frank told her. 'He seems to know something about Seumas and his sidekick, Jaimie Wotsits. Maybe he can get them to pull their heads in for a couple of weeks.'

'Miaow,' Squishy agreed and trotted up to the front door. She turned and looked back at him.

'Well, come on, I've never been in a Catholic church before,' she seemed to be saying.

Frank stepped warily into the church of St Mary's. Squishy poked an exploratory head around the open front door.

'It's not that I'm nervous about being in a Catholic church, Squish,' Frank whispered. 'Only they terrify me. Especially the nuns.'

'I know what you mean about the nuns,' Squishy whispered back with an Irish accent, 'they often scare the wits out of meself too.'

Frank almost screamed as he realised the voice was coming from behind him. Turning around he found a large man wearing a brown habit with a white rope belt around his middle. The man smiled, bent down and tickled Squishy.

'I can't stand that hymn, All Creatures Bright And Beautiful,' the man confessed. 'But I do have a soft spot for kittens. Considering most of the feline world grow up to be ruthless killers, I've never quite understood why that should be the case.'

'You'll be the parish priest,' Frank suggested.

'Father Brown at your service.' He held out a huge hand. 'And you'll be Detective Inspector Summers.'

Frank shook the man's hand, hoping that his own wasn't lost forever in the man's massive paw.

'You have the advantage of me, Father,' he said. 'I presume it is "Father" – the correct way to address you?'

'It's politer than some of the titles we've been given. Come, let's go to the vestry. It's considered impolite to the Lord to hold normal conversation in His house. I've never understood why. I'm sure He can hear us quite as clearly in the vestry or pub or library or wherever. After all, His first miracle was at a wedding, producing more booze.'

'You don't mind me bring Squishy into the church? My kitten?'

Squishy looked up at Frank as if to say, 'Me? I can go where I want. No need to make excuses for me. And anyway, the big man looks like he knows where the food is.'

'Squishy, is it? Well, now that's a lovely name. And no, I don't believe in letting in all sorts of animals who aren't house-trained, unlike some of the newer approaches, but a delightful young kitten-cat like Squishy? I can't help but feel the good Lord would tickle her under the chin and ask, 'Who's a pretty little kitten, then?' But perhaps,' he added, as they entered the vestry, 'I'm doing something equivalent to anthropomorphising. I can see Jesus doing the sort of thing I would do because I believe in a Jesus who is just like me, instead of asking whether I shouldn't be more like the real Jesus. Ah, here's Mrs Jones. Mrs Jones, you wouldn't be after knowing where we could find a saucer of milk for our latest non-convert, would you? Her name's Squishy. She's not Catholic but I don't think we'll hold that against her, will we?'

'Oh, what a darling little thing,' cooed Mrs Jones as Squishy took one look and rubbed herself against Mrs Jones' legs, calculating in an instant that, however nice the big man might be, this was the person with the key to the larder. 'I'm sure we can find a lovely saucer of milk for her. Come along, Squishy.'

'Not full cream,' Frank said, 'She's still a little young for that.'

Squishy paused for a second to look back at Frank. Her look stated quite plainly that she would be the one to decide on whether or not she was ready for full-cream, or even double cream. Then she followed Mrs Jones, tail flying high.

'So how did you know who I was?' asked Frank. Father Reilly gestured him to a chair, took out a bottle of whiskey and poured a goodly tot into each glass. he handed Frank one before sitting down.

'Tullamore Dew,' he said, before taking a dainty sip and sighing with enjoyment. 'It's one of those things I learnt as a young priest. About the only pleasure you're allowed is a touch of the amber liquid every so often. You won't be forgiven fornication. A liking for the wine, well, that's too close to communion. Cigarettes, tobacco, a pipe, cigars – well, I never did take to them things. But a whiskey from the Emerald Isle? You know, I was posted to a Scottish parish once, terrible it was, Catholics versus Protestants, they used to keep score of the hospitalised on the weekend, and the arrested. The police being Calvinist, it was mainly Catholics locked up. And then the word went out: 'he likes a dram'. That's what they said about me. And suddenly for the first time a Catholic priest could wander into a Scottish bar in that little town and order a drink because 'he likes a wee dram'. From that moment on the only question was whether Irish whiskey was better than Scottish whisky. And these were men who were serious about their whiskey. Had the Pope produced his own blend they would have suspended hostilities to test the quality.'

'To get back to the question, Father – how do you know who I am?'

Father Reilly winked.

''Tis a terrible memory I have, Inspector. I read about you. I have parishioners who tell me things about you. And then I hear things in the confessional. Which I can't repeat, of course. Trouble is, I can never remember which is which. So I don't repeat any of it. Then there's Vic Brown. He doesn't need a confessional to confess. He's always full of praise for yourself.'

'He's a Catholic?'

'Oh, yes. He once said to me, Father, if you want to choose the worst religion to be a sinner in, you have to choose Catholicism or Judaism. Except, of course, he didn't choose Catholicism, he was born into it.'

'Good old Vic Brown, eh? Ex-con making more money by going straight, and regretting it bitterly. I haven't seen him lately. What's he been up to?'

Father Reilly took a sip of whiskey and smiled at the glass.

'Sure and you know he went and bought a thousand cheap white t-shirts. Then he had 'I paid fifty quid for this lousy t-shirt' printed on them. Then he sold all of them – for fifty quid a go. In a single morning.'

Frank laughed.

'And I bet he didn't print more.'

'Nope. Some others tried, but it didn't work. The only t-shirts worth fifty quid were the original batch. And you know the really funny thing? Some people tried to sell theirs on for more. But they couldn't. People decided that a t-shirt that said it cost fifty quid could only be bought or sold for fifty quid. I will never cease to be amazed at the human mind and how it works.'

Frank spotted a familiar, cream-coloured piece of paper on the coffee table.

'I see the Cult of the Clueless have been calling here,' he said.

'Oh, yes. I wouldn't be surprised if we weren't their first port of call. While I was out, of course. They're not stupid.'

'What about them, Seumas O'Brien-O'Murphy-O'Connor-O and Jaimie? You do you know them, don't you?'

'Since they were just in high school. That was when I was posted here. They had just started learning how to disagree with some the Church's teachings. Since then they've come a long way. They've learnt to disagree with all of the Church's teachings. It's a pity they spend so much energy in flippancy. You see, they have a lot in common with serious theologians. Doubt and being – clueless, as they call it – is part of believing.'

'So you won't be going on the demonstration, then?'

'Demonstration?'

'The demonstration for religious freedom and having the Cult of the Clueless banned.'

'There's a contradiction in there somewhere,' smiled the priest. 'You aren't telling me seriously that there's going to be a demonstration against the Cult of the Clueless, are you?'

'Absolutely. Against all unbelievers who won't respect the godly. Friday next week, probably.'

'Silly. How very silly.'

'You don't agree with the sentiments?'

'Inspector, these people who get excited when others mock them, well – well, they don't truly believe. They can't. Look, if you really believe in an omniscient and omnipresent and omnipotent deity ... Well, if they truly believed, they would regard their mockers with compassion rather than getting all worked up. It's rather like the supporter of a top football club getting upset by an Accrington Stanley supporter telling them they couldn't play football.'

'An interesting analogy.'

The priest shrugged.

'I'm afraid I don't have time for zealots. There is too much work to be done, too much to discover. We still don't understand what God's ultimate purpose is.'

Frank raised his eyebrows.

'Perhaps you should join the Cult of the Clueless.'

'Perhaps I should,' agreed Father Brown.

'The demonstration is being organised by a bunch calling themselves the Righteous Once. We're expecting a counter-demonstration by the Clueless. It could get violent.'

Father Reilly's eyes lit up with enthusiastic laughter. He raised his huge hands.

'Then I'll join the counter-demonstration. Tis a long time since I boxed, Inspector. But whacking infidels around with my hands has always been a favourite pastime.'

'And infidels would be?'

'Anybody who doesn't understand good manners, Inspector.'

'You mean such as saying 'please' before punching their lights out?'

'You should have entered the priesthood, Inspector, you have a very quick grasp of theology.'

Frank stood up and finished his whiskey.

'Thanks for that, Father. I must be off. Much as I like the idea of seeing the Cult of the Clueless beat seven sorts of stuffing out of the Know-Alls, I have something more pressing to investigate.'

'The reason The Old Birds' army was formed? The attacks on the little old ladies?'

'Exactly, Father.'

'Well, if you need any help with that, just let me know. If anyone started terrorising my sainted mother, well ... I'd be taking me habit off and reverting to the status of barbarian for just a short while.'

'No-one mentioned anything in the confessional, then?'

Father Reilly gave a grimace.

'You know I can't answer that,' he said. Then he smiled. 'But there are ways of not answering it while still ensuring the truth came out.'

'I'll take that as a no, then,' Frank noted. 'Hello, here's Squishy,' Frank said as the housekeeper entered with a very satisfied looking Squishy following. 'You look like the cat got the cream, Squish.'

Squishy looked up at him as if to say, 'Of course I got the cream. What else do you think I came here for?'

'She's a darling,' said Mrs Jones, 'reminds me of a lovely little kitten I had when I was a little girl. Oh, by the way, Inspector, I picked some salad vegetables from the vegetable garden for yourself and your wife. We have some amazing late fruiting cherry tomatoes in the greenhouse. We grow them every year, and every year the good Father here pretends to be grateful while hoping I won't notice he hasn't actually touched any of them. So I end up giving them away to more deserving souls.'

'Fine food for rabbits,' commented the priest.

'Well, that's very nice of you, Mrs Jones. I can assure you my wife and I are most grateful, we do enjoy a home-grown fresh salad.'

'Inspector,' said the priest, 'it's that sort of comment that means I'll be getting the damned things next year again.'

Frank grinned.

'That sounds like a bugle call for retreat, before I become involved in a theological debate about green salad versus French salad. Come on, Squish, Let's go have a word with Vic Brown. See if he's heard anything on the grapevine.'

He paused.

'Say, Father, do you know if Vic Brown likes playing chess?'

'Vic? Yes, we have a game about once a month. He plays regularly at his pub. Like everything else he does, he's best at it when trying to do it badly. Why do you ask?'

'Ever heard of double chess, Father?'

'That's where a grand-master plays two games at the same time, isn't it?'

'That's the one. Anyway, must rush. Oh, by the way – do you think, if you were to have a word with Seumas they might agree to postpone their counter-demonstration for a couple of weeks?'

Father Brown shook his head.

'I'll try, but I can't see it, Inspector. If you want that done you'll need to get the demonstration postponed yourself. Surely you can do that? I would have thought that would have been in the police's remit.'

'Not really, not my level. But even if that had been possible, there's one other small problem. I'm on sick leave.'

Father Brown's eyebrows shot up.

'Forgive me saying so, Inspector, but don't you think you ought to go back to work for a rest?'

Frank laughed.

'See you later, Father.'

'And good luck to you,' said the priest.

Out at his car Frank paused before unlocking the doors, thinking. Squish miawoed at him.

'Vic Brown, Squish. He's the sort who would send someone a chess set as an anonymous present. He'd definitely pay for one to be made. He'd send it anonymously. But he wouldn't challenge anyone to a game anonymously. Would he?'

Squish sniffed at a weed, presuming it was a rhetorical question.

'Okay, let's go find out.'

Vic Brown sat at a table outside the Fisherman's Arms, gloomily watching the river Wellbury flow slowly past. An empty pint glass in front of him suggested that he hadn't quite made up his mind as to whether another would be a good idea, or whether it had been sufficient unto the day. A hand came over his shoulder and placed a pint of Beamish in front of him to settle the matter.

'Hello, Vic,' said Frank, putting Squishy on the table and seating himself opposite Vic. 'How's tricks?' Squishy sat down and regarded Vic Brown with the interrogative air of a cat trying to decide whether this human was going to be (a) a source of food, (b) a source of comfort, (c) require solace, (d) all of the above, or (e) need his empty shoes used as a litter tray.

'Mr Summers!' exclaimed Vic Brown, past master in dodgy Cockney accents. 'Cor, you didn't half give me a fright there, straight up, I never even heard you coming.'

'Of course, Vic, I'm not known as assassin Summers for nothing.' He took a sip of his pint, and then held it up to the air to better appreciate its quality, and perhaps wonder how many alcoholic drinks he was going to have to consume before the time came to start making dinner, a concern he had never had as a bachelor. 'Now, Vic,' he continued, putting the glass down, 'as you know, I'm booked off duty.'

'I heard, Mr Summers, I did send a bouquet of flowers to the hospital. Did you get them?'

'Yes, thank-you, Vic, My wife promised me she'd send a thank-you card. Did you get that?'

'Oh, yes, Mr Summers. It was lovely, it was, all hand-written. You don't get that sort of thing these days, like personally hand-written. Florist down near where I live, well, they have a professional script-writer in when people want things hand-written. You have to have a professional these days. People can't write no more. Specially what with this Inniternet thing these days.'

Frank smiled. There was a rumour that Vic Brown had once started a career in selling fakes, but had failed because he had insisted on correcting the mistakes the original artists had made. The exquisite irony was that Frank was quite certain the originator of the story was in fact Vic Brown. He was such a perfectionist as a fraud he'd made himself real.

'So true, Vic, so true. Anyway, since I'm off work, there was something I was hoping you could help me with.'

'And after the thank-you, she writes, "My husband has been booked off work for what is medical reasons, and if he comes to you asking questions, remind him he's supposed to be resting. Because if I hear you've been upsetting his blood pressure I'll be coming after you to ask questions." That's exactly what she wrote, no word of a lie, cross me heart and hope to die. And I don't think she meant polite questions. More the sort what don't need answers. Because it's poor innocent people like me what ends up suffering the slings and arrers even though we try to do what's right. If you know what I mean.'

He took a deep sip of the fresh pint and looked Frank innocently in the eyes, daring him to suggest he might even think of risking the wrath of the woman he had always called 'Mrs Inspector', long before Frank and Frieda had even thought of getting married.

Well. Frank, anyway.

'Vic, you're quite right. And I'm not here on official business. Like I said, I'm booked off duty. Thing is, my doctor said I need lots of exercise. You know, long walks, perhaps a bit of jogging, that sort of thing.'

'Ah, now why didn't you say so, Mr Summers, I know someone who deals in exercise bikes and –'

'So I thought, well, I could go on long walks to chat to these little old ladies who've been attacked. Re-assure them. Not actually do anything, of course, just to show the police are around. Of course, if I actually thought something was happening I'd radio in and request the two armed response cars we have waiting for just such an eventuality.'

'Two armed response cars,' Vic breathed in amazement. 'You mean, like with them Hechler-Koch machine guns an all?'

One of the reasons Frank liked Vic Brown is that the little man seemed to believe every word he was told was true. His biggest problem was trying to work out the boundary at which Vic would have to give up pretence at belief because what he was being fed was such obvious nonsense.

'Thing is, Vic, I need to be able to re-assure the poor little old ladies that we're looking out for them. Now you and I know we can't look after them all the time. They know themselves that's the truth, but they like to fool themselves to feel more secure. And who can blame them?'

Vic Brown gave a little half-shrug to indicate that, Yes, these little white lies might sometimes be necessary.

'So,' Frank continued, 'if I can tell them that I've spoken to someone from the criminal fraternity, well, you know, if they think that the coppers and the cons are working together on this ...'

Vic Brown made the face of someone who knew they were being led to their demise but couldn't find a way out before they got there.

'Look, Mr Summers, just so we understand each other, this isn't you getting involved with work or anything? Or, to put it plain, if Mrs Inspector finds out, she ain't going to be frying my giblets on her Aga?'

Frank gave him the puzzled look of the innocent and injured who only mean well.

'Vic, all I want you to do is to tell me you've thought about this whole business and have no information to contribute. That's all.'

'That's the trouble, Mr Summers,' Vic Brown said, 'I have thought about it. I've asked everyone I know, in a roundabout sort of way, and the answer's always the same. It's a crim mind at work. But it's not one of ours. And they're targeting one place. Aggie at the cemetery.'

'What makes you say that?'

'All the cases I heard of, most of them's been one-offs. Aggie's been continuous like.'

'And how do you know that?'

'Well, you know, Mr Summers, word gets around, people talk, you know.'

Frank guessed that Vic Brown had been wandering around the allotments. He had probably offered to buy up all their produce at the best price possible. But he didn't know about Martha Shaw.

'So what does your gut tell you? About who's behind the whole business?'

Vic Brown looked around to make sure that nobody could overhear.

'They're from the Smoke,' he assured Frank softly. 'I'm sure of it. Remember Hovis and Clovis? I ad the same feeling about them too.'

Frank knew. Anyone who was British and hadn't a Wellbury birth certificate came, according to Vic Brown, from 'the Smoke', or London. Vic Brown was the only person from London Frank had met who actually called it that.

'No names?'

Vic shook his head.

'Nah, too good for that. Them London hard boys is professionals.'

'Oh, well. Look, if you hear anything, you know how to get in touch.'

'Ah, come on Mr Summers, I can't go to the station, people will think I'm a nark.'

'No, Vic, I meant email. I thought you had my address.'

'Come off it, Mr Summers, I can't work one of those computers. Those things are for the youngsters. If I bought one it'd be hacked in seconds and I'd lose all me business secrets.'

'Good point, Vic, good point. Ah, well, I'm sure you'll find a way to bump into me by accident. Or I'll bump into you. You play chess on a regular basis at your local, don't you?'

'Yeah, Mr Summers, but not as good as you. I'm sure you could have been a professional.'

'Ever played double chess, Vic?'

'That's when a grand master plays two games at the same time, innit? Never had the chance, sadly. I would have liked to play a grand master.'

'Not to worry, I'm sure it'll happen some day. Come on, Squish, time to get dinner started.'

Frank strolled away with Squishy trotting behind. From what Vic had said he could conclusively conclude absolutely nothing apart from the probability that the spate of attacks revolved around Aggie and Martha Shaw.

Presuming Vic wasn't (a) lying (improbable) or (b) imagining things (highly likely).

'Sounds like Mummy's home, Squish,' Frank said just before six p.m. as he stood in the kitchen preparing that evening's dinner. Squish miaowed agreement and jumped off the stool to go greet Frieda, a human who had to be more interesting than Frank, who, for some strange reason, was busy tearing up lettuce leaves.

There was the sound of a briefcase being dropped, Frieda saying 'Hello, little Squishy', and then she entered the kitchen, Squishy in her arms. She stopped suddenly, aghast, pointing towards some packets on the kitchen table.

'Frank, nuts!' she exclaimed.

'Yes, Free,' he replied, holding up an object, 'and anaphylactic pen to ward off bad things.'

'Frank, no, we can't have nuts at the table.'

'Too late, we've already invited them.'

'Frank that isn't funny. That really isn't funny.'

He dried his hands on a tea-towel and put his arms around her.

'Free, as long we avoid perfectly harmless things I've eaten for years without a problem, you are going to be as skittish as a kitten on a hot tin roof during a thunderstorm with thousands of marbles raining down. Even if the doctors find out what the cause was, and it turns out to be some guano from a bat hardly ever found within a thousand miles you will be telling me to avoid nuts for the rest of our lives. And we don't want that, do we? I'm a copper, dealing with nuts is the fun part of the job.'

She looked at him for a few seconds, and then lay her head on his shoulder.

'You will be careful, won't you Frank?'

'Hell, course I will, Free, you don't think I want to go through that again. Especially not another stay in hospital. That was bloody awful, no matter how nice the staff were.'

He hugged her.

'And remember what Franklin Delano Roosevelt in his first inauguration speech as the 32nd President of the United States back in 1933. My firm belief is that the only thing we have to fear is fear itself – nameless, unreasoning, unjustified terror which paralyzes needed efforts to convert retreat into advance.'

She leaned back, looked and him, leaned forward, kissed him and laid her head on his chest.

'You memorised that, darling?'

'Second year uni exam. I expected a question on Twentieth century America and the emergence of empire.'

'And you got?'

'Spanish-American War of 1898 or British-American War of 1812. I had to blag it somewhat.'

She laughed.

'I'll bet you got a distinction, too. Okay, Frank, I promise to be less of a fuss-pot in future. I'd better put little Squishy down before she gets squashed.'

'Excellent,' said Frank, rubbing his hands. 'Your wine is over there breathing away. The legs of lamb have spent the day in the slow-cooker. The potatoes have been parboiled and are now in trays in the oven next to the lamb, waiting to be roasted in goose fat. Entrée of mushrooms on toast with a side helping of fresh green salad and cherry tomatoes; mushrooms waiting to be sautéed, I'll start the sauce just before they get here, salad's in the bowl with optional French sauce in the sauce jug. Soup, cucumber, a nice little peppery bite to it even if I say so myself – but not too much pepper, of course. Veggies to go with the main, carrots and peas – I was going to do Brussel sprouts, but that can wait until Christmas. Dessert, chocolate sort-of brownies with a base of sauce constructed mainly of syrup slightly cooked with a dash of vinegar, to be topped off with cold cream one side and hot custard the other. Cheese and biscuits with coffee and port to end. I'm sure I've forgotten something, but you always do. Feed them enough wine and port and they won't realise.'

Frieda smiled.

'Can't think of anything missing, darling. That dessert sounds lethal, though.'

'Oh, it will be. It's a recipe I picked up somewhere, can't remember where. It's the sort of pudding that drives needles through fillings.'

Frieda grimaced.

'I think small portions are called for.'

'Oh, absolutely. It's good old Epicurus again. The enjoyment of life, but not over-enjoyment. Enjoy good food, don't guzzle and end up overweight and sickly. Which reminds me, I haven't even started on those books dad sent.'

'Well, you won't be starting tonight. And you're still booked off work and going to take things easy. Now I'm going to change.'

Frank watched her go upstairs. He turned to look at Squishy.

'You're a lady, Squish, you going to change?'

Squishy raised an eyebrow as if to say "Hmmph! Typical man. No tuna" and then ambled after Frieda.

By the time Susan, Gertie, Wilf and Tom arrived – rather suspiciously together as if a herd instinct had brought them together because of a feeling of danger – Frieda had changed out of her work uniform and into her dinner-party uniform. The latter included a set of pearls.

'I'm verboten to discuss work,' Frank said once they all had their drinks of choice. 'But don't let that stop doing so yourselves. Go ahead, be our guests. Discuss any police work you wish to.'

The two men looked slightly embarrassed. The women gave him the type of look reserved for a particularly predictably naughty boy.

'Frank, stop that,' said Frieda. 'You know all shop talk is banned. This is our first dinner party together. Now, sit down and relax, enjoy yourselves everyone.'

'So,' said Frank as they took various seats, 'if we can't discuss work, how about this: Tom, if you were a chess piece, which would you want to be?'

'Chess piece? Well, I reckon a rook. I always played winger when I played rugby, so, yes, rook it would have to be. Straight down the side field, no funny business, anybody tries to stop you, you just go through them.'

'I'd be split,' said Wilf. 'My mind thinks like a knight, move sideways and other-ways. But I think I'd prefer to appear like a bishop. Preferably a cardinal. In purple.'

'I remember you calling the knight a horsey when we were young,' Susan said. Wilf sighed.

'Older sisters can be such a trial sometimes,' he noted, adjusting his cravat. 'And I did specifically order a younger sister.'

'What about you, Gertie?'

'Oh, queen, obviously. The most powerful piece on the board. What woman wouldn't?'

'Apparently the Ayatollah in Iran wants to ban chess,' said Susan. 'He claims it's because of gambling, which is a sin in Islam, but I think he just doesn't like any game where women have any power.'

'Gambling on chess?' asked Frank. 'I'm not sure I'd class that as gambling, at least not pure gambling. It's not a question of luck, after all. I mean, if I was to play a grand master I'd definitely bet against myself, there wouldn't be any luck involved.'

'But then if you'd bet against yourself you'd want to lose anyway,' pointed out Wilf.

'This interest in chess is because of that double-chess game you're playing against the Mason,' suggested Tom. 'I wouldn't mind ....'

His voice slowed and died as the temperature plummeted and three women looked at him in meaningful and unfriendly ways.

'Er, that is, um ...'

Frank laughed.

'This is a bit like that radio programme, Just A Minute,' he said. 'Though instead of avoiding repetition, deviation or hesitation you have to avoid mentioning anything that might remind me of work.' He stood up. 'Right, I'm going to get the starter going. I'll leave you to discuss whether we should have a game of JAM afterward.' He paused. 'Oh, by the way, did you hear about the bloke who got a job making chess pieces? They put him on knights.'

'Jam?' asked Gertie after he had disappeared to the kitchen. 'What sort of game is that?'

'He means Just A Minute,' said Susan. 'I think that's quite a good idea. I do pretty well when I listen to it.'

They looked at Frieda, who had her head in her hands.

'You okay, Frieda?' asked Susan.

'That pun was so bad it deserves its own special award,' said Frieda, looking up.

'Pun?' asked Gertie and Susan.

'Look, Frieda,' said Tom, 'sorry about that, it just came out.'

'Not to worry, Tom, I think we were a bit over-optimistic in hoping we could avoid that sort of thing altogether.'

'Oh, I'll avoid it from now on. After those looks you three gave me I'm pretty sure I'll never forget.'

'Knights!' exclaimed Gertie. 'Oh, god, that was awful.'

'Nights?' asked the others apart from Frieda.

After dinner they played a few rounds of Just A Minute. It turned out that Susan was quite right about being good at doing it while listening to the radio. She just wasn't very good doing it live with a few glasses of wine and port inside. Frieda turned out the clear winner. But then she was used to looking other people in the eye and making them listen without interrupting. And she didn't intend having to repeat anything, ever.

Later that night, after the others had gone, Frieda wrapped her arms around Frank and gave him a long, slow kiss.

'Now that,' she said once she had finished, 'was exactly what I thought a dinner party should be.'

'You know what, Free? I've had this brilliant idea for your birthday.'

'Now, Frank, careful of brilliant ideas. What is it?'

'We'll have a disco.'

'No, Frank! Certainly not. A disco! Really, the very idea.'

'With Abba and The Dancing Queen.'

'No disco, Frank,' she said, rather less forcefully.

'Mamma Mia.'

She sighed.

'That was something I'd hoped to go to on my sixteenth birthday, a disco,' she said. 'We had a trip to the Science Museum in London instead. It was very educational.'

'Thinking about it, we could have regular dinner parties based on musicals. And the kids will join in from the start. None of this handing them over to nanny nonsense.'

'That sounds like an excellent idea, darling,' said Frieda in a sleepy voice.

'No, we'll get Tricia along to look after them. She'll love it.'

Sunday

Pumping Pete; The demo is a go

'Mummy, mummy, can I go play in the sand-pit with the others?'

'Of course you can, Marie. Off you go, have fun.'

Tracey Phillips watched her daughter skip off to the sandpit about thirty feet away. She was sitting outside the Grove pub enjoying a Sunday pre-lunch drink with her daughter Marie and her husband Detective Sergeant Pete Phillips. Pete Phillips was sitting with a wary look on his face that suggested he had been waiting a while for an explosion which still hadn't come, but was probably waiting for him to relax before going bang.

His wife sighed as she watched her daughter cautiously joining the other children in the sand pit.

'She's doing ever so well now , isn't she?'

'She certainly is,' agreed her husband sincerely.

'We're lucky, aren't we?'

'We certainly are,' agreed her husband less sincerely. She might not recall the daily bemoaning of a fate that had led to her marrying the most useless copper this side of the Kremlin, but it wasn't something he was going to forget in a hurry. Having said that, it wasn't something he was about to remind her of in a hurry either, it might start her off again.

'To think we might not have known until she was all grown up,' continued Tracey Phillips. 'If the doctor's cousin hadn't also had dyslexia ...'

'Absolutely,' agreed Pete Phillips. 'Nineteen years old before anyone realised. Best part of her life gone, education ruined ...'

'And she's stopped having all those tantrums now,' Tracey Phillips noted. The "she" was her daughter rather than the doctor's cousin as might have been presumed from the flow, but Pete Phillips knew better than to point that out. The doctor had explained that Marie was quite an intelligent little girl and had not inherited a congenital stupidity from her grandmother on her mother's side as Pete Phillips had presumed but not actually made public in his wife's presence. Marie's problem was a slight form of dyslexia which stopped her from learning things as fast and easily as other children. That had made her frustrated and caused tantrums, the tantrums had exhausted her mother, who had taken it out on her father. Now that Marie knew she was a little special the tantrums had ceased, her mother was mightily relieved and her father made a small monthly contribution to the Dyslexics' Association in grateful thanks.

'Talking about that sort of thing, how's Frank Summers doing?' asked Tracey Phillips.

'I don't know, he's booked off since that attack. We've been ordered not to disturb him.'

'That'll be his wife the Inspector,' replied his wife. 'She takes good care of him. I hope you and the others aren't disturbing him.'

'Of course not, love.'

Frank had originally been 'Frank' to his wife because Frank had been the same rank as Pete when he joined Wellbury police station. Frieda, alternatively Fabulous or Frigid to the ranks depending on whether they were getting praise or a bollocking, had always been 'Inspector Garold' for his wife, until Frieda and Frank had married. She then became Inspector Summers. But Frank had been promoted, and he had become Inspector Summers. This created a social and hierarchical nightmare in her mind. Tracey Phillips had resolved it by calling Frieda 'the Inspector' and Frank 'Frank Summers'. Inspector Percy Hanson was 'your Inspector' to her husband, and 'Peter's Inspector' to others.

To Pete Frank was just 'Frank' and always would be. He regularly prayed that no-one else would be promoted for a while. It would just give him another headache.

'I need to powder my nose,' his wife decided. Want anything? Crisps? Another pint?'

'No, thanks, love, I'm okay.'

'I'll be back shortly,' she said, stroking his shoulder as she left. Pete Phillips sighed and stretched out his legs. He seemed to be living in married bliss. His daughter had decided he was 'Dear Daddy', his wife was now solicitous of his health – after all, he might not come back from a shift, just as Frank Summers seemed to tread the line between the here and hereafter with the style of a man on ice trying to outrun the cracks. It hadn't, of course, prevented her from making a comment about the probable differences between their demises, with Frank dying heroically, while her husband's body would be dragged from a cess-pit, and that of a brothel. But it was almost as if she did love him, from time to time. Inspector Summers – Inspector Frieda Summers – had pretty much ignored the crack he had made about the dog section – a major, serious miracle since, had it gone on his file, it would have ended his career prospects terminally. And the women at the station seemed to have Eric Johns in their sights rather than him. He wasn't aware of Churchill's definition of exhilaration as being shot at and being missed, but even if he had he would not have classed narrowly missing being taken out by feminists as being exciting.

So, all in all, things were looking pretty rosy. Of course he was aware that it was just as things seemed to be going swimmingly that they suddenly took a drastic turn for the worse, but what could possibly happen here, away from the station?

'Hello, Pete, how's things going?' asked Frank Summers, slipping into the seat opposite him.

Pete Phillips groaned and closed his eyes.

'Go away, Frank,' he begged. 'Please.'

'Well, and it's wonderful to see you too, Pete.'

'Frank, don't get me wrong, but Frieda's issued an ultimatum to anyone who even thinks of discussing business with you. Please, Frank, I'm here for a quiet lunch with the missus and little Marie. If the missus comes back from the loo and finds you and me here talking shop I'll be in all sorts of trouble.'

'Who said I wanted to discuss business? I was just doing some metal-detectoring down there, noticed you were here and thought I might as well pop up and have a pint and a chat. You know, there was quite a strong signal down there, just near that pine tree. I might bring along a spade next time.'

Pete Phillips sighed.

'Okay, Frank, what do you want to know?'

'Any more attacks? On old women?'

'Another half-brick over the back wall of Martha Shaw's place. Same MO at a woman named Mary Sweet. She lives at that complex of houses for the aged. Someone else there got a threatening letter. Alice Goodman. Retired school teacher. Could be an ex-pupil looking for revenge.'

'Mary Sweet. What is she? Or was she? Not another teacher.'

'No, just an ex-housewife. Husband died ten years ago.'

'No links then. Apart from being female and elderly. And not being harmed. Unlike Aggie.'

Pete Phillips took a draw on his pint.

'You've got a feeling about this, haven't you?'

'Logic, Pete, it's all down to logic.'

'And intuition,' he added.

Pete took a last drain on his drink and looked around for a waitress.

'If you're here for a pint and a chat you might as well have one. The pint, I mean.'

'I'd love to, Pete, but I'd better get going before your missus turns up. She might mention my presence to someone else, they might mention it to another person, you know. Then Frieda gets to hear about it and mis-interprets the situation. The only reason I'm here now is that she heard the Chief Constable might pop into the station and decided she wanted to make sure everyone's shoes were polished and their flies done up. I'd better get back before she does. See you later.'

Pete Phillips didn't bother looking to see where Frank disappeared to. Instead he looked at the pine trees.

'You okay, Pete?' asked his wife, sitting down opposite him.

'Sorry? Oh, yes, fine, fine. It's a glorious day, isn't it?'

'Your drink's empty.'

'Is it?'

His wife looked at him with some concern. If her husband hadn't noticed that his pint glass was empty there was definitely something wrong with him.

'You know,' he said, 'I might buy one of those metal detecting things myself. Never know when you might come across a Roman hoard.'

His wife frowned at him. Then she smiled. Men, for some reason, always needed these silly hobbies. And if Inspector

Squishy gave him a sorrowful look, miawoed at him, and nuzzled her head against his calf. He leaned down and picked her up.

'What's up, Squish?' He stroked her and his head pulled up as he heard the sound of the front door opening. 'And what is Mummy doing coming back in the middle of Monday morning?'

He went into the hallway to find Frieda standing there looking at him.

'Free? What's up? What's wrong?'

She put her arms around his waist and leaned her head on his chest.

'Let's go into the kitchen,' she said. 'I could do with a strong cup of tea and a sit-down.'

She took his hand and led him to the kitchen. She pushed him gently into a seat and switched the kettle on before sitting down next to him.

'There's no easy way to say this, Frank. Aggie's dead,' she said.

It took a few seconds for it to sink in.

'How?' he asked. She shrugged.

'Old age.'

'Not –'

'No. Doctor Wood did a preliminary autopsy this morning. I asked him to prioritise it in case it was murder.'

'When?'

'In her sleep. The allotment lot noticed she wasn't around at sunrise as she usually is, feeding her cats. They knocked on her shed door and found her in her bed. Doctor Wood said she wouldn't have felt a thing. Went to sleep and didn't wake up again. Not in this life, anyway.'

There was a silence.

Frieda Summers approved of her husband gallivanting around the countryside with some silly metal detector, then why shouldn't her own husband? After all, it would keep him from mischievous devilment.

And chasing other women.

Her suspicions were quite unfounded. Pete Phillips had never chased after another woman. Not since the day of their wedding. At first out of principle. Later because he feared that they were all like his own wife.

Late that Sunday afternoon Frank lay slumped on the couch in a posture that is only possible to achieve by slowly slipping down millimetre-by-millimetre until the coffee table is in reach of the feet. As it was Frieda's coffee table, and she was tucked up next to him with her head on his shoulder, he wisely refrained from using it as a foot-rest as he had been used to do in his own flat. Frieda hadn't actually banned him from doing so, but his own mother had made sure that he understood that gentlemen do not do such a thing, and Frieda was bound to follow the same line. In fact he and his father had developed a rule that a gentleman did not do such things while his wife or mother was present. If a woman is not present to observe him, however, a gentleman cannot be doing anything wrong.

Logically.

Just then the telephone in the hallway rang.

'That'll be work,' Frieda sighed. She got up and walked towards the hallway.

'How do you know?' asked Frank.

'Social calls on my personal mobile, urgent or normal calls on my work mobile, non-urgent secret and top secret calls on my work landline, or if at home, on my home landline, it's more secure.'

'Too many telephones for my liking, Squish,' Frank muttered as he heard Frieda answer the phone. 'What say we do a bit of channel hopping. There's got to be something more interesting than this lot.'

He had got to channel 549 when Frieda returned and dropped back onto the couch.

'Anything interesting? Percy organised a blockade of Wellbury again?'

'That was the Chief Constable, Frank. You'll have to meet him sometime or other now that you're a detective inspector.'

'Can't,' said Frank, sitting up, reaching forward for a handful of popcorn and dropping it in his mouth. 'I'm booked off sick, remember.'

Frieda slapped his shoulder lightly.

'I know we're not supposed to talk business, but it'll be in the paper soon. I can tell you that the demonstration in support of religious tolerance and banning the Cult of the Clueless has been given the go-ahead. For the moment.'

'Oh, good. I've been looking forward to that. Though I was hoping it would be a Christmas Special rather than this early in the year.'

'I'm sure you have been.' She sipped her tea. 'Yuk, this is cold. I would have liked to have you at my side. It could turn nasty.'

'Oh, don't worry, Free, you know me. I might be booked off, but I'll be out there somewhere keeping an eye on things.'

'That's why I wanted you by my side. So I could keep an eye on you.'

Frank poked his tongue out at her.

'Seriously, darling, you will take care, won't you?'

'Of course I will. You know I never take unnecessary risk[...]

'For a man who never takes unnecessary risks you see[...] land up in hospital an awful lot.'

Frank rubbed his chin.

'Nuisance, really, I've been doing my level best to stop [...] nonsense. Or at least postpone it. We've got this pe[...] behind the attacks almost bottled up. If we have [...] concentration distracted by the Cult of the Clueless and [...] Righteous Once, whoever it is could slip through unnoti[...] Certainly won't be the first time that's happened.'

'I'll keep an eye out for any potential public order reason[...] defer the demonstration for a week or two months. In [...] meantime I'll pop over and see Aggie tomorrow morning.'

'I'll ... I'll, er, go metal detectoring tomorrow.'

'Give Martha Shaw my regards.'

'Will do.'

Frieda smiled and lay her head back on his shoulder.

Monday

Departure; Mason (9); Zack

With Frieda having left, Frank finished off various c[...] washing up the breakfast dishes and putting them [...] putting away the last of the clean laundry from the we[...] wash, hoovering the lounge carpet free of any sugges[...] popcorn. As he moved through each room Squishy fo[...] rubbing against his legs and generally getting in h[...] Eventually he stopped in the kitchen and paid h[...] attention.

'What's wrong with you, Squish? You haven't even [...] your tuna brekky. Don't tell me you're coming d[...] something?'

'So, she was right then.'

'Right?'

'She has gone to join her brothers and sisters in heaven. And in October.'

Frieda stood up as the kettle whistled to announce its boiling.

'Yes, I suppose so. Tea?'

'Please, yes.' He stroked Squishy. 'I think Squish knew. She's been acting strangely. Almost as if she's upset about something'

'I asked the allotment people to keep an eye on her cats. They said they'd make sure they were fed and watered.'

There was another silence as she poured hot water into a teapot and brought it and cups to the table.

'I suppose we'll have to arrange the funeral,' Frank said.

'The council have said it will be on Thursday.'

'Thursday? So soon?'

'Not really. She had no relatives. They have a process.' She shivered. 'It's all very impersonal, but they have a process. Pauper, one, cremation, one. They never knew her. She doesn't mean anything to them. She's just part of the paperwork.'

'I suppose paupers aren't very well known, Apart from to other paupers.'

They sat in silence for a while.

'Well, at least she wasn't friendless,' Frieda noted, taking a sip of her tea.

'And if it wasn't other humans she always had her god and her animals.'

'She never did say which religion she was.'

'I presume they'll get the Anglican vicar to give a service. She lived in an Anglican cemetery. The funeral will be given by the state, and the state religion is C of E. In England, anyway.'

'She used to call the vicar a priest. That sounds Catholic.'

'Doesn't really matter now, does it?'

'I think it does. I know funerals are more for the living than the dead, but – it's a bit like the slaves in America, in the Deep South, they would always dress their dead children in the smartest clothes they could find, even though their live kids were in rags. I suppose it's wanting to give them something in death you wished you could have given them in life.'

'I seem to recall reading something similar about the Boer War camps.'

'That reminds me. She asked if she could be buried in the grave nearest her hut. She said something about the current occupant being restless, and leading him to god.'

He put his cup down.

'I'll have a word with Father Brown. Maybe if we can get an inter-denominational service going it might quieten down some of these religious nutters.'

Frieda smiled.

'That reminds me of one of the reasons I fell in love with you, Frank. Your eternal optimism.' She sighed. 'I'd better get back to work. I didn't want you finding out by accident.'

He kissed her.

'Why don't you take the rest of the day off, Free? I would.'

She smiled.

'Yes, I know you would. No, I'd better get back. I've got two couples coming in who want to register a protest about the planned protest march. If I can get only a few signatures opposing it I can get it deferred. I'll be expansive with my estimates of the number of people protesting against the protest.'

'Now that would be good news.'

'There's only one thing that worries me.'

'Which is?'

'One of the couples is called Cromwell.'

'Well, I suppose someone has to be.'

'No, Frank, that would be okay if it was your case. I prefer a bit more neatness to mine.'

White: The Mason's move. 9.O-O right-hand castle

Black: Frank

'Frank, it's your wife here.'

'I recognise the voice, I hear and obey, oh mighty one. Have you interviewed Cromwell yet?'

'Very funny Frank. As it happens they've postponed it until tomorrow. It's really irritating, I'm running out of time.'

'I could come in and protest against the protest. Technically I'm a civilian again.'

'Don't tempt me, Frank. Anyway, that's not what I called about. Your mason's been in touch again.'

'Oh, dear god, why couldn't he put it away for a while. We really do not need his nonsense at the moment.'

'Frank –'

'Yes?'

'Well, it does indicate that he doesn't know about what's happened. There's nothing in his email to suggest so.'

'I can think of several suggestions for him, all very impolite. What's his latest move?'

'I think I know this one. It says '0-0', that's zero, zero, and then 'right hand king-side castle'. That's swapping over the king and castle like we discussed, isn't it?'

'Indeed it is. Another defensive move. Interesting.'

'And then he says, "Beware the crooks, Inspector, if you know what I mean."'

'Beware the crooks? What the hell is that supposed to mean? That he's a crook? I know for certain he's a kook.'

'Frank, he could be hinting that he's someone you sent to jail once.'

'Sounds like a mental institution would have been more appropriate. Just a second.'

He took the piece of paper out of his pocket, picked up a pen and marked the move.

'Mmm. He's really keeping himself closed, isn't he? Are you at the chess board now?'

'Yes, Frank, I've made his move. Looks like he wants to pull his king into a corner where he can defend it more easily, just like you said.'

'Indeed. Classic move. Trouble is, it isn't a classic game. Right, let the cavalry out for a recce. Try this, Free: o-Oscar sixteen, that's numeric one-six, hyphen n-November fourteen, that's numeric one-four. o16-n14.'

'Okay, you're moving your left-most knight out in front of your king bishop's pawn, right?'

'That's the one. Tricky things, knights. Or should I say, horsey. You can never be sure where they'll be after a couple of moves. and with him pulling his horns in for defence I might just get a chance to create havoc in his back line.'

'Okay, Frank, I'll reply to the email as soon as I get back to my office. Is there anything you want me to add?'

'Such as?'

'Oh, some words of wisdom such as "Beware the Ides of March"? To match his weird utterances.'

'Excellent idea, Free, why didn't I think of it?'

'I only mentioned it because I knew you were going to think of it sooner or later.'

'You know me only too well. Good thing we got married, Free, or I'd be in trouble the whole time like I used to be.'

'I'm sure married life isn't going to slow you down that much, Frank. What do you want me to add?'

'Mmm. Let's see ... Summer beaches reach karma as the eternal susurrus ebbs and flows?'

'Ssssuper, Frank. See you later. Take care of yourself.'

Frank put the phone down and looked at Squishy.

'You know, Squish, I really must work out a way to politely say, "And when I finally get my hands on you I'm going to punch you in the face, several times." What do you think?'

Bill Dughaille

White: The Mason

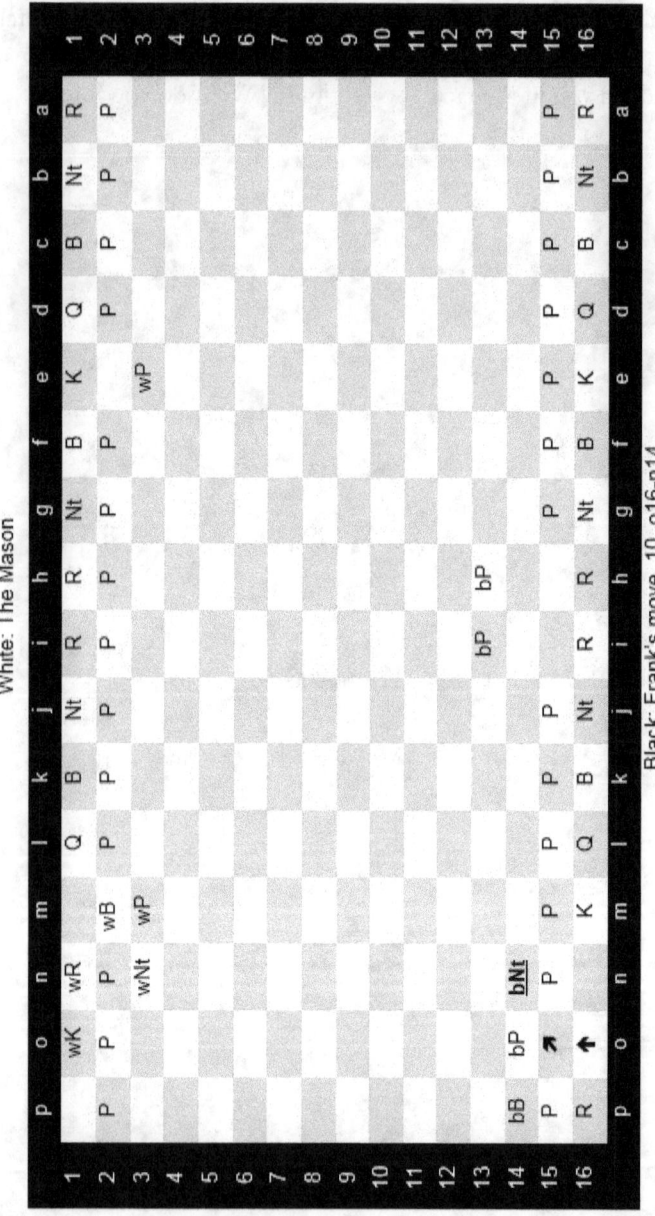

Black: Frank's move. 10. o16-n14

210

That evening Frank began preparing dinner by automatically switching the radio on. An advert for carpet cleaners had just finished.

'And that was especially for those of our listeners whose wives clean their own carpets,' Came Zack's voice. 'Now, tonight we have some really interesting guests.'

'Oh, god, no, not the Prat,' said Frank, reaching out to switch stations. He looked at Squishy. 'Oh, what the hell, do you want to see how he gets clobbered tonight, Squish?'

Squishy nodded. Frank left the radio on and attended to the business of preparing chicken in a white wine sauce with parsley.

'Now what you listeners can't see is that I am behind a newly installed glass screen which protects me from violent guests. We've always tried to maintain an informal setup here, but I'm afraid my life insurance was going through the roof. But we don't have to worry about tonight's guest because he believes the world is about to end soon, isn't that true, Mr Miller?'

'That is correct.'

'That's because you are ... ?'

'I'm Mr Miller, yes.'

'No, what I mean is that believe that the world will end soon because you are a ... millellinialimist?'

'Ah, I see. Well, to be exact, I am a dispensational premillennialist.'

There was a pause.

'A ... could you say that again?'

'A dispensational premillennialist.'

'Ah. My notes say that you are into scatology.'

'Eschatology, that is correct.'

'That's the study of cats?'

'It's to do with the end of times.'

'That's Dickens, I recognise that. It was the end of times, it was the ... start of times?'

'No, I don't believe Dickens ever wrote about the dispensations.'

'Dispensations?'

'The human story will be divided into seven dispensations, or phases. We are now in the sixth. The seventh will see the end of the world, and the ascending of the true followers to heaven.'

'The apocalypse, in other words.'

'Some call it that. There will be a period of tribulation, followed by Armageddon, and that will be the end of days.'

'Ah, yes, Armageddon, as in Armageddon-out-of-here? Ha ha?'

'No, I don't think that's what Armageddon means.'

'Ah. I see. Do you have a date for that?'

'Personally I always presume it will happen on Friday. Friday evening, to be exact. That way I can be confident of leaving a tidy desk for the weekend.'

'So that will be this Friday?'

'Possibly. Possibly the next. When I was younger I was far more confident that it would be this Friday, but now that I'm older I've learned patience.'

'How do your colleagues, your family feel about this?'

'Well, my manager always tells me that, if the world does end this Friday, I can take the rest of the week off. I think that's what he calls a sense of humour.'

'Ah, yes, a sense of humour. Do you have a sense of humour, Mr Miller?'

'No.'

'Ah. I see. So, what about your family, then, how do they feel about your ... beliefs.'

'My parents preceded me to heaven. I have never married, for obvious reasons.'

'Of course ... What obvious reasons?'

'It hardly seems worth getting married before Friday if the world is going to end, and not much point if it does so afterward.'

'Yes, not much time to exchange the wedding presents you didn't like, is there, ha ha? Er, you don't mind my little jokes, do you, Mr Miller?'

'Is that what they are? Speaking personally, I never take offence at anything anyone ever says. If the world is going to end soon there isn't much point, is there? It only gives you indigestion, anyway.'

'No, I suppose so. Well, listeners, you heard it here first on Zack's prime time Views of the Day. We'll just go to a commercial and thank you Mr Miller.'

Frank looked at Squishy.

'There's definitely something strange going on, Squish. A religious weirdo being reasonable and Zack getting through an interview without being thumped.'

He pondered for a few moments.

'No, something's going to happen, Squish, Zack not getting thumped goes against the natural order of the Cosmos. That just means that negative energy is being stored up until it explodes.'

Squishy nodded wisely.

Tuesday

Counter demonstrators; Mason (11)

'A Mr and Mrs Cromwell and a Mrs and Mr Thomas to see the Inspector,' Eric Johns told Tricia over the internal phone.

'Okay, Sergeant, the Inspector's expecting them. Could you send them up with a constable?'

'Okay, Tricia.'

Tricia dialled Frieda's extension.

'Your excuses for denying the demonstration are coming up,' she told her.

'Sorry, Tricia, I didn't quite catch that. "Concerned citizens eager to be of assistance to the constabulary" is what you said, wasn't it?'

Tricia giggled.

'I knew there was a better way to put it. Shall I show them straight in?'

'Please. And make sure we've got tea and coffee for them, plus chocolate digestives.'

'Chocolate digestives? They must be important.'

'Ammunition always is. It's one of the first things you learn on the force.'

'Ah, so that's what they are, ammunition.'

'Yes, but don't tell them.'

'Right,' said Frieda once they had sat down, 'I understand that you're concerned citizens who feel the demonstration for religious tolerance shouldn't go ahead. You're concerned about a breach of the peace, correct?'

The four looked at each other.

'Er, no, Miss, errm, Inspector, we seem to have our wires crossed,' Fred Cromwell said 'We want to join the demonstration, sort of, but we don't want to be marching with the Righteous Once. You see, we feel they're too, too ... what's the word, Dora?'

'Fundamental,' replied Dora Cromwell.

'Fundamentalist,' said Ruby Thomas.

'Aye, fundamentalists,' agreed her husband.

'I see,' said Frieda, drumming her fingernails on her desk in a staccato tattoo. 'Yes, we do indeed seem to have some crossed wires. Yes, indeed.' She continued drumming for a few moments without taking her eyes off all of theirs. 'So you were planning on a parallel demonstration, as it were?'

'Well, that's it, in a nutshell,' said Dora Cromwell. 'We walk parallel like, on the opposite side of the road.'

'I see. Well, unfortunately there's the small question of police resources, which are nowhere near as infinite as could be desired.'

'Oh, we won't be any bother, Miss,' said Ruby Thomas, 'you see –'

'You already are a bother, Mrs Thomas,' Frieda said in an entirely reasonable tone which threatened to become entirely unreasonable at the slightest provocation. 'Now you are becoming a bigger one. If the relevant authorities still permit this march to go ahead – and I will recommend against that – there will be one march and one march only. You can take the lead, you can walk at the back, I don't mind, but, stragglers ... stragglers never have a good time of it, do they ... poor things.'

She smiled at them. They looked back with the faces of people who are determined to have their own way, although under current conditions they might decide to go elsewhere, perhaps somewhere safer and healthier and do it there where no-one can see them.

Frieda stood up.

They stood up.

Frieda pressed a buzzer.

'We'll come up with a plan' said Ruby Thomas. 'We might have to speak to some people, but we'll find a way.'

'I'm sure you will,' agreed Frieda as Tricia entered the office. 'Tricia, please show these people out.'

Frieda stayed standing until the door shut on them. Then she sat down, picked up a pencil, and broke it in two.

'Rubbermats,' she said.

She picked up a chocolate digestive and looked at it.

'Comfort eating is never a good thing,' she said, and ate it.

White: The Mason's move. 11. g1-h3

	1	2	3	4	5	6	7	8	9	10	11	12	13	14	15	16
a	R	P													P	R
b	Nt	P													P	Nt
c	B	P													P	B
d	Q	P													P	Q
e	K		wP												P	K
f	B	P													P	B
g	♘		⇘P												P	Nt
h	R	P	**wNt**										bP		R	
i	R	P										bP			R	
j	Nt	P													P	Nt
k	B	P													P	B
l	Q	P													P	Q
m		wB	wP												P	K
n	wR	P	wNt										bNt		P	
o	wK	P												bP		
p	P													bB	P	R

Black: Frank

'That'll be Mummy, Squish,' Frank told the kitten as the phone rang. 'I can always tell when it's her. Hello, wonderful wife.'

'Hello, my husband. Do you always answer the phone like that?'

'Only when it's you calling.'

'And you knew it was me.'

'You can ask Squishy, I said to her that it was you before I answered.'

'I forgot, you're psychic.'

'That, and you've got caller identifier on your landline.'

'Ah, of course, damn, I'd forgotten that.'

'So, has Cromwell called?'

Frieda sighed.'

'I'll tell you about that later. Frank, we've had another email from our mason friend.'

'That soon? That's interesting. That suggests he's got more time on his hands. I wonder why that is.'

'Monday and Tuesday? A weekend would make sense, but Monday and Tuesday? Maybe he's booked off like you.'

'Maybe. His emails always turn up in the morning. I wonder where he's posting from. Home? School? University? Hospital? Some anonymous hi-fi hot spot? Maybe an e-café.'

'And from what? PC, mobile, laptop, tablet? Smartphone?'

Frank sighed.

'Sherlock Holmes never had these problems, Free. You know, what we need is a computer geek who can inject a virus in the e-mail and take over his computer device. Get it to send us his location. Tell you what, Wilf is a software developer, much as you wouldn't know to look at him. Maybe he can do something. Or knows someone who can do something.'

'Yes, Frank, and it's a good thing that Tom is a barrister, because we'll be needing one just after we send in our resignation letters. When they throw the book thrown at us for half a dozen various laws.'

'True. Pity, I rather fancied that idea. What his latest move, Free?'

'G-Golf, numeric one, hyphen h-Hotel numeric three. g1-h3'

Frank took his piece of paper out.

'Hmm, he's advancing a horsey on his left hand side, king's horsey. Interesting.'

'Frank, we need to have a discussion about your use of the word "interesting".'

'It's out of character. He's a defensive player. Defensive players under-utilise their knights. Horsies, I mean. Unless ...'

'Unless what, Frank?'

There was a silent pause.

'Frank? Unless what?'

'You know, Free, I think he's going for another castle. Get the knight out, push the bishop forward a space or two, and he's clear to castle again.'

'Another defensive move?'

'Bloody daft one. He'd be castling into the centre of the board, not towards the corner. That happens in double chess.'

'I see what you mean. If his king's in the centre he's got two flanks to protect as well as his front.'

'Precisely. I think he's taking the shortest castle because it's easier. He's got three pieces to get out if he wants to castle on his queen-side, and one of those is his queen. Defensive players protect their queens as long as possible purely because the queen is the most powerful piece. With that sort of player I go for a queen exchange as early on as possible.'

'Queen exchange?'

'That's where both sides lose their queens but neither gains any advantage. With people like our mason friend I like to give them the choice of taking my queen knowing that in doing so they'll lose theirs. If they back off they're retreating and wasting a move. It's also extremely psychological. If a tank general who has two hundred infantry but no tanks is up against an infantry general with no tanks and one hundred infantry, the infantry general normally wins because the tank general doesn't know how to fight with infantry. A defensive chess player normally doesn't like playing without a queen.'

'You almost make me sorry I didn't take up chess at school, Frank. It sounds almost exactly like office politics.'

'Most of it is psychological. People think John McEnroe had temper tantrums during tennis matches to put his opponent off. He was a rank amateur compared to chess masters. They're even polite while they do it. Talking of which, has our fruit-loop included any witty comment in his email?'

'You won't believe this, Frank.'

'Oh, I'll believe pretty much anything to do with tomato-boy. What is it?'

'He says, and I quote, "It's been a hard day's knight but worth the anvil. Your move, Inspector". That's knight with a k for kilometre, the piece he's just moved.'

'Anvil? The thing blacksmiths used to use?'

'Presumably. I did an Internet search; it could also refer to a Canadian heavy metal band, apparently. Though if he's making obscure references which only the invention of the Internet could make sense of, well, we might as well give up.'

'It's typed?'

'It's an email, Frank. How else do you create an email?'

'Well, it struck me that maybe he's misspelling words. But most email software would highlight that. Unless he was using a digital pen.'

'No, Frank, I can spot a typo or mis-spelling at a hundred yards. There's absolutely nothing wrong with the words he's using. They just don't make very much sense the way they're put together. Not unless you understand whatever code he's using.'

'Well, we might as well keep him going. What do you think I should do next?'

'You mean on the chessboard?'

'Yup.'

'Frank, you're supposed to be the chess expert.' Frieda paused. 'Okay, I get it, I suggest something completely idiotic, and then you explain to the little woman why it's completely silly.'

Frank took a breath before replying.

'Free, this is your hubby speaking, I would never do that to you. Apart from which I like hearing how other people think. One of the reasons I used to beat others at chess at university was because I knew how they thought, not because I was a better player. Anyway, I know you're extremely intelligent so whatever you say will come with a great deal of thought.'

There was a moment of silence as a woman who knew she was very intelligent grappled with the question of whether her husband should also have pointed out her physical charm, just in case anyone might think he had married her purely for her brain.

'I think you're going to castle on the left, Frank,' she said finally. 'The way is clear between your rook and king.'

'That's what I was planning,' said Frank. 'Trouble is, he knows it. What I really want is some totally unexpected move which will turn out to be pure genius.'

'You mean like Napoleon's march on Moscow?'

Frank sighed.

'Pretty much. A mark of genius from the old master, except it turned out to be a disaster on an epic scale. Okay, Free, send this reply: zero hyphen zero, left hand king-side castle. That should do it. Oh, and add, "Enjoy Amsterdam, but don't take any nooden wickels".'

'Nooden wickels. Wooden nickels. Got that, Frank. Any significance to the bit about Amsterdam?'

'Bugger all, but hopefully he'll think so. With any luck it will turn out that there's a heavy metal band called the Amsterdam Wickels performing in Wellbury in three weeks' time.'

There was a pause.

'Frank?'

'Yes, Free?'

'Remember that concert we went to?'

'Course I do. Best concert I've ever been to, bar none, including Glastonbury. And the Isle of White. Not to mention –'

'Yes, Frank. The problem is, well, we haven't been to any concerts since.'

'Give us a chance, Free, we haven't exactly had the time, what with getting married and loonymooning and getting shot at in light aircraft. Tell you what, I'll make a note of it and stick it on the fridge.'

'Why the fridge?'

'Isn't that where married couples always stick thing to remind themselves?'

'Sounds more like something they do in American movies.'

'Where do you normally keep your reminders?'

'In my head, Frank.'

'Okay, how about the front door? Outside? We'll see them whenever we leave, and whenever we come home again.'

'Don't you dare, Frank Summers. The fridge will be fine.'

White: The Mason

	a	b	c	d	e	f	g	h	i	j	k	l	m	n	o	p
1	R	Nt	B	Q	K	B		R	R	Nt	B	Q		wR	wK	
2	P	P	P	P		P	P	P	P	P	P	P	wB	P	P	P
3					wP			wNt					wP	wNt		
4																
5																
6																
7																
8																
9																
10																
11																
12																
13								bP	bP					bNt	bP	bB
14								R								
15	P	P	P	P	K	B	Nt		R	Nt	B	Q	P	R	K	P
16	R	Nt	B	Q	K	B	Nt	R	R	Nt	B	Q	↓	R	K	↑

Black: Frank's move. 12. O-O left hand king side castle

Wednesday

The first hoard; Mason (13)

'Another rock through a window last night,' the Chief Inspector said as they strolled slowly along the riverbank. Frank was idly moving the metal detector to and fro, more out of habit than disguise. The Chief Inspector was carrying his fishing kit and a collapsible spade, much to Frank's amusement.

'Another old woman?'

'No, a man dressed up as an old woman. Chap called Arther Purbright. Does a comedy routine. Parts of it he dresses up as an old woman. He was on at the Blue Bliss. Apparently he was still dressed that way when he left the place. Had a few drinks afterward and felt too tired to get changed. Decided to walk home, fell asleep on his couch in the lounge.'

'Too tired, eh? Not too tired to see who threw the stone, by any chance?'

'Didn't even know it had happened until he woke up this morning in the early hours, lying on the front-room couch, dying of thirst and covered in glass. Took him a while to work out what had happened. Thought he must have broken something himself at first, without remembering. It was only after he concluded that that didn't make sense and found that the glass came from the window that he called us in. According to Harry and Allison he was a rather strange sight, wig still on, but skew-whiff.'

'Well, that is interesting.'

'The wig?'

'No, the fact that whoever did it didn't know that she was actually a man.'

'Bit of a jump in logic, Frank. It could be someone who knew of him and disapproved of him dressing up as a woman.'

Frank made a face.

'Yes, I suppose so. Or some kids spotted him staggering home and thought it would be fun to throw things at him. Our usual problem. Which are the real attacks and which are just imitations.'

'Just so. Speaking of imitations, did you know that we're being followed?'

'Chap in an anorak, brown trousers, brown shoes, carrying a metal detector in his hands? Keeps trying to hide by running from tree to tree. Couldn't be worse camouflage'

'That's the one. Anyone you know?'

'Nope. My guess is that he really is a metal-detector hobbyist. Probably jealous of his patch. I've spotted him a couple of times over the past few days.'

'Are you sure about that?'

'Pretty sure. He looks mainly harmless.'

'Why doesn't he come up and speak to us then? These hobbyists are normally more than willing to bend a fellow fanatic's ear.'

'Well, let's test it, shall we? I'll pretend to have found something, and you –'

'I what?'

Frank chuckled.

'I was about to say, you dig it up. But I don't have to pretend. I really have found a signal.'

'Of course you have, Frank. You aren't going to catch me that way again.'

'No, I have. Just here.'

'Well, in that case, Frank,' the Chief Inspector said, handing over his folding shovel, 'you can dig it up.'

He sat down on the grass bank while Frank commenced digging. A passing couple with a little girl paused to watch.

'What's he doing, mummy?' asked the girl.

'I don't know, darling.'

'What's he doing, daddy?'

'I don't know, darling.'

'I'm from the water board,' said Frank as he dug. 'We're looking for a missing pipe. It seems to have been moved by someone during the night.'

'That's interesting,' said the man. 'We've been having problems with our drains. Maybe you'd know something about drains.'

Frank gritted his teeth.

'Not me,' he said. 'I'm just the workman. You'd better ask the supervisor over here.'

'Our drains get blocked once a month,' the man said to a surprised Chief Inspector. Do you think it could be the full moon?'

'Drains?' the Chief Inspector replied after a pause. 'No, I'm afraid you'd need to speak to someone from the drains department about that. Specialist subject, is drains.'

'The wife thinks it's the moon. You know, like with waves and stuff.'

'Could be. It's a powerful force, the moon. But, like I said, you need to speak to the drains department.'

'What you going to do when you find the pipe?' asked the little girl, staring at Frank.

'Ah, well, that's the question, isn't it,' he replied. 'You see it could explode.'

'Explode?' asked the parents almost simultaneously.

'Oh, yeah. Effluent all over the place.'

'Effluent?'

'Muck for miles around. Takes weeks to wash it out of your hair.'

'I thought you said it was a water pipe.'

'Sewage pipe.'

'But that's just a drain.'

'Oh, no, a drain's domestic like. Now sewage, that's different. There's a lot more of it, for a start.'

'You said it could explode?' asked the woman.

'Any moment now. They blow, quite suddenly. Just when you don't expect it.'

'Darling, don't you think we should move away,' suggested the woman. The man nodded.

'Yes, your mum might turn up at the flat any moment. Better get moving.'

Frank and the Chief Inspector chuckled as the three hurried away. They heard the man say, 'Pity they didn't know anything about drains.'

'That's a good one. About water-pipes,' said a voice behind Frank. He turned to find the man in an anorak behind him. 'I usually say something silly about buried treasure. Being sarcastic, of course. But you'd be surprised how many people believe you.'

They looked at each other.

'Harry Winters is the name.'

'Frank Summers. And this is Chief Inspector Hal.'

'Thought I recognised you. Couldn't work out what you were doing here. On a case, are you? Or just detectoring? Only, this area's being pretty much done to death. If you see what I mean. Everyone I know starts off along here. Nothing to find, mind.'

'That will be me too, then,' said Frank. 'No, we aren't on a case. I'm off work for a couple of days, thought I might see what the attraction is in metal detectoring. I picked up a signal here and thought I'd see what it was.'

'You can't have done! I've been over this part lots of times. When I take the dog for a walk. Take the detector with. Never had a signal in years.'

'Well, if you don't believe me, have a go yourself.'

Harry Winters eagerly switched his machine on, put his earphones in place and scanned the hole Frank had been digging.

'Blow me down! You're right and all. There is a signal.' He looked at Frank from underneath his eyebrows. 'Look, your shout. But – mind if I dig a bit? I've never found anything big.'

'Pleasure's all mine,' said Frank, handing the little shovel over. Harry Winters laid his detector aside and began digging with a careful frenzy. Frank and the Chief Inspector watched, the latter shaking his head at how Frank had managed so easily to get out of digging his own hole.

'Here we go!' exclaimed Harry Winters, going down on his hands and knees, pulling earth out with his hands. He brought out a little disk, his hand shaking. 'It's Roman! I swear it's Roman!'

Frank leaned forward to look. The Chief Inspector jumped up and joined him. All either could see was what appeared to be a corroded piece of earth-wrapped metal.

'It's beautiful,' whispered Harry Winters, brushing dirt off the object. 'Claudius, I bet.' He looked up at Frank. 'You've got the luck of the devil,' he said admiringly. 'You're a born natural. I've heard of people like you.'

'Er ...' said Frank. Harry Winters pressed the coin into Frank's hand, put an earphone to his ear and switched his machine on again.

'There's more!' he cried, threw the machine to one side and resumed digging, eagerly but gently pulling up the earth with his fingers. 'Here's another! And another!'

'That's wonderful,' said Frank, raising his eyebrows at the Chief Inspector. 'Shall we leave you to get on with it? We have an urgent appointment elsewhere.'

'What? No, your shout, Inspector. I know my responsibilities. Your shout. But thank you, oh thank you for letting me dig.'

'Precisely,' chuckled the Chief Inspector. 'And as a police officer Inspector Summers knows his duty. Don't you, Frank? Er, any more down there?'

It turned out, despite Harry Winters digging down as far as he could, that only a dozen coins had been buried or lost there. Each one was reverentially handed over to Frank as if in a formal ritual.

'Let me buy you a pint,' said Harry Winters as they watched him fill the hole. 'The Fishermans is just along the way.'

'We'd love to,' replied Frank, 'but we have do have to be somewhere else. Rather urgently.'

'Of course! You'll want to report the find as soon as possible. Quite right. Just what I would have done.' He coughed and looked at Frank sideways again. 'Could I ask a little favour?'

'Well, you can ask.'

'Could you, when the press interview you, you know, mention that I was with you when you made your find? Only, thing is. You see. The other chaps might not believe me. And the wife. She thinks it's silly as it is. I don't want any of your fame, of course. Richly deserved. You're a natural. But. As I say. The other chaps. And the wife.'

'Mr Winters,' said Frank, 'if the press ever come calling I shall send them to you for an eye-witness description of the event.'

'Will you?'

'Oh, yes, trust me, I will. And now we really must be going.'

After a series of commemorative and earnest handshakes they took their leave of Harry Winters, Frank's stride slowed down by the more ambulatory style of a chuckling Chief Inspector.

'Sometimes you can be a real Philistine, Frank,' he said. 'You might just have discovered important evidence of Roman occupation of Wellbury. Even if you haven't, you've made his day for him. Or week, or month, or even year. First time he's been around to see a treasure hoard uncovered.'

'More like a few coins dropped by a travelling salesman. And I'm more interested in catching whoever it is attacking defenceless old women. Or whoever they are. I don't have time for discovering ancient Roman coins. They'll just get in the way. And they won't work in the coffee machine at the station. Bollocks, bollocks and bollocks again, I really don't need this at the moment.'

'What will you do with them? The coins?'

'I'll give my dad a call. He'll know the etiquette. I think they need to be declared treasure trove or something.'

'And if they do turn out to be Roman? Could be worth a bob or two.'

'I'll give them to dad. He and mum would love that. Anybody popping in for a visit will be bored to death by the evidence of how wonderful their son is.'

The Chief Inspector shook his head.

'Most people would be thinking how much money they'd be worth,' he said.

'Most people don't use the brains they were born with. A few old Roman coins are hardly likely to set the world alight. You'd be lucky to get more than a few quid for them.'

'That's not how the media are likely to report it.'

Frank stopped.

'Oh, bloody hell, I'd forgotten that. Oh, damn, damn and blast and damn again! If Phil Walthers gets his hands on this ...'

'Which he will do.'

'Say what you like, he's good at his job.'

'Indeed.'

'I do not believe this. Why me? All I'm trying to do is solve a simple series of attacks on old women. I do not need Phil Walthers at the moment. Let alone the glorious hippies. And the Cult of the Clueless.'

'Cheer up Frank. You know what they say.'

'Yes, just as you think things couldn't get any worse, they do.'

'What, you might accidentally discover even more buried treasure?'

'Yes. They used to call me lucky at university. In an ironic way.'

White: The Mason's move. 13. f1-d3

Black: Frank

Frank switched the radio on before lunch to see what the latest casualty score was. After a few minutes of adverts an announcer came on to say:

'Our listeners will be devastated to hear that Zack tried a tantric dance at the top of the stairs last night, tripped and achieved cosmic concussion for which he is being treated in hospital at the moment. So tonight's Driving Hour will be presented by Julia.'

'See, Squish,' Frank told the kitten, 'you can't avoid your cosmic fate. Zack the Prat has been destined for a lifetime of being beaten up, and if he manages to avoid someone else doing so he has to do it himself.'

Having finished lunch Frank wrapped the old coins in a few layers of tissue paper, wrote his parents address on an envelope, popped the coins in, sealed it and put a stamp on it. He was about to stroll down the road to the letter-box when the phone rang.

'Frank? It's your wife here.'

'Hello, Free, what's up? Don't tell me that mason man has been in touch again?'

'Got it in one, Frank. His latest move and missive. Looks like he's on a roll.'

'He's got chess diarrhoea, if there is such a thing. What's his latest?'

While speaking Frank took out his battered piece of paper.

'In terms of latest move, or latest weird pronouncement?'

'Let's take the move first.'

'Foxtrot-numeric one-Delta-numeric three. f1-d3.'

'Foxtrot, eh?'

'Don't even think of going there, Frank. But it looks like you were right. He's clearing his line for another castle.'

'You know what I think, Free?'

'You think he might try to walk that king down to the one in the corner. Minimise the defence he needs for both kings.'

'It's a distinct possibility. It'll take quite a bit of time, but if he can keep me from attacking in the meantime it might be worth it.'

'Which you aren't going to do – give him time, that is.'

'Not if I can help it. No, I think I'll castle on the right into the corner and then run an attack straight down the middle with my centre rooks, see if I can blow a hole in his defences. That means I've got to get my right hand bishop queen and knight out of the way. So, let's go with b-Bravo-fifteen, that's numeric one-five, to b-Bravo–fourteen, that's numeric one-four, b15-b14.'

'Knight's pawn one pace forward. Why not two?'

'His bishop on Mother-2 could have it for free.'

Frieda's eyes followed the path from square m2.

'Ah, yes, I didn't see that. Easy to miss on a crowded board.'

'Easier to miss if you're only used to playing normal chess. He couldn't do that on a normal chess board.'

'So, would you like to know his latest unintelligible bon mots?'

'Go on, Free, don't keep me in suspense.'

'Must rush.'

'Must rush? What the hell's that supposed to mean?'

'He's in a hurry?'

'Yes, but ... It makes sense. That doesn't make sense. He normally comes up with something which, if we knew what the hell he was talking about, would contain the wisdom of Buddha several times over. Probably.'

'I know, Frank. Isn't that the way you'd play it if you wanted to confuse him?'

'Yes, but my style is copyrighted. He can't steal my style.'

'I know, darling, there should be a law against it.'

'Well, sod him. Send "Talk wall" along with the move.'

'"Talk wall?"'

'That's "walk tall" slightly muddled up. Should get him going for a while.'

'Okay, Frank. I'd better be going. Look after yourself ... and talk wall.'

'You too, Free, talk wall.'

Frieda shook her head as she ended the call.

'Talk wall?' asked Tricia.

'It's something we should all do, Tricia. Talk wall. Every day, all day.'

'I shall spread the news,' said Tricia solemnly. 'And one day we will all be able to talk wall.'

'And when I get my hands on our Mason friend, he'll know a lot about walls, but talking isn't something he'll be doing a lot of.'

'I thought detectives liked making people talk.'

Frieda gave her a look.

'Very well, he will talk. And then he will shut up. Or I will bounce him off a wall. Several times.'

'What if Frank gets to him first?'

'Then he will be a very lucky man. He'll die quicker.'

Hordes

White: The Mason

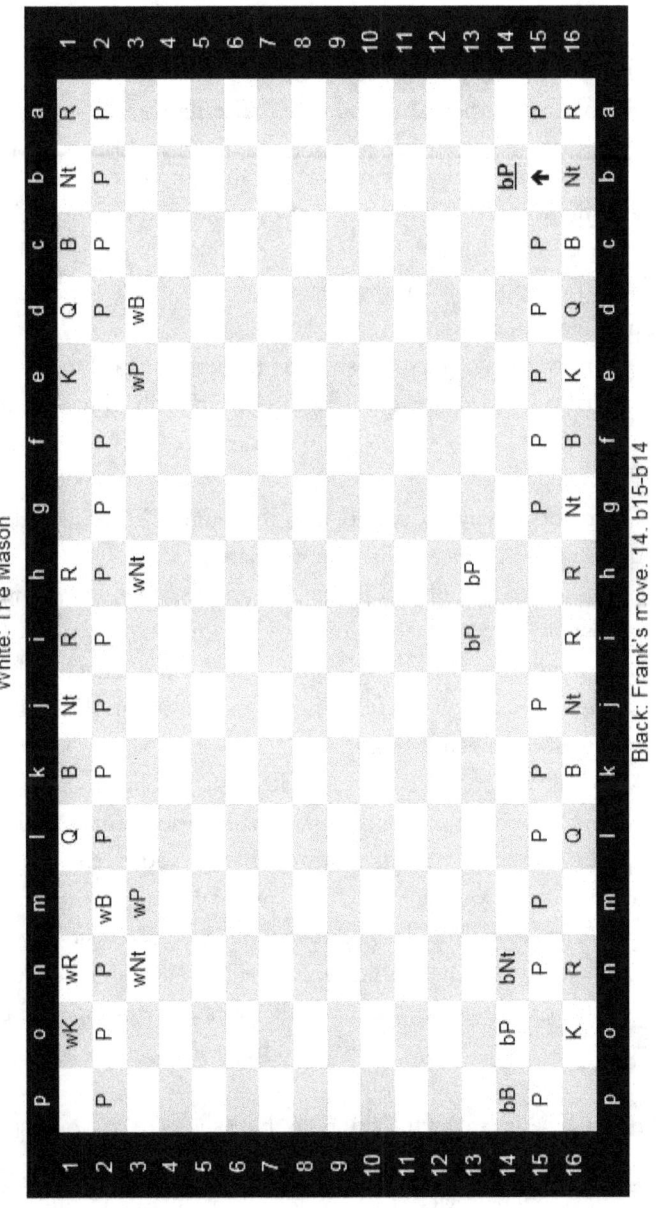

Black: Frank's move. 14. b15-b14

237

Thursday

The penny drops; The funeral; White flag time

'The funeral's at two,' Frieda said as she put her coat on prior to going to work. 'I'll meet you at the church at quarter to.'

'Right you are,' Frank replied. 'Looks like it's going to be a pretty miserable day. Appropriate.'

She gave him a kiss.

'Cheer up, Frank. It's what she was looking forward to.'

'Intellectually you are quite right. Emotionally, I'm not too sure.'

She smiled.

'You're beginning to sound like your father.' She gave him another kiss. 'I must be off. See you later.'

After she had gone he mooched around for a while, followed by Squishy who seemed to realise that something was wrong. After wandering around the rooms a few times, checking that the weather was still overcast, he found himself in the hallway looking at his metal detector.

'What say we go have a word with Martha Shaw?' he asked Squishy. 'For absolutely no reason than it's something to do.'

Squishy miaowed. It was warmer than it had been, but the garden outside was still wet from overnight rain, and, anyway, it was ages since she had gone visiting. And the inside of the car was dry and her table tennis ball should still be there. Frank put the metal detector on the back seat and opened the front passenger seat for Squishy to hop in.

'They say it's an awful thing to be ashamed of your son,' Martha Shaw said in her kitchen. Frank sat and sipped a mug of her over-brewed tea. Squishy roamed around the cupboards, inspecting this hitherto undiscovered part of her queendom. It was full of fascinating new smells, none of them dog.

'I've never understood why,' she continued. 'Or why it should be your son rather than your daughter. I've often wished I'd had a daughter rather than a son. Anyway, he was a bad lot. His father was a bad lot. That's it, end of story. No use in pretending otherwise.'

Frank suspected that this was a point of view Martha Shaw put to herself every day of her life.

'Funny, that,' she said. 'The job – if that's what it's called, it's the word he used – he was sent to prison for was quite a success in financial terms. Very expensive jewellery. If he hadn't committed suicide – well, I can't say that I would ever have respected him, but if you're going to do wrong, at least do it properly. Trouble is, like his father, he was second rate.'

'Twenty-five year sentence, at least fifteen years inside,' Frank said, 'and then nothing to look forward to apart from living on the dole, because he'd never get a job with his record, or trying another job with all the police watching his every move. Not much to look forward to.'

'Oh, no Inspector, he probably wouldn't have served even eight years, long enough as that is. No, it was the gang leader who got twenty-five years. He was the one who fired the shot. No, my son was given a twelve year sentence, and he would have got less if he had revealed where he had hidden the jewellery. That shows you how simple the others thought him to be. they trusted him with the jewellery. Thought that no-one would suspect him. They certainly didn't trust each other. I have to give him that. He never did tell anyone where he had hidden the stuff. Probably couldn't remember, knowing him.'

Frank put his mug down slowly.

'They never recovered the jewellery?'

'Never. Took his secret to the grave.'

'Which happens to be in the cemetery.'

'Yes. But I never visit.'

'You don't know whereabouts it is? In the cemetery?'

'No.'

'I think I know where it is. I think it's very close to Aggie's shed. The two people targeted most often were you and Aggie. She even said something about the person buried near her being unhappy.'

'I don't understand.'

'Now it all makes sense. This was all fifteen years ago, wasn't it? He was jailed fifteen years ago, wasn't he?'

'Well, yes, but –'

Frank looked at her.

'When did you start your vegetable patch, Mrs Shaw?'

She looked at him.

'About fifteen years ago,' she whispered. 'Oh, my god.'

'Precisely, Mrs Shaw.

'But that's ridiculous! Nobody could think –'

'Far too many people are doing some very strange thinking in Wellbury at the moment, Mrs Shaw. And my guess is that our mystery stone thrower is one of them. Can you remember who the gang leader was? Who else was involved?'

Martha Shaw put her mug down.

'The leader was called Godfrey de Boullion. I remember because it was such a strange name. And apparently he came from a wealthy family. No need to go around robbing people. They sent him to a psychiatrist for tests. Legally sane, I think they decided.'

'Would you recognise him if you saw him again?'

'Never saw him to start with. Never went to the trial.'

'His face wasn't in the newspapers?'

She paused as she tried to recall.

'If it was it didn't stick,' she decided.

'And you said that one of the officers on the case was a Detective Sergeant Summers?'

'Yes, but why –'

'Things are beginning to fall into place, Mrs Shaw.' He strode to the door. 'My guess is that he's out there somewhere, and this business of frightening old women has everything to do with finding those lost jewels. And he thinks I'm the other Summers.'

'You think they might be hidden here?'

'I don't care where they're hidden, Mrs Shaw, all I'm interested in is where our friend thinks they are, and I reckon that's either your vegetable patch or your son's grave. And I'm also rather interested in when Godfrey de Boulloin got out, if he is out. Come on, Squish, we've got work to do.'

Frank put his telephone on hands-free and dialled Pete's mobile number as he started his car.

'Pete? It's Frank. Can you talk?'

'Ffff-Philippa,' Pete replied, 'how wonderful to hear from you. It's been ages.'

'Someone else there, I take it.'

'Yes, yes, that's exactly right. Terrible weather for the time of year.'

'Okay, Pete, I'll make it quick. Martha Shaw's son was sent down for robbing a jeweller's about fifteen years ago. Part of a gang. Gang leader's name was something like Godfrey de Boulloin. I need to know all about the case. Who else was involved, how long they got, where they are now, that sort of thing. Oh, and find out if one of the officers was named Summers. Got it? See if you can get something together and bring it to the funeral.'

'Yes, yes, we must get together again soon. I'm in a meeting at the moment, so I'll have to get back to you on that one. I'll do that as soon as I can, okay?'

'Okay, Pete, speak to you soon.'

'An old friend of the family,' Pete said to Inspector Hanson. 'Haven't seen her for ages.'

'You are the most useless liar I have come across,' Percy replied. 'What did Frank want?'

Pete sighed.

'There's a case he wants to know about, happened about fifteen years ago. Jewellery heist. Martha Shaw's kid and someone called Geoffrey da Balloon.'

'Godfrey de Boulloin. I remember it well. I was a detective constable at the time. I was on the team that nicked them.'

'Was there a sergeant Summers on it at the same time?'

'Ah, my goodness, yes, I'd forgot about Frank Simmers. He was the one who arrested de Boulloin. Funny thing is, Simmers was going to be charged with bribery a few weeks later, disappeared off to Spain or somewhere before they could arrest him. De Boulloin could have jumped ship if he'd paid a little bribe, but presumably he didn't have the readies.'

'Will the notes be on the computer?'

'Could be. They should have digitised everything from the last fifty years. Why?'

'Well, I could just email Frank the file, then.'

Percy raised his eyes skywards.

'I don't know, you youngsters these days. One of these days there'll be a power failure and you'll have to learn to use a pen and paper again. Good thing too, it might encourage you to use your brains.'

Frank was a natural back-row person, whether it be classroom, lecture theatre or church. Frieda was a natural front-row occupier, the sort to lead by example. They compromised by Frieda deciding that they would sit in the front.

The service was jointly led by the parish vicar and Father Brown. Father Brown gave a short eulogy in which he extolled the life of someone he had never met. And then it was over, the coffin wheeled out to be taken to the crematorium, the mourners slowly exiting out into the winter sun. Father Brown and the parish vicar stood in their vestments chatting to their shared parishioners. Phil Walthers stood to one side, discreetly holding a small camera.

'I'm just going to pop down to Aggie's shed quickly,' Frank said to Frieda. 'Just to make sure it's secure.'

'Okay, Frank,' Frieda replied, before turning to Father Brown. Frank walked swiftly and guiltily away towards Aggie's shed. When he got there he checked that it was padlocked and the small window secured, just so that he could honestly say that he had not lied to his wife. He took the chance to take out an envelope Pete had slipped to him just before the funeral service. It was short and to the point:

"Confirm Godfrey de Boullon sent down fifteen years ago. Got out two months ago. Sidekick Robert Shaw committed suicide in prison. Percy confirms there was a Detective Sergeant Summers, says he was the one who arrested Boullion. Will get notes from computer and email them to you."

Frank smiled a grim smile of recognition at the confirmation. Then he paused. If Pete emailed the notes to his work email then the first person to read them would be Frieda.

He gave a mental shrug. That wouldn't be until the following morning. Plenty of time to come up with a plan on how to handle that.

Then he moved over to the grave that Aggie had pointed out. It was obviously one she had tended, though there wasn't much she could have down about the puddle of water which lay in a depression on it. The name on the headstone read, "Robert Shaw", with date of birth and death given. No 'Beloved son of' or 'Dearly departed father'.

'Got you!' thought Frank. Then he looked around with a feeling that someone was watching him. He couldn't spot anyone. He turned back to the grave and looked at the puddle. His skin went cold.

For a second two people looked back, one a young girl with a twelve-year-old-Aggie's face, smiling, the horrendous scar gone. The other was a young man, scarcely more than a boy, terrified. Aggie seemed to be holding his hand, as if to calm him.

And then the puddle was just a puddle again, reflecting the passing clouds scudding lightly across the sky.

He looked at Aggie's shed, and then back at the grave.

'Sleep well, Aggie,' he said. 'Or whatever it is you're going to do wherever it is you're gone.'

And then he remembered someone he should never have forgotten.

'And say hello to Jean when you meet her there,' he added. Then he walked quickly back to the group outside the front of the church.

Frieda was laughing at something Father Brown had said, and he was luxuriating in the vanity of a man who enjoyed making an attractive woman laugh even though he knew it was probably a sin. Frieda turned as Frank came up and the smile disappeared and she gripped his arm gently.

'Frank, what's wrong? You look as if you've seen a ghost. Have you got your epi-pen with you? Are you okay, darling? Do you need to sit down?'

'I'm okay, Free. I've just seen a ghost. Or an illusion. Or delusion. I'll tell you about it later.'

'A touch of the Tullamore, Inspector,' said Father Brown, palming him a small whiskey flask. Frank took it and just as smoothly took a deep sip without anyone seeing, before palming it back to the priest.

'Thank you, Father, just what the doctor ordered. I feel better already.'

'Encounters with the spirit world are always better when it's the right kind of spirit,' replied Father Brown. 'Right, time for me to be off. I've got confessions at five. Probably won't be anyone there, but you never know when his Holiness might pop in just casual like. Be seeing you.'

They said their goodbyes and watched him go.

'Are you sure you're okay, Frank?'

'I'm fine, Free. I just looked into a puddle and thought I saw a young Aggie looking back. Trick of the light, but it caught me unawares.'

Frieda shivered.

'Yes, I suppose that would give me the heebie-jeebies if I wasn't expecting it. What say we make our goodbyes and head on home before it gets dark?'

He paused. In his bachelor days an occasion like this would definitely have been followed by a couple of pints in the nearest pub.

'Good idea, Free. Let's get home,' he said.

'What do you fancy for dinner?' asked Frank as Frieda drove them home, Squishy asleep on his lap. 'Bit late to be cooking anything. We could order some take-away pizza.'

Frieda glanced at him. Take-away pizza was a favourite of his and his father's. His mother refused to allow his father to indulge in such unhealthy pursuits. Personally she was in agreement with her mother-in-law. It was just as quick, if not quicker, to put something together, take-away meals were always expensive for what you got, and they were invariably too rich, guaranteeing indigestion during the night and the following few days. Never mind what preservatives they put into them, and her doctor had been very impolite about companies that used such things.

'We can pick up something on the way,' she said. 'But not for me, I'm not really that hungry.'

'On the other hand, maybe just fry a few thin potato slices, some scrambled eggs, touch of herbs, toast, chuck in some baked beans – shouldn't take long.'

'I think I'll have a cheese and tomato on a thin base,' Frieda replied, pulling in to the pavement outside the row of small shops near to their home, directly opposite Alfredo's Instant Pizzas. 'If there's one thing I can't stand, it's baked beans.'

'Now that's an interesting question,' Frank said as they got out, holding a bleary-eyed Squishy. 'I wonder what they eat.'

'What who eats?'

'Martha Shaw and the others.'

She looked at him. She shook her head.

'It's going to be impossible to keep you off this case, isn't it?'

'Keep me off the case? I haven't touched it. I've kept well away from it.'

'You're a terrible liar, Frank Summers. Come on, let's get the pizzas and get home.'

Frank smiled.

'I think I'll have extra pepperoni on mine,' he said. 'Squish likes a bit of pepperoni.

'Only a little, Frank, she's a small kitten and it isn't good for her stomach.'

'So,' said Frieda, delicately stealing a slice of pepperoni from Frank's pizza and popping it into her mouth, 'has the Great Detective any clues?'

'What strikes me is that none of the woman have actually been hurt, apart from Aggie. And I'm beginning to wonder if that was intended to happen. I suspect that it was an unfortunate accident.'

'Physically, you mean?'

'Yes. It's all long range stuff. Throwing things from a distance.'

'You think that's significant?'

'Absolutely. Unfortunately it makes things a lot more difficult for us. It's the sort of thing kids might do, throw a stone at someone's house and then run like hell. But which of the attacks have been planned, and which have been just kids being nasty?'

'You think some of them have been planned? It's not just an outbreak of anti-old women hysteria?'

'A bit like Old Salem? No, I can't see it. I can imagine it happening, but this doesn't have the same feeling to it. That sort of thing needs someone to start muttering about witches, and I haven't heard anything like that, not even from Zack the Prat, nor the various religious oddballs floating around.'

He pushed his plate away. Frieda had insisted on plates. She had been prepared to permit take-away pizza, but there was no way they were going to eat out of cardboard boxes in her house.

Their house.

'The question is, is there a connection between the attacks and our mystery chess player?' He drummed his fingers on the table. Frieda stood up and took the plates to the sink.

'What does your instinct tell you?' she asked, turning the tap on.

'I don't believe in instinct, Free, you know that.'

'Of course not. So what does your logic tell you?'

'Logic tells me that the latest attacks have taken place very shortly after Mr Chessman came up with his gibberish. But logic also tells me that the first attacks took place before Mr Chessman started his nonsense. So is he copying something that he heard of, or are the things totally unrelated?'

'I suppose you'll want to come to the station to have a look at all the reports. Or have you found out everything without that?'

'You mean I'm allowed to come to the station?'

Frieda sighed, drying her hands on a tea towel.

'I suppose I was silly to imagine I could keep you away. And I'll feel better if you're somewhere I can keep an eye on you. I forgot the old dictum: keep your friends close, your enemies closer, and your husband in your arms so he can't get into any trouble.'

He grinned.

'In that case I can now tell you I know everything. Who is attacking little old ladies and why.'

Frieda's eyes narrowed.

'Frank, if you tell me that you've identified the culprit and arranged for him to be arrested without my knowledge ...'

'Oh, I don't know where they are, but I know who they are.'

'So the past fifteen minutes have just been flim-flam to keep me distracted?'

'No, not really. Our mason friend could be involved.'

'Okay, come on, Frank, spill the beans.'

Frank grinned back at her.

'And if you point out that I don't like beans I'll whack you with a frying pan.'

'Okay, Free, okay. Right, Mrs Shaw had a son called Robert. He got involved with the wrong sort, they tried on a jewellery heist, someone got killed, he was sentenced to eight years. He committed suicide shortly after starting his sentence. The jewels were never recovered. The gang leader, Godfrey de Boulloin, was the one who killed the jewellery assistant. He got twenty years. He was let out after fifteen for good behaviour. That was two months ago. I believe he got it into his head that Robert Shaw left the jewels somewhere where his mother could find them, and that they are either in her house or she buried them in her son's grave. He needed time to go through the house undisturbed and or dig up the grave. That meant getting Mrs Shaw and or Aggie out of the way.'

Frieda sat down.

'I don't suppose you've got any evidence for this Frank?'

'Absolutely none. But there's something else. One of the officers who arrested Boulloin was a Detective Sergeant Summers. Fast forward fifteen years and he might be a detective inspector. And lo and behold, Boulloin discovers there is a detective inspector Summers in Wellbury. And jumps to a natural but wrong conclusion.'

'And sends you – as Inspector Summers – a double chess set as some sort of a test?'

'It's decidedly possible. Maybe not as a test, maybe as a diversion, something to muddy the waters. This Detective Sergeant Summers might have had a passion for chess. Maybe Boulloin learnt carpentry in the nick and came up with this idea. I'm not saying that definitely is what happened, but it's a possibility. And I can't think of another option for this chess nonsense with the cryptic comments.'

She put her elbow on the table, cupped her chin in her hand and regarded him for a few seconds.

'If someone else had come up with that theory I would have sent them packing with several fleas in their ear. However, since it's you, Frank, and we're now married, and you'll be insufferable for the rest of our marriage if you're right and I don't believe you ... Presuming you're right, what's our next step?'

'I don't know. I only came up with the theory this morning talking to Mrs Shaw. Then I checked the grave closest to Aggie's shed after the funeral to check that it was the young Shaw's. I only, er, received information about Boullion this afternoon –'

'From Pete Phillips.'

'Now, Free, no names, no pack drill. Anyway, it answered the question, why did these attacks suddenly start at the same time. Now we need to keep an eye on both places to catch him red-handed.'

'With the jewels?'

'I don't think the jewels are in either spot. I think it's Boullion's wishful thinking. But we've got to nick him in such a way that he can't pretend the attacks were nothing to do with him.'

Frieda stood up.

'We don't have the resources to run standing patrols, but for the moment I'll tell them to re-institute the hourly checks on Aggie's place. Until we can come up with a better plan.'

'We've got to come up with a honey-trap,' Frank said, standing up. He looked at the sink. 'Free, you've done the dishes.'

'You are a clever detective, aren't you?'

'But, Free, you should have told me. Allowed me to give you a hand.'

'You were so deep in cogitation I didn't want to disturb you. Anyway, you've being doing the cooking and helping with the washing up over the past few weeks. I was beginning to think I wasn't needed in the kitchen. But one proviso about being back at work, Frank: you're partnered with Gertie.'

'You mean she gets to babysit me.'

'I mean you're partnered. That means looking after each other as well as looking after work. I have no doubt that you'll disappear very quickly if she tries to mother you.'

Frank grinned.

'Do me a favour, Free.'

'What's that?'

'Don't tell anyone else that you've agreed to my being at work.'

'You aren't going to be at work. You're just going to have a look through the reports. And try to come up with a plan.'

'No, what I mean is – well, keep them all thinking they mustn't talk to me about work. I feel a good wind up coming on.'

She shook her head and smiled at him.

'You have a nasty sense of humour, Frank Summers.' She paused before adding, 'I like it.'

Friday

Heralding the hoard; Singing detective; Mason (15)

'Now Phil Walthers has gone too far,' Frank said, flipping through the Wellbury Herald at the breakfast table on the Friday morning.

'What's he done now, darling?'

'Listen to this: 'While long known for his hard work and acute intelligence, it can be revealed that Detective Inspector Frank Summers is also regarded as a man of great luck. This has yet again been proved by his discovery of a hoard of ancient Roman coins along the banks of Wellbury River, a place which has been picked over by many others without such good fortune. Indeed his nickname amongst his colleagues is said to be the Lucky Detective. One of those colleagues, who wishes to remain anonymous, pointed out that, apart from finding ancient treasure where no-one else could, Inspector Summers has found much more modern treasure in his recent marriage, as reported in this newspaper not so long ago.' Well, really! What nonsense!'

'Oh, you don't agree that I'm a treasure?'

'Now, Free, that's not fair. You know what I mean.'

Frieda giggled.

'Yes, that bit about hard work and acute intelligence is obvious nonsense.'

Frank sighed.

'You're enjoying this, aren't you?'

'Absolutely, darling.'

'It wasn't a hoard. It was only ten or twelve coins. And we don't know what they are yet. They could be Victorian rather than Roman. Probably are.'

'Don't worry, Frank. I'm sure everyone at the station will sympathise.'

Frank groaned.

'Oh, god, no. I'll be called the Lucky Detective for the next three years. It reminds me of school and uni. I was called Biscuit because they decided I was a Jammy Dodger. Took me years to escape that.'

'Biscuit? I think that's sweet.'

Frank gave her a special glare.

'Well, it could be worse. You might be known as the Singing Detective. Though not for long. Not once you opened your mouth and sang, anyway.'

Frank grinned again.

'Free, you're a genius. Anyone calls me the Lucky Detective and I'm going to sing at them.'

'Just not while I'm there, darling. There's only so much a wife should be expected to put up with.'

'And I might go sing at Phil Walthers, too.'

'After I've discussed his ley lines with him, Frank.'

'If I wait until then there won't be much left to sing at.'

'Ah-ha!' exclaimed Pete Phillips, coming across Frank and Gertie in the corridor. 'It's himself, the Lucky Detective!' He paused as a thought struck him. 'Bloody hell, Frank, how did you get in? If Frieda finds out we'll all be for the high jump.'

Frank gave him a look which provided no encouragement at all.

'Look, Frank –'

'Midnight!' declared Frank, singing, 'and all around me is so quiet! The moon seems to have lost her memory! She is smiling at me!'

'Now, Frank,' said Pete Phillips, backing away while Gertie covered her ears, 'just a joke, you know, just a joke.'

'It was suggested that I should sing at anyone who came up with that nonsense. As a deterrent. Is it working?'

'Bloody hell, Frank! It's banned by the Geneva Convention, I'm sure. Cruel and unnecessary punishment. Promise you won't do it again.'

'Promise you won't call me that stupid name again.'

'I promise! I promise!'

'Promise me that you'll spread the word. Anyone else tries it they get sung at. And the next is Freddie Mercury.'

'I promise! I promise!'

'Good,' said Frank, clapping a hand on Pete Phillips's shoulder. 'We understand each other. However, as it happens, I do have a rather good baritone when I put myself to it.'

Pete Phillips watched him walk away with Gertie following, very unfeminine little fingers clearing out each ear. They went down the corridor and then out of sight. He shuddered at the thought of Frank's baritone. He shuddered even more at the thought of Frank imitating Freddie Mercury.

'Scarramoo! Scarramoo! Will you do the fandago!' came from somewhere down the corridor.

Eric Johns hove into view, tottering.

'Bloody hell!' he muttered. 'That was the most frightening thing I've encountered since the mother-in-law took up choral singing.'

'I can think of something a little more frightening, Eric,' said Pete Phillips.

'And what's that?' Eric Johns asked, his own little finger trying to clear all trace of Freddie Mercury from deep in his ear passages.

'Frank's in the station. Frank isn't supposed to be in the station. Fabulous has so ordained. So it's up to you to go to Fabulous and confess that you've just seen Frank in the station where he isn't supposed to be.'

'Ah, would do, but the reception needs manning, I'll leave informing the Inspector up to you,' Eric Johns replied, moving at a speed rarely achieved by someone of his portly stature.

'And I've got a time-sheet to complete,' muttered Pete Phillips. 'Several, actually. And they need doing behind locked doors.'

'Where to, Sarge, I mean Sir,' asked Gertie.

'I fancy a cup of coffee in the canteen,' Frank replied, a smile twitching at his lips. Gertie looked up at his face.

'You really do have a nasty sense of humour, Frank,' she said.

Frank's arrival in the canteen appeared to coincide with the existing occupants finding a reason to finish up and be somewhere else. Only Agnetha behind the counter and Sam Nightingale sitting at a table reading a magazine while finishing an apple seemed relaxed about his appearance. By the time they'd ordered and got their trays the canteen was almost empty.

'Hello, Sam,' he said, putting his tray on her table. 'Mind if we join you?'

'Go ahead, sir.'

'You don't appear to be bothered by my presence, unlike the others. What's the magazine about?'

Sam smiled.

'If you're going to enter the canteen openly the Inspector must know you're here. If she didn't you'd be skulking from room to room. And you wouldn't have Gertie baby-sitting you. Sir.'

'Good deduction, Sam. Strange how others haven't noticed the obvious. So, what's the magazine?'

'Biking in the USA. They have an organised trip following the route of Easy Rider. Allegedly.'

'You don't think it's true?'

Sam shrugged.

'I'd have to look into it. I haven't actually seen Easy Rider. It's just the photograph from the movie looked interesting.'

'I've always wanted a motorbike like that. Then again, I've always wanted a racer with swept-down handlebars, a Corvette like the one in the Smokey movies, a state-of-the art Jag, a huge touring caravan, a canal boat to tour, and so on.'

'On a policeman's salary?' asked Sam.

'Yes, that's a part of the problem. Also the question of time. Hello, here comes the boss,' Frank said as he noticed Frieda entering the canteen. She took a tray and was met at the counter by Agnetha.

'Do you want me to leave, sir?' asked Sam.

'You obviously have the same distrust of senior officers I have, Sam. Don't worry, you'll know when to leave. When you see me heading for the hills.'

'Seems very quiet in here,' Frieda noted as she brought her tray to the table and sat down. 'Was it something Frank said?'

'He said "Hello", ma'am,' Sam said, smiling.

'Yup, that ought to do it.'

'Cream and jelly?' asked Frank, looking at Frieda's tray. 'I think I might need to try that.'

'Hands off, Frank. It's for little Frank. Or little Frances.'

Sam's eyebrows rose.

'You're – you mean – Um- Sorry, Inspector, none of my business.'

'I am, and it will become your business. Can hardly go around looking like a Zeppelin without people doing silly things like asking you if you want to sit down and can I get you a glass of water or a cup of tea, or would you like me to do that for you, and the rest of it.'

'That's confirmation come through?' asked Frank, having finished his toasted chicken-and-mushroom and eyeing his son's/daughter's cream and jelly with gluttonous thoughts. Frieda enjoyed a mouthful while putting an arm around it to confirm that is was out of bounds, even to her husband.

'Indeed. I had a call this morning.'

'Well, that's a relief,' Frank said, giving up on the jelly and cream. He turned to Sam. 'We didn't want to announce it until everything was a hundred percent. Free's family have an inherited defect in which they imagine things.'

Frieda looked at him through narrowed eyes as she sucked on her spoon.

'You were adopted, weren't you, Frank?' she asked.

Frank was about to reply when Frieda's mobile made a pinging sound. She took it out and looked at it. She put it down again and finished off the jelly.

'Battle stations,' she said once that was done. 'The Mason's sent his latest move. 15. zero-zero. And Frank is now going to tell us what that means.'

'He's castling on the short side again, just as I thought. Come on, let's go have a look at the chess board.'

'Sure you don't want to play it in your head?' asked his wife sweetly.

White: The Mason's move. 15. O-O left hand king side castle

	a	b	c	d	e	f	g	h	i	j	k	l	m	n	o	p
1	R	Nt	B	Q	⇩	**R**	**K**	⇧	R	Nt	B	Q		wR	wK	
2	P	P	P	P		P	P	P	P	P	P	P	wB	P	P	P
3				wB									wP	wNt		
4					wP			wNt								
5																
6																
7																
8																
9																
10																
11																
12																
13								bP	bP							
14		bP												bNt	bP	bB
15	P		P	P	P	P	P	R	R	P	P	P		R	K	P
16	R	Nt	B	Q	K	B	Nt			Nt	B	Q				

Black: Frank

258

'Like you said, castling on the short side,' said Gertie. You only need to get two pieces out of the way, bishop and knight. The other side it's bishop, knight and queen. I always go for the short castle, I don't like having to move my queen out of the way of my king. It's normally a wasted move.'

'True, Gerts,' said Frank. 'And in single chess that makes sense. The problem here is that he's moved his second king towards the centre of the board. Makes it more difficult to defend. I'd move both to the centre or each to a corner.'

'I hate to mention this, sir, but –' began Sam Nightingale.

'But you've noticed that my right wing is too blocked up to castle either way? Yes, that's one of the drawbacks of only having one go at a time.'

He rubbed his jaw.

'Whaddya say we tickle that white bishop just a little bit?' he asked, motioning to the bishop at m2. 'Free, I think my next move is going to be c16-a14.'

Frieda looked at him, and then down at the board. She moved the black bishop to a14. Its line of attack flew straight towards the white bishop on m2, at what seemed like yards away.

'Straight exchange offer,' Sam noted. 'Bishop for bishop.'

'If he takes it,' Frank said. 'Then I take his bishop with my knight. That just leaves my queen to move before I can castle on my left. And if he's the nervous type, as I think he is, he's not going to like losing pieces, even in a one-for-one exchange. You've got to be prepared to take the losses to gain a strategic advantage.'

'And what, Field Marshal Hague,' asked Frieda, 'will you do if he doesn't take the bait?'

Frank grinned.

'Then I'll take his bishop anyway,' he said. 'He'll be forced to take mine with his queen, and he's going to like that even less.

Nobody likes having to waste the power of queens on pesky little bishops.'

'As Marie Antoinette once didn't say to Cardinal Richelieu,' commented Frieda. 'Would you like to know what his bon mot is today?'

'Does it involve fruit?'

'No.'

'Bats?'

'No. He mentions Aggie. Or refers to her.'

'Aggie? What the hell's he got to say about her?'

'He says: I was most disturbed to hear about the unfortunate passing of the old dear in the cemetery. Please pass on my sympathies. Ask not, of course.'

Frank's eyes narrowed.

'Ask not, of course? Ask what not, of course?'

'Um ...' said Gertie.

'Well, Gertie, do you know what it means?'

'Ask not for whom the bell tolls,' suggested Gertie. 'Someone mentioned it on one of my OU courses.'

'Of course,' said Frieda. 'But is he referring to Hemingway's book, or the original poem?'

'Either way it shows he's not an uneducated cuss,' said Frank.

'Cuss?' asked Frieda.

'I've decided to employ some of Georgette Heyer's terminology instead of the more earthier Anglo-Saxon ones I'd prefer. It makes me feel better. But you notice something about that?'

'How does he know about Aggie?'

'Exactly. The only place I've seen it mentioned is in the Herald. Which means either (a) he's involved in somewhere like the allotments where it's common knowledge, or (b) he's local and takes the Herald.'

'Your deduction is unassailable, oh great one,' said Frieda. 'But what does it actually tell us?'

'Bugger all,' said Frank.

'Now that's a Georgette Heyer I would like to read,' said Sam.

White: The Mason

File	1	2	3	4	5	6	7	8	9	10	11	12	13	14	15	16
a	R	P												bB	P	R
b	Nt	P												bP	↖	Nt
c	B	P												P	↖	
d	Q	P	wB											P	Q	
e			wP											P	K	
f	R	P												P	B	
g	K	P											P	Nt		
h			wNt									bP		R		
i	R	P											bP	R		
j	Nt	P											P	Nt		
k	B	P											P	B		
l	Q	P											P	Q		
m		wB	wP										P			
n	wR	P	wNt										bNt	P	R	
o	wK	P											bP		K	
p	P	P												bB	P	

Black: Frank's move. 16. c16-a14

Saturday

Attack on the Porridge Place

'Finally,' said Frieda after they had finished a leisurely breakfast which she had cooked, 'a whole weekend for us together.'

'Want to bet on that?' asked Frank.

'We'll start with getting the domestic stuff done. Put the washing in, then do the shopping.'

'Funny, that, that's what used to happen when I was single. Get a whole weekend off, plan all sorts of things, and end up doing the mundane domestic stuff. Well, the Saturday morning, anyway. Could always go down the pub for the afternoon, especially if there was some football or rugby on.'

'And in the afternoon we can go house-hunting.'

'Aren't Arsenal playing Tottenham this afternoon?'

'It's Chelsea versus Man United. I've a list of houses we can view, I just have to call the estate agents to confirm. If,' she added, 'you're interested, darling.'

Frank shot her a look.

'Now that's not fair, Frieda, you know I love you and would do anything for you, that's just taking advantage.'

'Okay, no problem, I'll forget about the idea if you want.'

Frank sighed.

'Okay, okay, Free, you win, we'll go look at these houses then. But I warn you, you'll regret it. DIY is hard-coded into the genetic make-up of the modern human male. Everything we look at I'll be full of ideas on how to change it, how to improve it, how to ...'

'Decorate it? Lovely idea, Frank, new decorations are what the modern female lives for.'

They looked at each other for a few seconds. Then Frieda's work mobile phone rang. She checked the screen for the calling number.

'Rubbermats. It's the station. Still, can't be serious, it's not my landline. Our landline. The landline. Hello, Inspector Summers?'

There ensued a series of communications in which Frieda said 'Yes?' several times, and 'Are you sure twice', ended with 'Okay, I'll be there in fifteen minutes.' She switched the phone off and looked at Frank.

'Trouble?' he asked.

'The Porridge Place has been attacked. A group of protesters tried to burn it down.'

'The Porridge Place? Protesters? What on god's earth were they protesting against? Don't tell me the cardboard muesli from Manao is made by child slave labour?'

'Not funny, Frank. Apparently the protest was made by New Age travellers who object to the gentrification of the Old Town.'

'Gentrification of – Are they bloody mad? Some parts of the Old Town are the most expensive properties in Wellbury. Others are slums which should be bulldozed and rebuilt.'

'I think the protesters were actually professional Londoner protesters who read about the Porridge Place and decided to have some weekend fun with the yokels.'

'But, Free, that's uniform's job. There's no need for you to go in.'

'One of the properties we were going to see was in the Old Town. But now I have to go in to work, so we'll have to postpone that. Thanks a bunch, Frank.'

With that she picked up her keys and stormed out, leaving a bemused Frank looking at the door. Squishy looked at him with the eyes of a female which said, 'There, see what you've gone and done now. Gone and upset poor Frieda for absolutely no reason whatsoever. And where's my tuna?'

'Remember when it was just you and me, Squish?' Frank sighed. 'You and me against the world. I carried you around in the pocket of that old leather jacket. I punched air-holes in with my pocket knife so that you could see out and breathe without being seen. We lived in my little flat then without a worry, didn't we? You didn't mind not having a garden or anything. Maybe we could go back to that, what say, Squish?'

Squishy cocked her little head, raised a paw, licked it, used it to clean her face, and then went out to see if the little girl next door was available to play. Squishy had memories of the life she had lived prior to finding herself dumped on Frank, and, nice as he might be, she had no intention of going anywhere close to them again. And having a garden was much better than living in a flat.

Frieda didn't return until late that afternoon. Frank had spent the day doing the washing, shopping, all the domestic tasks he had spent years as a bachelor practicing on how to avoid.

'Well, that's that, Squish,' he told the kitten curled up on the couch, watching him wipe clean the front of the television. 'And if I never have to do that again for a thousand years, it'll be two thousand too soon.'

There was the sound of Frieda's key in the front door lock.

'We'll get a cleaning lady in,' he told Squish. 'Couple of days a week. She'll be company for you. And entertainment, judging by how much you've enjoyed watching me slave myself to the bone.'

Frieda entered the lounge and stood looking at him for a few moments.

'I went to the zoo this afternoon,' he said. 'They only had a dog. It was a Shitsui.'

She smiled briefly.

'Okay, Frank, I owe you an apology, I shouldn't have lost my temper and blamed you for something that wasn't your fault.'

'There's a slight problem with that statement, Free.'

'Which is?'

'It suggests that you'd be quite happy blaming me for something which is my fault.'

'Well, I wouldn't put it exactly that way ... Frank, there are three things I need to talk to you about. I was thinking on the way home how often in the past I'd done the same journey glad to be on my way to my own private space, away from the office and the politics. The trouble is I have the same sort of thought, then I remember that we're married and I'm no longer on my own, and I feel sort of, well, like I'm betraying you by wanting to be alone.'

'Let me guess, you wouldn't have the same sort of thoughts if you were going home a different way, or to a different home?'

'Well, it did rather strike me that –'

'Okay, Free, we'll go house-hunting at the first available opportunity.'

'You mean that?'

'Absolutely. I'll get no peace otherwise.'

She hugged him.

'It'll work out, Frank, I know it will.'

'Course it will. What was the second thing, while I'm signing away my free time?'

'Arsenal beat Tottenham two-one. I heard the result on the round-up on the way home.'

'Two-one? Brilliant! But you said it was Chelsea versus Man United.

'They drew.'

'Damn! I could have watched the Arsenal game on the telly.'

'Frank, you never watch Arsenal play, you're too afraid they'll go four-nil up by half time and then lose five-four.'

'True. But they are good at that sort of thing. So, what's numero trois?"

'Uniform picked up a couple of our London protestors. They were quite loose-lipped. Apparently they've been staying in a squat in the Old Town. One of the other residents who egged them on was an ex-con. They were somewhat irritated because apparently he was full of it beforehand, but didn't turn up for the show.'

'And you're going to tell me his name after a drum roll?'

Frieda smiled.

'Godfrey de Boulloin,' she said.

'Well, well, well,' said Frank. 'Let me guess, when they went round to the squat to have a little word he'd gone?'

'Correct.'

Frank rubbed his jaw.

'You were expecting that?' asked Frieda. 'That he'd have disappeared.'

'Yes, I was. The question is, did he make a mistake in winding them up, or was he deliberately leaving his calling card for us to find?'

Sunday

A stroll in the park

'Right, Frank, I know exactly what we're going to do today,' Frieda said as they cleared the breakfast dishes away.

'Go house-hunting?' suggested Frank.

'No, I know you don't want to look at houses, Frank, so we'll put that on hold until you're ready.'

'I'm ready, Free, I'm ready. In fact I'd rather get it over with, if it has to be done it has to be done.'

'No, Frank, you made me forget something the doctors at the hospital said.'

'I made you forget?'

'Yes, one doctor – Doctor Harris I think it was, the one who looked a bit like Omar Shariff – said that research tends to suggest that stress can play a large part in problems such as anaphylactic shock. And, of course, in things like eczema.'

'Eczema? Well, I suppose theoretically stress probably plays a part in all illnesses.'

'Precisely.'

'But that's negative stress.'

'Exactly. So, until we get your results back we'll leave house-hunting off the agenda.'

He looked at her suspiciously.

'And instead we're going to do – what?'

'Go for a walk in the park.'

'Go for a walk in the park?'

'White's Folly, in the centre of Wellbury.'

'White's Folly.'

'The restaurant should still be open,' Frieda said.

'They have boats there, don't they?' asked Frank.

'I thought you'd like those, Frank. Indeed they do, though they lock them up for the winter. Should still be a few weeks before they do that, though.'

'Funny, that, I think the only times I've been there was either on a case or to have a go on the dodgems at the fair.'

'It happens that way if you aren't careful. I stayed with an old friend in London once when I was on a two-week course. She was also a police officer. She could tell you the way to walk to the local Underground station, the quickest way to drive to her work, but she couldn't tell you a single thing about anything in the other direction. She just never went that way.'

'Well, then, sounds like an excellent idea. How do we get there?'

Frieda smoothed a map out on the table.

'Walk up this road, down here, onto the river path here, up to the Old Town, through the Old Town, come round the left. That way we'll enter at the top and be on our way back at the same time.'

'About twelve, fifteen miles. I could definitely do with a walk like that. Too used to jumping in a car these days. So, what do we need? Daypacks, water, small emergency aid kit with something for blisters, maps, cameras, umbrella just in case – what else?'

'I'll make some boiled egg sandwiches just in case the restaurant is closed.'

'Mobile phone?'

'I'll take my personal one, switched off. The work one can remain here for a few hours.'

Frank grinned at her and gave her a hug. Frieda giving up the umbilical cord to work was a sacrifice of the first order.

'I was thinking of Laurie Lee and his book, As I Walked Out One Midsummer Morning,' Frank said as they walked along the pavement, past modest suburban terraced and semi-detached houses, 'what it must have been like in a time when it was quite normal to walk everywhere. Dick Whittington and his cat going to London.'

'You mean the days before everyone had cars, and countries didn't have enough nuclear weapons to destroy the world several times over? Oh, halcyon days.'

'Yes. Thing is, we all know exercise is good for you, walking is free, for the moment, keeps you healthy, keeps the blood pressure down, psychologically it relaxes you, but what happens? We end up, at best, driving down to the gym for exercise and then driving home again.'

'Talking of different times and exercise, I remember reading the story of White's Folly shortly after I'd arrived in Wellbury. I found a copy of Wellbury's history in a second-hand bookshop.'

'How did it get its name?'

'Apparently sometime in the mid-1880s the head councillor of the then little town of Wellbury, a man named Principal White, and his deputy councillor, a man named Patience Wood – those names stuck in my head – they decided on having a park landscaped and a lake dug to provide recreational space for the public and workers from a new factory which had been built nearby. Quakers, I think. White had made his own personal fortune and was happy to pay for a lot of it, there was a lot of that sort of paternalistic altruism going on in those days. Unfortunately he might have been good at business, he wasn't too good at getting a lake dug.'

'More Calamity Jane than Capability Brown?'

'Precisely. They wanted the Capability Brown result but weren't prepared to pay for someone who knew what they were doing. I can just imagine one of them asking that good old question, "After all, how difficult can it be to dig a pond?" Anyway, over two hundred men worked for months with picks and shovels. They used dynamite to shift most of the stuff below a few feet, it was pretty much bedrock. The rubble was moved in carts, horse-drawn or by cattle or donkeys. They took most of it to the far side of the park to make an artificial hill overlooking the lake. After about three years the work was complete and all they were waiting for was one of Wellbury's famously wet winters to fill the lake so that an official spring opening could take place.'

'Let me guess. It didn't rain.'

'Not a drop near the lake. For ten years Wellbury had a drought which seemed to centre strangely over the centre of the park, right where the lake was. They had regular prayer meetings begging for rain, but Councillor White went to his Maker believing his big project to have failed, according to the history.'

'What did he die of?'

'Well, that's where things become confusing. One account says that one night he went to the deepest part of the huge hole with all his portable wealth, and buried it there in propitiation of the gods of weather, even though he was supposed to be a committed Christian. As soon as he had done that the heavens opened and he drowned in the flood.'

'And the treasure is still buried there today, right in the deepest part of the lake.'

'Indeed. But the other story is that it was the deputy Councillor, Patience Wood, who implemented a plan to divert part of the river Wellbury to fill the hole. It filled the lake but emptied the river. It also drowned Councillor Patience Wood as he stood in the path of the oncoming water, having failed to take into account the fact that he was at the bottom of a dry lake and couldn't swim.'

'And our friend Councillor White was with him at the time?'

'The book doesn't say so. Apparently it rained solidly for three weeks, the lake filled up, it became a favourite site with shops and restaurants and travelling fairs and they all lived happily after.'

'Up until people discovered cheap travel and Benidorm.'

'Something like that. The book was published just before the Second World War. From what I've heard most of the attractions never recovered. The bandstand fell to pieces. The restaurants closed and never reopened.'

'Until now.'

'Until a few years ago, anyway. The travelling fairs and circuses never quite stopped camping there for a week or so. I think finally some of the modern councillors stopped and thought, "You know, maybe we could make better use of that."'

'Otherwise known as, "Well, if people are going to spend their money, they'd be far better off spending it with us"?'

'Pretty much so. I hear they're thinking of putting a huge screen up to show things like world cups. Glastonbury, Wimbledon. Anything where large crowds might want to turn up. Large crowds need feeding and watering, so they lease out the restaurants, fast food places, burger vans.'

'Beer tents.'

'Of course. And there's the proposed Wellbury Oktoberfest.'

'Wellbury, which isn't German, doesn't make its own beer or sausages.'

'I suppose you don't have to be Greek to run a marathon. Well, here we are, the entrance to White's Folly.'

'I wonder if they had an arch here when it was built,' Frank mused as they entered via a road wide enough to accommodate two large, horse-drawn carriages.

'I think so. It's been a while since I read it, but the book has some black and white photographs. I seem to recall seeing an arch with tall gates.'

'Probably melted down during the war to keep people's patriotic vigour stirring.'

'Let's stroll across the grass.'

'Good idea. I think I recognise one of those yoga trees.'

'Yoga trees?'

'In that yoga forest over there.'

'They do rather look like a forest, don't they – if painted by a Dadaist.'

'I wouldn't mind learning painting just to do that shot.'

'Would that be before or after learning to play the violin?'

Frank grinned.

'Let me think about that. I might need more time off work.'

They came across a young woman in a leotard standing upside down on a mat.

'Good morning, yogini,' said Frank, 'are you feeling the force?'

'Morning, sir, morning ma'am,' replied Sam Nightingale, 'the nadi is coming along nicely.'

'Nadi?'

'Channel of energy, sir.'

'Well, we'd better leave you alone to develop your chakra,' said Frieda, taking Frank's arm.

'Yes,' said Frank, 'we're trying to decide on whether to channel a dim sum or a chicken Masala. See you later, Sam, peace and love.'

'You shouldn't interrupt people in the middle of yoga, Frank,' Frieda said as they walked on.

'Don't see how we could avoid it. If we waved she'd feel she needed to wave back, and then she'd just fall over.'

'She just wiggle a few fingers at you as I would, Frank. How did you know a female yogi is a yogini?'

'I went out with one once.'

'Now why doesn't that surprise me? Every time you reveal some hidden talent or knowledge it turns out that it involves some ex-girlfriend.'

'She was of particularly short duration.'

'Not attractive enough?'

'She was about thirty-five. She was looking for herself. I've always felt that, if you haven't found yourself by the time you're twenty-one you probably never will. Besides which, maybe she would find out she was a mass-murderer, or a lesbian, or a nun. Be a bit of a downer on any relationship.'

'Twenty-one? That's a bit young, isn't it?'

'I don't think so. You might not have decided what it is you want to do, though even that I'd find that surprising. You might change your lifestyle, or goals, or whatever, but you should know who the basic you is by that stage.'

'And you knew what you wanted to do at twenty-one.'

'Absolutely. I knew what I wanted to do when I was eight. I wanted to have fun.'

'You would,' she said, giving him a look. She looked back to the thinned forest of yogi-yoginis. 'It's just struck me what these people are doing. It's the suryanamaskara. It's a salutation to the rising sun. Twelve asanas – that's posture or position.'

'A bit late for the rising sun, isn't it?'

'I think you're allowed a certain leeway in the winter. Oh, rubbermats, just a second.'

'What?' asked Frank as Frieda turned suddenly, hunted in her handbag, and came out with some large sunglasses which hid most of the top of her face and a chiffon scarf which, thrown around her neck and over her shoulder, hid most of the rest.

'See that oak tree, Frank?'

'The one with the yellow ribbon around it?'

'And the hippy playing the guitar underneath it, along with the dancing sylphs.'

'Ah, so that's what they are.'

'That's the one who decided I was their queen because my office lies band on the centre of two ley lines.'

Frank laughed out loud and then tried to smother it with his hand.

'Come on,' he said, 'let's wander over and see if they recognise their monarch.'

'Don't you dare, Frank Summers. Come on, let's get away as fast as we can.'

They managed to get past the group under the oak tree by Frieda hanging on to Frank's arm on his far side while admiring the view at an angle. Frank was out of breath from trying not to laugh by the time they had cleared the recognition danger zone.

'Frank, I don't think you should be laughing at them. I'm sure they're very sincere.'

'It's not their sincerity I'm concerned about, it's their sanity. There's a certain Catch-22 about religion; if people aren't willing to die for their beliefs they can't really believe them. If they are, then they're crazy anyway.',

'Hmmm.'

'Hmmm?'

'I was about to say yoga isn't compatible with killing people, but I think Sam would be comfortable with both under certain conditions.'

'So how come you know so much about yoga? Asanas and all the rest,' asked Frank.

'I used to belong to a yoga class. I was going through a rather tough time at the station I was at, and my psychiatrist told me to get out and join some activity groups. She suggested ones like yoga or hill-walking. I was already doing karate, ju-jitsu and tennis, so I chose yoga. Then one night, after a really bad day I was in the middle of a class, trying not to think about work, when I forgot it was yoga and changed into ju-jitsu mode. The class leader was very understanding about it, when he got his breath back, but he walked with a limp for weeks, or so I'm told. I was a bit too embarrassed to go back afterward.'

'You know, I think I might take up yoga. I've heard it's good for you. Lowers your blood pressure, makes you sleep better, that sort of thing.'

'Indeed –'

'So long as you avoid maniac police officers, that is.'

'Frank!' She punched his arm lightly. 'It is actually good for stress levels. I've often wondered whether I shouldn't encourage everyone at the station to take it up.'

'Now that's a sight I'd pay to see. Eric Johns adopting the Lotus positon.'

'Yes, I suppose that's what holds me back. There are some forces of nature it's best just to accept.'

'Unless you're training them as the Dirty Dozen about to drop into Normandy just in time to assassinate a few German officers at Rennes. Though I'm not sure what role Eric would play in that.'

'You know, if ever there was a movie which should have been re-made with an all-female cast that was it.'

'You as Lee Marvin and Susan as Charles Bronson? Who would play the psycho, Telly Savalas?'

'We might have to slightly adapt the story. I wouldn't want some religious maniac like that on the team.'

'But all the team were murderers of some sort. Or they'd been given the death penalty. Anyway, what about the bit where

Charles Bronson gets beaten up in the gents? Are his attackers also women? Military police?'

'Well, I haven't really thought about that. Maybe. Shall we have a go on the boats?'

'Do they come with torpedoes?'

'Do you ever take anything seriously, Frank?'

'I've never taken anything, seriously, Guv.'

'Frank! Answer my question.'

'Free I got married. What can be more serious than that?'

'I certainly hope you take marriage seriously, Frank.'

'Course I do. Epicurus probably said something about it. The more serious something is, the less time you should waste worrying over it. Just get on and do it.'

'And you come to that conclusion, how?'

'Well, all the other philosophers believed in the gods. Well, the majority. They were fanatical about paying attention to the gods. Epicurus's opinion was that, sure, he gods existed, but they weren't overly interested in humans, so you really shouldn't worry about them. Just enjoy life and leave the gods to enjoy their lives.'

Frieda considered the idea. It sounded awfully untidy.

But a day of boating and various innocent pursuits, however childish, would be one more safe day towards Frank's results.

And she'd never been boating before. But she was sure she'd be good at it.

And it allowed them to do something together they couldn't have done on their own: accept that there wasn't much they could do about Mason or de Boulloin for the moment.

Monday

Frank has an idea

'Free free?' Frank asked, entering the outer eyrie to Frieda's office, manned by her secretary, Tricia-Leigh.

'Inspector Summers,' Tricia-Leigh replied with a polite frown to show that she thought little of Frank's alliteration, 'is available, Inspector Summers.'

Frank winked at her and knocked on the door. He entered at Frieda's bidding, not noticing the blush on Tricia-Leigh's face.

'Free, I have an idea,' he said, closing the door behind him.

'I hope it's a good one, Frank. At the moment I'm trying to work out a roster for this demonstration, and it's not looking good. We're going to have to ask for help from the neighbouring divisions, and that becomes political.'

'Oh, I don't think we'll need any help.'

Frieda looked up at him over her reading glasses. She took them off, put them down on her desk, linked her fingers together and rested her chin on them.

'You have a plan.'

'Did I ever tell you how sexy those glasses make you look?'

'Tell me your plan, Frank. And afterward you can remind me of the sexy bit.'

'It involves a little co-operation from Phil Walthers and the judicious use of a few ley-lines.'

Frieda sighed. Then she listened as Frank explained. Finally she put her glasses back on again and looked at him over the top of them.

'You think he'd fall for that?'

'We don't have anything else.'

'If it works I might claim wife's privileges,' she said. 'After work, of course. Go to it, oh husband of mine.'

He kissed her and left. She picked up her telephone.

'Tricia, see if there are any concerts available. I'd like to book a couple of seats for myself and my husband on Saturday.'

'He doesn't deserve you, you know,' said Tricia-Leigh.

Tuesday
Setting the long arm of the lure; ITBMA (17)

The editor of a newspaper, especially if he is also the chief journalist and chief photographer, cannot have any private, me-time. Phil Walthers being Phil Walthers, had exactly that: Tuesday lunch hour was reserved for himself, in his own private alcove in the Hangman's pub. It was an unwritten agreement that this was one place and time he was never, ever to be disturbed. Not even – especially even – by Mrs Blower.

'Now, Mr Walthers, I think we should have a chat,' Frank said, slipping into the alcove. Phil Walthers closed his eyes and counted to five.

'Frank,' he said, re-opening them, 'I'm sorry, but this is my private time. If you wish to castigate me for some things I've written about you, well, I shall be available at the office in one hour precisely. Until that time I have to decide whether an Australian Burgundy is superior to that of a French Burgundy. My meal is a simple choice this week. Ham and egg pie, with home-made parsley mayonnaise. A good simple English repast.'

'Ham and egg pie? With home-made parsley mayonnaise?'

'Precisely.'

'With a dash of mustard?'

Phil Walthers paused.

'I would not normally consider such a thing, but now that you come to mention it ... interesting, I shall have to try that.'

'Mind if I order some? I'm starving. And it's been ages since I had a really good ham and egg pie.'

Phil Walthers scrutinised him.

'You promise not to mention work?'

'Absolutely.'

'Not even Roman coins?'

'Sod Roman coins. Does the pie come with gravy?'

'If you wish to be a Philistine, yes. Two ham and egg portions, please, Cynthia,' Phil Walthers told the waitress.

'Mine with gravy,' added Frank. 'And parsley mayonnaise.'

'It's one of those things,' he added once the waitress had gone. 'I've been doing a fair bit of cooking recently, but ham and egg pie? I wouldn't even think of it. It's the sort of thing you have to eat out.'

He grinned at Phil Walthers.

'You like a story of buried treasure. How do you fancy the story of jewels from a robbery fifteen years ago lying somewhere around Wellbury?'

Phil Walthers paused. Had he not just said that this was his unassailable hour alone? No work. Nothing apart from the careful and deliberate enjoyment of a simple meal.

Buried treasure?

Ridiculous.

'Jewels?' he asked.

'Diadems, if you want.'

'Diadems,' said Phil Walthers, rolling the word around to gain maximum pleasure from such a little used and precious thing.

'Lovely, sparkling diadems. And those things princesses wear.'

'Tiaras,' breathed Phil Walthers.

'Involving the discreet use of words such as filigree.'

'Filigree.'

'And sparklers if you wish.'

'Around Wellbury?'

Phil Walthers looked at him cautiously. He trusted Frank, but this sounded suspicious, very suspicious. It was entirely possible that Frank was having a mind storm of some sort. And he was well aware of Frank's medical history.

And it was his personal time.

Definitely.

'Frank, I told you, this is my personal time. I do not discuss business in this hour. However, perhaps I might pass on the Crème Caramel today.'

'Well, I'm not going to. I hear the Crème Caramel is particularly good today. And here comes the ham and egg pie.'

Phil Walthers tried to compose himself to his ritual of experiencing the delights of a simple repast. Napkin in the right place. A delicate and brief dusting of salt and pepper, purely for form's sake, a sort of obeisance to the gods of kitchens and cooking history. Taking up the knife and fork slowly, almost reverentially. A brief pause to appreciate the enjoyment ahead.

An enjoyment reduced by Frank's tucking in with gusto, using only a fork and spurning the napkin. In anyone else Phil Walthers might have decried such a barbaric approach. With Frank it only made him feel that he was missing some of the pleasure.

Frank finished well ahead of Phil Walthers. He sighed, put his fork down, and stared dreamily into the distance, not uttering a word until the other man had completed his delicate consumption.

'Very well, Frank,' Phil Walthers said, 'dabbing at his lips with his napkin. 'Shall we continue?'

Frank handed over a sheet of paper as the waitress appeared with their Crème Caramels.

'Henry Shaw and Godfrey Boulloin,' he said. 'They were involved in a jewellery heist fifteen years ago, along with two others.'

Phil Walthers nodded as he put his glasses on to read. He waited until the waitress had left before replying. Frank started on his Crème Caramel.

'That was a big story then,' Phil Walthers said.

'All four were picked up a few days afterwards. But they never found the jewellery. This is lovely.'

Phil Walthers took his glasses off and looked at Frank.

'Of course,' he said. 'I'd forgotten about that. I used to do an anniversary story about that for a few years afterwards. Where are the jewels now? That sort of thing. And then I – got bored with it, I suppose. It was pretty obvious that, whatever happened, the jewels would have been cut up and sold off by then, or something to that effect.' He paused. 'But you don't think they were.'

'The thing is, the jewels were given to Martha Shaw's son to look after. He never revealed what he had done with them. Then he committed suicide in prison. Now de Boulloin is out, and I believe he's somewhere in Wellbury, looking for them.'

'Of course! Martha Shaw! If anyone was likely to know it would be Martha Shaw. You think she does know?'

'No, I'm pretty certain she doesn't. But I think de Boulloin thinks she does. I think he was trying to frighten her out of her house. And I think he was trying to frighten Aggie out of the cemetery because her shack is close to where Henry Shaw is buried. And maybe, just maybe, Martha Shaw had him buried with the jewels.'

Phil Walthers stared at him.

'I don't believe it,' he said. 'It's perfectly obvious, now you come to say it, but – well, it's the sort of thing I should have spotted.'

'Ah, but your see, that's the difference between us. You're always looking for the truth. Facts. Something that can be printed.'

'And you?'

'I'm always looking for what people believe to be true. A subtle distinction, but an important one.'

'Do you think the jewels are buried somewhere around Wellbury?'

'No. But, to be honest, that's irrelevant.'

Phil Walters sighed.

'Pity. There was one piece I've always wanted to see. A necklace of red gems shaped like cherry tomatoes, with leaves. It sounded so hideous it deserved to be seen.'

'Cherry tomatoes? I seem to be being haunted by the things.'

'Not if they've been split up and sold off. So what's your plan, Frank?'

Frank grinned at him and leaned forward.

'Don't you think that someone burying such important objects would, however much they might not realise it, be guided by supernatural forces?'

Phil Walthers picked up his spoon and took a small serving of Crème Caramel. He was struggling with an internal battle in which his mind told him both that Frank was talking nonsense and that Frank rarely talked nonsense. Well, not when he was serious. Which wasn't that often. But he might be now. Indeed, he did look serious now. Or perhaps he was taking the editor of the Wellbury Herald for a ride. Which he was quite capable of doing. Or maybe not.

'Ley-lines,' murmured Frank, having finished his own pudding.

'Ley-lines? Really, Frank, this is too much.'

He looked down at what he was eating. Frank had a horrible look in his eyes which reminded him of Dracula with a sense of humour.

'I don't think Frieda was too impressed with your article a few weeks back. Encouraged all sorts of undesirables from places like London. And when Frieda is unhappy, well, you know ...'

'If you're talking about those yobs who attacked the Porridge Place, I am publishing an article thoroughly excoriating such behaviour. We can't have such people coming to Wellbury to indulge in senseless violence.'

'Oh, not only them, there are all sorts of aged hippies turning up in some strange places. Religious nutters intent on creating havoc. Women's groups threatening violence. I hear even the Boy Scouts are thinking of trying a protection racket instead of bob-a-job day.'

'I hope this isn't a case of the police leaning on the press, Frank?'

'Can't be, I'm booked off ill, hadn't you heard?'

'Frank, I think people underestimate you. At least I have. What is it that you want?'

'The Herald comes out on Thursday morning most weeks,' Frank said. 'Just enough time for people to rush off and buy themselves state-of-the-art metal detectors. Not enough time to do anything else, the days are too short. But I suspect they'll all be out at first light on Friday. Along with others.'

'Such as this religious demonstration which starts at nine o'clock on Friday.'

'Which will, strangely enough, purely co-incidentally, follow the ley-lines as discovered in Wellbury.'

Phil Walthers looked up with a grim smile.

'You want the Herald to assist you in torpedoing the religious protest?'

'Oh, no, Mr Walthers, you know me better than that. I just thought I'd mention that Wellbury police are rather concerned about hordes.'

'Hoards?'

'Yes, hordes. We don't want to lose control of them.'

'And these hoards are somewhere along the ley-lines.'

'We believe the hordes will follow the ley-lines, yes.'

'And where in the ley-lines do you expect these hoards to appear, specifically?'

'Well, it's difficult to be precise, but we're expecting them to appear in the early hours of Friday. Quite possibly in the cemetery. Or nearby.'

Phil Walthers considered. Finally he nodded.

'You think Godfrey Boulloin will come out?'

'Exactly. He'll be out there somewhere, terrified that someone else will discover what he thinks is rightly his. And once he is out, and we spot him, we'll have him for the attacks on old ladies. Especially Aggie.'

Phil Walthers smiled. He put down his spoon and held a hand out for Frank to shake.

'The staff of the Wellbury Herald will be proud to participate, the little that they can, in so noble an enterprise. I shall even go so far as to purchase metal detectors for myself and Mrs Blower. As subterfuge, of course.'

Frank grimaced.

'No, Mr Walthers, anything but Mrs Blower. There are too many things that could go wrong as it is.'

'Inspector, if you know of a way of deflecting Mrs Blower, then please let me in on the secret.'

Frank made a few movements with his mouth as if trying to remember how to speak.

'Don't tell her?' he suggested finally.

'Oh, I shan't tell her. But doesn't your wife discover things you don't mean to tell?'

'Not yet she hasn't.'

Phil Walthers returned a grim smile that said, 'Don't worry, she will. Eventually.'

White: The Mason's move. 17. b2-b3

Black: Frank

'Inspector Summers asked me to tell you she's down in the interview room where the double chess board is, Inspector Summers,' Tricia told Frank as he entered her office. 'She said, ITBMA.'

'ITBMA? I've heard of ITMA; It's That Man Again, World War Two radio show. Let me guess: It's That Bloody Mason Again?'

'Apparently so, Inspector. Except that the Inspector didn't use the word "bloody".'

'Excellent. I'm just in the mood for kicking some butt on a chess board. Coming down?'

'Oh, yes please! I haven't seen the board for ages.'

Down in the interview room they found Frieda, Gertie and Sam looking at the double chess board.

'He's pushing another pawn forward,' said Frieda, ' his left knight pawn: b2 to b3.'

Frank studied the board for a few moments.

'He's opening up a path for his bishop,' said Gertie.

'Could be. Bishop to b2, knight to c3, rook pawn to a4. That would allow him to advance on my right flank.'

'You're certainly right about him being cautious, sir,' said Sam. 'Talk about one step at a time.'

'I think it's time to start taking casualties. And giving them. His bishop looks ready for taking.'

'Before you do that, would you like his latest bon mot?' asked Frieda.

'Oh, go on then.'

'Remember Inspector, clue as a cucumber.'

'Clue as a cucumber? What is it with this nutter and his fruits?'

'Can't be a nutter if it's fruits, Frank,' said Gertie. 'It would have to be a fruiterer.'

'Actually it's been vegetables – tomatoes and cucumbers – so that makes him a vegetabler, sir.'

'Maybe it's something to with salads,' suggested Frieda.

'It could be a reference to five a day – does the number five ring a bell?' asked Tricia.

Frank looked around him at them all and shook his head slowly.

'Let it never be said that Wellbury's finest couldn't come up with the weirdest theories without the slightest evidence.'

Frieda coughed modestly.

'Good point well made, Frank,' she said.

Frank sighed.

'Right, oh fruity one, your bishop is toast.'

They watched as he took the white bishop.

'You know, I don't think I've ever had that,' said Tricia.

'Had what?'

'Cucumbers on toast.'

Frank grimaced.

'Cucumbers on toast? If this is Godfrey de Boulloin then he has a sick mind. Cucumbers would make the toast soggy.'

'Frank, darling,' said Frieda, 'I hate to mention this, but if it is Boulloin, then we're dealing with a murderer. And he seems to have a certain fascination for you.'

White: The Mason

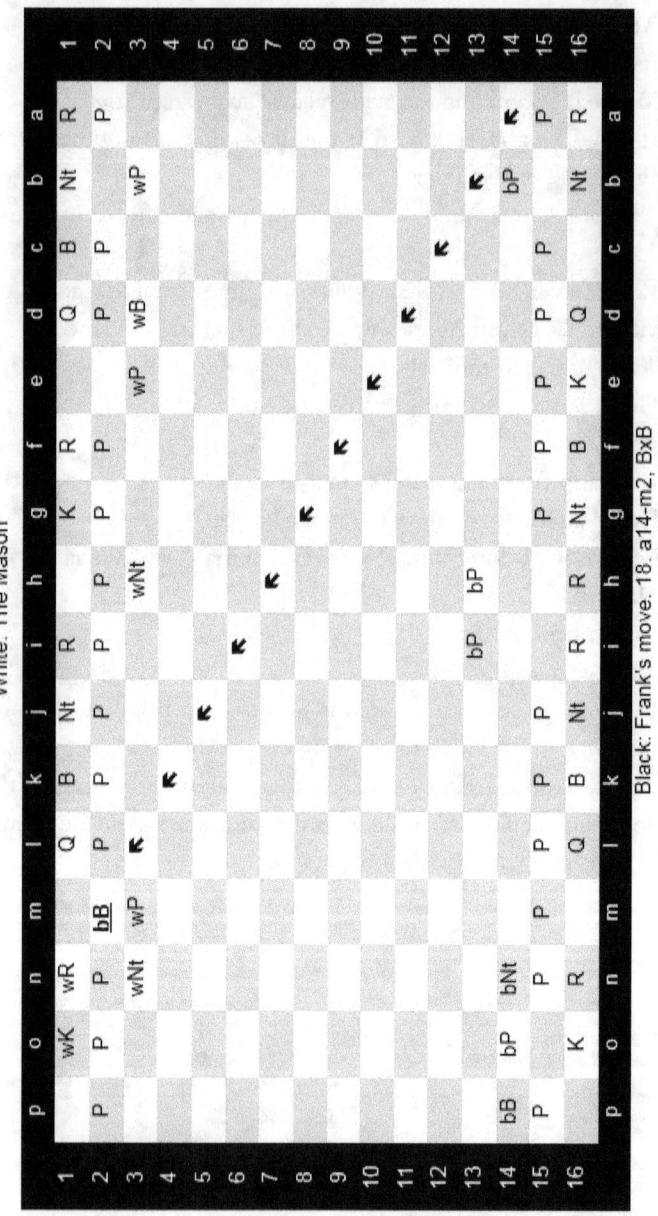

Black: Frank's move. 18. a14-m2, BxB

Wednesday

Frank's plan; Mason, reverse ferret

'Ready for the briefing, Frank?' asked Frieda.

'Ready as I'll ever be.'

'You have given briefings before, haven't you, Frank?'

'Of course. Admittedly the last one started off as "Once more unto the breach dear friends" and ended up as "Let's go nail the bastards", but it worked.'

Frieda sighed.

'Come on, then,' she said.

They passed through reception on their way to the briefing room. Tom and Wilf were sitting on the bench waiting for Susan and Gertie.

'You two are becoming a fixture,' Frieda noted.

'Yes, miss,' said Wilf.

'I don't like people cluttering up reception, it makes the place look untidy.'

'No, miss.'

Frieda gave them another couple of seconds of eyeballing before turning towards the briefing room.

'Just one thing, you two,' said Frank, 'do not, whatever you do, believe anything anybody says about ley-lines.'

'Ley-lines?'

'And especially not buried treasure. It's all complete nonsense.'

'Buried treasure?'

'Good, so long as we've got that covered,' Frank said and followed Frieda.

'What was that all about?' asked Frieda in a whisper.

'They're both educated and intelligent. Imagine if something mentions buried treasure and one of them says, "Ah, but Inspector Summers told us that was nonsense".'

'The other person will respond with something like, "Well, that proves it must be true".'

'Exactly. And anyway, we wouldn't want those two wasting money on metal detectors and wandering around the cemetery uselessly, would we?'

'I think I'd prefer them wandering around the cemetery than cluttering up reception.'

'That's one of the drawbacks to my plan. Too many people hunting non-existent treasure and Boulloin might slip through the net.'

'Speaking about that, I've been thinking. Your plan is that you and Gertie are going to be looking after Martha Shaw's place.'

'Yep. Percy and Pete will be doing the cemetery.'

'Where do you think he's most likely to turn up?'

'If he turns up? Martha Shaw's place. The cemetery is too public.'

'In that case, would you mind if I took the cemetery with Sam? Percy and Peter can hold the fort at the station.'

Frank's eyebrows raised.

'You can't do that. Not in your condition.'

'Frank, I'm only a few weeks' pregnant. It isn't a disease or a crippling condition. I could mention the name of someone else I know who shouldn't be doing anything. Anyway, I'll have Sam with me. She's got black belts in half a dozen of the more lethal martial arts, and she's more than happy to use them.'

'But who will co-ordinate things?'

'Percy, like I say. I'll have my radio. You've got your radio. It is working, isn't it darling?'

'Of course it's working, Free. It only stops working when it gets bored.'

'Ah, I wondered what the cause was. Anyway, I have a feeling that he's going to turn up at the cemetery. He must have read about Angie. I'm surprised he hasn't made his move yet. Providing your theory is correct.'

Frank paused. He gave another grin.

'Ten quid says he turns up at Martha's place,' he said.

'Make it fifty. I can spend it on having my hair done.'

'Fifty it is. That'll buy quite a few pizzas.'

'Listen up now,' said Frank, standing in front of the assembled police officers in the operations room. 'We all know the saying about a battle plan not surviving its first contact with the enemy forces, and our battle plan is pretty dodgy to start with. All I can say is that there is one aim: find Godfrey Boulloin and nick him.'

'Well, at least there is a plan,' murmured Steve Right.

'You said something, Steve?' asked Frank, doing an amazingly accurate rendition of Frieda had she been speaking.

Steve coughed.

'Nossir,' he said, 'just a tickle in my throat.'

'Well, I suggest you take something for it. Because constables Steve Right and Sidney Feeler have been assigned to escort the demonstrators tomorrow. From 08h00, just in case there are any early birds.'

'What? Just the two of us? There's supposed to be thousands of them. Sir.'

Frank smiled.

'I can confidently predict that they are unlikely to number in double figures.'

Glances were passed. Inspector Frank Summers, nice bloke, good in his own way, was a walking disaster when he was confident.

'Okay,' Frank resumed, 'this is how it stands. We have two problems. One is the demonstration for freedom of speech by the Righteous Once, which we expect the Cult of the Clueless and The Old Birds' army to confront, along with a number of other groups. Peacefully, of course. For about ten seconds, after which our peace-loving free-speechers in the Righteous Once are likely to pile into the other two groups, including their allies. The other is our friend Godfrey Boulloin. As you probably know by now, he was the leader of a gang jailed for the jewellery heist fifteen years ago. He got out a couple of months ago. We believe that he thinks that Robert Shaw, his sidekick who committed suicide, left the proceeds with his mother, Martha Shaw. Boulloin seems to have the idea that the jewels are either buried in Martha Shaw's vegetable patch or in Robert Shaw's grave. Or possibly hidden in Martha Shaw's house somewhere. He's been trying to drive Martha Shaw out of her house to give him time search the place thoroughly. And he was trying to drive Aggie out of the cemetery to get at Robert Shaw's grave. This is the theory.'

'Hell of a lot of work digging up a grave that settled,' noted Percy, as if speaking from experience.

'Indeed. And he's got to do it in one night because someone is going to start asking questions when they find a grave dug up. Can't blame everything on the police and zombies. So, we have to do two things: stop the demonstration turning into an all-out fight, and be waiting to nick Boulloin as soon as he comes in range carrying a shovel.'

'What about evidence?' asked Pete. Frank gave a wry smile.

'We don't have any. Unless we catch him in the act of either throwing something at little old ladies, or digging up Shaw's grave, he can tell us to whistle. So we're going to put a little pressure on him. The Herald will tomorrow reveal that the jewels are buried somewhere along the ley-lines in Wellbury. And that we'll be digging them up as soon as we get our kit together. Not explicitly, just enough to let people lead themselves up the garden path.'

The men and women sitting in front of him looked at each other. Then they looked back at him.

'So,' Percy said, 'we're going to let the good folk of Wellbury know that there's some buried treasure out there just waiting to fall into the wrong hands.'

'And the ley-lines are pretty much anywhere you want them to be,' added Pete.

'I believe the Herald might just site them running through the cemetery this time. All those spirits wandering around, lonesome as a cloud. They generate amazing energy which aliens can see because of their advanced eyesight.'

There was a pause as they tried to work out if there was a joke in there somewhere.

'Which means,' Sam Nightingale noted, 'half of Wellbury will be out digging holes, and Godfrey Boulloin will have to get there before they do.'

'Precisely,' said Frank. 'We'll have one team in the cemetery waiting for him, another at Martha Shaw's place, from about 07h00. One or two constables standing outside the front of the cemetery looking bored. One constable overnight at Martha Shaw's place just in case. And if the plan works, half of Wellbury out and about at first light looking for the jewellery, which will reduce the hordes in the demonstration to a manageable half dozen, maybe a dozen. And Steve and

Sid, I want you to count the protestors very carefully, several times, we always get criticised for getting the numbers wrong. And don't let them move too fast, someone might pull a muscle and then we'll need ambulances and all sorts of stuff. And don't forget, stop on the red man and go on the green.'

There was a pointed silence. Finally Sam coughed politely.

'Um, sir, what do we do if the plan doesn't work?'

'Well, Sam, then we go to plan B.'

'Which is?'

'Everyone gets called back to the demonstration and at the first suggestion of violence we climb in and clobber them.'

'I didn't hear that, Frank,' murmured his wife.

'Now that,' said Pete Phillips, 'is my kind of plan.'

'Right,' said Frank, sitting at his desk, 'Let's see what you make of his, Mr Mason. Move number 20. Bishop n14 takes Bishop d3. 20. Bn14xBd3. Press Send, and there, it's gone.'

'But you don't have a bishop on n14,' Gertie said. 'Do you?'

'Not until Squishy knocked over the pieces.'

'Squishy knocked over the pieces?'

'Yup. Just after we received our friend's latest move. Which he hasn't sent. That should muddy the waters quite nicely.'

'What was his latest move?'

'Hmm. Good point.' He scanned the paper. 'a2 to a4, I reckon. Rook pawn advances two spaces. Since he hasn't advanced a single pawn two spaces so far it'll be totally out of character. Should confuse him even more when he hears about it.'

His computer made a pinging sound.

'Well, well, well,' he said. 'Looks like our friend is online. Let's see: 'I haven't made my move yet, Inspector. Number 19.'

Quite correct, Mr Mason, you haven't. Very confusing, isn't it?'

He leaned back.

'Aren't you going to answer?' asked Gertie.

'Oh, tomorrow should be good enough. Let him stew for a while.'

Gertie shook her head in disgusted admiration.

'I'd go mental if I had to wait a day for a reply to that.'

Frank sighed and put his hands behind his head.

'It's the modern world, Gerts. Rush, rush, rush.'

'I don't think it's the modern world, Frank. I think you're just an old-fashioned bastard with a mean streak.'

'Well, there is that, too.'

Thursday

The Mason, querulous; The Herald

'Right, Gerts, what say we reply to our mason friend? He should be nicely stewed by now.'

'Twenty-four hours. Yes, I think I'd be cooking nicely if I hadn't received a response by now.'

'Depends on how old he is. If he's over fifty he probably won't be too bothered. Under thirty – well, apparently some of the younger generation have panic attacks if no-one responds to their text messages in thirty seconds. Right, let's see.' He began typing a reply: "Your move number nineteen received yesterday at 05h30 Zulu stop a2 to a4 stop needed to reset the board after kitten Squishy knocked the pieces over stop query stop stop stop."

'What's with the stops?' asked Gertie.

'Old telegramese, Gerts. Telegram sentences used to have the word stop separating them. I guess you've never received a telegram. I know I haven't.'

'But the "stop stop stop" at the end? And the word "query"?'

'That's my version of his cucumbers. And tomatoes. I just use stops.'

'So you aren't pulling all the stops out?'

'Gertie, if you've picked up my sense of humour ...'

The Wellbury Herald appeared slightly later than usual that Thursday, just before lunchtime. The headline 'Police Desperate To Safeguard Hoards!' caught most people's eyes. According to the article it was believed that Wellbury police had identified areas where hoards were likely to be found, and there was a suggestion that one or more of the hoards were connected to a jewellery heist which had taken place years before, which many Wellburians would remember. The same ley lines which were now inciting people to play out their religious and spiritual beliefs had almost undoubtedly influenced people over the centuries to bury their precious artefacts along those lines. This could well include the young Robert Shaw – one of the gang members, and the only one who had known where the jewellery was hidden - in his choice of hiding space for the jewels. An examination of the astrologic relations of the planets, the moon in the quarter of Venus, and the onset of the Age of Aquarius were all in direct alignment as they had been fifteen years before. Fifteen was, of course, a mystical number, and the fact that the people who had been in Wellbury fifteen years ago were now fifteen years older was, some might believe, a sign of discovery. However the police were taking no chance, and the hoards would be fully protected prior to an urgent police operation due to begin at nine o'clock precisely on the Friday. Inspector Summers refused to rule out the role his luck had played in both the discovery of the Roman hoard so recently (as reported in the Herald) and his careful and professional analysis of the likelihood of further hoards which had revealed the disturbing news. He also refused to confirm that they had used the help of export astrologer Mr Sam Knut (believed to be a direct descendant of King Cnut, or Canute) to pinpoint the direction of the ley lines, nor that they could well be, as many believe, be pointing directly towards the old cemetery. Cemeteries have traditionally been holy places, often associated with burial gifts, so it was entirely possible that the young Robert Shaw might have instinctively buried the jewellery – of great value – in that area. Inspector Summers hadn't been immediately able to confirm that, since the insurance had already been paid out over twelve years before, the jewellery now legally constituted treasure trove, which any finder could keep.

Normally Phil Walthers would have insisted on the addition of several question marks, but in this case he had to agree with Frank that the jewellery had never been found, and must, thus, definitely be out there somewhere. Probably a few continents away, and spread over a few continents, but out there somewhere. At least it was more physically real than ley lines, and he hadn't forgotten that Frieda Summers was still intent on having a word with him about those as soon as she got the chance. He didn't believe in propitiation of the spirits, but Frieda wasn't a spirit.

As for the "treasure trove" claim, that was quite true. Inspector Summers hadn't been able to immediately confirm it because he hadn't been asked to, immediately or otherwise.

Any sensible person would have realised that it was complete nonsense, but it hadn't been written for sensible people.

It probably wouldn't have made a difference. All across Wellbury people were making excuses for a longer lunch hour, taking the afternoon off or having an early weekend. Those who left early enough managed to grab the last few metal detectors from an increasingly bemused shop-owner who hadn't the fortune to be in the delivery area of the Herald. Others found themselves ranging farther afield, many returning late at night. And having an early night.

Black Friday
The hunt

04h00. A dark Friday October morning. Frieda was first up in the Summers' household, by all of four seconds. It allowed her to shower while Frank attended to Squishy's pleas that she was a starving little kitten and why didn't Frank and Frieda get up this early every day like she had always encouraged them to. While Frank showered Frieda dressed and went down to the kitchen to prepare breakfast, a Full English to keep them going.

'Black suits you, you know,' she said as she put the plates on the table and they sat down. 'I've always thought polo-necks do something for a certain type of man.'

'Suits you too, madam,' he grinned. 'And that polo-neck of yours definitely does something for you. Though as a copper I can't help but notice that you look dressed for a spot of cat burglaring. But a very well dressed cat burglar.'

'Cat burglars do not normally wear mascara.'

'You might start a craze. What was the name of that movie with Cary Grant and Grace Kelly?'

'To catch a thief. When I first saw that I empathised with Brigitte Auber, the girl who played Danielle. I think most girls go through an age when they're besotted with an older man, so I think I understood how she felt. Trouble was, it made me also want to have strawberry-blonde hair like hers. Oh, and a pert little snub nose.'

'You have a lovely nose.'

Frieda looked at him.

'You know, if Cary Grant had said that to Grace Kelly on screen I'm sure it would have come across as extremely romantic. This time of the morning, about to go on a stakeout, I'm not so sure.'

'Okay, how about, you look as sexy as all hell in that outfit.'

Frieda paused.

'Better,' she said, 'though even better would be if you weren't mopping up your egg with a slice of bread as you said it.'

After breakfast they washed the dishes just as any normal married police officers might. Then, just before leaving Frank slipped a balaclava hat into his pocket.

'If I have to wear this I'll end up looking like a reject from the SAS. Somehow I've always seen as myself more like Lawrence of Arabia. Flowing white clothes out in the desert.'

'Just make sure you aren't wearing it if you've called in support, Frank, they might think you're the one needing a truncheon over the head.'

'There is that. I don't think anyone would make that mistake with you. You still look like you're in charge, even in that get-up.'

Frieda placed a black scarf over her head and flicked one end back over her shoulder, leaving only her eyes showing.

'And later I might do the dance of the seven veils,' she said.

Frank grinned.

'You don't look like a Cairo dancer, Free,' he said, 'you look like a desert assassin.'

She stuck her tongue out at him. Somehow, with the scarf in the way, it didn't quite work.

'Shall we go, madam? Our various escorts will be waiting.'

In the pre-dawn darkness Frank and Gertie slipped through the gap in the brambles in Martha Shaw's front garden and worked their way silently around to the back door. A light was shining from a chink in the kitchen window. Frank tapped softly on the door.

'Come in, Inspector,' Martha Shaw called.

'How did you know it was me?' he asked, ushering Gertie in before him. He was about to add something when he realised that Martha Shaw was not alone. Georgina Scythe and Mildred Smith sat at the kitchen table, mugs of tea in front of them, a hockey stick next to Mrs Scythe.

'You know Mrs Scythe and Miss Smith?' asked Martha Shaw.

'What are you two doing here? You'll have to leave, I'm afraid. We have a police operation on the go.'

'Which is why we're here, Inspector,' boomed Georgina Scythe. 'To catch that – that thing.'

'Keep your voice down, Mrs Scythe! What are you talking about?'

'You know perfectly well what I'm talking about, Inspector. Though I can't say that I agree with using a free press to spread such a story about. However, if it achieves its aim then I shan't complain.'

'It was that obvious?'

'It was to us. Judging from the number of idiots wandering around in the early hours carrying metal detectors or whatever they're called – well, it appears to have fooled most others.'

'Well, I'm afraid you are going to have to leave, Mrs Scythe. This is no place for you. Godfrey Boulloin might well be armed.'

'So am I,' Georgina Scythe replied, holding up the hockey stick. 'And I'm sure I don't need to point out that trying to forcefully evict myself and Mildred from a perfectly legal social visit will undoubtedly undermine your operation. You wouldn't want that thing scared off by loud noises, I'm sure.'

Frank sighed. He looked at Gertie. She shrugged her shoulders as if to say, 'She's got a point'.

'Where's the constable?' he asked.

'In the lounge.'

'Better check on him, Gerts. Tell him he can be off. Tell him to make sure anyone watching will see him leave.' He turned to Martha Shaw. 'So how did you know it was us?'

She nodded towards the little black and white television.

'Closed circuit television,' she said. 'I had it put in about ten years ago. It only covers the side, unfortunately.'

'Pity. I don't think our friend is likely to waltz up the side path. Speaking of which, we'll need all lights off in about an hour. And then you'll have to go do your shopping, Mrs Shaw. Again, making sure anyone watching sees you leave.'

'Shops won't be open by then.'

'I'm sure there's an all-night petrol station somewhere, Mrs Shaw. Pretend you're an insomniac for a few hours.'

'Blast!' muttered Frieda, peering through a crack in Aggie's shed. 'What are those two idiots doing here?'

'Who?' asked Sam, peering through another crack covering the back.

'Wilf Pleadle and Tom Gregson. The last people I would expect to see wandering around a cemetery with metal detectors. Or a metal detector, singular. How did they get in?'

'By the back like we did?' suggested Sam. Frieda frowned.

'Tom! Wilf!' she called in a low voice. 'Get out of here!'

Tom looked around for the source of this voice. Wilf had his concentration on the earphones he was wearing.

'Who's there?' Tom asked.

'Quietly, Tom! Over here, the garden shed. Quickly!'

Tom took Wilf's arm and hurried them over. Frieda opened the shed door and pulled them in.

'Inspector Summers! What are you doing here? Hello, Sam.'

'More to the point, what the hell are you two doing here?'

'Looking for the lost treasure. The jewels. Wilf thinks they must be buried around here.'

'Did you miss the point where Frank said anyone talking about buried treasure was talking nonsense?'

'Well, um, well, we thought that might just be double bluff ...'

Frieda sighed.

'You're going to have to leave. We're expecting someone called Godfrey Boulloin to turn up as soon as the officer on the gate leaves. As soon as he does we'll have the handcuffs on him.'

'What, just the two of you?' asked Tom, amazed.

'You mean just us two weak women?' asked Sam. 'Perhaps you'd like a one-on-one sometime.'

'Oh, yes, Miss, please, Miss,' said Wilf.

'Shush!' said Frieda. 'That's enough! Come on, you two, out.'

'Someone's coming down the lane,' whispered Sam. 'I can hear them.'

They sat in silence, listening. it took a few seconds before they heard what Sam had heard, the sound of someone whistling.

'Must be someone on the allotments,' said Sam. 'I can't see them.'

'That's how we got in,' said Tom. 'Slipped through the allotments. Wilf almost woke their chap up.'

'Well, I'm not in the army, am I? I'm not used to padding around in the darkness looking for someone to garrotte.'

'It's getting light,' said Sam. 'These two will have to stay here. Boulloin will smell something if he sees them coming out of here. If he hasn't already seen them.'

Frieda sighed. Why, she wondered, did this sort of thing always happen to her? Though usually it was Frank who caused her problems. Instead she now had two overgrown schoolboys to take care of, while Frank and Gertie were no doubt bedded down securely at Martha Shaw's house, the picture of police professionalism.

Constables Steve Right and Sidney Feeler stood at the bottom of the steps leading to the large doors of the Old Town Hall. They had adopted the posture of good-natured but thoroughly bored coppers who were hoping that either (a) their scheduled break would come soon, or (b) something amusing would happen which would allow them to nick someone.

'Eight-thirty,' noted Steve, looking at his watch. 'The demonstrators should be turning up any time now.'

'Hope some of them have remembered to bring some tea,' muttered Sidney. 'It's bloody perishing here. Why do they always build Town Halls in the wind?'

'Oh, look, it's Mr Walthers. Come to take pictures of freezing plods, Mr Walthers?'

'I have come to record for posterity the great demonstration in favour of tolerance,' Phil Walters replied acerbically.

'Somehow it doesn't look as if we'll be overwhelmed with the crush.'

'Surely it's not newsworthy, then?'

'You've heard of the saying, "Dog bites man" isn't news, but "Man bites dog" is?'

'Can't say I have. Have you, Steve?'

'Nope. Where did this happen?'

'What?'

'This man who bit the dog.'

Phil Walthers sighed.

'I think I'll stand a bit further ahead. Close to those Japanese tourists. I forgot my wide angle lens.'

The two police officers watched him trudge up the road.

'Japanese tourists, eh, Steve. What do you make of that?'

'Daft beggars. Where did they come from?'

'Japan?'

'I thought I saw something,' declared Georgina Scythe, on her knees behind Frank, who was looking through a chink in the curtains. Martha Shaw had gone, and the kitchen was in darkness.

'Just a cat,' said Frank. 'Do me a favour, Mrs Scythe. Take that hockey stick out of my back.'

'Sorry.'

Frank glanced at Gertie. He could see that she was trying to stifle a fit of the giggles.

'If Frieda asks, this didn't happen,' he told her.

'You don't suppose he's crawled into the vegetable patch without our noticing, do you?' suggested Mrs Scythe. 'Maybe he's tunnelling away already, keeping his head down.'

Frank considered this.

'No, I don't think so.'

'Probably not,' he added.

'We'll look complete idiots if that's the case,' Mrs Scythe commented. 'At least you will.'

'Thank you for that comforting thought, Mrs Scythe.'

'Someone coming through the allotments,' called Sam. 'Creeping through. Looks like a woman, from the way she's moving.'

'A woman?' asked Frieda.

'Carrying a metal detector.'

'There's another one coming, from the other side. Also female.'

'Tom, you and Wilf keep an eye on the front,' Frieda said, turning to join Sam. 'And don't even think of any smart comments, Wilf.'

Wilf closed his mouth.

'They're converging,' said Sam. 'They'll meet any second now.'

'It looks like Mrs Thomas and Mrs Cromwell,' noted Frieda. 'They're supposed to be demonstrating for religious freedom in half an hour. On the other pavement.'

'Looks like they prefer buried treasure. Strange, I didn't expect women to turn up. More boys with their toys.'

Wilf and Tom exchanged embarrassed glances.

'Here we go,' said Sam. 'The meeting of minds.'

'Mrs Thomas!' they heard a voice exclaim.

'Mrs Cromwell!' replied the other.

There was a pause as they watched the two women trying to conceal their metal detectors behind their backs.

'Thought I'd just pop in and check me aunt's grave,' said Mrs Thomas.

'My uncle's,' replied Mrs Cromwell. 'It's just past that shack.'

'So's me aunt's.'

Another pause.

'You're here for that buried treasure, aintcha?'

'It might appear that way.'

'Tell you wot, we'll share it fifty-fifty. Better that than letting someone else get in ahead of us. Wotcha say?'

'An excellent idea, Mrs Thomas. The fewer people who know the better. Including our husbands.'

'Damn right, Mrs Cromwell.'

They listened as the two women hurried past. Frieda turned around and watched them through a crack in the shed wall.

'I just hope they lose themselves somewhere on the far side,' she muttered. 'Otherwise we might as well give up and go home.'

'A man's coming!' whispered Sam. Frieda shuffled back to her.

'Here we go,' said Steve. 'One bloke carrying placards.'

'One bloke? Not exactly the start of the revolution, is it? Does he look like he's got some tea with him?'

'Doesn't look the tea sort. Good morning, sir, bride or groom?'

'What? What are you talking about?' demanded a small man overwhelmed by half a dozen placards he was carrying.

'Sorry, sir, are you the demonstration or the counter-demonstration?'

'I, officer, am leading the demonstration for respect for religious tolerance and freedom of speech and death to non-believers.'

'Ah, I see, sir. Would you care to give me your name?'

'Certainly not. We live in a free country. I do not have to give my name up to any police officer because he has a whim.'

'Absolutely, sir, I just thought I'd be polite and ask. See, if we have to ask you to pause for traffic or anything like that, well, shouting "Oi, you in the front, hold up a mo", well, it sounds rather rude, if you know what I mean.'

'Well, of course I'm not scared of giving my name, I act for a higher power, earthly dangers hold no fear for me, constable. I am Deacon David Danish, leader of the Righteous Ones. Are you laughing at me, officer?'

'Of course not, sir,' said a voice in front of him.

'Wouldn't dream of it, sir,' said a voice above him.

'Now, if you could move to the right here, sir, this is where the kick-off line for the march is. The protestors against the march will be standing over there.'

'Protestors against the march? I understood that all protest against our protest was going to be banned.'

'Oh, no, sir, couldn't possibly ban protestors protesting about a protest. We'd have to ban people protesting against the protestors protesting the original protest, and where would we be then? We'd end up arresting innocent people like those Japanese tourists, and then we'd have an international incident on our hands in no time.'

'Well, you'll have to have a lot more of your lot if they start causing trouble. My people have strong feelings.'

'Yes, sir, we have plenty of other officers on call. Er, expecting many, are you?'

'Thousands, officer. Thousands. The day of the reverent is dawning. Judgement day is nigh and He will not stay his hand against the idolaters, the unbelievers and the disrespecters.'

'Right you are, sir. Er, before Judgement day comes, you haven't brought any tea with you by any chance?'

'It's getting light,' noted Gertie. 'He'd better come soon.'

'Perhaps he isn't coming,' suggested Mildred Smith.

'Do try to be positive, Mildred.'

'Mrs Scythe, could you keep your whisper down to a shout?'

'Sorry, Inspector.'

'There is one thing that worries me.'

'Only one, Sarge? I mean, sir.'

'If there's nobody here, and nobody at the cemetery, they'll all be at the demonstration. With only two constables to keep order.'

'And if that happens, said Gertie, 'somebody is going to be asking, whose bloody stupid idea was this?'

'Cheers Gertie, thank you for your support.'

'My pleasure, Frank, sir.'

Frieda groaned.

'Mr Thomas,' Sam said. 'And, oh, look, coming along on the right, Mr Cromwell. Both carrying metal detectors.'

'They're supposed to be somewhere else carrying placards. Honestly, men! You can't even rely on them to turn up at a simple demonstration as they promised to.'

'Thomas!'

'Cromwell! What are you doing here?'

'Same as you, I reckon. Looking for some buried treasure.'

'Fifty-fifty?'

'No need to tell the little women.'

'We'd better get on with it. There are loads of cars parked out the front. As soon as that constable goes it's going to be like a circus in here.'

'It already is a circus,' muttered Frieda. She turned to Tom and Wilf. 'Can you see those other two – their wives?'

'No, they've moved out of sight.'

'Pity. I was looking forward to them meeting.'

'I think they might get lost in the crowd,' said Sam. 'Everybody appears to have suddenly realised the way through the allotments is open.'

Frieda put her eye to the gap. Dozens of people had materialised and were pouring through the allotments, like First World War soldiers advancing through a mist, only without the sound effects. As they realised that they were not alone they began racing each other, jumping over runner beans and cloches. Hoods which had been raised over heads made them look like an army of monks. It wasn't long before the hoods came free and the monks turned into normal looking people carrying metal detectors while doing the sprint.

The allotment guard had woken and was waving his arms at them, telling them that they couldn't come in.

'We're not coming in,' shouted one as he raced past, 'we're trying to get out, you pillock.'

'Keep your eyes open for Boulloin,' said Frieda. 'I don't think he'll be in that lot, but you never know.'

'Haven't seen him yet.'

'Interesting,' said Wilf. 'You can tell who the Catholics are. First sight of a crucifix and they pause to make the sign of the cross.'

'Yes,' said Tom, 'I've just seen one fall over his metal detector while doing it.'

'You can spot the non-Catholics, too,' said Sam. 'They seem to think they should do the same, only they don't know how. Looks like most of them are waving a hand across their faces to ward off the evil spirits.'

Frieda closed her eyes. Someone was going to have to explain this to the Chief Constable, and she just knew that person would be her.

'Finally,' said Steve as a group of men appeared, 'these must be some of the real protestors. I was beginning to feel embarrassed for the little fellow over there with his placards.'

'They don't look like protestors to me,' commented Sidney. 'They don't have that – well, protesting look.'

'Good morning sir,' Steve said, 'here for the protest, are we?'

'In a manner of speaking,' replied Seumas. 'We're the counter-protestors. Cult of the Clueless. This is Jaimie, uncle Tom, major Tom, and Tom the Feck. Tom the Feck is an honorary member on account of him actually being a Ranter.'

'A Ranter?'

'Indeed, officer, one of the few left, and as fine a manner of a Ranter as ever lived. Swear something to the nice officer, Tom.'

'Fecking good morning to you, officer,' Tom the Feck said, doffing his cap.

Sidney looked at Steve. Steve looked at Sidney. They shrugged and turned back to the COTC.

'Did you bring any tea?' asked Steve.

'No, but we brought some Bishops,' said Seumas as he and Jaimie slipped a can to each of the police officers.

'Very kind, sir,' replied Sidney as he and Steve palmed the cans and hid them in their helmets. 'We shall avail ourselves of refreshment as soon as we're out of sight of any senior uniforms.'

'Just one other thing, sir,' said Steve, 'may I ask why this gentleman is wearing what appears to be a colander on his head?'

'Oh, I forgot, this is Oh And Litmus.'

'Oh And Litmus?'

'Yes.'

'And the colander is?'

'Spaghetti,' said Oh And Litmus.

'Seumas and Jamie looked at each other. They turned back to the police officers.

'It's a colander,' said Seumas.'

'For protection?' suggested Steve.

'Meatballs,' said Oh And Litmus.

'Perfectly right, sir, I was just about to say that, meatballs,' said Sidney. 'Now, if you could all take your place across the street there, we'll get this demonstration going shortly.'

They watched as the group shuffled and strolled across the street, Seumas giving Deacon Danish dagger eyes.

'What did they say his name was again?' asked Steve. 'The one with a colander on his head?'

'Is that some sort of a test?'

'How do you mean?'

'See if my memory still works.'

'Nah, I just forgot his name.'

'Funny, that, you'd think you'd remember the name of a bloke wearing a colander.'

'Well, it ain't a special colander, is it? My wife's got one just like that.'

'He's got to come,' murmured Frank.

'Unless he knows we're here,' suggested Gertie. 'Or he's at the cemetery.'

'He hasn't turned up there yet.'

'How do you know?'

'Frieda would have radioed me straight away.'

'To keep you informed?'

'To claim her fifty quid.'

'You have a bet on this?' asked Mrs Scythe.

'Competition between spouses, Mrs Scythe. My wife hates losing.'

'I dare say you aren't too fond of it either, Inspector Summers. Indeed, I don't know whether I'd bet on your wife, as a fellow woman should, or on you, as a financial realist might.'

'I don't mind losing against my wife, Mrs Scythe, but I shall be severely not very happy if I lose against Boulloin. I want him and I intend to have him.'

'At this rate, Inspector, it looks like you might have to pop out and find him. He doesn't appear to want to come to you.'

'Looks like that's the last of them,' said Sam.

'And no Boulloin.'

'Maybe Inspector Summers has caught him,' suggested Tom.

'Inspector Summers ... would have informed me had that been the case.'

'How much?' asked Sam.

'Fifty pounds.'

'Ouch. That's a lot to lose.'

'Well, we would be keeping it in the family.'

'And you'd earmarked it already?'

'I was hoping it would fund my next visit to the hairdresser.'

'That would pay for a manicure too.'

Frieda sighed.

'So much for Frank's brilliant plan,' she said. 'It doesn't appear that Boulloin's fallen for it.'

'What now?'

'Give it another half hour. If he hasn't turned up by then I'll radio Frank. We'll get ten or so uniforms to check everybody around here in case he's slipped past us somehow.'

'Oh, no,' groaned Steve, 'don't tell me that's what I think it is.'
'A Catholic priest and one of them Muslim priests, I reckon,' replied Sidney.

'An Omam.'

'Eee-mam, I think.'

'He-man?'

'No, Ee-mam.'

Steve sighed.

'Well, at least that little fella will finally have some company, I'm beginning to feel quite sorry for him, all on his tod. Good morning, Father, Imming, you'll be joining the protest for religious tolerance, I take it?'

'Indeed we will,' replied Father Brown. 'We'll be marching with the Clueless and the Old Birds.'

'Um, but Father, they're the counter protestors.'

'And we shall be counting ourselves amongst them. I'm a Doubter, and the Imam here is a Sufi. Come, John, I can see the clueless over there.'

Steve and Sidney watched them walk away. Steve looked at Sidney. Sidney looked at Steve.

'Well, let's just hope no trouble breaks out then,' Steve decided.

'Sufi,' commented Sidney. 'Sounds like a Julie Andrews song. I could do with a song and a bit of tap-dance. Warms you up, both physically and psychologically.'

'Leave it out, Sidney. We've got enough problems with this lot, we don't need chimney sweeps and milk maids and nuns added to the brew.'

'Nice word that, brew.'

'Should've brought some straws. Long ones.'

'And those Australian helmets.'

'Option one,' said Frank, 'somehow he knows we're in here and isn't going to appear until he knows that we've definitely gone.'

'You could go and leave Mildred and I to detain him,' suggested Georgina Scythe.

'I rather think not, Mrs Scythe. Option number two, he's guessed our little plan and intends to lie low for a few days.'

'But then he runs the risk of losing the jewellery,' Gertie pointed out.

'If he gets nicked for attacking little old ladies it won't matter whether he loses the jewellery or not. He'll still be on parole. Can't spend it inside.'

'If he's laying low there's not much we can do.'

'No. But there is option three. He is out there trying to get to it before anyone else, but it isn't here or in the cemetery. The question is, where? Where else would he think it might have been hidden?'

He looked at his watch.

'I think I cocked this one up,' he said. 'I should have asked Mrs Shaw more questions. Such as whether her son had a girlfriend at the time. Or an ex-girlfriend he could rely on. Or even a boyfriend. That'll teach me to rush in with all guns blazing.'

'There is a tide in the affairs of man,' said Mrs Scythe. 'You took it at the flood, Inspector, just the way I would have. We just have to accept that sometimes it doesn't work out the way we want it to.'

'Can you hear singing, Mrs Scythe?'

'Singing? No, I can't say that I can.'

'Well, then, Mrs Scythe, it ain't, as they say, over yet.'

He switched his radio on.

'Free?' he said softly.

316

'Frank?'

'It's a no-show here.'

'It's a full turn-out here, Frank, Uncle Tom Cobley and all. Unfortunately we're missing the key player.'

'We'll wait until Martha Shaw gets back. Then we'll head back towards the station.'

'Okay, Frank. We'll finish up here. See you later.'

He switched the radio off. Georgina Scythe looked at him.

'Aren't you supposed to say over and out and that sort of thing?' she asked.

'Probably.' He stood up and stretched. 'I've never bothered.'

'Well, Inspector, it seems we won't have the delight of belting several sorts of nonsense out of him. However the day is yet young. We still have a protest march to protest against. Come along, Mildred.'

'Try not to beat them up too badly, Mrs Scythe. I'm sure they don't deserve it that much.'

'Ah, there you are wrong, Inspector, they have been oppressing women for thousands of years. Now they have thousands of years of retribution to take.'

'Can we go play with our toys, now, Miss?' asked Wilf. Frieda gave him a glare.

'I could suggest several things you can do with your toys, but I will restrain myself. Get along with yourselves.'

The two men opened the shed door and hurried away like two schoolboys released from detention.

'I think it must be something in the water,' the others heard Wilf say. 'Either that or they grow some strong women in these parts.'

'Cheeky sod,' said Sam. 'But cute in a way. So, what now, ma'am?'

'Back to the station. I'll get a few uniforms to keep an eye on things. If they see anyone digging up buried treasure they can nick them. If they see anyone digging things up without finding buried treasure – well, it will probably be good for the flowers I would imagine.'

'One Judgement Day nutter,' muttered Sidney, 'and it's almost quarter to. If no-one else turns up he's going to have to march by himself. And I ain't carrying those placards of his.'

'Hang on,' said Steve, 'here come some more.'

'Oh, god, three old women, one in a mobility scooter. If ever you want a religious nutter, look for the old women. Good morning, madam, are you here for the peace protest?'

'No, young man, we are here for the war protest.'

'War protest?'

'Yes, if any of those silly religious men start their nonsense we're going to war.'

'Have you seen any cyclists, officer?' asked Mildred.

'And we don't take no prisoners.'

Steve looked at Sidney. Sidney looked at Steve. They turned back to the three women.

'Did you, by any chance, and this is an official question I have by law to ask you, bring any tea, perchance?'

'Certainly not, young man, we are here to protest, not to have a picnic. Come, Mildred, Marjorie, let us join the others. And I will be asking questions of those TOBs who haven't turned up.'

The two constables turned at the sound of clinking noises behind them. They found a family of four setting up folding chairs and a table.

'Do you mind if we ask you what it is you're doing, sir?' asked Steve.

'We're spectators,' answered the man. 'We want the kids to see a real life demonstration. They probably won't get many chances. Closest we got when we was kids was stuff on the telly from foreign parts. Me dad used to go on about the demos he went to as a young lad. Real ones with real rocks being thrown about.'

'Spectators?'

'There'll be others along shortly. We're a club, really, go all over to do things.'

'Well you can't do it from here, sir. I'm afraid this is a police area.'

'We brought some tea and something to eat,' the man said, bringing out a Thermos.

'Ah.'

'No girlfriends, Mrs Shaw?' asked Frank.

'Not that I knew of. And if he had a girlfriend that Boulloin person would have known more than I did. So he would have got in touch with her first, wouldn't he?'

'Maybe he did. Maybe she convinced him that she knew absolutely nothing about the jewels.'

'Too many maybes for my liking, Inspector.'

'True. Unfortunately that happens a lot in our job. You'll be okay by yourself?'

'Don't worry about me, Inspector. I've been taking care of myself for a long time now, and I'll be doing it until the day I die.'

'Nine-thirty,' noted Steve, looking at his watch. 'It was supposed to be a nine-o'clock start. I'm sorry, sir,' he called to the Deacon, 'but we're going to have to make a move or we'll run out of time. The march has to be over by eleven or we'll be making traffic jams.'

Deacon Danish sat on the town hall stairs, dejected head drooping, placards dropped on the pavement.

'They betrayed me,' he sobbed. 'Even Mohammed. They must have gone searching for the gold. Oh! To worship golden idols!'

'There, there, Thumper,' said Seumas, coming up next to him and patting his shoulder, 'I'm sure they would have been here if they knew what an effort you made.'

'Judases! They could have told me they weren't coming.'

They were joined by the protest protestors and the Japanese tourists. Seumas looked down at the little man sitting with his head in his hands.

'Oh, the hell with it,' he exclaimed. 'Tell you what, Thumper, we'll give you a hand with these placards. Come on, everyone, grab a placard and let's get this protest on the march!'

The others gathered around.

'This is absurd,' commented Georgette Scythe. 'I like it.'

'Remember what Nietsche said,' said Jaimie.

'Fiddlesticks to Nietsche,' replied Georgette Scythe.

'No, that was Kierkegaarde. Nietsche said, There's no such word as Kant in my dictionary.'

'Feck,' said Tom the Feck, 'a Ranter must, by nature, be a protestor.'

'Islam is a religion of tolerance,' noted the Imam as he picked up a placard and read the message.

Steve looked at Sidney. Sidney looked at Steve.

'Well, the sooner you buggers get this protest over, the sooner we can get back to the station for a mug of, er, tea. Come on, Steve.' They bent down and picked up a banner each.

'Come on now, look sharpish you lot, heads up, chests out, put some pride in it.'

Phil Walthers shook his head one final time and started taking pictures of the protest which would be known later as the Wellbury March.

Eric Johns raised his eyebrows as Frank and Gertie entered the station.

'Everybody seems to be wearing black today,' he noted. 'Is there something I should be aware of?'

'Just a stake-out which didn't work, Eric. Everything quiet around here?'

'Quiet as the graveyard.'

'From what I hear the graveyard isn't that quiet at the moment. Frieda back yet?'

'Up in her office. She looks about as happy as you do.'

Frank and Gertie left him humming to himself, skimming through a tabloid newspaper. He congratulated himself on never having had the urge to become a detective. They were out at all hours in all weathers. He had a comfy desk job with set hours, and the only task he had had to perform so far that day was to release an overnight drunk. A very quiet drunk who left meekly. With some foreign surname which sounded like a cube of Oxo.

Frank stood looking out of the window in Frieda's office. Frieda sat behind her desk, Gertie in one of the chairs, Sam standing near the door.

'Well,' said Frank, 'at least the demonstration went off without a problem.'

'Went off with hardly any demonstrators,' noted Frieda. 'Most of them were running around the cemetery with metal detectors when we left. So, yes, at least that part of your plan worked.'

Frank turned and smiled.

'Daft bunch. I was thinking that, if Martha Shaw buried those jewels with her son, somebody would have to dig down quite a way to recover them. Not the easiest of tasks, and certainly not something you could do without someone noticing.'

'And illegal without a permit.'

'Mmmm.'

'Thinking, Frank?'

'Nope. Mind's a blank. I just can't figure out why Boulloin didn't turn up. If the theory is correct – that he was trying to frighten away Aggie and Mrs Shaw for long enough to do some digging – then he definitely wouldn't have stayed away knowing that half of Wellbury were about to turn up with shovels in their hands. But he didn't turn up. Which suggests that the theory is wrong.'

'Maybe he didn't know. Perhaps he isn't the type who reads newspapers or listens to the radio.'

'If it is him he must try to keep up with the news. How else would he know our reaction to these attacks?'

'He could be lying in a bedsit reading cheap novels or watching television,' said Sam. 'After all, if it is him he's been working mostly at night.'

'Good point, Sam. I'll ask Percy if he can spare Pete Phillips to do the rounds of cheap bedsits and rooms to let.'

Martha Shaw heard a noise behind her as she weeded her vegetable patch on her knees. She turned to find a man bending over her. He had crewcut hair, tattoos on his arms, and a carving knife in his hand.

'Don't make a sound,' the man said. 'Get up and walk over to the back door there.'

She stood up slowly and moved to the door, keeping half an eye on the man.

'Inside.' She stepped inside. 'Now, sit down there with your hands on your knees where I can see them.'

She did as she was told. The man turned another kitchen chair backwards towards her and straddled it.

'Now, Mrs Shaw, you're going to tell me where that stuff is.'

'You must be Godfrey de Boulloin. Though I don't remember your face.'

The man chuckled.

'Godfrey's far away,' he said. 'In another life, you could say. But before he went there he told me all about it. Since he won't be coming back I thought I might as well have those jewels myself. And his very recognisable name kept the coppers on the wrong track. Now where are they? The jewels?'

'I don't know where they are.'

'Now, Mrs Shaw, I really don't like hurting people. But you'll tell me sooner or later. Everyone has their breaking point, believe me.'

'I have no doubt that you're right. But I still don't know what my son did with whatever it was he stole.'

'He wrote you a letter before he topped himself. I know, one of the lads took it when he got out. Godders told me.'

'Yes, and I burned it without reading it.'

'You what?'

'I don't know what was in it, but I can guess. Another snivelling rant about how life had been unfair to him. He sent quite a few of those. Had I known that it was the last one he would send I would probably have read it, but I didn't.'

323

'I don't believe it. A letter from your own son? And you never read it? What sort of a mother are you?'

'You never met my son, did you, Mr – whatever your name is.'

'No.'

'He had the ego of his father without what little brains my husband had. He thought he was cunning, but he was just a sneak. Underhand. Even at school. Even as he was growing up I often wished he had died at birth. Sometimes I wished that I had smothered him, for my good, if not that of society.'

The man's jaw dropped.

'That's a horrible thing for a mother to say.'

'He was a horrible thing. Simple as that. He was a good advert for abortion.'

The man blinked.

'Blimey, you're a real hard one, aren't you?'

'Sometimes you have to be. Now, I am going to make a cup of tea. You will have to decide what you are going to do, but if you think the jewels are around here you're mistaken. They certainly aren't in the vegetable patch, I've dug that down to bedrock.'

'Don't try anything, now.'

She ignored him and set about filling the kettle. He gnawed at his thumb.

'You must have some idea where they are,' he said.

'If I did I would have got rid of them years ago. As you can see, I'm hardly living a life of luxury.'

'You would have sold them?'

'Naturally. Wouldn't you?'

'Yeah, but you're ... '

'I'm what?'

'Well, you aren't a crook or anything. I mean, that's stolen goods we're talking about. You would have given them in, wouldn't you?'

'Perhaps. Possibly, then. Not now. Now, for various reasons, I don't give a damn. Anyway, the question is immaterial. Whatever my son did with them no-one has been able to find them in all these years. Either he hid them too well or someone disposed of them. Though quite why so many people are wandering around with metal detectors I don't know. Maybe that's got something to do with it.'

'What? Metal detectors? What people?'

'It was in the news yesterday.' She nodded towards a copy of the Herald on the table. He snatched at it and skim-read the front-page article.

'Bloody hell!'

'I take it you don't read newspapers.'

'I was otherwise detained yesterday.'

He threw the paper to one side and leaned over, his elbows on his knees.

'Bloody hell!' he repeated.

'I haven't heard of anyone finding anything,' she continued, 'and I very much doubt whether anyone will.'

'What makes you say that?'

'Just what I said a few moments ago. If they haven't been found in fifteen years they aren't likely to suddenly turn up now. Unless they're in someone's attic and they decide to have a clear-out.'

'Whose attic?'

'Who knows? My son didn't have any friends that I knew of, not what you would call friends, but perhaps he left the jewels with someone to look after, someone who didn't realise what they were looking after. Or perhaps he hid them in a drain or culvert somewhere. Perhaps they're lying under a car-park somewhere.'

'A car-park? Where?'

'Mr – what is your name?'

'Call me Bert. That'll do.'

'Well, Mr Bert, tell me, were you the one who threw the rocks through my front window? And the ones over the back?'

'Yeah, well, sorry about that. I was just trying to scare you off for a night or two so's I could get into your garden without being disturbed. I didn't mean to hurt you or anything.'

'And the rock that hit Aggie?'

'That was an accident. I just wanted to scare her away so's I could have a look at your son's grave. Godders – Godfrey – told me he reckoned you might have buried them there. He said you was strange that way.'

'You are a remarkably stupid man, Mr Bert,' Martha Straw said as she turned towards the shrieking kettle.

'You wot? Now you'd better watch what you say, missus. Just remember I've got a knife here, and I've used it before and I'll use it again if need be. You're the only one who knows what I look like, and that could be a problem for me.'

'I wouldn't say all men are remarkably stupid, but the one I married was, and his son was even worse. And it strikes me that you're in their league. You look at me and you see a little old lady in her kitchen making a nice cup of tea, don't you?'

'Eh?'

'Tea, Mr Bert, requires boiling water. Have some.'

She took the lid off and flung the kettle at him. He looked at it coming towards him, stunned. He jerked his arm up just as the boiling water hit his face. He fell back onto the floor, eyes closed, screaming, trying to brush the scalding liquid from his face. She picked up her spade, stepped over, and brought the flat side down on his head as hard as she could. His screams collapsed into a gurgle, and then he was silent.

She looked at his body for some seconds, as if pondering on whether to give him another blow. Then she turned towards a drawer and took out some gardening twine. She tied his arms in front of him, and his ankles together. Having made sure the knots were tight she recovered the kettle, filled it with water, and put it on the stove to boil once more. Following that she mopped the floor around him. Once that was done and the kettle boiled she made herself a cup of tea, fetched a garden fork in from outside, and sat watching him, sipping at her tea. It was some twenty or so minutes before be began to come to, groaning. It took another five for him to recover sufficiently to remember where he was and what had happened. All that time Martha Shaw looked upon him in silence.

'You tried to kill me!' he exclaimed as her face swam into focus. 'Bloody hell! My face! I'm burning to death.'

'I'll fetch a mirror in shortly,' she said. 'I believe the word is blotchy. Though I wouldn't worry too much, you weren't exactly an oil painting beforehand.'

'You're crazy! You're mad!'

'Well, that would be open to interpretation. There are a number of people who would think that I should have killed you straight off, and I don't believe any of them are regarded as mad.'

'Straight off? What do you mean, straight off?'

'I mean that I'm wondering whether you'll make good compost for my vegetable patch. Blood is very good, of course, full of protein. They sell it in boxes, you know, blood and bone. In powdered form. Fresh is much better, of course, much better. Old battlefields are famous for their lush growth. But not too much in one spot, not for vegetables. I could slit your throat just a little and make you crawl around, a bit like a walking watering can, only with blood. That should do it.'

The man named Bert opened and closed his mouth a few times.

'You can't do that! That's murder! You'll never get away with it.'

'I don't see why not. The police are looking for Godfrey Boulloin. Who is apparently in a different world. No-one knows you're here.' She sipped her tea. 'When one hasn't a television and doesn't get out much one has to make up one's own entertainment, you know. Would you like a slow and lingering death, or something a bit faster? But that's my decision, really, isn't it.' She sighed and put her cup down. 'It all depends on how entertaining you are, really.'

'Enter- enter- You are mad!'

'Shall we try with the fork first? Make a few holes and see how much blood comes out? Not too much, not in the kitchen, I've just mopped up.'

'Get away from me!' he cried, crawling to the back door on his knees and elbows as she stood up and lifted the fork. 'Help! Help! Someone help, she's going to kill me!'

'Now, now,' Martha Shaw said, following his scrabbling body out towards the vegetable patch. 'No-one will hear you, they've all gone to work. They've got these lovely little white collar jobs for little white collar men and white collar women. In little boxes, all the same. There's a song about that.'

'Help!' he screamed as he felt the prongs of the fork in his buttocks. 'Help me! Help me, someone!'

'A bit closer to the right, Mr Bert, that's where the broccoli is going in. They do very well with a good dose of bone meal.

Keep away from the cabbages, I promised one to a police officer and I wouldn't want him cooking it with your blood on. It's not in the recipe.'

'Help! Oh, please someone, help!' whimpered the man, his voice going, his strength ebbing.

'Of course hair is a problem,' Martha Shaw continued, sitting on an upturned bucket, 'I find it never decomposes fast enough. I don't know why that is. But it does mean I might have to shave you beforehand. Well, shear you, anyway.'

'Please, no, please, please, please ...'

'Fortunately you aren't too fat. Fat does tend to be another problem. I could burn you, I suppose. But I don't think I could stand the smell.'

'Please let me go, please let me go,' the man pleaded, his eyes closed.

'Shall we cut a slice of you off to see?' asked Martha Shaw as the sound of a siren came dimly through the brambles at the front. 'We could watch it burn together. Wouldn't that be nice? What bit do you think will be best?'

'Oohh, nooo,' moaned the man, oblivious to the sound. 'Please, please, no ...'

'Oh, that is a nuisance,' said Martha Shaw as Frank came crashing around the corner, Gertie immediately behind.

'Mrs Shaw? Are you okay? Someone phoned saying they could hear screams coming from here.'

'Well, I am a bit put out that you got here so quickly, Inspector. I was hoping to have a little more fun with this – thing.'

The thing looked up and realised that he was no longer alone with the madwoman.

'Help me! Help me! She's going to murder me! Please, you've got to help me.'

'He's the one who has been attacking helpless little old ladies. He's not Godfrey de Boulloin. Calls himself Bert. I think he might have done away with Boulloin'

'Is he, now?' asked Frank, squatting next to the man. 'Would that be true, sir?'

'You've got to help me! She's mad! Stark staring raving mad!'

'Is she, now? She looks like a perfectly harmless little old lady to me. Now, tell me, are you the one who has been going around frightening the poor old dears?'

'I didn't mean to harm them! That old biddy was an accident! This one's the one who needs locking up. She threw boiling water all over my face.'

Frank raised his eyebrows at Martha Shaw.

'Indeed, I did. I thought it fair return for his holding a knife on me. You'll find the knife in the kitchen.'

'I wasn't going to hurt her. It was just for show. And she stuck a fork in me.'

'It's the problem of not having a telephone, Inspector. I knew my voice wouldn't carry sufficiently, so I had to use him as a loudhailer. I think it worked rather well.'

'It certainly seems to have done the trick,' said Frank. 'Now, I think we'll start with your real name, please sir.'

'I need to be taken to a hospital! My face is burning off!'

'Oh, don't worry, we'll get someone to have a look at you. In fact I know the very person.' They turned as two uniformed constables came crashing round the corner.

'Ah, Sid, Steve. Put some handcuffs on him, untie that string, and take him down to the station. Get the doctor to have a look at him. Oh, he's our rock-throwing, little-old-lady frightener.'

'Is he, now?' asked Steve, the look of sympathy on his face disappearing. 'We'll take good care of him, sir.'

'Now, Inspector, would you like a cup of tea?' asked Martha Shaw as the man named Bert was taken away. Frank turned to her, about to decline.

'Ah, well, that would be lovely, Mrs Shaw,' he decided instead. 'I could do with a cup after that. I'm sure you could, too. You must have been pretty shocked.'

She smiled thinly as they walked back to the kitchen.

'Terrified, Inspector. Until I realised just what a stupid man he was. And he had a hangover, just like my husband always had. And then I suppose all the anger came out. At last I had something I could hit back at. And then, once I had him tied up I enjoyed myself enormously. A little payback for those poor little old ladies too frightened to go outdoors. You see, the worst thing is that he just doesn't understand. He says he wasn't intending to harm anyone, but the damage he did was very real. Innocent old women too scared to go outdoors, trapped in their houses and flats? And what will the courts give him? A suspended sentence? A – what do they call them, ASBO, an anti-social behaviour order? No, he needed a good lesson. And I certainly hope I gave him one.'

'Sit down, Mrs Shaw,' said Gertie, taking the kettle from her trembling hand. 'I'll sort the tea out.'

'Thank you, my dear, I do feel a bit wobbly.' She sat down and then beamed at Frank. 'Do you know, I suggested that I should cut a bit of him off and we could watch it burn together. And he believed me.'

Frank smiled, and winked at her.

'Now, Mrs Shaw, you need to try to relax and not talk too much. Especially not to two police officers who will have to stand up in court and relate what they had seen and heard. What we can remember, of course.'

'I hadn't thought about that. I suppose I'll have to go to court too?'

'Probably. But it depends on whether or not our friend makes a full confession.'

'Don't say a word, Marti,' boomed a voice from the kitchen door. Georgina Scythe flowed in, followed by a nervous Mildred Smith. 'Not a word until your lawyer gets here!'

'Georgina, what are you doing here?'

'That young lady gave me a call,' the other woman replied, nodding at Gertie. 'One good thing about those blasted mobile phones. Said you'd been attacked.'

'Mrs Shaw very bravely fought off her attacker, took him prisoner, and presented him to us,' said Frank. 'And now, it's time Gertie and I got on with work. You'll be okay, Mrs Shaw?'

'She'll be fine,' decided Mrs Scythe. 'Now, Marti, none of that tea nonsense, what you need is a good brandy. And it gives me an excuse to have one too. And just by coincidence I have a bottle of the good stuff here.'

'All's well that ends well, then, sir,' said Gertie as she drove them back to the station. 'Looks like your luck is still in.'

'Would you mind not mentioning my so-called luck, Gertie?'

'Sorry, Sarge, sir. But things did finally turn out your way, didn't they?'

'Apart from our mysterious chess opponent. But, yes, I'm glad we got that sorted. Though I'm not sure whether "we" is the right word. In fact it could be argued that all that Wellbury police force has achieved is to create a run on metal detectors. But I don't think we should mention that too loudly.'

'No, Sarge, sir, probably not. And I'm sure that Wilf will get bored with his soon enough. Either that or I'll hide it away somewhere.'

Frank rubbed his jaw.

'The thing is, if our friend Bert was behind all the attacks – all of them – that means that our chess fiend is probably just some harmless lunatic.'

'Harmless lunatic?'

'Yes, I don't think we need bother with him any longer.'

'Ah, Frank,' said Frieda as he walked into her office, 'good work in nailing that odious little – thing – this morning'

'All credit goes to Martha Shaw,' Frank replied. 'My calculation of when he'd hit was slightly out – by about two hours.'

'Not at all, Frank. There was one thing you couldn't know. At five in the morning – overnight, actually – our friend Bert, calling himself Godfrey Boullion, was spending his time in our very own cells. He was arrested late yesterday afternoon for being drunk and disorderly. It seems he was getting depressed with so few results and our getting in his way he decided to start drinking earlier than intended and just carried on.'

'Bit of a bummer. If he'd been on time I'd be claiming my fifty quid.'

'There's another thing, though. Our famous mason. He's sent another email.'

'Anything interesting?'

'Oh, very interesting. That plan you had, sending him a move that was impossible.'

'He's complained, has he.'

'He's sent a photograph showing his board as evidence. He's using a large piece of paper instead of an actual board, and you can see why. Let me show you.'

She turned the screen. Frank studied it for a few seconds and then grinned.

'Oh, yes! The perfect shot!'

The screen showed a large piece of cardboard very similar to Frank's paper, with only one piece out of position. Plus alongside it a key to a hotel room, with the key-holder showing the room number and hotel's name.

'I think I'll go have a word with our mason,' Frank said, standing up.

'I've asked Pete Phillips to keep an eye on the hotel, just in case he thinks of checking out before you get there. Percy's in contact with him.'

'We've got him,' said Pete Phillips over the radio. 'He's in his hotel room right at this minute. And it's got Internet access. It has to be him.'

'Well,' said Percy Hanson, 'what are you waiting for? Go in and get him.'

Pete Phillips hesitated. He didn't know why, but something felt slightly wrong. Still, Percy was an inspector, and an order was an order.

'Right, sir,' he said. 'And if there's someone on reception I might even ask for a key.'

There was someone on reception. Someone who refused categorically to allow Pete Philips to go anywhere without a search warrant. They were still disagreeing when Frank turned up with Gertie and Sam.

'What's going on, Pete?' Frank asked.

'This young woman says we can't go anywhere without a search warrant.'

Frank looked at the young woman behind the reception desk and gave her his best 'carefree young bachelor currently available smile', forgetting that he was now married. He showed her his warrant card.

'Inspector Frank Summers,' he introduced himself. 'We'd like to have a quiet chat with the gentleman in 33C. We're pretty sure he isn't violent – well, largely sure – but we don't want to take any chances. So if you have a spare key we could borrow ...?'

The dismissive look on her face made it clear that any slight attraction the bachelor Frank Summers might have once had thoroughly disappeared.

'I said search warrant, and I meant search warrant. I don't care if he's a sergeant and you're an inspector and the others are generals or admirals, no search warrant no entry.'

Frank smiled at her. He pointed to the corner.

'Oh, look,' he said, 'a squirrel.'

She whipped around, hand to mouth.

'A squirrel? Where? Where?'

It took a few seconds for the truth to sink in. She turned around to find Pete and the others looking back to where Frank had just disappeared up the stairs.

'Oh, no, you don't,' she said, 'I'm calling the police.'

'Look,' Pete said, pointing to another corner, 'another squirrel!'

'I'm not falling for that one again,' said the receptionist.

'That's not a squirrel,' said Gertie, 'it's a rather large spider.'

'A spider!' squeaked the girl, managing to turn around and sit on the reception desk with her legs tugged up in one fluid movement. 'No! No! Where?'

It took a few more seconds for the silent sound behind her to alert her to the fact that she was now on her own. She turned to confirm it.

She sighed.

She sat down in her chair, picked her mobile up and texted her best friend. It would be a waste of time phoning the police, and least her friend would commiserate with her. And they could exchange gossip.

Up on the third floor the others caught up with Frank waiting outside room 33C. He held up a hand for silence. He knocked quietly on the door.

They held their breaths as the sound of a man asking who on earth that could possibly came through the door as it opened.

'Inspector!' exclaimed the man who had appeared.

'Mr Sampson!' exclaimed Frank.

'What a surprise! I was going to call on you, but I thought you'd be far too busy to spare time for an itinerant salesman.'

'You were going to call on me?'

'Yes, the misunderstanding with the chess game. I can't think how it happened. I thought perhaps someone had accidentally sent an email to you which collided with one of mine and got confused, but my son tells me that's just silly.'

Frank looked at the other man beaming back lopsidedly through his pebble glasses.

'Now just a minute, Mr Sampson, I think there are one or two questions I'd like to ask you.'

'Ah, yes?' He looked behind him. 'Well, I would invite you in, but it's only a small hotel bedroom, no room to swing the proverbial, eh? Perhaps we could retire to a local hostelry for a drink – unless you're on duty, of course.'

'I am most certainly on duty, Mr Sampson. And before we go anywhere I'd like some answers. Such as why you signed yourself "Mason" on your emails?'

The man looked puzzled at first, and then turned red.

'I didn't, did I?'

'Don't tell me you don't know how you sign your emails.'

Sampson wrung his hands a few times while opening and closing his mouth.

'Um. Well, it's a little embarrassing, really, Inspector. Because the answer is, no, not really. You see, I suffer from a slight degree of dyslexia. Well, a severe form of dyslexia, actually. I asked my wife to set up an automatic signature on my email account. A few weeks back it got lost while I was on the road so I fixed it. Or at least I thought I'd fixed it. Because I don't actually see it each time when I press the send button, well, I didn't think to look. Because it's automatic, you see. And anyway, I'd probably read it as Sampson because that's what I thought I'd set it up to be. I do that sort of thing, you know.'

'You expect me to believe that, Mr Sampson?'

'My daughter's got that,' offered Pete. 'Dyslexia. Not as bad, though. She's having extra teaching for it.'

Frank gave him a look which told him quite clearly who was running this particular investigation.

'Oh, yes,' said the other man seriously, nodding his head, 'it's somewhat of a trial. But I try to keep my chin up and sing. You must tell your daughter not to worry too much, things will work out.'

'This wife you've suddenly acquired - I thought you lived with your mother,' said Frank.

'Oh, yes,' beamed Sampson, 'my wife and mother get on like a house on fire. They're best of friends.'

'I've never understood that saying about a house on fire,' offered Pete, 'I mean, a house on fire is burning down.'

'Right,' said Frank, glaring at Pete as Gertie's mouth screwed up, 'well, how's this for something you'd better have a good explanation for. How did you know I was booked off? And how did you get hold of my wife's email address and why did you send all the emails to her?'

Sampson blinked.

'But I didn't,' he said. 'I sent them to inspector dot f dot summers at wellbury police dot org. I knew the last bit was right, I saw it in an article in the Herald, it was asking for witnesses.'

'Precisely,' said Frank, 'that's not my email address. Mine is just frank-dot-summers.'

'Not your email address? Oh, really, Inspector, you can't really expect me to believe that your wife is also Inspector Frank Summers? I mean, I know my children think I will fall for any practical joke going, but that's really too much.' He chuckled.

'I'm not joking, Mr Sampson, that is indeed my wife's email address. Her name's Frieda, hence the 'f.''

Sampson's mouth opened a couple of times again before managing to say something.

'Oh, dear, that is a coincidence. But how was I to know? Still, no harm done, look on the bright side, that's my motto. I mean, obviously, apologies to your wife, but it was kind of a genuine mistake.'

'That's your motto,' Frank said very, very slowly. 'And I suppose, were you to type that out it might come out as 'that's my tomato'?'

'Don't be ridiculous, Inspector,' Sampson chuckled, 'I wouldn't ... I didn't, did I?'

'Yes, Mr Sampson, you did. Along with "Clue as a cucumber", "Vintage is mine, sayeth the lard", "Ask not" and "It's been a hard day's knight but worth the anvil".'

Sampson sighed.

'I must have switched the auto-correct on again by mistake,' he said. 'People can normally work out what I mean if I make a spelling error, but the auto-correct ruins that.'

'And when you emailed "Beware the crooks if I were you Inspector, if you know what I mean". Let me guess, that should have been "rooks".'

'I didn't, did I?'

'You did indeed, Mr Sampson.'

'Well, I was only concerned that you were leaving your central rooks a little open.'

'And "Clue as a cucumber"?'

'Well, if I remember properly it should have been "as cool as a cucumber". I think.'

'"It's been a hard day's knight but worth the anvil"?'

'I'd been studying the board late at night, but I thought it was worth the candle. It's an old saying, when people used candles, I —'

'Yes, I know the saying about candles, Mr Mason, I mean Mr Sampson. What about "Ask not, of course"?'

'Well, ask not for whom the bell tolls, the famous poem.'

'I knew that,' said Gertie.

'"Study as she goes"?'

'Um, probably should have been steady.'

'And "The vintage is mine, sayeth the lard."'

'I meant "The advantage is mine, sayeth the lard." I am a little overweight, I thought you'd understand the reference. I was just trying to say that, in my opinion, I had the advantage at that stage.'

'But what was the chess game all about?' asked Pete.

'It was just a chess game,' Sampson shrugged. 'I make chess boards as a hobby, it's usually very relaxing. Every so often I'll make a double one just for something different. I don't have a problem seeing the pieces, and using double sets sort of levels the plane field, if you see what I mean.'

'Did you just say 'levels the plane field', Mr Sampson?'

Mr Sampson beamed.

'You noticed, Inspector! I knew you would. Most other people don't get my puns. My children are forever groaning at them.'

'Plane?' asked Gertie. 'That's a pun?'

Sampson chuckled.

'Plane as in carpentry. Yes?'

'No,' said Frank. 'Now –'

'How old are your children, if you don't mind me asking?' asked Pete Phillips.

'Angie is twelve, she's the oldest, then there's Sookie, she's ten, and little Phillip, he's eight. The girls all mother him, he's the baby. I've got some photographs here, if you'd care to see?'

'I'd love to,' replied Pete Phillips, 'I've got some of my daughter, Marie. She's just turned four herself. We only found out about the dyslexia a couple of weeks ago. It's made an amazing difference.'

'I think we can put the mutual admiration society on hold for a while,' said Frank as sternly as he could. 'You've put us to a lot of bother, Mr Sampson, and I'm afraid I'm going to have to ask you to accompany me to the police station.'

'Oh! I'm not under arrest am I? I didn't mean to cause any bother. I'm sure –'

'You aren't under arrest, Mr Sampson, but we do have the matter of a chess game to finish off.'

Sampson clapped his hands.

'I'll get my jacket!' he exclaimed and scuttled back into the little bedroom.

'And,' Frank said under his breath, 'you'll have a chance to meet the missus again. I just know she'll want a few words with you.'

Frieda did indeed decide she wanted words with Mr Mason-Sampson when Gertie and Sam came to her office to report that Frank was not only back with the Mason but preparing to continue their game in the interview room.

'He's what?' she asked.

'Taken Frank's bishop with his queen,' Gertie replied.

'I didn't mean that, I meant what does Frank think he's playing at. I'm going down there myself.'

'The thing is,' said Gertie as she and Sam trailed Frieda, 'it turns out that he's dyslexic.'

'The Mason is dyslexic? He'll be cured once I've got my hands on him. I'll make sure he sees straight.'

'His name isn't Mason,' Sam put in. 'It's Sampson. He was in hospital with Inspector Summers.'

'Sampson? Bug-eyed little man, tries to be nice to everyone?'

'That's the one. Apparently he didn't realise he was sending strange messages. His wife set his signature up for him, something went wrong and he thought he'd fixed it himself. He didn't realise he'd changed it to Mason.'

'His wife?'

'And they have three darling little children who fortunately don't have dyslexia,' Sam informed her battleship vanguard. The vanguard slowed down.

'His wife helps him with his computer and they've got three darling children,' Frieda noted.

'He and Pete Phillips were swapping photographs,' Gertie said.

'Pete Phillips has three darling children?'

'No, he only has one daughter, Marie, but she's got dyslexia too.'

'Not as bad as Mr Sampson's, apparently.'

'Pete Phillips' daughter has dyslexia and he never told us? Why ever not? I'm sure there are ways to help, the Federation must know some.'

The other two wisely stayed silent.

'Right,' said Frieda, 'let's see about this.'

She sailed into the interview room followed by her two escort destroyers. Frank and Sampson were engrossed in their game. Sampson had brought a little telescope-type tube which he used to review the board before making his moves. He looked rather like a little portly Nelson at the battle of Trafalgar. They were being watched by Percy, Pete Phillips and constables Sidney Feeler and Steve Wright. Percy and Pete fell back a few steps at Frieda's entrance, while Sidney Feeler and Steve Wright took the opportunity to perform a side-step followed by a full-on retreat out of the doorway Frieda had just used. Frank looked up.

'Oh, hello, love,' he said. 'You know Mr Sampson, I think. Mr Sampson, my missus.'

Anthony Sampson jumped to his feet and held out his hand.

'Inspector Mrs Summers!' he exclaimed. 'My goodness, I am terribly sorry, Inspector Mr Summers was telling me how I – unintentionally, I hope you understand – unintentionally confused the issue. I really should have asked my wife to check that signature of mine, but the trouble is you don't think you might be wrong when you don't think you're wrong, do you?'

'Of course not,' said Frieda, a woman for whom the concept of being wrong didn't exist.

'And your husband was so positive and supportive, always replying with messages like "Walk tall". That really meant a lot to me. And remembering that I'd mentioned we were going to Amsterdam for the weekend, even though I'd forgotten I'd mentioned it, and then that puzzle about the stops, which I knew meant pulling out all the stops, and –'

'Er, yes, I'm sure he is, you know, that way. But, Mr Sampson, now you should sit down and rest yourself,' said Frieda to the amazement of Percy and Pete. 'And I see you haven't been offered any tea or coffee, what can I say, you can't get the staff these days,' she added, looking at Pete and Percy to make sure they understood exactly what "staff" she was referring to. 'I'll get that organised.'

'Coffee, please, love,' Frank said, without looking up. Frieda reacted with a glare sufficient to slice pressed steel, and then relaxed and patted his shoulder.

'Coffee it is, my sweet,' she said, and left with Gertie and Sam, the last two taking a last look at the chess board.

Percy and Pete looked at each other. They each put a finger over their lips and resumed their study of the game.

As the day wore on little groups of officers popped in to see the state of play. On the one hand Frank was a fellow police officer and to support the other person would be a betrayal of your colleague and mate. On the other he was going to give that poor little fat bloke with the dodgy eyes a right good thumping, and one could hardly fail to feel for the underdog.

On the third hand he was taking an awfully long time to beat the fat little man.

In the end it was a close run thing. Sampson built up an impressive advance on his left flank, moving his pieces slowly but purposefully towards Frank's lines. Frank pushed his centre pawns forward while apparently randomly sending other pieces out close to Sampson's rear lines. They acted like scouts observing an enemy force without appearing to constitute a threat, but unnerving in that they were there. Eventually Frank's centre pawns and roving queens broke a hole in the centre of Sampson's lines, and Sampson's middle king proved his downfall. He desperately tried to manoeuver it out of danger without sacrificing other pieces, but that and his unwillingness to move it off his back line meant that Frank was able to carry out a move peculiar to double chess.

'Checkmate,' he announced, moving his queen to Sampson's back row. The observers crowded in to see how he had done it.

'That's not checkmate,' noted Pete Phillips as Sampson softly pounded his knee. 'He can still move his kings out of the way.'

'Yes,' said Sam, 'but he can only move one out of the way. The other stays in check, so, checkmate for one of them.'

'A schoolboy error,' moaned Sampson, 'how many people have I caught out with that move, and here I am, hoist with my own petard.'

After several minutes' cogitation he reluctantly moved his right-hand king to safety, sacrificing the left-hand one and apparently leaving him free to launch a full-scale attack with his left flank, now relieved of its duty to protect a king.

But Frank never gave him a chance, relentlessly attacking Sampson's right-hand pieces, checking his remaining king wherever possible, forcing it to move, taking out pawns to leave a clear field of fire. Sampson did manage to build a strong defence with his queens and rooks, but it was a Maginot Line of a defence, powerful but in the wrong places. Sampson's king was eventually checkmated by Frank's two queens while trying to flee down the right-hand side of the board.

'Well, Inspector, I thoroughly enjoyed that,' Sampson said, shaking Frank's hand. 'I can't remember the last time I had such a good game.'

'It certainly was an interesting experience,' Frank replied. He looked around the room to discover that it was fully occupied by, amongst others, Frieda, Sam, Gertie, the Chief Inspector, Pete, Percy, a number of constables, and Agnetha from the kitchen. Even Squishy sat on the windowsill, head cocked, looking at the board. She seemed to be saying,

'I could play better than that.'

'So,' said Pete to Percy as they walked down the corridor, 'what happened to the Summers character?'

'Summers? You mean Frank?'

'No, the Detective Sergeant who nicked Boulloin.'

'Summers? I told you, his name was Simmers, Frank Simmers. I-India, not u-Uzbekhistan. Actually, we called him Charlie for some reason. Funny, that. the things you remember.'

'Ah ... yes ... of course. He's probably forgotten about it now.'

'He's probably in a jail somewhere now. Or flogging dodgy insurance. He was that sort of chap.'

End of the three weeks

Diagnosis

'Tricia, you are looking gorgeous,' Frank said, striding into Frieda's outer office. He leaned over her desk and gave her a kiss. 'Or more gorgeous than ever, I should say,' he continued, opening the door to Frieda's office. Tricia looked back, goggle-eyed, trying to point out that Frieda was busy. 'Darling, give your hubby a kiss,' she heard as the door closed. Frieda's mouth also remained open after Frank kissed her. She too appeared to be attempting to mouth something.

'All sorted,' Frank carried on. 'I'm in the clear.' He paused as he sensed someone behind him. He turned around very, very slowly, to find the Chief Constable leaning against the bookcase, saucer in one hand, cup of tea halfway to his mouth, an unusual look of surprise on his face.

'I don't believe you've met my husband, Chief Constable,' Frieda said, having recovered.

'No, I don't believe I've had that pleasure.' He put the cup on its saucer and held out a hand. 'I've been looking forward to meeting him ever since I first heard of him as a Detective Constable. Frank Summers has a remarkable ability to be somewhere else whenever I've turned up.'

'Ah,' said Frank, shaking the other man's hand. 'In fact, come to mention it, I must really –'

'Do sit down, Inspector. You appear to have some news for us. Or is it for your wife's ears only?'

'Well, I –'

'Sit down, Frank,' said Frieda. 'What is it?'

'Well, er –'

'Frank!'

He sat down. Then he grinned and took a folded-up sheet of paper from his jacket pocket.

'I'm in the clear,' he repeated, handing it over to Frieda. She scanned it quickly.

'What is it?' she asked looking up with worry in her eyes. 'It looks like a medical report. But I don't understand it.'

'It's quite simple. I'm allergic to aspirin. Well, strictly speaking, a combination of aspirin and that beer I was drinking.'

'Aspirin?'

'That's what gave me the attack. Ironic, if you think about it. I'd feel one of those terrible migraines coming on, I took whatever pills were nearest, and if they happened to be aspirin, or contain aspirin, they would have knocked me for a six. Anaphylactic shock. Bang! That's me done for. Now I know. So long as I avoid aspirin and that brand of beer together I'll be fine. A clean bill of health.'

'But, Frank, I gave you some of my tablets when we were over in France. You didn't have an attack then.'

'They didn't contain aspirin. It was the stuff dad gave me that gave me the attack. And the beer. I wouldn't have taken it if I'd known what it was anyway. Ever since I was six years old and mum gave me a half of aspirin for a fever, I found it tasted revolting. Made me even sicker than before. Since then I've always just automatically avoided it.'

'Oh, dear,' said Frieda after a pause.

'Oh, dear?' asked Frank.

'I'd better get along,' said the Chief Constable, putting his cup and saucer down on Frieda's desk. He held his hand out again. 'Nice to have met you, Inspector. Don't be a total stranger in future. I don't bite. Not that much, anyway.'

'Er, yes, right, sir,' Frank said, jumping up. He watched the Chief Constable leave. Then he turned back to Frieda and clapped his hands.

'Brilliant!' he exclaimed. 'You don't know what a relief that is.'

'I think I do,' replied Frieda, smiling. She stood up to give her husband a kiss and a hug.

'We're just going to have to be careful how we explain it to your dad,' she said. 'We don't want him blaming himself.'

'Damn! I hadn't thought of that. He will, you know. Perhaps we'd better just tell him that it was the beer. Or the sunlight. Or something.'

'Don't be silly, Frank. I'm not taking the chance of you scaring me half to death again. I will make sure everyone knows exactly not to give you aspirin.'

She paused.

'Frank, every case you've been on you've ended up either injured or almost dead. I hope you aren't going to do that to me this time.'

'Free, don't be silly. I'm now a happily married man. I am fully committed to a life of domestic bliss. I will even train myself to looking forward to your mother coming to stay.'

'You don't like my mother.'

'I have absolutely zero dislike for your mother. It's just that I don't like the way you grit your teeth every time your mother calls.'

Frieda paused and re-arranged the blotting-pad on her desk.

'Free, we'll go house-hunting,' Frank said.

Frieda looked at him

'I won't enjoy it, and I don't think you will either, but we'll go house-hunting, because ... well, just because.'

The weeks go by
Playing house

Some weeks later Sunday came and Frank and Frieda prepared themselves for what had become a regular event: going to view houses which they could look over, agree with the estate agent that it definitely had possibilities, making a circling gesture with their index figures against the head once the agent's back was turned, and afterwards agreeing with each other that the amount being asked was quite ridiculous and would never get a buyer stupid enough to pay so much, nor a bank so silly it would lend that amount for such a poor property. A few days later the estate agent would call to tell them that the property had been sold for more than the asking price, but he had just had a new property come on the market, one he or she could describe as a very desirable do-upper.

And then the circle would start all over again.

And then late one winter's afternoon in November Frank and Gertie were driving back to the office under the rapidly darkening sky. They had been attending a case of little interest on the far side of Lords Acres and Frank had decided to drive to remind himself how it should be done. Just by coincidence he chose Dukes Avenue as a short cut. They drove past a house with a For Sale sign on the front, giving it scant attention. If the houses that Frank and Frieda had looked at were apparently worth a small king's fortune, or even a king's small fortune, somewhere in Lords Acres would require a nabob's nabob's fortune.

Then he slammed on brakes, causing Gertie to mutter an epithet.

'Frank, what the –' she began as he went into reverse. 'You're not having a fit, are you?'

'That for sale sign,' he said, 'I've just realised something.'

'A for sale sign in Lords' Acres? Did you win the lottery or something? Several times?'

'Recognise the entrance?' he asked, stopping the car.

'Of course! Martha Shaw. She's selling up?'

'Let's go find out. Grab a torch.'

They made their way through the narrow path through the brambles, their torches throwing beams along the way.

'Hope she isn't alarmed by people at the back door,' muttered Frank as he knocked on it.

'She'll have seen us on the CCTV.'

'Who's there?' came a hesitant voice from the kitchen.

'Frank Summers and Detective Constable Gregson' Frank called back. 'Inspector Frank Summers, you remember. From Wellbury police.'

The door opened and Martha Shaw looked out from the brightly lit kitchen.

'Come in, Inspector, Gertie. I wasn't expecting anyone. I've got nervous about unexpected night-time visitors. Actually, any unexpected visitors. The CCTV isn't working. Would you like some tea?'

'Love some, Mrs S. But it's only really late afternoon.'

'It's dark, that's night. Never could stand winter. Take a seat.' She put the kettle on. 'I learnt not to let it bother me, but since – well, Georgie and Mildred pop around every couple of days. Reminds me of what it was like to have someone to talk to.'

'You've put the house up for sale?'

'Yes. Georgie and Mildred talked me into moving in with them. Their house is a lot bigger than it looks. There are some allotments nearby. And a decent pub. And we don't plan on stagnating there. We're off on a Mediterranean cruise in four weeks. Sun and sea for a month. It's another reason I hate winter, it's hell on my arthritis. The following winter we might do somewhere like Thailand. Imagine. Me and Marti and Mildred in Thailand.'

'Can I ask you how much you're asking for the house?'

'Well, it's hardly a secret, Inspector.' She named an amount to which Frank might have responded 'You what?' had he not already had his surprise at house prices permanently disabled. Gertie's mouth hung open.

'Do me a favour, Mrs Shaw,' Frank said as he accepted a mug of strong tea, 'don't accept any offers until I've had a chance to speak to my wife.'

Martha Shaw looked surprised. Gertie's mouth hung opener.

'Inspector, you do know how much work it requires? Not even the estate agent has found a euphemism which will stretch that far.'

'We'll have to think about it. But the thing is, my wife wants a place we can both call home. First thing people do in those circumstances is redecorate. Pull walls down. Put walls up, move the upstairs loo, move the stairs, repaint the front door, that sort of thing. If a house is in perfect condition it's a waste of money, but people do it anyway. So moving into somewhere which needs it in the first place makes sense.'

'It's still a lot of money. I didn't think police officers got paid that much.'

Frank grinned.

'We get good mortgage deals because we've got the best life assurance going.'

'Well, I'm quite happy to delay any decision for a few days. I haven't had any offers anyway. The sort of people who buy property in this area expect it to be immaculate.'

For a moment there was a smile on her face.

'And then the wives redecorate,' she added.

'Blimey, Frank, I mean Sarge I mean Inspector, you must be getting paid a lot more than I thought,' Gertie said the moment they were back on the way to the station.

'Not really, Gerts. If we can get a mortgage our combined salaries should just about cover it. Then it's a question of hanging on until inflation reduces the value of the repayments. I remember my folks talking about how much their house cost them – something ridiculous like a few thousand quid. In those days it that was something like ten years' salary for my dad. Today it's not even half that.'

'You reckon?'

'That's the theory.'

'And Frieda's going to like the idea of all that building work?'

'It's either that or continue house-hunting for another five years. Or until the kids leave home and we can downsize.'

Which was pretty much what Frieda said when he suggested it. The following day they went to view the house and agreed a price with Martha Shaw. Within a week they had a mortgage agreement which Frieda arranged one lunchtime, based on the estimate of the sale of her house and Frank's flat. The various bank officials had been most helpful. As she put it, mortgage advisors might start with a patronising attitude to the pretty little woman, but that rapidly ends when you introduce yourself with 'Inspector Summers, Wellbury police, and is that your illegally parked car outside?'

Though Frank did ponder on what the reaction would have been had he also been there to follow up with "And I'm also Inspector Summers. I'm the friendly one. But don't let the smile fool you. And this is our kitten, Squishy. She can get real nasty."

Their first Christmas together came and went – they spent it with Frank's parents – and by January they were the proud owners of the oldest and most dilapidated house in Lords Acres. They were getting used to having builders pop in to give a quick quote, only to spend much time muttering 'tsk, tsk', tapping walls and shaking their heads sadly. They all said something along the lines of, 'Well, we don't know what it's like behind the plaster/wallpaper/ceiling, we could be looking at three/four/five times the cost.'

With the eagerness of someone unused to DIY Frank took it upon himself to start removing loose plaster and wallpaper so that they could see what was behind it. He was doing so one Saturday afternoon in the library while Frieda was busy in the kitchen while talking to what was by then known as The Bump. Suddenly there was the sound of several bricks falling down and a muffled swearword. Frieda held her breath. It would be typical of the man to get himself critically injured at this stage.

'Frieda,' he called, 'could you come here for a moment?'

'What is it?' she asked, coming into the room. He was standing in a pile of bricks nursing his shin while looking into a hole. 'Have you – Frank, what on earth have you done? That hole wasn't there before.'

'Nope. Nor that thing,' he said, pointing.

Frieda looked into a hole which might once have been part of a serving hatch, had not the back been of solid brick and the whole immovable. Amongst the contents was a large object of porcelain-ware with a dusty bundle of papers inside, tied up with string. On top of that was a skull.

'What on earth? It looks like a strange shaped bowl.'

'Which will make the skull on top - what?'

'Very, very dead?'

'It's a priest's hole, I reckon,' said Frank. 'One ex-priest and his bible. Probably hid away and they forgot about him somehow.'

'Except for a few minor points.'

'You mean, like vertebrae, and all the other bits and pieces? Fibula, tibia, etc.'

'Precisely. I think whoever it was had their head chopped off and thrown in.'

They regarded the scene for a few moments.

'That porcelain thing rings a bell,' said Frieda. 'I'm sure I've seen a picture of something similar before.'

'Probably used to hold the blood.'

'Could be.'

Frank blew some dust off, taking care not to touch it.

'There's a name written on it. Can't quite make it out.'

'Don't blow any more dust off, Frank, I think it might be a scene of crime.'

'Have to get Susan in, I suppose.'

Frieda nodded as slowly as she could.

'A forensics expert, anyway,' she said.

She paused.

'I've got a feeling that this is going to be a lot of trouble, you know.'

She paused again.

'And it will all be your fault.'

Then she added,

'Darling.'

End of Book Seven

Oh, And By The Way

To clear up one or two points ...

Frank did change his password. Originally it had been Voluptuous1. Frieda suspected he would change it to Voluptuous2, but a quick test disproved that. In fact he changed it to VoluptuousT00.

Mohammed didn't go on the search for jewels in preference to the demonstration. After a long shift of waiting on demanding infidels he had overslept. He tried to explain this to Deacon Danish, but the Deacon had lost his religious drive and had taken up plane-spotting.

TOBs was disbanded. Martha, Mildred and Georgette took up travelling with a vengeance. Martha began travel-writing, while Georgette learnt what a blog meant, and keeps a very popular one entitled "Bloody Foreigners".

The Fisherman's now has a banner adorning one of the walls. It reads "Death to Religious Intolerants". TCoTC still hold regular meetings. Every Friday Seumas, Jamie, Uncle Tom, Major Tom and Tom The Feck can be found debating the serious issues of the day.

Oh, and Oh And Oh And Linus.

Follow Frank, Frieda, Susan and Gertie in *Painter 8*. The object that Frank and Frieda have discovered appears to belong to the early Avant Garde school. The probability is that the skull is that of one of a group of artists who had used the house as a base sometime between the end of the First World War and 1969, quite possibly the painter of the picture. The object itself is either a priceless work of art or the ravings of a madman – or madwoman – according to taste. Either way it's potentially worth a good deal of money, and that attracts people who would like to have a good deal of money and aren't too concerned about the legality of the methods they employ. There are also the academics, a French professor from a New York University and an American professor from the Sorbonne, and the students from around the world for whom the porcelain bowl, if it is the original, is the Art World's equivalent of the Holy Grail.

most-disliked Wellburians, from nagging neighbours to estate agents ... and the police, at a poorly performing number ten. But Frank fails to realise that there is a graver danger closer to home. Three women have decided that he is their responsibility: his boss, his constable and the local pathologist have agreed to become best of enemies. Now they intend to re-arrange his fate the way it should be. And they aren't asking anyone's permission.

Fakes, Fraud and Deception

The third in the FFSG series.
Detective Sergeant Frank Summers is in the doghouse, despite having recently arrested an internationally sought con-artist. And since he is in the doghouse he has no intention of pointing out that there is something very strange about the attractive French police woman who has come to interview the arrested man, not to mention the two detectives claiming to be from Scotland Yard. Oh, no, he is going to stay well out of the way this time. Definitely.

Jokers

The fourth in the FFSG series.
The doctors have pronounced Detective Sergeant Frank Summers physically fit following recovery after his shooting, but his colleagues fear that his sense of humour was extracted along with the bullet. They are, as always, more than willing to interfere in his life in the pursuit of a good cause. If that wasn't enough, a bunch of criminals calling themselves the Joker Gang are laughing at him, the university students are creating mayhem during their rag week, and someone called

The Shocker is trying to kill him. The only advantage is that it take his mind off of the ultimatum the three women in his life have given him, one that he has only until the Sunday to resolve. Or leave town.

Prophecies

The fifth in the FFSG series.

Detective Sergeant Summers is under a hex, otherwise known as his colleagues. First they don't want him to get married, then it is imperative it must happen. Then they decide that a prophecy has been made which threatens the wedding. They don't believe in prophecies, but aren't sure that prophecies understand that. So they'll have to Do Something About It. And if their bumbling efforts aren't enough to ensure he never makes it to the altar, he has to cope with visiting aliens and resident ghosts. He does have tiny Squishy to protect him, but what match can even this plucky little kitten be against a prospective mother-in-law?

Loonymoon

The sixth in the FFSG series.

The Inspectors Summers have tied the knot and embarked on their honeymoon in a small family-run hotel in Normandy. She has very definite ideas of what she wants out of a honeymoon: to set a seal on their love, and to form a foundation for life-long devotion. He just wants to nick a French police officer's kepi. He had a Bobby's helmet nicked from him once by a French girl while he was on crowd duty one New Year's Eve in London, and now he intends to return the favour. Neither is about to achieve their aim unless they can solve the mystery of the woman in the bath and the missing heroin. Which means pitting their minds against the French Inspectors Simenon. That's Mr and Mrs Simenon, whose marriage has gone beyond the rocks and is now beating itself to death against humdrum reality. One or either or both or neither could be the guilty crumpet. More importantly, is their marriage a portent of what could become of the Loonymooners? Ultimately the decisive question could well be: which side do the peas go?

Others:

The Window

Little does Jim Allbright realise just how much paperwork his letter containing a simple enquiry to his local council is about to produce, nor the strange events he will experience as a result of the 'system'. But if the system cannot be beaten the interchange of letters can be used to have a little fun and get to know some of the people struggling behind it, especially the woman who signs herself as 'Sandi (pp the Administrator)', and perhaps, one day even meet her.

Diary of a Sane Man

In a cross between 'Last Of The Summer Wine' and 'One Flew Over The Cuckoo's Nest', set against a backdrop of the brave new world of New Labour's end of honeymoon, Fred is the Last Cynical Optimistic Realist.
Believing that he's found the perfect niche – three square meals a day plus all the newspapers he can read just for

occasionally pretending to be mad – he's not going to be the one to rock the apple cart. Oh, no.

Safe from the wiles of women and the woes of the world, he's not going to rock the boat. Oh, no.

No, he's just going to sit and observe, and comment quietly on the insanity of life outside.

Well, maybe just little one tug of the loose strand of wool on life's jersey ...

Did you know they elected a monkey as mayor in Hartlepool?

The Weekend At Longwood

A whodunnit in the classic sense, set against the backdrop of World War II and the trials, tribulations and romances of nine suspects.

A group of friends get together during the last weekend of August 1939 at the rural retreat named Longwood, just a few miles from Portsmouth. They are there to celebrate the last time they will see Georgina Riley, famed American novelist and socialite, for some time, as she is scheduled to leave for her native New York in order to marry her childhood sweetheart. During the afternoon they good-humouredly assign to each other the most suitable names of the nine muses, the daughters of Zeus and Mnemosyne:

Calliope: the muse of epic poetry and rhetoric

Clio: history

Erato: love poems and mimicry

Euterpe: lyric poetry

Melpomene: tragedy

Polymnia: hymns to the gods and heroes

Terpsichore: dance

Thalia: comedy

Urania: astronomy, astrology and prophecy

The following morning Georgina is discovered in her bedroom covered in blood, her throat slit, barely alive. Her American maid is dead. A tiara Georgina had been flaunting the day before has disappeared.

Detective Inspector Rudman arrives to investigate. But with Georgina in a coma and no solid evidence there is little he can do apart from haunt their lives. With Germany's invasion of Poland a week later they disperse across the land, some to the air-force, some to the army, others to reserved civilian jobs.

But Rudman does not give up. Wherever they are he can be found. Whatever other duties he is tasked to, he will find time to keep tabs on them. Whatever the defeats and victories of the Allied cause, he has only one aim: to find the person responsible for the murder done that weekend in Longwood.

The war ends; some of the Muses have survived, some not. Some have prospered, some married, some matured, others have found despair. And then comes invitation to spend another weekend at Longwood. The message is that Rudman has found the evidence he has been looking for.

And so one of the surviving couples motor slowly down to Portsmouth, remembering the original weekend, the trials and the tribulations of the past years, and wonder: what will be revealed during the coming weekend at Longwood?

Firelight

A modern-day tale of an ordinary family gathering at Christmas; the good, the bad, the dysfunctional and the forgotten.

George Browne and his wife Winifred have retired to a large, run-down pile in the country. Rumour has it that it was once the abode of a mad aristocratic family with a penchant for Satanism, and that both they and their victims still haunt the corridors. Other rumours are that it was a lunatic asylum for much of the nineteenth and twentieth century, and bodies of the inhabitants are buried around the large gardens in unmarked graves.

The Brownes are an unremarkable retired couple who, depending on who you might ask, have bought it as an investment, or alternatively as somewhere with enough bedrooms to accommodate their children, grand-children, and the little baby great-grandchildren. Too often in the past excuses have been made at special times, the most common of which has been of the 'I don't want to put you to any trouble' variety. That excuse can no longer hold water.

Now it is approaching Christmas. Winter has set in, but the house is snug with oil heaters and real fires. As the various relations arrive, or don't arrive, it becomes clearer why invitations might have been refused in the past. The men of the family believe in having their way. The women of the family are strong-willed in their own different ways, and have various means of getting what they want.

The guests of the family - friends, boyfriends, girlfriends, wives and husbands - discover that their partners have a totally different side to them as the explosive hatreds of long-nurtured fights and feuds simmer to the surface before quickly boiling over.

One evening Winifred Browne encourages them to each tell a story as they sit in the lounge with the large fire warming them, the television off, no access to broadband, computers or mobile connections. Reluctantly at first they begin. As each evening passes: with different members taking turns, they announce in stories the feelings and hopes they cannot voice in public.

Finally it's the turn of Winifred Browne. Her story will be the one that tells them who they are, where they come from, and maybe why they have turned out the way they have.

For further details on these visit:

www. dughaille. info

Appendix: How the game turned out

Previous moves:

Mason:	1. P m2-m3:
Frank:	2. P h15-h13
Mason:	3. P e2-e3
Frank:	4. P i15-i13
Mason:	5. B n1-m2
Frank:	6. P o15-o14
Mason:	7. Nt o1-n3
Frank:	8. B n16-p14
Mason:	9. 0-0 : right hand king-side castle
Frank:	10. Nt o16-n14
Mason:	11. Nt g1-h3
Frank:	12. 0-0: left hand king-side castle
Mason:	13. B f1-d3
Frank:	14. P b15-b14
Mason:	15. 0-0: left-hand king-side castle
Frank:	16. B c16-a14
Mason:	17. P b2-b3
Frank:	18. a14-m2, BxB

The rest of the game:

Mason:	19. l1-m2 QxB
Frank:	20. P e15-e13
Mason:	21. B c1-b2

Frank:	22. Q d16-f14
Mason:	23. P j2-j3
Frank:	24. Nt b16-c14
Mason:	25. Nt b1-a3
Frank:	26. 0-0-0: Right hand queen-side castle
Mason:	27. P o2-o3
Frank:	28. P l15-l13
Mason:	29. P c2-c4
Frank:	30. B k16-o12: Threatening the white queen
Mason:	31. Q d1-c2
Frank:	32. B o12-n13
Mason:	33. P l2-l4
Frank:	34. n13xd3 BxB
Mason:	35. c2xd3 QxB
Frank:	36. B p14-o15
Mason:	37. R a1-e1
Frank:	38. Nt n14-o12
Mason:	39. B b2-c1
Frank:	40. B f16-c13
Mason:	41. Q d3-c2
Frank:	42. P h13-h12
Mason:	43. P d2-d4
Frank:	44. P i13-i12
Mason:	45. Nt a3-b5
Frank:	46. Nt o12-p10

Mason:	47. P a2-a4
Frank:	48. P h12-h11
Mason:	49. B c1-a3
Frank:	50. P i12-i11
Mason:	51. P b3-b4
Frank:	52. Nt p10-o8
Mason:	53. P a4-a5
Frank:	54. P i11-i10
Mason:	55. Nt b5-d6
Frank:	56. P k15-k14
Mason:	57. P c4-c5
Frank:	58. Q f14-m7
Mason:	59. R n1-l1
Frank:	60. P h11-h10
Mason:	61. P b4-b5
Frank:	62. Nt o8-n6
Mason:	63. P b5-b6
Frank:	64. P h10-h9
Mason:	65. Q c2-a4
Frank:	66. P i10-i9
Mason:	67. P a5-a6
Frank:	68. Nt n6-l5
Mason:	69. P a6-a7
Frank:	70. P i9-i8
Mason:	71. K g1-h1

Frank:	72. P j15-j13
Mason:	73. P f2-f4
Frank:	74. P k14-k13
Mason:	75. P e3-e4
Frank:	76. P k13-k12
Mason:	77. P a7-a8
Frank:	78. P h9-h8
Mason:	79. P b6-b7
Frank:	80. P j13-j12
Mason:	81. P c5-c6
Frank:	82. Q l16-j14
Mason:	83. P d4-d5
Frank:	84. Nt j16-k14
Mason:	85. P g2-g4
Frank:	86. P h8-h7
Mason:	87. Nt d6-c8
Frank:	88. P h7-h6
Mason:	89. P e4-e5
Frank:	90. P i8-i7
Mason:	91. P f4-f5
Frank:	92. P i7-i6
Mason:	93. P a8-a9
Frank:	94. P i6-i5
Mason:	95. Nt h3-f4
Frank:	96. P i5-i4

Mason:	97. j3-i4 PxP
Frank:	98. i16-i4 RxP
Mason:	99. P h2-h3
Frank:	100. P h6-h5
Mason:	101. P g4-g5
Frank:	102. R i4-j4
Mason:	103. R e1-e4
Frank:	104. j4-j1 RxNt
Mason:	105. i1-j1 RxR
Frank:	106. Nt l5-k3
Mason:	107. Q m2-l3
Frank:	108. k3-j1 NtxR
Mason:	109. R e4-e2
Frank:	110. R h16-i16
Mason:	111. P i2-i4
Frank:	112. o15-e5 BxP
Mason:	113. B k1-j2
Frank:	114. e5-f4 BxNt
Mason:	115. l1-j1 RXNt
Frank:	116. h5-i4 PxP
Mason:	117. h3-i4 PxP
Frank:	118. i16-i4 RXP
Mason:	119. f1-f4 RxB
Frank:	120. Q j14-h14: check
Mason:	121. K h1-g2

Frank: 122. Q m7-h2 check

Mason: 123. K g2-f1

Frank: 124. Q h2-h3 check

Mason: 125. K f1-e1

Frank: 126. h3-j1: QxR and checkmate: the Mason can only move one king, the other is mated

Mason: 127. K o1-o2: King on e1 removed. The Mason is now free to let his left flank loose.

Frank: 128. Q h14-h1

Mason: 129. f4-i4 RxR

Frank: 130. Q j1-p1 check

Mason: 131. K o2-p3

Frank: 132. p1-n3 QxNt

Mason: 133. P l4-l5

Frank: 134. Nt g16-f14

Mason: 135. R e2-e4

Frank: 136. Q h1-p1

Mason: 137. R i4-n4

Frank: 138. Q n3-o2 check

Mason: 139. K p3-o4

Frank: 140. p1-p2 QxP

Mason: 141. K o4-o5

Frank: 142. Q p2-p9

Mason: 143. R n4-p4

Frank: 144. Q p9-o8 check

Mason: 145. Q l3-o6

Frank: 146. o2-l5 QxP check

Mason: 147. K o5-p6

Frank: 148. Q o8-n8 check

Mason: 149. B j2-o7

Frank: 150. n8-n2 QxP

Mason: 151. Q a4-b3

Frank: 152. c13-m3 BxP check

Mason: 153. K p6-p7

Frank: 154. Q n2-n9 check

Mason: 155. K p7-p8

Frank: 156. Q l5-p9 checkmate

www.ingramcontent.com/pod-product-compliance
Lightning Source LLC
Chambersburg PA
CBHW071204250626
47159CB00001B/199